Contents

Dedication

To Big Mama, Mama, Ma'Dear, Big Daddy, and Daddy many thanks for soft whispers, little shoves, and angel kisses.

CHAPTER 1

Searching for A Real Love

asual sex had become about as satisfying as a cold shower on a winter night in Chicago when the woman I was with asked me, Don stroke'em and leave'em Stokes, if I loved her. I laughed and said, "Love you? Hell, I can't even elucidate a good reason to still be here." Until I met Niki the only difference between good sex and great sex was what happened next. Even a player like me knows you don't get to choose if, when, or how another person loves you.

Niki cursed me the hell out and threatened bodily harm while she whacked me with her thousand dollar Christian Louboutin pumps. It was the rawest passion she had shown since I meet her. I held her down on the bed. She welcomed my late effort by wrapping her skinny legs around my back. I rolled away when I realized I didn't have another condom. It would be just my luck to get her pregnant. She took my slight as another jilt and came at me with curses and threats again. I got the hell out of her apartment before she could beat me with her stilettos again. Niki Jones is one of the most beautiful women in the world, but her bedroom skills are lacking, and this is not the first time her attitude has gotten downright scary.

I hopped in my Ferrari and called my favorite groupies while I made my way to my best friend's party. If these women were paying attention, I wouldn't have to explain why I don't know diddly-squat about love. If it wasn't for my son, I wouldn't have anyone to show for my so called great loving. Men in my position don't have to use the "L" word to get what we want. It boggles my mind when women flip-out when you tell them the truth. No one will ever accuse me of lying—I don't have to lie. Hell, I would like to be in love, but most women

1

either have hidden agendas or they are smart enough to know better than to buckle up with men like me.

After tonight's episode with Niki, I finally had to admit that using women only for my pleasure has become a waste of time and energy. Sex never bored me like it does lately even though the women have gotten a helluva lot kinkier over the years. It was just as well that the twins didn't answer.

I programed my iPod to Santana's Greatest Hits and let the hot African, Latin and jazz beats rock me. I zipped in and out of traffic on the heels of a yellow cab as I made my way to Sloan's Tribeca loft.

Sloan and I go back to freshman year at GW. He was born rich and wild so we're cool. He recently took over his father's advertising firm. We're co-owners of a real estate investment and development company, an urban clothing line, and a jazz and R&B label. This cocktail party is for our key executives.

My melancholy mood didn't change when I entered the party. John Coltrane's soothing rendition of Soul Eyes was playing in the background. My shoulder was throbbing where I'd gotten whacked, and I was still trying to understand how a woman could go from trying to do anything to pleasure me, to threatening to kill me with her shoes.

Instead of mingling I hung by the window and nursed a cognac and a Cuban cigar. I tried and failed to ready myself to deal with a bunch of music moguls and what's hot rhetoric. While I was checking out Sloan's panoramic view of the city, a Steve Urkel looking brother made a grand entrance with two beauties on his arms. One of his queens was chocolate, slim, short, and smiling. The other was vanilla, plump, tall, and somber. Her contradictions pulled me in and held my attention—her peachy skin and wild curly hair, her baby fat voluptuous body and the seductive innocence in her eyes. Chocolate's short pink dress enhanced her curves and smooth dark skin. And although Vanilla's low-cut black wrap-around-dress was struggling to cover her generous finger-licking-southern-fried-chicken curves, it was perfect on her. She made baby fat look sexy-hot, and the fire in her diamond earrings and tennis bracelet meant she either had her own bank or Urkel was a very generous sugar daddy. Her neck, legs, and toes were naked and my mouth watered at the thought of tasting them. I gave her an eight for what I could see, and a ten for what I imagined.

Sexy innocence had my attention physically and emotionally, and I'm not a man who is easily roused these days. I wiped drool from the corners of my mouth when Vanilla made eye contact from across the room. She licked her pouty lips and smiled. I've been a player for so long—I'm like a dentist—I forget the names, but show me the teeth and the memories return.

Vanilla winked and looked away when her eyes met mine again. I shook off her pickup and turned back to the view. She joined me by the window a few minutes later. A server offered us Cristal or Courvoisier. I straightened my tie, checked my cufflinks, made sure my lapel was straight and braced for her pickup when she took two cognacs. Vanilla didn't look my way when she tossed both drinks down. She didn't even frown. I said damn to myself when she sat the empty snifters back on the tray and turned back to the view. A few minutes later she sniffled. I got a glimpse at her reflection in the window. Tears were making a mad dash down her cheeks.

"Are you okay?" I asked.

"The view is breathtaking," she said. She sucked in a deep breath and wiped at her tears.

It pained me to see her cry. I didn't know her, although she looked familiar. Her juicy lips quivered when I wiped mascara from her baby soft cheeks. I wished my johnson was her favorite flavor popsicle. She frowned as if she was reading my mind and wiped at the smudges herself.

"Please don't tell me you're crying over the view."

I expected to hear one of those all-men-are-dogs line since she didn't seem to be feeling my vibe.

"My husband died in a terrible car crash over two years ago. Sometimes I think about Charles and lose it. When our eyes met, I had a sudden urge to warn you about something. I'm not sure what, since this is my first time meeting you. Maybe it was the way you looked at me from across the room. Your stare made me smile. It reminded me of my Charles and my warnings to him."

"Warnings?" I chuckled to myself and wondered what game she was playing.

She looked up at me with those big heartbreaking eyes and said, "Sometimes I get feelings that I can't shake, and other times I get full blown visions. I had a vision the morning Charles died. I warned him, but he thought I was being silly, and then…, and then…, it was too late." She looked away and wiped at the tears rolling down her cheeks again. "You know what--forget I mentioned it. I didn't mean to disturb your peace."

Our eyes met again, and as I removed mascara from her cheek, I realized that she was Dr. Gina Mae Hill. I had read the Essence Magazine article about her and Charles's life together and the foundation she helped set up in his name to honor him. Gina was about twenty to thirty pounds heavier than her picture in the magazine last year, but it damn sure was her.

"If I died tomorrow nobody would miss me, except my mother, my son, and maybe my best friend Sloan," I said. Considering all the women I've been intimate with it didn't feel good to admit that there wasn't a special lady in my life. Groupies don't count and after what happened tonight nor does the supermodel I was with earlier.

Gina looked dead into my eyes and said, "That's pitiful, Donald Stokes. It sounds as if it is time for you to trade lap dances for slow dances."

I chuckled. My own mother called me a man-whore when pictures of the twins giving me a lap dance appeared on the covers of the tabloids. "Slow dances, huh?"

She smiled and said, "Yup. Get your old two steps in order. Find someone nice. Hold her close. Feel her energy. Let her feel yours. Watch your steps. Don't rush. Find someone you understand and trust and love will work itself out."

"Is that right?"

"It worked for me."

"Your husband must have truly been special."

"He was. He was a big fan of yours," she said, and she blushed and looked away when she said, "And so am I."

Considering how she was blushing, I wasn't sure how to digest that bit of personal information.

"We loved sports, music and each other… I miss Charles more than words can explain."

Gina knew who I was and she wasn't on my jock. I gave her bonus points as I swept my eyes over her again. Not bad—sad sexy eyes, great cleavage, the twin peaks even look real. Plump, but damn alluring. I'll sink into Gina's soft sexiness anytime. I slapped my imaginary wrist and reminded myself that I had vowed to change. Gina didn't strike me as the one night stands type even though I was sure she was up to something. Her cheeks and chest got rosy with prickly heat again. If I didn't know better, I would swear that she was reading my mind.

Her friend rushed over and ended our stare-off. "Here you are, Gina, are you having a good time?"

"I'm not up for this yet, Rolonda. Give me your keys. I know it's important for you to be here, but I'm out."

Rolanda's hands found her hips and her head did a semicircle when she said, "Girl, don't even think about leaving this party before you meet Sloan."

"I'll say hello to him on my way out. Thanks for trying to hook us up, Ro. You and Edward can stay. I'll call a cab."

Ro shifted her head around and looked at me as if I was a vulture swarming over prey when she asked, "What did you say to her, Don?"

Gina blushed and flashed a smile my way. "Give me your keys, Ro. I have to get outta here."

Ro looked at Gina as if she was nuts, but she gave her the keys. Gina snatched them and dropped them in her purse. Then she extended her hand to me. I clutched it and willed her to stay.

"Thank you for the generous donation you gave to Charles's Foundation. I'm sorry about rushing out. Your donation was greatly appreciated. You're a good man, Donald Stokes, slow down and you will find someone special."

Gina flashed a smile my way before she strutted away like a gazelle without saying goodbye. She has a nice ass and great legs and a helluva stride. And judging from the way she rebounded from her grief and read me like a dirty magazine—I'll put my money on her being a lady in the streets and a whore between the sheets.

Rolonda looked at me with evil eyes again and said, "Don Stokes, what did you say to her? Do you have any idea what I had to do to get Gina out of her big quiet house in country ass Connecticut? I dragged her to this party to meet Sloan. Don't you have enough sluts chasing you?"

Normally the scorpion in me would have put her in her place, but my mind was on Gina's ass and I didn't have a quick defense.

"You ruined all my hard work! Gina fantasizes about getting with a bad boy like you. She is so naive sometimes, which is why I would never let her get involved with you!"

Rolonda stomped her feet on Sloan's hardwood floor and growled like a pit bull. My mind was stuck on Gina's fantasies. Whatever she was saying to Sloan had put a huge grin on his face, but it was blocking my image of my cock buried deep in her pussy and her long legs wrapped around my back.

Rolonda's nerdy boyfriend rushed over to reclaim her. I excused myself. Gina gave Sloan her business card and scribbled something on the back. I felt a tinge of jealously for the first time since we have been friends. Nothing was going my way tonight

Sloan is a redbone like Gina. He blushed like a virgin staring at his first piece when he tucked Gina's card in his wallet and tapped it for luck. It's not unusual for either of us to sleep with someone we just met. We both vowed to change. Gina has most of the qualities we both seek in our mates. I flashed Sloan a peace sign and eased out the door a few minutes after Gina.

When I stepped off the elevator, she was sitting on the sofa crying. Sloan's doorman said he had helped her get to the couch. I sat down and wrapped my arms around her. She rested her head on my shoulder. I rubbed circles on her back and made promises I didn't know enough about her to make. One touch of her soft skin and a whiff of her wild raspberry smell made me want my slow dance.

"Shh," I finally said. I wiped her cheeks with my thumb just to see if her lips would quiver again. They did, and Mr. Johnson perked up.

"It's late. You shouldn't be on the streets of New York like this."

She sniffled again. "I'll get it together before I call a taxi."

"Where are you headed?"

"Corner of Fifty-eighth and Fifth."

"I'll take you, okay?" I didn't know if I was being a Good Samaritan or if I thought I had a chance of melting my ice cube in her lemonade. It seemed like the right thing to do at the time.

Black Magic Woman/Gypsy Queen blasted through my car speakers. I reached to switch to my standby Trey Songz. Gina slapped my hand and chastised me with a nonverbal look that reminded me of my mother. The guilty boy I used to be could only grin when she winked.

She leaned her head back and closed her eyes, and judging from her facial expressions she quickly entered Santana's world. She made screwball-faces like a guitar player and from what I could tell she wasn't missing a cord. The seatbelt could barely contain her as she gyrated her hips and played her thighs like congas. The pat, pat, pat sounds of flesh pounding flesh made me picture our naked bodies slapping skins again. Gina didn't miss a beat when the song segued into Samba Pa Ti, and she didn't say a word until I parked in front of Rolonda's building. It didn't matter her dance had spoken a language that would make even a mute man draw the same conclusions. I was feeling some shit I don't know anything about again long before Gina threw her arms around my shoulders, pulled me to her firm soft full breasts and fucked me with her tongue!

She hopped out my car before shock would let me reciprocate. Then she leaned in the opened window. I smiled at the perfect view of her black lacey overstuffed bra.

"Thanks, for the ride. I'm, uh, sorry if I ruined your evening," she said with a satisfied blush on her face.

I hadn't rebounded from her grandmotherly hug and that tongue kiss so I wasn't surprised when her smile made me want to feel her pouty lips some other places. Niki had tried everything and all Gina had to do was blush.

"Maybe our paths will cross again under better circumstances," I said as a black Land Cruiser with tinted windows creeped by us blasting a remix of "Real Love." I was almost yelling when I said, "Perhaps when you're feeling better you can teach me how to slow dance or salsa or meringue or whatever you were doing in your seat."

A mischievous smile graced Gina's face, and I was thankful for the cool breeze coming through the window.

Her eyes were on the SUV. I didn't know how to read the knitted eyebrow look on her face when she said, "That song takes me to another place and a better time."

"Oh, yeah, so can you bring a friend, my night wasn't going all that well until I meet you."

Our eyes met and she blushed again and said, "I don't know if you're ready, Mr. Stokes. You cannot force these things y'know." The SUV turned at the corner and sped away.

"Now I'm curious. I don't know if I can keep up, but I would damn sure like to try. You were putting some moves on my seat that would put my favorite lap dancers to shame."

She blushed and said, "Actually I was probably doing some sorta ceremonial dance."

I raised my brow and flashed another inquisitive look.

She leaned deeper inside the window and whispered, "I shouldn't tell you this, but sometimes I can't begin to explain the thoughts that flash through my mind." Our eyes locked and the sexiest smile I've ever seen washed across her face.

"The first time I experienced Black Magic Woman I was in junior high school. My parents had gone to Chicago to attend a funeral. I don't remember who, but I remember being angry with my sister not so much for letting her new boyfriend spend the night, but for swearing me to secrecy. My sister is thirteen years older and in those days, she treated me like a child. She still does but that's another story. Her new boyfriend, a guitar player himself, talked her into letting him stay over so they could take care of me together, as if them playing house had anything to do with me. Anyway, I went to bed early because I didn't want to know anything to tell. We lived in Mississippi, and my parents are still as old school as they come.

Sharon was blasting the music so I was semiconscious when my sister's headboard started keeping time with the beats. By the time Black Magic Woman came on I had closed my eyes again, but a powerful vision of a young black woman dancing kept me from sleeping. At first I thought I was having a vivid vision of my sister getting it on because the girl was ebony and beautiful and sexy like my sister, but then I sensed that it was me dancing on their sexual energy. God, I can't believe I'm telling you all this. Anyway, I couldn't tell from the music if it was from Africa, Cuba, Haiti, or Brazil, because the girl was wearing a grass skirt and her breasts were bare. She was dancing around a group of men and teasing them like the flames of an out of control fire."

Gina waved her hands in front of my face like a witch casting a spell. I moved away and pretended that I couldn't stand her teasing.

"She scorched them with her love heat, and backed away, all while her hips moved in hypnotic circles like what I was doing. That girl hypnotized all those men with her spellbinding movements. And when the song and dance ended, she had sapped all their energy without touching any of them. They all fell to the ground, and I had my first orgasm." Our eyes meet again.

"I meant to say, my soul had been touched, and I was sweaty and exhilarated even though the first time I had that vision I couldn't begin to describe what had happened. It made me awfully curious though." Gina blushed again. "I was reliving that vision when you--" She stopped talking and blushed. "I'm so embarrassed—I didn't mean to go on and on like that."

"Hell, if I had known you were feeling all that, I would have pulled over. I usually walk away from women who can't stop yakking, but my guess is that story says a lot about you, and your kiss made me awfully curious as well." Even though I hadn't figured her out yet, I somehow knew that would make her blush.

"Sometimes my visions are pretty outlandish. My grandmother used to tell me that I have stronger than normal reactions to the spiritual energy in people, and music and life." She blushed again and said, "I see that skeptical look on your face. I'm not saying I'm a psychic or anything remotely close, and I hope you don't think I'm crazy, but most of the time my warnings are on point so slow your roll, big boy, before you zoom by what you're looking for."

All I could do was chuckle. Gina's tone was soft and teasing again. I suspected that she was teasing to make light of the strange truths she had revealed about herself. She showed me her best belly dance move again and I didn't care one way or the other. I was smitten.

"Don't laugh. Visions and warnings don't come to me often, but trust me, I'm not crazy. Shucks, if I wasn't still in love with Charles I could turn you out and show you how love feels. That's what your massive woman hunt is about, right?"

The way Gina was reading my mind or too many tabloids was unnerving. My business is all over the entertainment news. Maybe Sloan said something. He's the only person who knows about my plan to settle down and our lists. We got drunk to celebrate our decision to bite the dust, and while we were planning our exodus from playboys to husbands and fathers, we made a list of the top ten qualities we desire in our mates. Gina looked at me as if she knew I was comparing her to my wish list.

"I know you are wondering if I can back-up my big talk. You do know that curiosity killed the cat," she said. She winked and strutted away.

"Yes, but satisfaction brought him back," I yelled. My tongue wagged like Michael Jordan's while I enjoyed every sway and wiggle of her hips. "And with a walk like that——"

I thought she heard me when she spun around on her heels and staggered. She held her balance like a skater, and screamed, "Get down, Don! Get down now!"

Squealing tires silenced my, "What?"

Gina ran into the building and disappeared so fast you would have thought she had on Air Jordan's instead of stilettoes. The black SUV from earlier did a pop-a-wheelie around the corner and damn near took my bumper with it. A small gloved hand with fur around the wrist stuck a Glock 9mm gun out the half opened tinted window, aimed in my direction, and opened fire!

CHAPTER 2

She Must Be Crazy

My life flashed before my eyes in five seconds or less. When a gun is pointed in a man's direction he quickly rethinks his life choices. The first thing he thinks about is his kids, his woman if he has one, his mother and everything and everybody he has ever done wrong. I did more praying in five seconds than I've done the last five years. The last time I told Mom I was going to stop chasing skirts, she joked about it taking a brush with death to put me on the straight and narrow.

I eased up on my elbows like a punk and peeked out the window when the sounds of the gunshots and SUV faded to silence. Gina was nowhere in sight, but the glass door to Roland's apartment building looked like a pile of diamonds twinkling on the sidewalk. I was shaken, but not hurt. Thank God for bullet proof windows. Sirens headed in my direction sounded like rumbles of thunder chasing flashes of lightening as they got closer. I revved up my engine. Was there any point in sticking around to answer questions about a shattered glass door? Most of what had happened hadn't fully registered in my mind. I went through a quick set of what ifs. Gang bangers? Hip hop rivals? Wannabe gangsters? A drug deal gone bad? Carjackers? A lover's spat? Some bitch I'd done wrong trying to scare me? This damn sure wasn't the only time Niki had shown her violent possessive side. Whatever it was or wasn't I didn't have any answers. If that bullet had really had my name on it, I would have died thinking about Gina's legs wrapped around my back. Not a bad way to go until it hit me that I didn't have her number, and Sloan did.

I ran upstairs and turned on my computer the minute I got home. There were four hundred matches for Gina Hills. I clicked on the article from Essence

Sloan had sent, the websites for her dental practice, and the foundation. Gina's emergency number was for dental emergencies only. It was late, and I had to get up early. I don't give away half a million dollars every day so if nothing else I can reach her at her dead husband's Foundation or her office during business hours to make sure she is okay.

I reread the tear-jerking article about Gina and Charles's long and loving marriage. Charles, a civil rights attorney, had set up a foundation that would reopen and represent mishandled civil rights cases. They had planned to name the foundation after Gina's grandmother but Charles died before it was official. Gina named the foundation after Charles and she pledged to continue to make it a success. I called Sloan back last December and told him I was sending a check for five hundred thousand dollars since Uncle Sam was going to get it anyway. That article made me think about my father's accident, but more importantly it triggered my desire to be in a relationship based on love. Gina got under my skin when I first read the article and again tonight. She is obviously still in love with Charles and interested in Sloan, but her innuendoes and warnings still made it hard for me to sleep. Every player knows that when women tempts you with a juicy steak, and dare you not to bite, they are only checking to see if you can pass their litmus tests. You damn right I'm curious, Gina, but even if I had your number I would be afraid to call you after whatever the hell happened tonight.

As soon as I got comfortable in my bed, the phone rang and I not only wanted Gina's number, I wanted her. She had called Sloan in a panic and begged him to call and check on me. The lawyer in him tried to figure out what the shooting was about. After he established that I was okay and none of the shots had hit me or my car, we assumed that the bullets probably weren't meant for me. We decided that the worst case scenario was maybe some chick wanted to scare me. My mind went straight to Niki. Sloan went on and on about how wonderful Gina was after he calmed my nerves. I didn't bother to ask him for her number.

My press outside of basketball has not been good, which is why I'm hesitant about the publicity things my agent has set up for me. My needs at this point are basic. Give me a sweet lady, shelter and a bunch of kids and I'll be straight. I know my needs are contrary to my recent actions, but the first promise I made to God last night was to find me a sweet lady and treat her right.

Instead of playing cards or video games during the flight to Los Angeles, I tried to relax. I had fallen asleep when Rick King sat down and nudged me in the side. Rick is my boy. Ted renegotiated him a fantastic contract last year. I'm interested in the same type of deal, but Ted keeps steering me towards movies and shit.

Rick was married to his college sweetheart when we became teammates three years ago. His infidelities on the road caught up with him two years ago. We got caught in a hotel suite with a couple of honeys. The honey Rick was with was sixteen and she had pot, which she said was Rick's. The drugs and her age complicated matters. Rick would have gone to jail, but the girl I was with took the payoff and confessed to setting us up. Rick's wife stuck by him, but as soon as the charges were dropped she gave a new meaning to the old cliché if you play you must pay. She moved back to Atlanta with Rick's two sons and half his money. She blamed me for Rick's indiscretions. Rick is my boy, but a dick is like a horse--you can lead it to water, but you can't make it drink.

I pretended to be asleep when he nudged me in the side again. "Wake up, man. Don't I get a chance to win back the Benjamin's you took from me on the last road trip?"

I was having a sweet daydream about slow dancing with Gina.

"Who was she? It must have been good if you're trying to catch up on your Zs now."

After all the mess Rick has been through with his wife, I thought he would have had enough of this playboy shit, but he is so deep into the groupie thing it's like a rites of passage that is written into his new contract. Rick is one of those awkward looking brothers. Everything about him is big--feet, hands, teeth, butt, head--nothing cute, he's almost scary. He's the type of brother the girls used to make fun of, or cross over to the other side of the street to avoid until he became a star. I hope he isn't blowing his money; this shit isn't going to last forever.

"You know me, if baby girl doesn't have it together, why waste a whole night?" I wiped the sleep from my eyes and stretched. "You wanna hang with me and check out some movie stars?"

"Hell yeah." He flashed his classic toothy grin. "Who we gonna hook up with?"

"Trevor Noah."

Rick frowned. "Who else is gonna be there?"

"I don't know. Are you down or what? I was supposed to read for a part playing Candy Webb's cheating boyfriend, but I spoke to Mr. Hudlin, and he said the part was mine if I wanted it."

We checked into the hotel using our aliases. Most of the time I'll use the name of the woman I was with last, but I decided to do Niki a favor and keep last night private. And thoughts of Gina Hill had kept me awake all night so I decided to keep that private as well.

I called Mom and Jason and reminded them that I love them. I didn't mention that some bitch may have shot at me. I guess I'm not buying into Sloan's theory. I called room service and ordered lunch. My stomach didn't give a damn about the time change, that's why I hate coast-to-coast runs. I took a nap even though I was still pumped from the night before. In addition to the interview I had practice.

The ringing phone woke me up. The front desk was calling to let me know the studio's limo was waiting downstairs. I splashed water on my face and called Rick's room.

Rick and I chatted with Trevor backstage before the interview began. Dude is funny as all hell, and he is smart. It didn't take long for the conversation to turn to my private life. I was glad I hadn't mentioned my silly feelings for Gina to Rick or the shooting. Rick was feeding Trevor story after story about our dealings with groupies--hearing it from someone else made me question my character. If I'm as bad as I sound, it's no wonder why Mom and Gina told me to slow my ass down. Everything Rick said was true, but after last night none of it needs to be within the public domain.

My gut tightened as though I was a little boy again. I wished I hadn't let Ted talk me into doing the interview. He's always telling me I'm handsome, and smart, and that I can be a movie star, but being a star isn't all it's cracked up to be. What if somebody out there wants my ass dead, just because I fucked their wife, or girlfriend, got what I wanted and got the hell out, some random fatal attraction shit, who knows?

Trevor gave me a brief introduction before I went on stage. By the time I sat down, I was cool, calm and collected. The women in the studio audience screamed when I walked out. One woman was in a frenzy.

Trevor welcomed me to The Daily Show and said, "Don, you have quite a reputation with the ladies." I prayed that he wouldn't give any details. "We were talking backstage and you said you were ready to settle down. Why don't you tell our audience the type of woman a man like you could become serious about?"

The only time I had thought out the specific details was over Sloan's and my drunken lists. "Well, Trevor, I'm almost thirty-two-years old. I've meet more than my share of beautiful women over the years. Don't get me wrong—I'm into beautiful women, but beauty to me is more than physical appearances. I dig fit women who have a little extra cushion in the right places. It also helps if she is intelligent, spiritual, dependable, honest, drug free and well-grounded. Wholesome women with interesting personalities who are not afraid to do their own thing tend to get me going. It would also be a plus if they love children." Okay, so I described my mother. Who else is a man supposed to turn to when he's in trouble?

The screaming woman shouted, "Here I am, baby!"

"Do you hear that, ladies? You don't have to be beautiful, but you must love children. Speaking of kids, you do lots of good things for the youngsters in your community. Tell us about some of the programs you work with."

I smiled. That was an easy question. "I run a summer basketball camp for boys and girls in Chicago where I grew up. Everything is free for the kids. I also work closely with the Make-A-Wish Foundation. We go to hospitals and help make dreams come true for terminally ill children." I waved at the screaming lady while the security guards escorted her out.

"I've lost a few friends to the drug war so I also support programs that provide alternatives to that lifestyle. I go to schools as often as I can and tell kids how important it is to study and put their hopes into completing their education. Playing professional basketball is a difficult job. I remind the kids that it takes hard work and dedication to do anything worth doing. It doesn't matter if you want to play ball, rap, dance, cook, or be a doctor or lawyer, education, discipline, and patience are the keys to the life you want."

"How do you stay in perfect condition?" Trevor asked.

The ladies screamed when he said condition and every time I smiled. I'm baffled about having that effect on women. When I ask them about it, they say my smile and my dimples drive them crazy. How someone could get that worked up over dimples is beyond me. I see myself as being rather average looking. I love to party, but I don't abuse my body. I'm leery of women who get too excited by my looks and who I am. The problem is: that includes all the women I've met since I've been playing professional basketball except Gina. Ted is pushing acting down my throat because this could be my last season.

"I work out every day and play as often as I can," I said. "I play in a few celebrity games during the off-season. The proceeds help to raise money for various charities that help children, and they help me to stay in shape."

"Since you are a man of position and means, before we wrap it up we would like to hear your take on the shocking comments Trump made about women."

"What is even more shocking, Trevor, is that this guy could actually be our next President. I travel all over the country and sadly there are a lot of people in America who agree with his politics of fear and anger. This is just another blatant example of how justice in this country is really applied. Conscious and unconscious presumptions of Black men being dangerous and guilty are always out there. Even a rich Black man like myself, would be judged harshly and criminally if I treated women with such disregard, and I certainly wouldn't be rewarded with the Presidency."

The audience clapped. Trevor thanked me for joining him and that was it. We chatted for a few more minutes after the recording. It had been easier than I had expected.

I looked over the script on the way to practice. The only reason I would consider the part is Candy Webb--she has a reputation for being as sweet and as bad for you as her name.

The twins and I hooked-up when I got back to the city after my five games and thirteen-day road trip. Bee and Tee are caramel colored beauties with a sensuous mix of lust and passion. I went home after practice the next day. The phone was ringing, when I opened my door. My caller ID indicated that, Niki, the pissed off model, had called thirty times. I waited until I heard, "Whassup, Don? This is Candy Webb," before I picked up the receiver.

She was in the city. She called to see if she could change my mind about doing the movie by bribing me with dinner and whatever else jumps off. I couldn't do the acting thing and spend the summer with my son.

Candy is a knock out actress with what I call soul sister looks--a chocolate beauty with natural hair, a tiny waist, and more than a hand full of booty. She has a man but I know a proposition when I hear one.

We decided to meet at Zen Cafe even though my gut was telling me to slow down. The restaurant's relaxed romantic atmosphere would provide the perfect setting for me to get to know Candy before giving her what she wanted.

Candy air-kissed me on both cheeks when she arrived. She is only five feet tall, but her peppery personality on screen makes her appear taller. We ordered Jamaican martinis and sipped on them while we browsed the menus and each other. She is much more glamorous in person than the crackheads and hoes she plays so well in the movies, but she was trying too hard to be sexy and provocative.

I like naturally sexy things about women. Most of the time it's something they probably wouldn't think is sexy at all. Sometimes it's the way they look at me, or the way they walk, or move in their seat when they are nervous. It's more of a reaction to me than anything physical that gets me going. Sometimes it's as simple as their voice, their smile, or the way their eyes light up when they look at me. They can't fake any of that shit, which is why it flicks my switches. Gina tickled all my nerves and some--maybe I should call her up. I wasn't connecting with anything different about Candy other than the physical.

After two martinis Candy said, "I've heard some nice things about you, Don."

"They're not true," I said. Most women can't wait to talk about a good thang, and I've been good to more than my share.

"I think you're a terrific ball player--naturally I follow L.A., but since I'm a native New Yorker; I have to check out the home team."

"So you like basketball?" I asked while we exchanged predatory looks.

"I like you," she answered and her full lips curled into an informative nasty girl smirk. She took another sip of martini, and I proceeded with caution. My nasty boy had resurfaced as well even though I was honestly trying to change. I wanted to feel Candy's lips wrapped around me, but after my last episode with Niki, I didn't want to rush things. My business is all over the tabloids as it is.

"So, you like to watch me play?"

"I'd like to play with you."

"You think you can hang with a pro?"

She leaned back and chuckled. "You jocks crack me the hell up. I got game." She stood up. "Let's go to your place I'm staying with my boyfriend--he's working."

"Oh, shit!"

Gina's words flashed through my mind, but it was hammer time!

We started undressing in my elevator. Candy had on an orange silky dress with a matching orange sweater. The orange looked great next to her smooth dark skin. I removed her sweater. Her large dark areolae were pressing against the thin fabric. I kissed her and ran my hands over her small perky breasts. I prefer bras--the challenge of hooks and snaps, and the thrill of unwrapping them like a child with new toys is turn on number one.

We made it to my oversized blue leather sofa and it was on. Candy wasn't into foreplay, but I cruised her body and introduced myself to it until she whispered, "Cut the bullshit. I want what you want! Save the mushy stuff for your old lady."

A woman who knows what she wants--incredible turn on number two. I had a pocket full of condoms, my American Express card, and my reputation to uphold.

Candy yelped, "Harder! Deeper! Faster!" and Mr. Johnson being the pussy addict that he is enjoyed pleasing her. Her instructions made it easy. It was a quickie, but she was happy so who the hell was he to complain? Candy fell asleep afterwards and I lay awake and reprimand Mr. Johnson for jumping in too soon.

Candy woke up hours later when I flicked on the TV. I was ready to slow dance. She wanted to hurry home to Link. We ended up in my guest room. I walked her downstairs and put her in a cab around three a.m. Candy blew me a kiss when the cab drove away and I felt like the ass side of a booty call.

I went back upstairs and lay across my bed while I played my messages. My goods were in my hand, and my mind was on Gina's sexy innuendoes. Foreplay! That's what her story and dance had been. Before I could dwell on my new revelation, one of the messages form Niki said, "I think I'm pregnant. We'll talk when I get back from doing the Paris shows."

When I first meet Niki, she said, "Don't ever assume I'm just a beautiful girl from west Texas. I go after what I want, and I damn sure know how to get it."

"I'm fucked! I should have listened to her warnings. The bitch is crazy!"

CHAPTER 3

Little Girls, Gunshots, and Blue Eyes

he truth is I wasn't reading Don's mind. I was reading his energy, but even that is not something I can do to everyone. And it definitely is not something I can do all the time. It's much too draining. Charles was the last stranger I connected to that deeply. It's what drew me to him and what put a wedge between us toward the end. My instincts have always been good, and I'm great at reading body language and eyes. Premonitions are much harder to explain. Sometimes they come to me in my dreams, and other times I can touch someone and full blown visions will flash in my mind. Don kept imagining himself making love to me so I kissed him and tried to scare him off with my crazy dance story. My vision of him being in the path of a pissed off ex-lover wasn't nearly as scary as the vision of him loving me. I'm so confused, I'm not sure if I saved Don's life or put mine in danger. I still feel guilty about not being able to save Charles. I was just so angry with him about my visions of him with his paralegal.

Don hit twenty points the other night. I guess that means he's okay. As for me, I haven't stop thinking about him since I kissed him a month ago. Well, okay, I can picture myself screwing him. Don is completely wrong for me, but even grieving widowers have needs.

Rolonda made me another date with Sloan to help me get over my lust for Don. I like Sloan, but I postponed our date. I can't decide if dating him will help me get over my strong feelings for Don or if it will create a scandal if my visions come true.

Don was sending as many mixed signals as me. I stole that kiss to prove that my visions had to be wrong, but if I hadn't hopped out of his car when I did, there is no telling what would have happened. One kiss and my whole body is still yearning for him. I hadn't had any yearning at all since Charles died, now I'm in trouble.

Rolonda doubts that I can handle a man like Don, but sexing him isn't what scares me. I'm a suddenly single thirty-nine-year old woman who has had a boyfriend or a lover since I was six. Charles used to call me his undercover wild woman, and trust me, he wasn't referring to my hair. He could barely keep up with me after he was diagnosed with high blood pressure and high cholesterol. If he had listened to me and his body sooner, he wouldn't have been losing his edge. Their quickie on his desk was good for his ego, but it wasn't enough to break up our happy home. Ro can doubt all she wants. I know what to do when opportunity knocks. The problem is my visions tend to come true. My therapist is probably right about me repressing my childhood nightmares because the truth in them is too traumatic to relive.

Ro bought me a Mr. Wonderful. She thinks I'm just horny. She's right. After I kissed Don, I renewed my membership at Gold's Gym. There is nothing wrong with being confident enough to hit it, quit it, and get on with it, if my opportunity does come again. I requested Patrice Young the only African-American on staff to be my personal trainer.

Patrice had a perfect combination of muscles and feminine curves with a pretty face to balance everything out. She had a blond weave, long blue nails and a ghetto fabulous confidence that challenged me. She gave me two forms to fill out; a food diary and a goals sheet. I omitted screwing Don from my goals sheet, and the Snickers bars and donuts, Laura, my dental receptionist brings in every day from my food diary. Patrice looked at my questionnaire and asked if I had just had a baby. I said fibroids and it was that time of the month. She said I must have a slow metabolism. I faked a smile and said, "In that case, we should start by working on it." I called her a trick in my mind and challenged myself. She isn't the only hussy who can look good.

Patrice looked me over again as if she accepted my dare. She said we had a lot of work ahead of us as if she needed to lose fifty pounds. I carry my weight well. I'm five-feet-ten inches tall and stacked in the right places, or so I'm told. She promised to have me looking like her in six months or less. She looked like Catwoman in her tight black workout gear. I even pictured her holding an imaginary whip over me while she made me sweat my fat away. I was overdoing it, but she was right, I used to have a body like hers. Her biker shorts were showing off her tight butt and her shapely legs, and she was so sure of herself. I used to be sure of myself before Charles had an affair and died before I could confront him. Now I'm at Patrice's mercy.

When I got home, I headed straight for my Jacuzzi. John Coltrane's Soul Eyes made love to my ears as I soaked. The stars seemed closer through the windows in my vaulted ceiling and I felt closer to heaven and Charles when a warm glow of light seemed to join me in the tub. I could smell Obsession cologne--the scent Charles was wearing the last time we made love. Maybe it was my imagination or maybe it was his spirit loving me for old time sake. Whatever it was it calmed me as only my Charles could do.

My mind floated back to the last time we were together. I faked my way through a triple play that morning. Our friends often called Charles and me the Huxtable's. Charles was a high profile civil rights attorney, and a caring father and husband until Theresa charmed her way into the picture. I was a good wife, mother, lover, friend, and a successful dentist. Our son Kevin is a great baseball player, saxophonist, and artist. He's a slacker in school, but a good kid. And Myesha is a talented dancer, piano player, and my good student. She can be a drama queen, but she can pull off sweet when it matters. Charles looked like Marvin Gaye with thick goofy looking glasses, Kevin looks like Charles. Myesha has my face and long legs, but she has dark skin and silky long hair like my mother and my sister Sharon.

Rolonda and Sharon go crazy over Ibaka, but my secret Santa has always been a throw down with Mr. Donald Stokes. Sometimes I'm not sure if I had that vision of me and Don or if it was wishful thinking on my part. I taunted Charles with threats about hooking up with Don for some real satisfaction that morning, and boy did that make him jealous and get his adrenaline going. I tried my best to convince Charles to leave the next day, but now I know I went about it all wrong. Sex was never his Achilles heel--that is mine. Charles never believed I could have premonitions. Lawyers and cops need proof of everything. He always said hunches were for detectives and paranoid wives. Charles swore that he was coasting because he didn't want Myesha and Kevin to hear their mother scream-ing, but I knew better. Charles promised me some good old fashion make me wanna holla loving when he got home the following Friday, but Friday never came. He was such a gotdamn workaholic, and so was that bitch who seduced him. Charles always did things by the book. Spontaneity was wasted on him after he became a father and a successful attorney. Theresa probably made a move on him. I should have told him that I knew about their little tryst on his desk. He wouldn't have admitted any guilt, not Attorney Charles Kevin Hill, but knowing that I knew would have compelled him to stay home and prove that he loved me and our children more than anything in this world. I knew he still did. We would have made love like we used to do before we had to worry about our kids hearing me scream, mortgages, our careers, networking with the right people, and home wreckers, and he wouldn't have died in that awful car crash.

I shouldn't have let him go. If I don't know anything else, I know that when-ever I get the heebie-jeebies something usually happens. I almost never know exactly what. Most of the time the dreams and visions come long before the event. Things come to me in metaphors most of the time. But that morning, and when I met Don, I knew for the first time in a long time. I used to be better at predicting stuff when I was young. Nobody believed me then either. People have a hard time believing what they can't explain. I have a hard time knowing what I know, such as the little girl who looks like me in my dreams telling her father not to take the shortcut to the ice cream parlor moments before they stumble upon a lynching, or Charles having an affair with his paralegal at his firm, or the mere possibility of me falling madly in love with a womanizer like Don Stokes.

When I was a kid the more I talked about lynched boys, dead men, and a man touching my privates, the crazier my family thought I was. I learned the hard way to keep my damn mouth shut even though it didn't stop the night-mares and dreams. A dozen or so boys used to visit me often and tell me sto-ries about how they had been murdered. The dreams and visits stopped after Charles helped solve some of their cases. I secretly dropped the hints those boys had given me to Charles. It was those suggestions that helped him solve those cold cases and helped him make a name for himself.

The nightmares started again when Charles crossed the line with Theresa—the nightmares, the visits, the heebie-jeebies. I knew crazy thoughts like--Sharon getting pregnant by a boy she had just met and telling her ex-boyfriend the baby was his, or Charles dying in that car accident, or me telling Don to get down moments before the shooting started, were not just random thoughts. I tried to warn all of them. I just wish people weren't so quick to call me crazy.

The light in the Jacuzzi with me seemed to caress me until I felt a surge of ecstasy, and then it disappeared. I smiled thinking that sleep was going to come easy for once. My sister Sharon had forced me to see a therapist after Charles died. My therapist has more "issues" than me, but telling me to keep a journal and do things around bedtime that make me feel good was the best advice she gave. I didn't need Mr. Wonderful tonight. I slipped on a silk nightgown, said my prayers and had my nightly cup of spiked chamomile tea.

I fell asleep quickly, but my dreams were filled with the nightmare about the little girl who looks like me. The girl and her father bounced over Sweetwater's back roads at top speeds in a blue Chevy pickup truck. The girl's head rested on her father's lap and her feet dangled over the seat like the boys I see hanging from bridges in most of my nightmares about the girl. The girl's pink dress and face were bloody. She was semiconscious at best. My adrenaline rushed every time her father, who also looked like my father, stroked her cheek and prayed in pig Latin or some language I couldn't understand. That part didn't make sense. My father is more of a gambling and drinking man than a church going man. The dream ended this time with the girl dying in her father's arms. Her mother's screams mixed with mine woke me up.

The first and last time I made love to Charles I visualized this part of the dream. I've prayed for years for that to be all that it is—a bad, bad dream or a metaphor for losing my virginity, or for having sex too soon with Charles, or for using sex to make him love me knowing that I wasn't his type—anything but something that could have possibly happened. It would fill in a lot of blanks. It would prove once and for all that the little girl, like those boys, was real. It would prove that I'm not crazy.

Patrice made me keep a food diary and she weighed me every week. The hardest part was eliminating sugar, because I was addicted, and drinking at least eight ten ounce glasses of water daily, because I had to go too often. Patrice worked me out three times a week. I alternated between her Zumba classes, walking or running on the treadmill or the elliptical machine, and weights the other days. The first month I worked out every day and did everything she told me to do. I was driven every time Patrice looked at me as though I was a balloon getting ready to pop, and I looked at her and thought, I used to have a tight ass, flat belly and perky breasts like yours, and I will have them again, dammit.

Like many women I crave chocolate, ice cream or booze when I'm unhappy. Instead of giving in to temptation I treated myself to soaks in my Jacuzzi, jazz, and aromatherapy. I stopped drinking, and my cravings for junk food were under control unless I had PMS. Working out and cutting out caffeine loaded sweets made me tired enough to sleep better, although there were still nights when nothing helped. The pounds came off quickly at first. I felt better as I reclaimed my old body. I forgave Charles mostly because I missed him more than ever. It wasn't doing me any good to stay angry with a dead man whom I still loved and would have easily forgiven anyway.

Patrice was filled with pride two months later when I dropped the first twenty pounds. She invited me to her small office to give me a reward. Her office had just enough room to fit a desk, a file cabinet, two chairs and a "Just do it!" poster of Michael Jordan. She smiled when she gave me a ten-pack of mini Snickers bars from her desk and told me it was a ten-month PMS supply.

Sweets are just as addictive as alcohol and drugs when you're craving love, romance, or just plain old get down and dirty sex. Eating one small candy bar once a month would be like getting finger fucked at this point in my life. I got over my chocolate cravings when I realized sweets were just a tease for what I was hungry for—a strong chocolate man like Don to do the do and go home after I'm satisfied. It's an unusual request to ask of God, but after loving Charles it seemed greedy to ask for more.

Sex with Mr. Wonderful is shallow even with me visualizing Charles or Don in the bath with me. Sloan called me again. Maybe I should take him up on his offer. I need some loving sugar like my big Mama used to tell me to give her. A few hugs, a little conversation, and cuddling up next to Don or Sloan wouldn't be bad even if it were just for one night. I've forgiven Charles for falling for Theresa, but since I kissed Don I can't stop feeling guilty for trying to make Charles jealous instead of confronting him with the truth.

Sex isn't the most important thing that I need from a partner, or even the thing that I miss most about Charles. My real hunger is for emotional love, but it comes at a higher cost, and it is ten times harder to find. Charles believed in me. He didn't always believe me, but he understood me, he was patient, he encouraged me, he protected me, and he always supported my dreams for us and our children. Sure, he was a good lover, but all I had to compare that with was a lot of heavy petting with, Bobby, my elementary and high school boyfriend. I dated other guys, but Bobby and Charles were the loves of my life. I was in love with Bobby from the first grade until the twelfth, and Charles and I were lovers and best friends for twenty years. They say we should be thankful if we ever find true love. So, yes, I thank God every day for every moment I spent with Charles even though he failed me in the end. They also say you can't love somebody else until you love and understand yourself. I'm like the crab that represents my birth sign—tough on the outside and soft on the inside. I've never been comfortable with or fully understood any of my differences, not even my pale skin. My dark skin family believed it was an opened door to anything I wanted. It was just another source of confusion for me.

My therapist wants to delve into my childhood because I'm still having problems sleeping. She says childhood traumas can resurface in adults and are often triggered by other traumatic experiences. Understanding my nagging childhood nightmares about the girl has become my number one priority. Those boys were lynched before I was born, I helped Charles prove it. What happened to the girl? Why would those women shoot at me and Don? That's what I need to know.

CHAPTER 4

The Things I Wanna Do to You

Patrice invited me to Buddy's to grab lunch after our workout. She wanted to show off her new Audi A5. Buddy's was chosen by The Hartford Courant as the best bar and grill in town because of its burgers and mixed drinks. Most people go there to get picked-up. I think that is what all the hoopla is really about. It is just a basic sports bar and grill. It has a 50's decor, with black-and-white-checkered tablecloths, low hanging Tiffany lights and TV sets scattered throughout.

Our waiter was a chipper, young blond surfer type. He took our orders and left after flirting with us. Patrice asked me if I ever pretend to be white, but she mostly wanted to know how many white guys I had dated. I can let far more important things slide without losing my cool, but those questions always catch me off guard. We could have been bonding like sisters if we walked by faith instead of by sight and judged people from the inside out. My dating history was pathetic between Bobby and our many breakups before I met Charles. The boys I dated, other than Charles and Bobby, were attracted to me based on their fetishes with my boobs, high behind, long legs, pretty feet, and pouty lips. I learned a long time ago that their goal was sex and my pale skin didn't have as much to do with it as some people believed. The few occasions when my path crossed with someone who favored my skin color over everything else, I quickly excused myself from the situation.

Patrice looked up at the TV and said, "Now there's a brother I would love to get with."

I turned around to check out who she was referring to. A rebroadcast of the basketball game I had watched with Kevin the night before was on. "Which one," I asked?

"Don Stokes, he is rich and handsome, and they say he's smart, but who cares about that with a man like him?"

I didn't bother to tell her I had met him. Even though I had blown it, envy would probably be a bitch with Patrice. The camera zoomed in on him while he prepared to shoot a free throw.

"Look, Patrice, I love his dimples. He has a great smile."

"Forget the smile. He has a great body and a fat ass wallet."

"Looks and money isn't everything."

"It's a damn good start."

Patrice admitted that she was living from paycheck to paycheck by juggling credit card payments. She knows she is living above her means. She says it is part of her game plan to hook-up with someone like Don. I tried to convince her that there is nothing wrong with hard-working ordinary men, but she said she is tired of white girls taking all our fine rich men. She argued that we should do whatever it takes to increase our odds. Her credit cards are maxed-out and she is driving a new car she can't afford so she can attract a rich man. Deception is probably going to attract deception so I reminded her that love is an emotion that is best when it is given freely, but she reminded me that all is fair in love and war and black women are losing big time.

I've had my shield up, but nobody has tried to knock it down. Sloan has called a couple of time, but I'm willing to bet that he has just as many women chasing him as Don. I guess if I want Don or Sloan, I had better get with the program. My emergency cell phone rang before I could concede to defeat. I had an urgent message from Dr. Troy Devaux, a world-renowned forensic odontologist and a detective. He is often called to disasters where bodies need to be identified. He had worked closely with the team assigned to identifying the remains of the people killed on 9/11.

My voice trembled when I said hello to Troy. He answered as casual as blue jeans and T-shirts. He wanted to meet at my office after I finished my lunch.

Patrice and I continued our conversation about love and money. Her chances of using her God-given talents to make enough money to live the way she wants are a lot better than plotting to hook up with Don Stokes. If she wants to get with him for sex, her chances are much better. Hell, even I had a chance at that. Patrice was surprised that if given the opportunity I would indulge in casual sex with someone like Don. She probably thinks I'm a prude, but if Don had asked me that night, he would've had to beg me to have mercy on him. My sister, Sharon, and Rolonda sleep with younger men for their own gratification all the time. I'm old enough to date like a man as well. Sex, love, and money are three separate needs. I've been loved and I have my own money, so why not? I wanted to say more to Patrice about saving for her future, but I sighed and prepared myself mentally for Troy's urgent news. He had been checking into cold cases of rapes and murders in Mississippi at my request.

Natural light cast romantic shadows through the lacy curtains covering my office windows, but my gold and burgundy Laura Ashley upholstery reminded me of Big Mama's funeral home parlor. The lynched boys and Big Papa used to keep me company while Big Mama did her work. My family thought my ability to communicate with the dead was cute child's play until I gave Big Mama a message from Big Papa that I wouldn't have known otherwise, about how his head had gotten chopped off over a cockfight. Big Mama paid more attention to me after that. I don't know if my office reminding me of those times is good or bad, but I did love hanging out with my great grandmother. She was a wise old lady.

I put my feet up on the cherry credenza Charles had given me and day-dreamed about the day we christened it. I'm holding my own even though I still cry sometimes when I think about Charles.

Troy showed up early with a lovely bouquet of yellow roses. The flowers' sweet aroma helped me to switch to my Southern hostility routine.

"Why thank you, Dr. Devaux. You called me up and got me all fidgety because you wanted to bring me these lovely flowers?"

He flashed a cocky grin. The twinkle in his ocean-blue eyes reminded me of the men in my nightmares touching little girls inappropriately.

Before I could ask him about his research he grinned again and his eyes flickered like a flashing police light. "Are you seeing anyone yet," he asked.

I put the flowers on the counter, and gave him my once-over. He was tall and slender like a runner. His short black hair had a gentle salt and pepper sweep. He had a strong mandible like Jay Leno. He was a shade or two tanner than I am, and his full pink lips looked inviting. But when he pinched his thick eyebrows together and smiled, the fine hairs on my back and neck stood up like the crowd when the judge enters a courtroom.

"I have two teenagers, a business, and a foundation to run. Dating is the last thing on my mind."

"I'd like to change that," Troy said and my stomach did a flip-flop.

"Why me?"

He swept his eyes over me. "I saw you working out at LA Fitness. You've lost a lot of weight. You look like a Barbie doll with a wild Afro. You're sexy as hell, Gina. Don't blush and pretend you don't know it."

Being sexy means I'm fuckable, not beautiful or even pretty. Whenever men say things like that about me, I always think about the time I overheard my father's drinking buddy ask my father where he had gotten a beauty like Sharon and a misfit like me. My father said he had been asking Ida Mae the same question for years.

Troy smiled wickedly and said, "I'm willing to bet that we will be good together." He closed the distance between us and placed his hands on my cheeks. "Your friend Ally told me all a about you."

Ally and I were classmates in dental school. She's president of our local dental society. She probably meant well, but she should have asked me before she spoke to Troy.

"Have you ever been married, Troy?"

"Never," he said and then he kissed my forehead and walked the kiss down my nose. His boldness made my heart pump faster when I stared into his eyes.

"Kids?"

"None."

"I don't have much time or energy for a relationship right now," I said. "I'm not sure if I want to get involved with a never married, no kids professional man with your good looks. Are you a workaholic, gay, impossible to please, in a witness protection program or what?" I teased. I always wonder when I meet a man like him.

His lips covered mine as if he hadn't heard a word I'd said. He pushed me deeper into his kiss. His hands slid up and down my back while our tongues did a tango. Our lips smacked when he pulled away. My eyes popped open. I would have slapped him but his boldness frightened me as much as it aroused me.

"We should get together whenever I'm in town for stimulating conversation, dinner, and sex," he said as his hands cruised from my back, around my waist and u-turned and groped my breasts. He kissed me again but this time I pushed him away.

"Stimulating conversation and dinner would be nice, but fucking? I don't think so." I used the f-word to remind myself as well as him what he was really asking for.

"Why not? I could make it good for you."

I stared at the lustful look in his eyes and waited for drool to drip from his inviting lips. For lack of a better excuse I said, "I'm old-fashioned when it comes to making love."

He laughed from his gut. "You're old enough to enjoy it without feeling guilty." I thought about my conversation with Patrice as he swept his eyes over my favorite casual gear—tight Levi's a fitted bodysuit and my favorite alligator boots. I counted to ten, but before I could speak Troy started talking and kissing me between each word again. I drifted into his kisses more than his words. Kissing is one of my favorite things to do in the whole world. Charles used to say my lips were made for kissing. Bobby and I would kiss for hours. Don's kiss was freaking unforgettable.

"I saw you dancing at the President's Ball at the dental convention last May. A woman that can move like liquid sex on the dance floor must have needs. Everything about you exudes sex. Your nipples are erect now."

I pulled away from his embrace and covered myself. He licked his lips in a provocative way.

"Are they pink like your lips or wheat-colored like your hair and eyes?"

"None of your business! I thought you wanted me to meet you here because you had identified a rape case that was like the case I told you about. Forget it, I have to go home to my children."

I snatched my purse up and attempted to leave. He grabbed my elbow, pulled me into his arms and kissed me again. God, he was a good kisser and the touch of a real man was invigorating. I sure could use some quick and fast sex, but I looked deep into Troy's eyes and turned him down.

"I'm not leaving until you agree to go out with me," he said, and the arrogance of his words and his forceful tone reminded me of the white men in my childhood nightmares again.

"I'll wait until you're ready for sex; as wet as your kisses are, it won't be long." He scribbled his private number on his business card. "Call me. I'll be good to you."

I didn't care who he was--he couldn't snoop into my private business and ask me for sex. I'm not desperate. Well, okay, I am but I'll pick the dick.

Troy laid his card beside the flowers. "I made an appointment to see you," he said and then he left. I threw the flowers at the door when it closed behind him.

His offer didn't sound so bad as I lie in my lonely bed later that night and reminisced about his kisses. Charles has been dead two and a half years. Everyone has been on my case about dating again, but would a no-strings-attached relationship with Troy, or someone like Don, or Sloan make me feel better, or would it give me new voids to fill? Can women really date like men and not get screwed? Sloan calls me every now and then. I love talking and laughing with him about music, politics, sports and how we handle people who mistake us for being mixed race. Now I want to screw him and his best friend. How crazy is that?

I woke up at three a.m. that night missing Charles in a special way. I clicked on the TV. Don Stokes was on The Daily Show with Trevor Noah. Don was wearing a camel-colored suit, brown shoes and large diamond-stud earrings in his ears. He ran his tongue over his lips and pursed them in the perfect position for a kiss. I listened to his interview and wished he had been as bold as Troy. His brown eyes made me feel warm and tingly inside as he whispered sweet nothings. His words kissed my neck and shoulders until my insides were like warm melted butter. I used Mr. Wonderful and imagined Don, Sloan, and Troy loving the life back into me. When I closed my eyes, there I was tying one of them to the post of an 18th century mahogany poster bed. The detail of the bed made it more of a possibility than a fantasy. I knew I would see that bed again. Their faces were like a merry-go-round fading from Don's to Sloan's to Troy's. One of them whispered my name and I took him places I had only known with Charles. We moved together until all our heated tangled bodies created a sweet musk in the air. I drifted deeper into the dream after I was satisfied, but I woke myself with a scream just before dawn. Troy's blue eyes were wide open. His chest had a hole in it as big as my fist. Blood was all over the little girl's pink dress and face. She had a gun in her hands!

CHAPTER 5

Coming Up Empty

I get excited about road trips with stops in Chicago. I can throw down in the kitchen, but nobody's food is as good as Mom's. Two days with Mom and Jason, and the fact that I usually play well in Chicago is just what I need to change the way I've been living.

The air in Chicago was bone-chilling, but the sight of Mom's bright eyes and rosy cheeks made my heart realize just how much I miss her and Jason. Most people don't believe she is my mother—I look like my dad. I had to kick many a butt when my buddies started playing the dozens. Mom is one of those big yellow heartbreaking women that Blues men like Muddy Waters sing about. She's the kind of woman who could walk into a bar and the whole place would get quiet and all eyes would be on her. Gina reminds me of her. There is definitely something about Gina Mae Hill that shook me even though I'm hesitant about pursuing her.

Sometimes when things are quiet, I think about Gina. I wonder how she is doing. I wonder if she's happy. Her chat with Sloan had left a lasting impression on him as well. Rolonda arranged another date for them to get together. Sloan is planning to take her for a ride in his father's private plane. He will take her someplace romantic for dinner, which will surly lead to them having each other for dessert. When he told me that, jealousy kicked in again. I let it slip that she had kissed me, but instead of telling him to back off I told him to be careful.

Snowflakes began to fall as we made our way home. Most people hate Chicago's winters. I grew up on the south side on Wentworth Avenue in a two-family house. Mom and I lived on the second floor and my uncle and aunt and their three daughters lived on the first floor. I started a snow removal business

34

when I was twelve. Most of our neighbors were from the South so they were more than happy to leave the shoveling to me. I made more than enough money to buy candy, marbles, baseball cards, and yo-yos, and Mom started a college fund with the rest. I hired two young boys on my street to help do the shoveling, and Don's Snow Removal Service was my first successful business; I've been an entrepreneur since.

My favorite foods were waiting when we got home. Mom's fried chicken is the best. She even made sweet potato cobbler. My room was spick-and-span and Mom had put the electric blanket on my bed to keep me warm. It has been just me and her most of my life. Dad died in his eighteen-wheeler when I was ten. He was one of few black men in those days who owned his rig. Mom suspected foul play, but she didn't have the money to check it out, which is why I upped my donation to Charles's legal fund.

Some people say I'm a mama's boy, but I say I love my mother and she loves me--if that makes me a mama's boy, then lucky me.

I filled my belly, and then I stretched out on the black leather sofa in the den and clicked on the large-screen TV. I channel surfed until I found BET JAMS. A video of a young rapper singing while five sexy women in skimpy bikinis danced, kissed, and rubbed him up and down while he did his thing was playing. Video whoring is appealing to brothers like me while we are living out our fantasies, but what's going to happen when the videos are over? What's going to happen after my last replay and their last hit? What then? I surfed until I found CNN. They were showing the latest fashions from Paris and out walked Niki doing her infamous catwalk. I continued to surf until I found a rerun of "Good Times."

I was relaxing before practice when Jason woke me up from the daydream I was having about Gina kissing me. People who don't know Jason is my son often mistake him for my little brother. Sometimes I feel more like his brother than his father, but we're cool.

He had a sly grin on his face when my eyes popped open. Jason is only fourteen, and he already has a thin mustache. He's tall, and his chest and shoulders have taken on a barrel shape. I asked him what was up. He said he had done it. I sat up until I could see his face clearly. I've missed so much of his growing up. We spend summers together, but that's not enough. I couldn't remember if I had talked to him about safe sex. I may not know anything about love, but after I got his mother pregnant, I never trusted women again.

"You told me I should use condoms no matter what she says. I liked it--I mean her."

"That's good, Jay." I tried to think of something cerebral to say. This was a big father-son moment.

"Have you ever been in love, Dad?"

I knew the answer to Jason's question, but I didn't want to admit to myself how the answer reflected on my character. "Well, Jay, you have to nurture love and give it time to grow. I'm too busy with basketball, business, and summer camp to let my heart sink into a relationship." Jason looked at me cross-eyed and I knew he didn't believe a word I had said. "Most women don't understand how much time and energy I have to spend doing other things."

"Didn't you say we should make time for the things that are important in our lives? Love is important."

"It is. But I guess I'm still searching for that special person."

"You've done it a lot. You didn't like any of them?"

"It's more complicated than that, Jay. I enjoy sex. But when you're in the position I'm in, you have to be careful."

"So, it's easy for you to get sex, but it's hard to find someone to love?"

"That's how it's been, but I'm trying to change. I'm gonna give up lap dances for slow dances. I want a grin on my face like yours. So, tell me about your girl."

"Her name is Diana. She's pretty, and she likes me, too." Jason talked about Diana timidly, but his face was beaming. I haven't beamed like that since I tapped my first piece. I was fourteen, as well, but love didn't have anything to do with it then either.

"Well, lover boy," I patted him on his back, "I have to go to practice, but when I get back we'll continue this discussion."

Mom has been dropping hints about moving back to Alabama after I settle down. She wants a few more grandchildren while she is young enough to enjoy them. I'm a player, but I suppose I should start planning for life after the last game.

❧

Coach did his usual speech about how we could beat Chicago if we played our game and didn't let Chicago set the tempo. We scrimmaged and ran through a few plays. My strong point is my shooting game. I try to establish my game early so I can get better statistics. This is a do or die season. My stats need to be great for me to continue to play and demand megabucks.

Rick wanted to hang after practice, and since Chicago is my city, it was on me. Instead of hanging out I invited him to dinner. I wanted to spend my time with Jason and Mom so I called ahead to let Mom know I was on my way with company.

The mahogany dining room table was set when we arrived, and the smells of Mom's special spices and pies were calling my name. She had made steaks with onions, homemade potatoes and gravy, string beans, homemade rolls, and an apple pie. We took off our coats and boots and headed to the table like starving children. Mom yelled at us like we were little boys and sent us back to wash-up.

I said grace even though I haven't been to church since my cousin's wedding five years ago. I've been praying a lot more since that shooting. I talk to God often about that crazy night. Mom was a Sunday school teacher, and Uncle Leon was a deacon at Mount Calvary where I spent many a Sunday and quite a few Saturday nights. I can hold my own praying; I simply mock Reverend Washington.

"Mrs. Stokes, you Southern women can throw-down in the kitchen," Rick said.

"Thank you. Perhaps you and Don should find y'all a couple of nice Southern girls and stop all that foolish running around y'all been doing."

"Their cooking will never come close to tasting as good as yours, Mom," I said as I put a couple of steaks on my plate.

"Y'all better stop running around before y'all get in some trouble you can't get outta. I didn't raise you that way, Donald."

"I hear you, Mom."

"How much longer do you think you can play ball and chase skirts every night? The Lord gives it and the Lord will take it away."

"Mrs. Stokes, I'm not looking for a wife. I have enough trouble with the one I had," Rick said between bites.

"That's because you're running the streets when you should be taking care of your kids."

"Mom! I'm sorry, man."

"The truth is the truth, and ain't nothing wrong with telling the truth. Jason and all these other boys look up to you, and since I'm your mother, it's up to me to point out what's wrong with how you're living."

I sank down in my chair. "Maybe you're right."

Mom got up to answer the ringing phone. She said a few words before she gave it to me. It was Sloan. He was in Chicago on business. Mom had already invited him over.

Jason and I were doing the dishes, and Mom was giving Rick an ear full about getting back with his ex-wife by the time Sloan arrived.

Mom had gone to night school and gotten her masters in social work while I was in high school sowing my wild oats. I always had good grades so she didn't have a clue until I messed up with Valerie. Mom still does volunteer work, but lately the only case she has been on has been mine.

Sloan asked for the honeys when I answered the door, but before I could answer he saw Mom and pushed by me to hug her. His parents took me in, and Mom takes everyone in. She didn't waste any time before she jumped on Sloan's case.

"I wish y'all would find the right combination with those honey bees you're always talking about."

"Lighten up, Mom, we're working on it."

"We have to take our time. The ladies we deal with aren't like you. They don't just see us--they see our bottom line. We have to be careful," Sloan added.

"I know, but y'all must be looking for the wrong things from your ladies, also. In my day when we lay down with someone they had to be special. Nowadays, young people do it in reverse. That's why you keep coming up empty."

Sloan tasted the food. "Mmmm, this is good. So, Mom, how can we tell if we're dealing with a good woman?"

"Eat your dinner, man--we can discuss this later."

"Hush, baby, Sloan wouldn't have asked the question if he wasn't expecting an answer. When you meet the right person, Sloan," Mom paused and looked at me, "Something inside you will click, but you need to slow down and learn to listen to what your heart is telling you. Listen to your heart, listen to what she says, and make sure that what she says and what she does is consistent. Understand?"

"Mom, will you let Sloan eat his dinner?"

"Oh hush up, and listen to what I'm saying. I'm going up to my room. Enjoy your dinner, Sloan." She stood up and kissed me on my forehead. "Goodnight, baby."

"What she said makes sense," Sloan said after Mom left. "You need to start turning down some of that easy pussy."

"Since when did you change? The way you are trying to seduce Gina is scandalous." I couldn't believe he was on my case after all the things we've done.

"I'm not putting any pressure on Gina." he said.

I gave him a raised eyebrow look that reminded him of who he was talking to.

"Okay, she's really hot--I would pop on a party hat and go for broke if I could get her to make a date and keep it."

"Gina is a nice lady. Maybe she knows you just want to fuck her."

The possibility of no longer playing ball and the party suddenly stopping bothers me. I don't trust women enough to open my heart to them, but I'm tired of waking up alone. I do want to settle down. This could be my last season. I'm not ready to quit but I'm starting to think about what I want to do after it's over. Sloan promises me lots of real work in our business after my last game. That isn't a problem. I thought I would have had a loving wife and a house full of kids by now. Nice women don't want to buckle up with a guy like me. Sloan thinks I should leave the groupies alone. He's right—we both should. They are getting freakier and slicker by the minute. Men like us can't even protect ourselves with condoms anymore. I know players who are paying child support right now because some freak put holes in the condoms, or froze their sperm. There are fourteen and fifteen-year-old freaks who look twenty-five, and they're getting us in all kind of trouble. Then there are the "he raped me, he hit me" set-ups.

Sloan and I used to think our biggest threat was getting AIDS but it is rough being a player these days. Most people think this is the life. But it's not easy to walk away from free anything-anyway-you-want it sex. Now I understand what Mom meant when she said all that glitters ain't gold. What if I get caught banging some girl Jason's age?

I went to the kitchen to get beers. Jason and Rick were in the family room playing video games. I asked Sloan if he was content with his singleness when I gave him a beer.

We thought we had life all figured out when we were in college. Sloan's parents and Mom tried to warn us, but we didn't listen. I used to laugh when Mom used to say nothing will bring a black man down quicker than drugs, alcohol and white women. I took a gulp of beer and thought about the countless number of women I've been with just for sex and the chill in my manhood suddenly felt colder than the beer as it worked its way through my organs in search of my brain. I wonder if women's fathers warn them about men with big dicks and a smile?

White women aren't that bad--they treat us like gods and all we need to do is sex them right. Black women weren't so easy back in the day, but they hate being outdone by white girls. Nowadays sisters are taking freaking to brand new heights. I dated my share of white chicks. The one I dated freshman year gave the best fellatio on campus. Things were cool until she started talking that love shit. I told her to do Sloan. She did. I told her to lick the dirt off my feet-- she turned it into a sexual act. That's why brothers love'em--it feels good for someone to honor your shit like that. She was pretty, smart and her father was rich, and she was a fiend for my sex. Women get hooked on my stuff and forget about the other needs in the relationship. She was as virtuous as a nun when she introduced me to her husband and their three daughters after a game a few years ago, and I played an innocent college friend well.

"So you didn't go out with Gina yet, what's up?"

Sloan smiled as if he knew something was fishy about my question before he said, "Not yet. We talk often on the phone. The jet is ready to go whenever she says the word. She's really sweet and funny and smart—I'm going to love every minute of hitting that."

We made eye contact and I must have flinched.

"You're not telling me something. You want Gina yourself, don't you?"

I swallowed a swig of beer. "I have bigger things to deal with right now. I may be outta New York soon anyway."

"So it wouldn't bother you if I waxed Gina's ass and moved on?"

"I didn't say all that. Gina is not the type of woman you can just dog out like that." I knew he was being crass to get a rise out of me, and hell if it didn't work. "She's not after your money. Gina is future wife material. She deserves way better than what you're offering."

Sloan chuckled, "I knew it! I was just fucking with you. I ran into Rolonda the other day. Gina keeps postponing our date. She says she has to work on herself before she starts dating again, but Rolonda thinks Gina keeps making excuses because of you."

"Me?"

"Look man, I like Gina—I like her a lot. But if you all already have something brewing, I might as well bow out now?"

"Gina is not over her hurt, man. And have you forgotten that she's a dentist." Sloan laughed—he is one of few people who know dentists scare the hell out of me.

"Stop making excuses man. Any fool could see something was happening between you and Gina at the party. Look me in the eyes and tell me you don't want her."

I couldn't.

"Don't think I didn't notice that you described Gina as your idea mate to Trevor Noah on The Daily Show."

"Get the hell out of Dodge, I was describing Mom!"

"Bullshit, you described Gina!"

"Well, Gina reminds me of Mom."

"Yeah, but you were smiling when you said it."

"That's because when you said she was sweet, and funny, and smart, and not digging for gold you turned three shades of red."

"Rolonda says Gina has been working out with a personal trainer. Gina has lost twenty-five pounds. Rolonda says some famous doctor is trying to ring Gina's bells. Ro told me I had better get it together fast if I am still interested. Now I know for a fact that we both are." Sloan opened his wallet and pulled out a business card. He waved the card in front of my face. It smelled like Gina's raspberry perfume. "The question is: Is it going to be me?" He waved it again. "Or you?" He made a u-turned with the card and made a sound like a jet landing. "It's going to be me unless you admit that you want her!"

I snatched the card so quick it ripped in half. Sloan looked at his half and frowned. I looked at mine and laughed. I had her handwritten cell phone number with two numbers missing.

CHAPTER 6

Crimes of Passion

I could be a Southern Belle or as freaky as I wanted to be with Charles. I always had to struggle to find my balance. I found my G-spot when I was twelve. Well, okay, Bobby found it, but if he could do that with his hands so could I. We used to call it Gina's spot long before I heard of Dr. Ernest Grafenberg. I didn't feel like a virgin when I finally did it, I sure as hell didn't act like one, and it didn't matter to Charles either way. Now I'm back to being like a child whose left brain is aggressive and freaky, and whose right brain is cautious and scared. I secretly checked my schedule every morning for Troy's name. The thought of casual sex with him makes me feel creepy. I'm horny as hell. I'm running out of ways to postpone my date with Sloan. I'm starting to like him. I want to fuck his best friend. Maybe Rolonda is right. Maybe I'm just not cutout to be an emotionless playgirl.

A UPS package came to my house the Monday before Thanksgiving. It contained two bottles of Merlot from France and a note from Troy. It said he was working in Paris with the team investigating the massacre, and he wants to share the wine when we make love. I crumpled the note up. Then I opened a bottle. My intent was to pour it down the drain, but it was good. It transcended the fruity simplicity of a medley of grapes and it had a clean firm edge. I found my cork bottle closer and used it, and then I put the opened bottle in the refrigerator and the closed bottle on my wine rack.

Sloan called to wish me a Merry Christmas. Rolonda had told him about my fantasies about Don, and Don had told him about our kiss. Sloan admitted that he likes me, and that he thinks Don likes me more than he is willing to acknowledge. Sloan wanted me to decide. I must have sounded too excited when I asked him exactly what Don had said. Sloan said he wanted us to remain friends, but he wouldn't tell me what Don said. Something about a bro-code. Then he said something weird about giving Don the rest of my card.

Troy's name appeared on my schedule after the depressing holidays had come and gone. It was a crisp Friday early in January. It was my half day, and he was my last patient.

I was sitting at my desk looking out the window when he parked his Lexus next to my Benz. He was wearing funky sunglasses that made him look intriguing, a pair of stone-washed jeans--without a belt, topsiders--without socks, a plain T-shirt, and no coat. It was thirty degrees and windy outside.

I instructed Laura to treat him like any other patient--a professional no-no. I waited in my private office and gloated over my rudeness while he filled out the registration forms. Laura and Doris were laughing; perhaps he was propositioning them as well.

Troy smiled the moment I walked into the dental suite, and the cold greeting I had planned got stuck in my throat. He showed me the tooth that was hurting. I couldn't find anything wrong with it, but by the time I replaced the existing silver filling with a tooth colored resin I had agreed to have lunch with him.

I lied about having an appointment to see my therapist so I would have an alibi if push comes to a shove. We drove separate cars to Ming Gardens on Main Street. Troy requested a fresh chili pepper on the side when he ordered. After the waitress walked away he whispered, "Did you know chili peppers are an aphrodisiac?"

"I've heard that but Charles didn't need them."

I wanted Troy to know Charles was going to be a tough act to follow.

He leaned in closer and whispered, "I can screw for two, three hours without stopping."

I frowned. I should have slapped his face and left, but as horny as I was I would probably make him a one minute man. He said he has a friend in London who loves every minute of it. I frowned and changed the subject to his work.

"Tell me about some of your interesting cases."

"Let's go to my place. I'll show you my slides."

"I have an appointment. Can't you tell me about them?"

"I could, but I've put together some incredible slides of cases I've solved involving crimes of passion. I would love to show them to you after your appointment."

"I heard you solved a lot of rape cases and homicides--how incredible can your slides be?"

"They are, trust me. The stories behind them are incredible. I'm talking Ted Bundy, Jeffery Dahmer, O.J. Simpson types of crimes."

"Those were some gruesome crimes. How can you sound so excited?"

"Putting the puzzles together is exciting."

"Well, their victims are still dead. I can't get excited about that. And O.J. was acquitted of murder." I didn't give a hoot about O.J., but I was disturbed by the way the case had polarized the country. It was definitely a wakeup call proving that America still has some serious racial problems.

"That's because the LAPD inadvertently destroyed crucial evidence which could have made it an open and shut case. Some of the samples appeared to be tampered with. That led to a reasonable doubt."

"So you're saying the jury made the right decision?"

"I'm saying they had a reasonable doubt."

"So how do you help solve these passion crimes?"

"I find and match bite marks and other clues that most people wouldn't recognize."

"Do you prey on all the widowers when you're done?"

"Ouch! That hurts. I take my work very seriously, Gina."

"Sorry. So, do you get a lot of work? How many rapists go around biting their victims?"

"More than you would think. Biting may be the victim's only defense. She might bite her assailant and he may react by biting her. Sometimes bite marks are the only evidence we have in crimes of passion."

"I wish you wouldn't call them that."

"I solved a case where the only evidence was a half-eaten apple. Did you know most serial rapist leave signature bite marks?" Troy paused to laugh.

I couldn't believe he was laughing about such a serious matter. In addition to being arrogant he is weird. I tilted my head and tried to figure out why I was attracted to him. "So, where are these signature bite marks?"

"Neck, collarbone, breasts, back, between the thighs--all of the places I'd like to kiss you."

I shot an evil look his way, but I didn't comment since those were just a few of Charles's favorite spots. Troy smiled and continued.

"A good set of bite marks can be as good as fingerprints. And the DNA in saliva is quite stable."

"So how do you make a match?"

He ran his long slender fingers through his hair, and I imagined him kissing and touching those spots.

"There are a few ways. If the bite marks are fresh it can be as simple as matching the marks with models of the suspect or swabbing the area to retrieve the DNA evidence needed to link the suspect to the crime. DNA doesn't lie--it's unique for everyone. Sometimes marks are not clean and clear to the lay person. That's when an expert like me is called. I'm good." He smiled naughtily.

"I bet you are." I shot him my best don't-even-go-there look, but I was born curious.

"I solved a case a couple of months ago--sixteen-year-old runaway who bit her assailant's penis and got away. I made a match--it was an open and shut case. Open and shut--get it?"

Troy had the same excited look when he talked about his work and sex.

"So most of your cases are open and shut?"

"Not at all. By the time the experts are called, critical evidence most likely has already been destroyed and that makes putting the puzzle back together three times as hard, if not impossible. These types of crimes are rarely isolated. We store everything in data banks and wait until they strike again. I can solve hundred-year-old crimes with the new technology. Criminals eventually get careless or arrogant. When they do, voila--ten crimes solved at one time, and my picture is in every major newspaper in the country!"

I frowned again. "Aren't you a little full of yourself?"

He leaned back in his chair and chuckled. "When you're good, you're good. I'm good at everything I do."

We ate our lunch while he continued to tell me stories about his work and his sexual escapades. He walked me to my car. I said goodbye and thanked him for lunch. He tapped on my window before I could pull away. I opened it while my car idled. I thought he was expecting another goodbye kiss, but he whispered, "I hear brothers don't go down. I'll lick and tease your breasts until your nipples are as hard as pebbles. I'll eat you until you're raw. I'm good, Gina. You'll see."

I turned beet red and sped away. It took him two weeks to call and say he was sorry. I told him to get lost, but he called every day. Laura was good at getting rid of him, until he faked dental pain in the tooth I had worked on. I replaced all his silver fillings with resin fillings while we tried and failed to figure out where his pain was coming from. He made sexual innuendoes about my nipples, the way I walk or what he said my eyes were saying but I wasn't. He knew how to make me blush, and he always made sure he was my last patient so I couldn't rush him out of my office. He invited me out to lunch or dinner after each visit, but I always gave him excuses about needing to be with my kids.

It was late February and Troy was still trying to get me in his bed. I haven't heard from Sloan since Christmas and Don sure as hell hasn't called. I wasn't surprised when I decided to let Troy turn my nipples into pebbles and kiss me there until I begged. I was so horny most days it wouldn't have taken much to achieve either if the bloody nightmares hadn't been coming almost every night again. Sometimes I wake up in a cold sweat and little girls with little pink blood smeared dresses sing "Amazing Grace" until I go back to sleep, and other times I dream about somebody with a post-bed loving me the way Charles used to. Troy has a possessive arrogance that is attractive on a professional level, but it is a turnoff in a lover. The next time Troy asked me out I said, fuck it—Don isn't going to call. Besides, Troy had tickets to a sold-out Alicia Keys concert at Mohegan Sun Casino.

CHAPTER 7

Young, Gifted, And OMG

The cashmere sweater I wore was supposed to keep my pebbles from showing, and the tennis bracelet Charles gave me on our tenth anniversary cruise was supposed to remind me why it is important to seek the things in a lover that make the heart beat to the same beat.

While Alicia sang my mind drifted to another time, another place, another love. And when she sang the words, "Tonight I'm gonna find a way to make it without you," I couldn't stop my tears. Troy wiped them away and whispered, "Everything will be all right; you can love again if you give yourself a chance." He tightened his arms around me and I relaxed in his embrace.

We went to Cheri's for dinner and drinks after the concert. Troy ordered a three-hundred- dollar bottle of wine, oysters, lobsters, and crab legs for both of us. I started "Gina's Rules" after I dropped thirty pounds. One of my rules is to have drinks or dessert as a treat, never both. I can't have ice cream and cookies or liquor and sweets the same day, and I convinced myself that I hate chocolate. I vowed not to have sex with Troy before hearing the "L" word, and he must use a condom and make a commitment. I'm flexible on the commitment part. My number one rule is--any rule can be broken if I can live with the consequences.

"I enjoyed the concert, thanks for inviting me," I said. Troy smiled wickedly as I sipped my wine and locked eyes with him. Cheri's relaxed colonial decor, reminiscences of Alicia's sultry voice, Troy's soft whispers of longing, the dim candle light, the soft glow of the flames in the old rustic fireplace, the chill in the air, the wine starting to kick in, and my need to be touched in a certain way, contributed to my changing mood.

Troy stared into my eyes and moved my hand in slow motion to the lips that would have tasted my cookies months ago if only he had a clue how to break through my barrier. He placed soft wet kisses on my hand. His chapped lips lingered when our eyes met. I imagined him kissing my breasts while telling me how much he loves me. I smiled and gave him a long searching glance. I saw pink blood stained dresses in his blue eyes. I blinked to try to force the images away.

"Thanks for joining me. I could barely hear or see Alicia for admiring your beauty," he finally said.

"Try again, buddy--I was there."

He held up his wine glass and said, "To us." Our glasses clicked. "I like you, Gina. I like you a lot." He cleared his throat and waited for me to say something.

"Those are famous last words," I said as I stared into his ocean blue eyes and saw my face tainted with blood, lots and lots of blood.

"What do I have to do to convince you that I care?"

"Be patient."

Troy begged for sex throughout dinner, and I played my usual game of chess and called checkmate at the eleventh hour. We chatted for a few minutes at my door. I deep kissed him and let him rub my butt and breasts until I felt like a tease, then I sent him home before he could make another plea.

We went out whenever he was in town. Patrice thought it was great that I was dating a high profile white guy since according to her, white women don't have a problem snatching up our finest. In my heart, I knew I was fronting with Troy. How am I supposed to forget that it was a white man who raped my great-great grandmother and made Big Papa watch. Then he chopped Big Papa's head off with that ax because he allegedly cheated the man at a cockfight! Big Papa was a medicine man. It was the money he made off his herbs and roosters that enabled him to buy his wife's freedom. Big Papa told me during one of his visits, that he had brought Grandma Ella Mae's and all their children's freedom before the war started except for Dora Mae's. Dora Mae was Ella Mae's first and it was obvious that she was Master's. Ella Mae and Big Papa loved Dora Mae the same as the others but Master made her price too high. My Big Mama was born to Dora Mae and a black man right after the war. My great grandmother lived one-hundred and eight years. Master's genes skipped a few generations, but they came back to whitewash my face. How am I supposed to forget my family's history? How am I supposed to let Troy love me with the fucking nightmares telling me night after night how white men used to view Black women. Have they changed? Not much else has. My history is too deeply rooted in the crimes of Mississippi for me to give myself to Troy freely. I somehow managed to raise my kids to love everyone. They didn't have to suffer through black vs. white, and light vs. dark skin issues the way I did in Mississippi. Myesha and Kevin are cool about me and Troy at least as far as race goes so I'm trying to forgive and move on as well.

Every time Troy takes me to expensive French and Italian restaurants for dinner and drinks, we get stares and double takes. And sometimes women recognize him and ignore me while they flirt with him and him with them. I used to get the same stares when I went out with Charles and the occasional bold interruptions. Troy thinks I'm paranoid. He claims that people stare at me because I'm sexy. I want to believe him.

There are just as many black people who hate to see the races mixing as there are white people who hate to see black men spoil white women. I see and feel it every day when I look into their eyes and they look into mine and wonder. But the real problem with Troy is the closer I get to sleeping with him the less interesting he has become otherwise. Fine dining is cool, but he's a bore. Other than being horny there is no reason to show him my true freaky colors.

One of my patients gave me rare tickets to a UCONN basketball game. I had taken care of his mother's dental pain while she was visiting him from Florida. Troy hates basketball. The only sport he likes is golf. Ally has been try-ing to get me interested in golf for years, so when Troy mentioned it, I suggested that we play even though I'm a lousy player.

It was a sunny, nippy day, but not bad for Connecticut in March. I hadn't played golf since dental school and it showed. Troy told me what to do and how to do it. That rubbed me the wrong way. I pretended that the golf ball was his head, and my putting improved. Troy was so annoyed with my inability to play he didn't even ask for sex.

I thought he had finally given up, but he called the next day and gave me the names and numbers of several golf leagues where I could learn to play. I told him to go to hell. He begged me to go out to dinner with him. I invited him to Q's Place for dinner and dancing in my hood.

Q's Place is owned by an ex-professional football player from New London named Quincy Patino. It's the favorite stomping ground of some of the best local and professional jazz bands in New England. Q's Restaurant serves the best mix of Southern, West Indian and Italian cuisine in downtown Hartford, and the ambiance and decor is New York chic without breaking the bank. Disc jockeys play a mix of old school funk and hip-hop between jazz sets, but I prefer dancing the night away in New York.

Troy was waiting for me at Q's Place when I arrived twenty minutes late. Since we were in my hood--I was on time. He had a naughty grin on his face and stars in his eyes. I was wearing a short, tight, low cut red dress. I was willing to show him the rest if he could dance with a little soul. If he couldn't dance, he probably couldn't fuck, and I wasn't going to waste my time. I had given up on love and commitment. It was time to get down and dirty!

Troy pulled me into his arms and laid a torturous kiss on me. I was in the mood so I put some oomph into it and we came ridiculously close to having each other for dinner.

"You look great. I can't wait to get you on the dance floor. I watched Soul Train for years. I have the running man down pat." I laughed, but before I could tell him the dance was outdated, and that I was more interested in slow dancing, we overheard two couples commenting on our kiss.

One of the women said, "When white men date black women they pick the fine sisters who have it going on."

"Uh-huh, girl, did you see that red Benz she stepped her high-yelluh ass out of?" her friend added.

The first woman pointed to a black man with his white girlfriend and said, "But y'all brothers are always getting some stank, fat, stringy haired wanna be blond when y'all crossover. If you're gonna bring home flour at least get Martha White."

Then one of the men with the women looked me up and down and said, "A brother don't stand a chance with a quadroon like that. Those bitches are as confused as the mixed blood flowing through their veins."

And the other brother added, "Man, a mulatto with tits and ass like that ain't got time for a black man as poor as us."

The men bumped fists. They stared at my chest and made derogatory lickety-kisses and grabbed their jocks. The light left Troy's eyes as I stiffened in his arms. I held him tighter to keep him from doing something stupid. I should have been used to other people's negative comments about who they think I am by now, but when my own people turn on me the words go straight through my heart like a long sharp dagger and rip it wide open. The way he rolled "mulatto" off his tongue and looked me up and down, you would have thought he had known me all my life. My mother, father, and sister are all as dark as the night and I'm as yellow so what? Didn't they say I was black? It's rare, but I'm living proof that it happens. They don't have any idea how it feels to have your own father question your mother. It bugs the hell out of me the way people take one look at you and think they know your story. I'm tired of trying to belong. I get it from blacks and whites. Charles has been dead over two years and not one black man has asked me out. Sloan doesn't count because Rolonda set the meeting up.

The maître d' was one of my patients. She had a waiter seat us quickly.

"Don't let them get to you, Gina. It doesn't matter what they say. I think you're beautiful, that's what matters."

Even Troy couldn't understand how free American people could think with such a slave mentality. But the same voices that have been telling me not to let myself fall in love with him have been telling me for years not to hate people who think like that because as painful as it is, I understand their slave mentality.

We were silent while we sipped wine and listened to Kevin's saxophone teacher's jazz band. The lighting was low and romantic, and my mind drifted back to the special occasions when Charles had brought me to Q's Place. We would have dinner and dance late into the night for our anniversary or my birthday, and then we would sneak in the house and try to make love without waking the babysitter and the children.

"I'd like to take you to Paris," Troy mused aloud.

"What?"

"Paris--things are different there." His eyes lit up. "Paris is beautiful. You'll love it. I'd like to treat you and your kids to a few weeks in Paris."

"Didn't I hear something in the news a few years ago about skinheads beating up Nigerian students in Paris, and weren't you just there investigating a massacre or bombings.? There is hate all over the world today. And with our new president a lot of countries are angry with Americans."

Troy ignored my questions and comments. "There are so many things to see and do there. I could take you all to the Eiffel Tower, the Arc de Triomphe, Notre Dame, and the Moulin Rouge. You could shop for the latest fashions, and we could dine at the best French cafes and drive along the beautiful country side and stop to sample the finest French wines. And if you were to get bored with France, which you wouldn't with me as your guide, but if you did, we could take a train ride and explore some of the other countries in Europe."

It was nice to see Troy excited about something other than sex and bite marks. "I'll think about it."

I sounded enthusiastic, but the idea of being at his beckon call in a foreign country for weeks boggled my imagination.

"I'll arrange everything. You'll love it. I will be in Europe next week. I'm going to be there about a month. Say, 'yes,' you won't regret it."

I had absolutely no experience with breaking up with men. Troy was okay for an occasional date, but it was going to be harder than I thought to engage in casual sex with him. The boys I went out with besides Bobby and Charles would have given me the boot long before now. Troy and I listened to the jazz, sipped wine, and picked over our food. When we finished, I laced my hand with Troy's and tried to look deep into his ocean-blue eyes. They would remind me of what I had to say and why. My heart raced and butterflies kissed the walls of my stomach.

"Troy...," I sugar coated my voice to make what I was about to say easier. "I can't pretend that situations like that don't bother me. It hurts to know that people still harbor so much hate. I care about you, but I can never fully express my true self without dealing with certain consequences. As a black woman, I'm judged by a different standard. I could stand tough and pretend nothing else matters, but it does—it does to me."

He sank back in his chair. "Come with me to Paris."

"The wounds are deeper than tonight. Running away to Paris won't heal my pain. I've had to deal with shit like that since I was a child. Most of the time I don't know where I belong. I can't deal with me, how am I supposed to deal with us? I've been avoiding dealing with any feelings I could have for you because I've been fighting all my life not to see people in terms of race." I stopped and laughed. "Most people think it is easier to look as if you can be any race. It's not. It's very confusing in America because everybody is placed into a little box and expected to stay in it." Troy twisted in his seat. I wanted him to understand that this wasn't just about him so I told him about my childhood nightmares. After hearing my story, he was sure something terrible had happened at Dead Man's swamp. He vowed to find out exactly what! I had poured my heart out, and Troy had the nerve to drill me about what else he thought I could reveal about the crime! He had dealt with post-traumatic witnesses before, and being the expert crime solver that he is, he kept pushing and pushing for more information. I was ready to scream when he suggested that we go to his place so he could make me feel better. He promised to check my story out and put my mind at ease, but instead of feeling relived I knew I had made a mistake.

I didn't hear from Troy for two weeks so I settled back into my normal routine until Kevin's saxophone teacher invited me to come to Q's Place to hear his band play. Omar was a child prodigy. Kevin has been his student for ten years, and that still makes him barely legal. Omar is a six-foot hunk with short locks. His skin is the color of peanut butter. He's a class act musician. He dresses artistically. He has an athletic body and he is irresistibly charming. I couldn't think of a single reason to say no when his eyes lit up and he asked me to meet him after his show.

I asked Patrice to come with me. She didn't have any interest in a struggling musician so I listened to Omar's band, sipped wine and let my mind play with the possibilities while Patrice flirted with the married owner of the club.

The band was excellent. They received a standing ovation. I intended to give Omar a congratulatory hug when he joined me at my table. I threw my arms around him and our lips and tongues came together like magnets. My hormones jumped up and down for joy. I told him I was sorry. He smiled and said it was okay, and his eyes lit up again. Omar has been calling me Gina since I can remember. I never noticed how comfortable he was with me until we kissed. I was surprised that I hadn't picked up on his crush sooner.

"I sent a demo tape to D&S Music--they signed me!" Omar said.

D&S Music rang a bell, but I couldn't place it. "That's wonderful, Omar." I removed my arms from around his neck, but he pulled me closer.

"Come and help me celebrate!"

There was no mistaking the bundle pressing against my leg. I was startled, but my hormones were wigwagging.

"Please," he begged.

I'm a sucker for "please" and my hormones must have thought they were sixteen again when I asked him where? The last time I checked this was the only party worth attending on a Saturday night in Hartford.

Omar kissed me again and told me to follow him. His kiss meant business, and my hormones weren't bullshitting either. We twisted and turned our way around Hartford's city streets. I couldn't believe I was following him. He pulled into a parking space at a newly renovated duplex located on the south end of town in a mostly Italian neighborhood. I pulled in next to him. His hand was on my waist while we walked up two flights of stairs that led to a small scarcely furnished apartment.

He penned me against the wall and kissed me the moment we walked in and closed the door. Omar's apartment reminded me of Charles and my first apartment. Omar's kiss and his strong young body pressing against mine reminded me of the hot unyielding passion Charles and I used to share.

Omar pressed his body closer to my old horny body and his strong tongue wrestled with mine hungrily. His nature rose and I instinctively pressed my pelvis to his and did a slow grind. He slid my zipper and my dress down in the same quick movement. My bra was off next. I've hated slips and stockings since I was in the first grade. I rarely wear them. I shivered like a virgin when his young eyes appraised me in my red panties and spiked-heels.

I got light headed as Omar kissed his way from my lips down to my belly button. I leaned against the wall and moaned. He hadn't invited me in properly. We hadn't spoken any words. I hadn't had a chance to think my way out of his bed. I wanted and needed him badly. He was quick, young, and hungry, like my

Charles when we first met. My moans were encouraging. He kissed from my sternum back to my neck and back to my awaiting lips. He moaned as I kissed him lustfully. He fondled my grapefruits in each of his big heavy hands.

"Oh my God, please," slipped from my lips. Omar slid a thick finger into my wet spot. My moans turned into a love ballad.

"Please, Lord, help me," I moaned. He continued to play me. I was helpless and then a sweet wave of ecstasy pulsated through my entire body. My eyes popped opened. This wasn't a dream. My head cleared as blood rushed back to my brain from my swollen center. I got a whiff of love in the air and got stiff in his arms. He replaced his finger with his mouth. I closed my eyes again. Wave after wave of ecstasy took over my entire body again. I moaned and shivered uncontrollably. Omar kissed his way back to my awaiting mouth. He had a satisfied smile on his face, and deep pools of lust in his brown eyes. He continued to kiss and tease my nipples with his nimble fingers until he realized I was crying. He whispered "Am I hurting you?" in my ear while he tenderly nibbled at it and sent more pulsating waves through my body. I wanted to finish what we had started. I felt like a high school tease when I removed his shirt and slid down to my knees. I pushed sweet Omar against his wall and pulled his pants to his ankles. He wasn't wearing underwear.

I asked him if he had a pencil-post bed; he said brass. I know what lust feels like, and I knew giving in to it, I'd better be prepared to live with the consequences. I grabbed Omar's hands, pent them against the wall, and took him deep. This was just for him. His love ballad was bebop to my ears. It didn't take long. He shuddered the moment I stuck a finger in his anus and sucked in hard. He uttered, "I can't... I can't... holy shit, damn, Ginaaaaaaaa!" My name sounded like the lyrics of an old slow jam as I tasted his salty sweet liqueur.

He looked a bit embarrassed so I kissed him one last time. I should have been ashamed, but in the moment, I felt young, beautiful, alive and oh so powerful. Satisfied. I dressed quickly. Kevin must never know that his mentor tongue and finger fucked his mother and she returned the favor! I tried to leave before my weak body overruled my better senses again. God knows I had already stayed longer than I should have when I let sweet Omar convince me to stay a little longer.

CHAPTER 8

Whip Appeal

Women made me offers everywhere I went after my appearance on The Daily Show aired. At first I didn't turn down anything. I pretended to be searching for that special someone, but like they say--if you keep on doing the same shit, the same way, you get the same f-ed up result. I was still waking up alone. Or with strangers I didn't give a damn about. Or worse with Candy. She was screwing me on the low while publicly dating Lincoln Moses, the nerd who co-starred in her last movie. Niki was still blowing up my phone declaring her love and desire to have my babies. She was offering what I wanted, but my gut just wasn't feeling forever with her. Never did. Never will. The twins were always available whenever I needed to get my freak on.

I made a triple double, tonight. Rick and I celebrated with a few shots of bourbon before heading home. I was still in a zone when Niki invited me over. The night was young. Why not checkout if she has honestly changed?

Niki greeted me in a shear robe. She kissed me and said something about sucking and swallowing me whole. I backed away, something wasn't right. Her eyes were glassy. There was a mirror on her coffee table with three powdery lines and a short red straw. Next to the coke was a pair of purple gloves with fur around the wrist.

My mind raced to find a way out without pissing her off again. I coughed several times like a longtime smoker and held my stomach. Then I bent over and moaned to make it look real. Niki came closer and made a gesture to help. I raised my arm to keep my distance.

"Don't get too close. There's a bug going around. Half the team has it. Oh, god I feel sick. I have to throw up!" She looked concerned. I rushed to her bathroom and locked the door.

I grabbed a cup and filled it with water from the toilet. Then I poured it back into the toilet while I made sounds and pretended to throw up. I flushed, and just in case she was near the door listening I moaned and groaned. "Oh god, this is bad, this is really bad."

I repeated my antics several times. Then I checked to see if she had mouthwash before I yelled, "Babe, do you have any mouthwash?" I wanted to pinpoint her location on the other side of the door. I grabbed another paper cup and rinsed loudly with Listerine. I splashed water on my face. And just before I opened the door I sprayed a generous amount of Lysol. It was easy to look nauseated because I was totally disgusted with Niki. I opened the door with caution. Niki was leaning on the wall outside the door just as I suspected.

"I'm sorry, babe," I said as I made my way to the exit door. "I'm gonna have to take a raincheck, you don't want whatever this is."

She blew me a kiss. I held my head down to hide my smile as I rushed out.

Mom and Jason came to New Orleans to help me celebrate making the All-Star Team. The game had been moved from Charlotte because of controversy surrounding North Carolina's "bathroom bill" better known as HB2. It's ironic that the NBA did what it had to do to be politically correct the same year the country, well the electoral college, elected the most politically incorrect president in the country's history.

New Orleans is one of my favorite cities. I love the food--gumbo, alligator, spicy shrimp, crawfish, po-boys, fresh pralines, and beignets. I played well, but not great. I spent as much time as possible with Mom and Jason. We did a swamp and ghost tour, took a cooking class and checked out The McKenna Museum of African American Art. Mom reminded me that wishing for a significant other to share my victories with wasn't going to make it happen. She said nothing will ever change for me until I open my heart and let someone else in. I felt like a child being reprimanded. We were having lunch at Melba's Old School Po Boys. Mom frowned and stared. I thought I had voiced my offence out loud. Then I followed her eyes to check out who or what she was staring at. And there she was—a fourteen years last seen ghost—Valerie—Jason's mother! I'm not sure if it was the hate in my eyes or Mom's that scared her away. She ran off again and never looked back. She was the reason for my heart of stone. Once again, Mom was right.

I ignored Niki's calls. She was only adding to my heart of stone. When people piss be off, I see red. It can get ugly when the Scorpion in me comes out. The sting can be lethal. I figured Niki would get the hint. But when I returned from the break, she had filled my machine with messages again.

"Hi, it's Niki again. I didn't want to tell you this over the phone, but since you haven't returned my calls I didn't know how else to tell you I'm really pregnant."

"No babe, the only thing you are is scary crazy. I feel like a fool for getting involved with you," I said mostly to myself but I needed to hear it.

I paced the room and tried to think of a way to get rid of Niki once and for all. I could almost understand how some men snap on women. Never say never until you deal with a delusional woman with tendencies toward violence and stalking. She needs to see a doctor before she hurts someone or someone hurts her.

My intercom buzzed before I could hit redial. Candy has a way of showing up at my weakest moments. I didn't expect to see her again after she announced her engagement. She was standing at my door wearing high heels, a trench coat and a pink teddy.

We didn't waste any time, we never do, she always has somewhere else she should be. She was doing her harder-deeper routine and I spanked her in more ways than one. While I was doing my who's the man routine she laughed like a hyena and said, "You know I have your ass whipped, Don. I belong to Link, but you can't resist me. Can you?"

I was hitting it too good to stop, but she made me think, and every player knows thinking and pussy is like drinking and driving. I spanked that ass again and she woke up in my arms the next morning with a smile on her face. I screwed her in the bright sunlight so she could see who was whipped before I sent her home to Link. Knowingly screwing another man's woman is as low as a man can go. I'm not a vindictive man, and I sure as hell don't have a problem finding women to screw. That realization was an epiphany. I vowed that the next time I get with a woman it will be about more than the heat of the moment. It will be about love.

After Candy left I grabbed an orange juice from the refrigerator and clicked on ESPN to check out my highlights. I gulped the juice down. While I marveled at my skills, I felt a sharp pain in my tooth and damn near slam dunked the ceiling. I'm not afraid of much, but if I had to start a list, dentist would be at the top.

When I was seven, I was awakened by a toothache and a swollen face. Mom gave me two cherry flavored aspirins for the pain and took me to the clinic the next day. The dentist was an older man who had no patience for kids. I refused to sit in the dental chair. He grabbed me by the arm and sat me down. His assistant held me down while the dentist pulled the abscessed baby tooth with pliers and no anesthesia. That shit hurt so bad, just thinking about it, makes my head hurt. I frigging went in my pants. Now just the thought of going to the dentist makes me break out in a cold sweat.

My tooth hurt every time I drunk something cold or ate something sweet. I ate on the other side to avoid setting the pain off. Then I made the mistake of drinking Gatorade during one of my games, and the pain started and my concentration was blown for the rest of the night. The pain got worse and lasted longer with each episode. I refused to call a dentist. I could control it with Tylenol or Motrin before the game and at bedtime.

My numbers have been slipping since the All-Star break and Niki's crazy nonstop calls about being pregnant knowing that she is not. I changed my number and only gave it to Jason, Mom, Sloan, and Rick. It's a bad time for me to be unfocused. I'm trying to get my rhythm back, but I couldn't buy a basket the last time we played Miami. I wanted revenge tonight.

We were up by twenty points at the half. It was a physical game. Rick and I were in foul trouble. Coach sat us out most of the third quarter. Miami tied the game at the top of the fourth. We responded with a perfectly executed play, which gave me an open three to put us back in the lead. I followed up with a stolen ball and an alley oop to Rick, which he slam-dunked. We were up by five when Miami's center burned Rick with a turnaround jumper. The lead exchanged hands several more times. Rick jammed another basket with one minute on the clock. He got called for a foul. He told the referee what he thought about the call and got hit with a technical. After the shots were taken, Miami was back on top. I hit a three to bring us within two, and Rick blocked a shot with four seconds on the clock. The score was 105 to 103 when Coach called a time out.

I'm the team's best perimeter shooter, but I was playing on pure adrenaline. When the buzzer sounded to resume play, the fans were going crazy. The noise made my tooth hurt more. We needed the win to get home court advantage for the playoffs. Rick put the ball into play. Everyone was depending on me. I had three seconds to get off what should have been a nice jump-shot at the buzzer. It was a fucking air ball. A gotdamn embarrassment.

Excruciating pain shot through my tooth, shit, my whole fucking body. My knees buckled, and I sat my ass at center court. I would have cried, but cameras were everywhere. I tucked my head between my knees and rocked until the pain eased up. I didn't want anyone to capture the tears in my eyes and assume it was the agony of defeat. I couldn't believe I missed that easy fucking shot. The play had been perfect otherwise. It was April Fool's day and the joke was on me.

A warm hand touched my back and Rick asked me if I was okay. I mumbled something about my toothache. He told me to take my ass to the dentist. I hopped in the shower before the reporters could stick a mike in my face. The warm water beating against my face relieved the pain. New York reporters and fans don't play hide-and-go-seek. They wanted answers. They believed they deserved them. I said something Mom told me years ago. "Some shots are like lovers, you want to make it, but it wasn't meant to be." I quoted the last part.

Candy was waiting in my lobby when I got home. I kissed her hand and told her to play at home from now on. She said some lame shit about Link not being like me—he's a "good brother." She gave me a peek at her purple teddy, then she handed me the matching feather. I dusted her nose with it and told her to work with Link—even good brothers want their women to be freaks in bed.

I went upstairs and took my last six Motrin and went to bed feeling sorry for myself. The pain woke me up the next morning. I was out of painkillers.

It didn't matter since they no longer stopped the pain anyway. I called the first dentist in the phone book. I hung up when the receptionist greeted me.

The phone rang again and startled me. Rick laughed when I told him about my phobia but he realized I needed help. He suggested that I try a female dentist. He assumed a woman would be gentler or at least I didn't have to worry about her holding me down in her chair. I didn't want to put my reputation on the line, but I had run out of excuses. The playoffs could make the difference between playing again next year, with whom, and for how much. I had come too far to blow it.

I tried to visualize myself surviving a dental appointment without embarrassing myself. Visualization helped me improve my game. I told myself that I wasn't afraid. They say if you tell your mind something enough times it becomes your reality. Rick didn't know any female dentists, and then it hit me. I had a perfect excuse to call Gina. If she wanted to hold me down in her chair, I probably would enjoy it. Before I could change my mind, I asked Rick if he would roll with me to Connecticut.

"Mo Money Mo Problems" was blasting in his background. "Sure, I'll go with you. You're my boy." He said. "I could have used your help last night, man."

"I'm sorry I let the team down."

"You can't make'em all."

"Yeah, but if I had made that shot I would be sitting pretty when it's time to renegotiate my contract. Everybody and their mama showed that clip. It didn't matter that I hit thirty points; everybody is going to remember me throwing up that f-ing air ball."

Rick moaned. "It'll pass. We're only human."

"We know that, but the owners pay us to be superhuman."

"Don't let it eat away your confidence. I'm gonna make sure you take care of your toothache so you can get your rhythm back."

"Thanks, man."

His tone of voice perked up. "Last night I hooked up with a couple of identical twins, named Bee and Tee. I could have used your help."

"Man, I don't mess around anymore." I chuckled and shook the fiery memories out of my mind. "Bee and Tee? Been there, done that."

"Sounds like a player is serious about somebody?"

"Not me, man. I'm concentrating on my game. I gave up my bad habits, the twins were tough but I went cold turkey." Valerie and Niki, and now Candy had put a bad taste in my mouth for women.

"I need to leave the groupies alone myself. I'm trying to work things out with my ex. I miss my boys. So, Don, are you ready to settle down on the OK Corral and have a couple of kids and shit?"

"I'm hanging up now. I'll call Dr. Hill and text you a time."

CHAPTER 9

Pain in My Heart

Omar has been blowing up my mobile phone since he found out Myesha and Kevin were in DC touring with the jazz band. I would be embarrassed by my behavior if the Big Os hadn't been so amazing. I got dressed. We had a drink and I critiqued his demo. Omar said he is willing to go as slow or as fast as I want to go.

I booked a last-minute trip to Mississippi to slow myself down. Mother has been visiting me all week in my dreams. I told Omar she was ill and that I had to go home and check on her. He touched my heart when he was genuinely more concerned than disappointed. He is a sweet irresistible young man.

Ida Mae and I aren't particularly close. Mother was always on my case about Bobby, in addition to trying to make me dress prissy and act like a lady. I was determined to be the free-sprit that I am at any cost. I didn't know how to tell her I hated pink. Ida Mae didn't give up easily so naturally I became very good at straddling the fence. I love my mother even though we butted heads on almost everything. When she came to me in my dreams I got worried.

It was eighty degrees when I stepped off the plane. I tied my wool blazer around my waist and pulled my suitcase along the sidewalk. Bobby Baker called me as soon as I stepped out on the curb. He was wearing a skycap uniform, and when he smiled his gold central incisor shone like the Northern star. He still had the smoothest blue-black skin I've ever seen, but his muscles had turned to flab. I was probably thinking about his big afro tickling my thighs and why I nicknamed him Bobby "blue balls" when I slipped and said, "Bobby blue…"

He flashed his golden smile again. "Baker, Gina. You had so many men you couldn't keep'em straight."

He looked at me and smiled as if he remembered how I looked with most of my clothes off. "You're still fine and I bet you're still tight with your sweet pussy."

I probably turned six shades of red as I walked faster. Bobby grabbed my suitcase and walked with me to my rental car. Sharon had told him about Charles. He asked me out and I would have gone because we have been friends forever. Jenny, the bitch I had caught him banging in the janitor's closet had caused our final breakup. She left him with their son when he didn't make it to the NFL. His second wife hated his son because he is mixed and she couldn't get pregnant. He had eight kids with his third wife, but he caught her with another man while she was pregnant with their ninth. But it was his Jeri-Kurl and that gold tooth that made me say, "I'm sorry things didn't work out for you in California, but you should never give up on your dreams."

Bobby looked at the pavement. "I'm sorry about the way I treated you. I was young and dumb, and you had it all together."

"I was chasing dreams the same as you."

"Well, at least one of us made it." Bobby smiled again as he appraised me. "You still look the same--sexy as all hell." He flashed that gold tooth again. He used to have the sexiest smile.

I stopped in the Hertz parking lot in front of a red convertible Mustang. "It was nice to see you. We need to find some new dreams to chase. Life ain't over until it's over."

He put my suitcase on the back seat and I gave him a hug and then I sped away. I hopped on I-20 West, which is a straight shoot to Sweetwater. The radio was preset on WOKJ, the oldies and blues station. Otis Redding's "Pain in My Heart" came on. I pumped up the volume and crept down Main Street so I wouldn't miss it. I made a right onto Cougar Road and drove faster as I passed Dead Man's swamp. The warm breeze dried the tears on my cheeks. I thought about Charles, Daddy, and Bobby. Most men don't know how to say they love you. Daddy thought it was automatic, and Bobby thought he could prove it on the back seat of his car. My sweet Charles didn't even understand everything about me, but he left a gigantic pain in my heart.

I pulled myself together when I topped the hill on Bobcat Road and saw the cartwheels at the end of the driveway and Ida Mae's prize magenta azaleas and pink lilies in bloom. The small yellow brick ranch with green shutters looked the same as it did before I moved to Connecticut. This was where I learned to shut the ugly things about the world and myself out.

Ida Mae and Daddy were surprised to see me. Sharon had taken over Ida Mae's job at the funeral home when she retired. It works out great since Mother can fill in when Sharon needs to take time off. I kissed my parents and went down the hall to take my things. My room still looked as if it had been decorated for a little princess. Pink shit everywhere. I wanted to tell them I had given away my virginity there, well sorta, nice Southern girls don't count oral. Ida Mae wanted me to be her sweet little innocent girl. I tried to live up to that image, but I haven't been innocent since I was in the first grade.

Ida Mae stuck her head in my doorway, "How're you feeling? You're getting awfully skinny."

"I'm okay, and I'm not skinny. How are you feeling, when was the last time you went to the doctor?"

"I'm fine. My pressure was good and Dr. Thelonious said I'll probably live to be a hundred like Big Mama, God rest her soul." She smiled and sat on my bed while I unpacked my suitcase. "Dr. Thelonious asked about you. You know he's sweet on you," She said as she gave me a little poke in the side.

I'm extremely ticklish so I was giggling when I said, "Marvin and I are just friends. We took a lot of the same classes at Tougaloo."

"Have you met someone you like to help you raise your kids?"

"I don't need help taking care of my children. I need somebody to keep me warm at night," I said to spite her. She would never say that to Sharon even though she moved back home and brought her daughter Erica with her my sophomore year in college.

"Why do you think I can't take care of myself?"

"Because you've always had us or Charles, God rest his soul, to protect you."

"I own and run a business and a multimillion dollar foundation, Mother. I miss Charles, but I'm doing okay."

"Sugar, if you would listen to me and wear nice dresses and perm your wild hair, you would have more than your share of men to keep you warm at night." I didn't bother to argue.

Sharon pushed Ida Mae out of her way and gave me a hug. Mother left us alone to catch up on our sister talk. Sharon laughed at my stories about Troy and Omar. Then, she pointblank told me that I wasn't sixteen anymore and I couldn't go around teasing grown ass men unless I'm looking to get raped. I'm always going to be Sharon's naive little sister, and Ida Mae's baby who needs protecting so I kept my grownup fantasies about Don to myself. Sharon's married friend Zack was taking her to Memphis for the weekend, and Mother didn't have a damn thing to say about it.

On her way, out Sharon said, "If Troy doesn't make your coffee percolate tell him that it ain't happening. And if Omar can hook your tight ass up with his fingers and tongue you better jump on that shit like Ida Mae's sweet potato pies and enjoy it for as long as it lasts."

I gave her a high-five and we giggled like teenagers.

"Did you know men reach their sexual peak in their twenties and we reach ours in our forties? You and Omar could go buck wild on each other."

"We could if all I needed was sex. I have to think about my kids, and what I really need is emotional support, and if he plans to move in he's gonna have to come up with some economical help, and if he wants me to have his babies, well, he can forget that, and he's so fine he deserves to procreate so that right there tells me that I'm not the one for him."

"You're full of shit, Gina. Get the dick. Be discreet and Kevin and Myesha don't have to know. These young men ain't looking to start a family with our old asses; they want us to teach them a little something, something so they can go back and blow some young girl's mind. You're reading way too much into it, baby girl. Get the dick, and go home with a smile on your face."

Daddy scared the hell out of me the next morning when he woke me up and asked me if I wanted to go fishing. I wiped sleep from my eyes, stretched like a cat and hopped out the bed. I pulled on my Levi's and T-shirt, brushed my teeth, and threw cold water on my face. Then I grabbed my wallet and a straw hat from the coat rack and ran outside.

Daddy was waiting in his Ford pick-up. I asked him if he had checked his glucose and taken his insulin. I was worried about him going into diabetic shock, and he was worried about leaving before Mother woke up. My hands found my hips and he said I looked and sounded like Ida Mae with her straw hat on while I scolded him about skipping breakfast.

"I see we're gonna have to do this your way."

I flinched, and then I went back in the house to get him something to eat for breakfast. Mother was at the table sipping her morning coffee. She flashed me a knowing smile. Mother and Daddy have been married fifty-five years and she knows him like the back of her hands. Daddy used to think he was slick, but Mother says he didn't get away with half the foolishness she let him think he was getting away with. I grabbed a banana and an apple from the bowl.

"Where are you and Johnny trying to slip off to anyway?"

"Daddy's taking me fishing--well, actually I'm taking him. We'll be back." I was so excited my lie didn't come out right.

Ida Mae smiled. "Make sure he eats and don't keep him out too long. He ain't doing as well as he pretends."

"And what about you, Mother? Are you sure you're doing okay? I had another dream about her last night. She had cancer. "When was the last time you had a mammogram?"

"Everything was fine when I had my full physical last month. Now get outta here before it gets too hot."

I started the car and switched the radio back to the blues station. "Every day I Have the Blues" was playing. We stopped at 7-Eleven to get me a fishing license. I bought some sandwiches for lunch and some water. Daddy bought a six-pack of Budweiser and two Moon Pies, chocolate for him, banana for me. He remembered. I shot him a dirty look because I knew better than to stop him in front of the white sales clerk.

We went out to his favorite spot, an offshoot of the mighty Mississippi. I touched the live worms without freaking out when Daddy showed me how to bait the lines. I was determined to make my first and probably only fishing trip with him a success. Maybe my dreams were mixing him up with Mother.

We floated around a couple of hours without catching anything worth taking home. We ate our lunch and washed it down with beer. I've never been much of a beer drinker, but I had to make sure he didn't drink too much. The beer and the rocking boat had made me woozy when Daddy spotted a net someone had illegally set. We rowed toward it. Daddy pulled the net filled with catfish up while I did look-out duty. We filled our coolers with fish and threw the net back in the water.

Daddy grinned and said, "Baby girl, I say we call it a day." I was close to passing out from the beer, the heat, the rocking boat, and the mosquitoes were tearing my ass up. I didn't argue. We high-tailed it back to the car. Daddy and I sang the blues all the way home. My head had cleared until we got home and Daddy stopped singing mid-sentence. His agape mouth made him look like he had seen a ghost.

Ida Mae and a woman who looks more like me than my own mother were standing in the middle of the driveway near a black Jeep with a Montana license plate. I followed Daddy's lead and took my time getting out of the car.

"I would never forget my best friend and favorite cousin even though you, Seddie Lee and Angie disappeared without a trace nearly forty years ago," Ida Mae said as Daddy and I approached them. Ida Mae and the strange lady had tears in their eyes when they embraced.

I turned around to look for Daddy. He was lagging behind. He obviously knew the strange woman as well. His ghost-face was now replaced with what looked and felt like malice when he said, "What the hell are you doing back in Mississippi, Pearl?"

Mother and the lady seemed stunned by Daddy's harsh tone.

"Why are you talking to Pearl like that Johnny Lee?" Mother asked. Before he could answer the teary-eyed stranger reached for my hands and called me Angie.

I was dumbfounded, but I managed to tell her my name was Gina. I waited for Ida Mae to say something but she looked as confused as me. Then Pearl said, "It's me, Angie. I'm your mother. Don't you remember me?" I looked toward

Mother again, but she was frozen in her tracks, and tears were in her eyes again. My gut told me that they both were my mother. Ida Mae had raised me, but I look more like her cousin Pearl than her.

Daddy pried Pearl's hands away from mine and said, "Big Mama said, our Gina, came out looking like you and Angie because Ida Mae missed you all so much the last month she was carrying Gina."

"Where is my god-baby," Ida Mae asked, and Pearl and Daddy's ghost-faces returned. "Angie used to rub my stomach and wish I was having a girl even though even Big Mama thought that I was carrying a boy. Where is Angie?"

Pearl looked at Daddy and then she spurted out, "Big Mama didn't tell you?"

Before Ida Mae could answer, "Daddy said, Ida Mae was having a very difficult time with the pregnancy and all after you left. She ended up having Gina three weeks early. Gina was colicky and she looked like a white baby. I can't lie and say her skin color didn't throw us for a loop at that time. It was a very difficult time for us considering everything that was going on at the time. That's all dead and buried--we survived it—that's the only thing that matters."

The frightened look in Pearl and Daddy's eyes must have filled in the blanks because they seemed to understand what the other was leaving out. "So, Pearl, what brings you back after all these years."

She looked at Ida Mae and whispered, "Cancer. Seddie Lee passed on a while ago, and I'm dying. I didn't want to leave this world without seeing you again, Ida Mae, and your baby—the one that was supposed to be my godchild."

"Why did you leave, Pearl?"

"Seddie and Angie got into a tangle with some white men. We had to leave in a hurry. Big Mama said there was no time for goodbyes. It was the hardest thing I've ever had to do—Big Mama said she would take care of everything else."

Daddy led me away with a mouth full of unanswered questions. We left Ida Mae and Pearl in the middle of the driveway hugging for old time sake.

CHAPTER 10

Hurts So Good

I dialed Omar's number. Don has been heavy on my mind since my discussion with Sharon. I hung up. I sorted the mail. Paid the bills. Picked up the phone. Called Omar. Put the phone down again, and then it rang. Frigging caller ID. I didn't check before I answered.

"I was just thinking about you, Omar." I said, but the deep sexy voice on the line identified himself as Don Stokes!

I lost ten bucks to Kevin when Don missed that shot last night. Don rushed through something about a toothache, a dental phobia and wondering if I could "hook a fearful brother like him up." He wasn't the first fool to pull that fake ass toothache rap so I said, "It's my day off, but I'm sure I can fit in a little hang time for you since you hooked a sister up with a shoulder to cry on, and a ride home last fall."

Don chuckled at my flirt. He deepened his tone and he sounded serious when he said, "Well, if Omar isn't treating you right, you can cry on my other shoulder."

"Before you go barking up the wrong tree, Mr. Stokes, I should remind you that I'm sometimes clairvoyant. I had a feeling you were going to call so I aborted my call to Omar, so if you're teasing me, I'll see right through you. See, I, uh, was only pretending not to know who you were because I wanted to make sure you were in fact who you say you are."

"Good come back." He dropped his tone another notch and said, "So, Miss Sometimes Clairvoyant, I don't have to tell you my offer is good, 'cause you already know, right?"

"It's true--I was thinking about how sweet you were that night, and uh, lots of times when someone is heavy on my mind, I will send my spirit and will them to call me, and sometimes I'll even wish a toothache on them if they take too long."

Don chuckled. "So that explains why my toothache stopped when I punched in your digits."

I grunted to let him know I was on to him as well. "Whatever, Big Man, I like a man who knows how to create his own shots anyway."

"Not so fast, Dr. G--it hurts mostly at night--that's when you were thinking about how I take it to the hole, right?"

"Damn! You're a better give and go player than I thought. Are you clairvoyant too?"

Don chuckled. I was way out of my league, but I didn't back down.

"I have to go to practice to work on my downtown shots, but I would be most grateful if you could hook a Big Man up late this afternoon. You're pretty good at crashing the boards yourself, Dr. G."

I gave him my emergency number, cell phone, home number, and directions, and then I said, "Remember, Mr. Stokes, toothaches are the least of my powers--I'm not a ball hog, but I'm much better at soothing pain than giving it." I didn't know where that came from but if he is game I'm ready to play.

He laughed as though he knew I was propositioning him. "I'll be there. I asked Rick King to come with me—Big Man may need some backup around you, Dr. G."

I laughed and said, "Swish!" I heard Don laugh before he clicked off.

After I hung up I pinched myself to make sure I wasn't dreaming. My assistant wasn't home when I called. I left her a message. The phone rang again a few minutes later this time it was Ro.

"Why did you give Don Stokes my number," I said. "I was only joking about screwing him. I knew it was a joke, but it was fun flirting with him."

"What in the hell are you talking about, Gina?"

"He's coming to my office. He even made up a lame story about having a dental phobia." Ro screamed then she swore up and down that she didn't have anything to do with it. She dared me to take him home, give him a home-cooked meal and jump his fine ass bones. I didn't know how I was supposed to do that with two kids and his friend Rick hanging around, but she offered to take Rick off my hands and she suggested that I send the kids to their friends' houses. She called me a pussy for using Kevin and Myesha as an excuse, but my kids are much more important to me than my nonexistent love life. Ro was talking about me living my life through my children. They had been my only reasons to continue living after Charles died.

"Charles is not coming back." Ro said. "You can't change what happened. It wasn't your fault so don't start with that crazy talk. I'm not saying forget about Charles, but you have to find a way to move on."

"Okay, Ro, if Mr. Stokes makes a move on me, I promise not to use the kids as an excuse."

"Don't blow it this time, Gina. You better make some moves of your own."

"Just make sure you're there when he breaks my heart."

"As long as, you have a wet pussy and work your magic, Gina Mae Hill, you can break a few hearts your damn self."

I hopped in my Mercedes, opened the sun roof, popped in my go-to Isley Brothers' CD with "Summer Breeze" on it and headed to the gym. The Isley Brothers and Barry White were the one thing Ida Mae and I could agree on, we both love them.

I've made a royal mess of my love life since Charles died. In the good old days, all I had to worry about was getting pregnant or a major heartbreak. These days a girl must worry about things like chlamydia, genital warts, herpes, AIDS, and HPV. Quickies can kill you these days. I would be content with Mr. Wonderful if he had soft lips, strong arms, and tickle fingers. I'm almost forty, and here I am trying to decide if I want a relationship or if I want to live life on the edge like Rolonda and Sharon. Sharon told me to shut the fuck up, I should be happy I still have options. Patrice and Ro told me to get with the program.

Patrice was in the parking lot talking to Quincy when I pulled in. I don't understand why she is wasting her time with an old married man when she could have had a juicy fruit like Omar. I wanted to sense-slap that girl. I've talked to her but it goes in one ear and out the other. At this rate, she is going to be an old maid chasing after money. She is not going to be young and beautiful forever. She better chase somebody with some ambition and come up together.

She caught up with me. "So, how was Omar?"

"He played great. You should have hooked up with him instead of wasting time with Quincy."

She showed me a thin sterling silver Tiffany lookalike bracelet Quincy had given her for their second anniversary. It looked like something Kevin would give his sweethearts.

After my work-out I sat on my deck in the warm sunshine, drank iced tea, and painted my toenails black while I waited and wondered if Don was going to come. My cell vibrated and when I answered and heard Don's silky smooth baritone voice again I couldn't speak. He thanked me again for seeing him on my day off and we flirted for a hot second. Ten minutes later I was at my office.

I waved at Don and Rick and flashed them a cordial smile. Don looked surprised but his smile warmed me as he checked out the thinner me. Don and Rick sat in Don's red Ferrari while I walked to the door. I concentrated on the movements of my hips since I was being scrutinized by their watchful eyes.

My navy-blue culottes stopped just above my knees and my light blue polo shirt was hugging my breasts in all the right places. It was a preppie look with enough buppie to seduce him without his knowledge. Thanks to Patrice and my Gina's rules, I had dropped thirty-five pounds since we met last fall.

I greeted Don and Rick in my reception room again. Rick shook my hand. Don kissed it. My eyes met Don's and it seemed as if he could see and feel my dreams. A tingle ran from the spot he kissed to the tips of my nipples, down deep in my G-spot, right down to the tips of my toes. Our souls seemed to connect as he swept his eyes over me. My nipples turned to pebbles and I blushed while my hormones did the freaky-deaky!

Don filled out the medical and dental history forms and insurance information while I set things up in the back. I put my hair in a ponytail holder, put on a lab coat, and changed into my white clogs. Don was ten times more gorgeous with clear eyes and daylight. The thought of his luscious lips kissing mine gave me a chill. I had to take deep cleansing breaths before I could re-enter my own reception area.

Don swept his eyes over me and smiled. "I'm ready," I said in a flirty tone. He matched my tone and said he was ready as well. I didn't know if he was flirting or if this was his normal persona so I led him to the dental suite. I washed and gloved my hands and put on a face shield. He looked at my professional armor and said he wasn't that dangerous. I laughed, and said, "A girl has to protect herself these days." I didn't know where I was getting the nerves, but I threw myself in his space and hoped he would bite. He said I didn't need to protect myself from him, but with the way I was feeling it wasn't him that I was worried about.

He had a big black hole in his lower left first molar. I panicked and checked the rest of his mouth, his uvula and his adenoids. I needed an x-ray before I could make a diagnosis, but I was sure that he was going to need a root canal or an extraction to get rid of his pain.

Little beads of sweat formed on Don's nose and upper lip when I gave him the bad news. A lot of big guys try to hide behind their macho attitudes, but when it comes to dentist, it seems as if the bigger they are, the more afraid they are. I didn't miss the tremble in his voice when he asked if it would hurt. His T-shirt was wet from sweat. I patted his damp arm and said, "Don't worry; I'll make you comfortable before I do anything." Our eyes met. "I won't hurt you. I promise."

Don smiled, but it didn't hide the fear in his eyes. I squeezed his hand gently and said in a calm sensual tone of voice, "You'll have to let yourself trust me. You're not afraid of me, are you? Sometimes I will use my Southern accent and call my patients endearing names to help them feel more comfortable with me. I wanted to call Don "sweetie" or "sugar" but I didn't trust myself.

"I'm not afraid of you, but trust is a different ballgame," he said.

"If you're not afraid, that's a good start. I'll give you laughing gas. It will relax you. Think of all the things I do to help you relax as my crossover moves. After I take an x-ray, I'll let you select some relaxing music. When you're comfortable, I can do the rest in a pain-free way, okay?" I patted him on the hand again. The coconut oil on his bald head and the citrus smell of his cologne had mixed with his body heat and he smelled like cookies baking. He smiled and I wanted a taste, a nibble, a crumb, or his whole damn cookie. It took all my strength to keep from kissing the small beads of sweat on his nose and upper lip.

"I, aghhrr, better take that x-ray."

The oversized digital x-ray on the computer screen confirmed the need for a molar root canal. Normally I refer my patients to an endodontist for molar root canals but there was no way in hell I was referring Don anywhere. I showed Don my personal iPod instead of turning on SiriusXM. He appeared to be fascinated as he looked through my selections. He described my taste in music as diverse, eclectic, and interesting like his. I can tell a lot about people from their musical tastes as well. I have a patient who is a musical therapist. I quizzed her and brought the books she recommended on the subject. I use musical therapy to keep my depression under control. My moods determine the types of music I listen to. This morning when I got up I played The Commodores' "Zoom" something told me it was going to be an emotionally charged day. I was about to tell Don what I was thinking until I heard Big Mama's voice in my mind saying, "Smart women keep some secrets for themselves." Don was staring at me as if he was reading my mind so I said, "Music has been my best therapy since Charles died. The rhythms soothe my soul. I also have a bunch of CD's over here if you don't see anything you like."

Don squatted and ran a long thick finger over my jazz collection. I intended to stoop next to him, but my bare leg brushed against his jeans and created a static electrical charge that popped. The shock threw me off balance, and I fell in Don's lap.

We stared at each other for a tense moment. I wanted him to kiss me. He didn't, but the feel of my ass pressing against his bundle of joy was a cheap thrill I will never forget.

"I slipped--I swear. Don't sue," I joked.

His hands brushed against my breasts and I didn't miss his almost squeeze when he stood up and pulled me up with him. I bit the inside of my lip to keep from smiling.

"Are you okay?" I asked.

"You're cute when you blush."

"I'm too old to be cute."

"Cute, pretty, sexy, alluring you're it, Dr. G., don't fight it," he said, and then he gave me "The Best of Sade" CD. "I was looking for some slow dance music before you fell."

I blushed again. Charles had made love to me many times with Sade's voice in the background. I felt naked in front of Don. Most men buckle under my gaze, but not Don Stokes. His stare is just as beckoning as mine. He didn't blink and nor did I.

He sat in my dental chair. I explained the procedure for a root canal and he started to sweat again.

"All I have to do is remove the nerve from your tooth and the pain will go away." I wanted to make it sound sweet and simple so I threw in, "You'll be able to sleep like a baby tonight." I rubbed his arm and looked deep into his eyes. "You have my promise."

"A good night's sleep would be great," Don said. But with the memory of my body pressing against his, my warped mind heard, "A night with you would be great," because his eyes were saying what I was thinking. He must have known I was reading him because he repeated, "Sleep--I need a good night's sleep."

I asked Rick to come into the suite while Don was under the influence. I was working alone and my mind was in Don's pants. I seated Rick in the chair reserved for moms and dads, and gave him the latest issue of SI and ESPN. I adjusted the mask over Don's nose and turned the nitrous oxide up until he looked relaxed. Then I put a Q-tip with pina colada topical anesthetic gel on it into his mouth.

"This jelly will numb your gums," I said before I injected the anesthesia. "Your lip and tongue are going to feel numb on this side." I touched his face. "Can you feel this? It should feel fat." I usually say "tingly" but that best described me.

"It feels great." I ignored his comment. Don is Mr. Flirt and he hasn't realized yet that he is dealing with Ms. Tease. I used a dental dam to isolate his tooth while I removed the nerve. I was sitting at the ten o'clock position, but Don's hot-cookies smell and the bundle in his pants were making me horny. I wondered how he could have a hard-on when it was obvious that he was scared.

Dentistry is very intimate for some guys, and then there are always the perverts who get off while I'm doing my thing. I switched to the seven o'clock position. I was having fantasies about slow dancing with Don. The first time a patient told me about his perverted fantasies I was mad as hell, but after I heard it from several more patients I wrote it off as an occupational hazard. After all, there is nothing between our laps and the patients' heads but a pillow, and if I can smell his cookies, he probably can smell mine.

I was back-filing when Don's hand rested on my thigh and he started rubbing it like an eager lover. Each stroke sent orgasmic type waves through my body. I adjusted my position and looked at Rick to see if he was paying attention. Sade's sultry voice was filling the air with a "Kiss of Life," and my mind drifted back to the first erotic dream I had about Don. I cleared my throat and got his attention, but that made it worse--now he was staring into my eyes as he rubbed. I adjusted my position again, but that allowed him a more sensitive position on my thigh so I stood up.

I took another x-ray and asked Don how he felt. He said great, so I turned the nitrous off, but when I sat down, his hand found my leg again.

"I'm almost finished. I'll put in a temporary filling, and we'll be done for today."

"Don't rush. I'm doing fine. This is the best dental visit I've ever had." Don continued to rub my leg so I finished in record time.

"Your lip and jaw will be numb for another hour or so," I said. He looked deep into my eyes and I forgot what else I needed to tell him. "Oh, I'll give you a prescription. You can fill it at the pharmacy next door, and uh, you should take the first dose before the numbness wears off." I removed my gloves and washed my hands, and then I led the way to my office.

I shed my lab coat and ponytail holder and shook my hair loose with my fingers while I strutted into my office. I wanted Don in the worst way and I was feeling confident enough to get him. I kicked off my clogs, wiggled my toes and crossed my bare legs. His eyes never left my legs and feet, and the smile on his face said he liked what he saw. With a boldness, I haven't had since my hot pants wearing days, I said, "Your move Mr. Stokes."

"Move?"

"Have a seat." He sat in the chair bedside my desk while I wrote his prescription on my computer. "You did well. I started the root canal, and since things were going well I removed all the nerves. I want to see you again next week to place the filling." I sugar coated "want" and threw in a little Southern charm like loaded dice. "If next week is not good, we can finish when your season is over." I wrote my home address and number on the back of my card and gave it to him.

He smiled at it and said, "Can we do the same time next Wednesday?"

"Let me check my calendar." I took my personal planner from my Gucci bag and looked away so he couldn't see the big ass smile on my face. "Next week same time will be fine"

Rick walked in and crossed his arms. With a knowing smile he said, "Making a date without me?"

Don and I smiled as though we had gotten caught with our hands in the cookie jar. "Can you recommend a nice restaurant where we can grab a bite to eat before heading back to the city. Now that my tooth is not hurting, I'm starving." Don said as he gave me a little wink.

"You all can go to Buddy's if you're in the mood to get mobbed or you could come home with me. I was planning to cook some catfish I caught. I felt like a fool lugging the cooler and Big Mama's cast-iron skillet on the plane." TSA patted me down and searched all my shit, but Don's smile made it all worthwhile.

"I accept," Don said. "How could I resist catfish that you caught?" His smile was seductive, and I was thinking that I wanted to have him for dinner, so I can only imagine how I looked when I started telling him the truth about the fish.

"I didn't exactly catch all those fish. I used to be a wimpy tomboy. I would dig up worms for bait for Daddy, but I couldn't stand touching the slimy little boogers. Yuck!" I shivered when Don looked at me and laughed. I knew I was frowning and making funny faces because that's how I am, or so I've been told. In my mind, I was touching his worm in ways that would have made Ida Mae disown me.

"So, how did you catch the fish?" Don asked and he smiled as if he wanted to do things to me that would make his mother disown him as well.

"I went home for the weekend because I didn't want to be lonely, I mean alone. Daddy's diabetes has been acting up, and I was missing my mother. I don't go home nearly enough. Anyway, after I got there, I got up the nerve to ask Daddy why he likes Sharon more than me. Of course, he denied it. I asked him why he never took me fishing. He thought I was afraid of worms and getting my clothes dirty, but that wasn't what we were afraid of, but we never talk about that."

"So how did you catch the fish?"

"Daddy woke me up early. We were going to sneak away, but Mother caught us. She doesn't miss anything. But Daddy and I went fishing anyway. We drank beer and I don't drink beer because it makes my stomach too full, but I had to drink it so daddy wouldn't." Don probably thought I was crazy. I wanted to kiss him, but since I hadn't figured out how to do it again and get away with it, I continued to yak. "Daddy and I bonded for the first time since I was in the first grade. It was nice. I can't believe I'm telling you this."

"And you still didn't tell me how you caught the fish."

I waved my hand. "Oh, that part isn't important. It wasn't about catching fish." Don smiled as if he understood, or at least wanted to. He shrugged his shoulders and looked at Rick.

"Do you make hush puppies?" Don asked.

"I'm really not all that great a cook, but I'll manage okay if I stick to Big Mama's recipe." Don shot Rick another questionable glance.

"Perfect. Is that cool with you, Rick?"

"Yeah, man, if it makes you happy, it's cool with me."

I emailed the prescription to the pharmacy and then I called to explain the situation. I didn't want Don and Rick getting mobbed but mostly I wanted to keep them for myself. While Don and Rick went to the pharmacy drive-thru, I dashed into the supermarket to get a box of condoms, K-Y His and Hers lubricant, and chocolate chip cookie dough. It's not like it used to be back in the day; a girl should be prepared these days.

CHAPTER 11

Under Your Influence

Charles used to swear that our house was sitting dead in the center of Connecticut. God, I miss that man. I want to be loved like that again, but I'm afraid to try. I pulled into the driveway and hit the automatic garage door opener. Don parked between my Benz and my Land Rover, my winter car. Driving in snowstorms scare the hell out of me. I replaced Charles's BMW with the SUV. My neighbors are surprised I can still afford to live here. Charles left a will, three insurance policies, and trust funds for the kids. Plus, we got a humongous settlement from the trucking company that caused Charles's accident. My practice is doing great as well. Charles left us financially set and emotionally devastated.

We entered my kitchen from the garage. I love my kitchen even though I'm not much of a cook. It's finished with the finest Italian tiles and it has all the newest gadgets. The kitchen is located between the deck and the family room. It's the central meeting area for the whole family.

I offered Don and Rick drinks. Don had juice after much banter on both our parts. Rick had a coke. I yelled for the kids to come downstairs. They were shocked to see Don and Rick in our kitchen. Don told Kevin and Myesha he was a big fan of mine after the wonderful way I had treated him at my office. I couldn't stop blushing. I sent them back upstairs to do their homework. Myesha left quickly. Knowing her she probably had someone on hold. Kevin said he didn't have any homework. I didn't want to have an altercation in front of Don and Rick so I didn't argue. Kevin bet Rick that he could beat him at NBA2K17. Don told Rick to go ahead while he helped me with dinner.

I'm trying to raise responsible children, but Kevin doesn't do his home-work, he doesn't clean his room, he stays out past his curfew, which drives me nuts, he smokes pot, and I'm almost sure that he has had sex in the house. Kevin and Myesha are tight. He was a big help when Charles died. I try not to be too hard on him. He needs Charles now more than ever because I've ran out of words. I don't know what else to do.

"So what do you want me to do?" Don said and brought me out of my muse. He licked and pursed his luscious-looking lips into the perfect position for a kiss. I might as well have been naked in front of him. The sexy smirk that blessed his face certainly read my emotions correctly.

"Cooking isn't my forte so your help will be greatly appreciated, sir."

"I'm not bragging, but I can throw down in the kitchen."

"I bet you can." I raised an eyebrow and flashed him a look that dared him to prove it. His grin let me know that he understood my innuendo. I giggled innocently and he laughed as though I had busted him as well. I kicked off my shoes, put on an apron, and gave him my "Kiss the Cook" apron. He stared at my feet and bare legs.

"I like the cool feel of tile under my feet. Why don't you try it?" The kitchen floor looks like hardwood like the rest of the opened area but it is a matching easy to clean tile.

Don kicked off his shoes. We moved around my kitchen in our bare feet and playfully teased each other while Don cooked the fish and I prepared the hush puppies. He was more comfortable in my kitchen than he had been in my dental chair. Now I was the nervous wreck. I burnt the hush puppies then I run the old blackened hush puppy trick. He didn't buy it. He cooked the second batch himself. I did okay with the bag of fresh garden salad, the rice pilaf from a box, and the cookies. Don said we made a good team. I got a glass of Troy's wine to calm my longings.

"I'm going to chill-out on the deck for a few minutes before calling the crew. Would you like to join me?"

"Sure," he said.

I sat on the double sized chaise lounge and patted the spot next to me. Then I took another sip of wine to keep my nerves calm. My foot inched its way to

Don's lap. I tickled my toes on his jean's zipper and tiptoed around his creator. He trapped my foot between his hands and stopped me when it was apparent that his sweets liked my message.

While he massaged my feet, I daydreamed about how his skillful hands had pleased me in my dreams. A moan was caught in my throat when he said, "It's nice out here."

I murmured, "It's nice in the summer and fall, winters too, but I don't like winters in Connecticut. I hate the snow, it gets too cold, and it last well into the spring."

"Do you still miss Charles?"

I got choked up, but I managed to say, "All the time." Then I gazed into space again. "Miss" didn't begin to express the voids.

"Are you dating, what's up with you and Omar?" Don asked.

"Nothing, he's Kevin's sax teacher."

Don stroked my cheek and stared into my eyes again. I shivered when his lips touched mine light like a feather. I wrapped my arms around him and deepened the kiss. My breasts were pressed against his chest and our tongues were doing a well-orchestrated waltz when Myesha's surprised gasp interrupted us. I didn't want the kiss to end but Don pulled away.

"Is the food ready? It smells good and I'm hungry," she said coyly.

"Set the table and let me know when you finish."

"Okay." She giggled and left.

Don stroked my cheek again and whispered, "I wanted to kiss you when you were telling me that silly fishing story."

"I thought you understood my story," I said with more of a pout than I wanted to own.

"I want to understand you." He helped me up and pulled me into his arms. We kissed again before we went inside.

Myesha had set the kitchen table instead of the dining room table. She looked at Don and me and shook her head when we walked inside.

"I figured since Don was kissing you like Daddy, and since you look happier than you have in ages--well, I thought it would be okay to make dinner informal." She smiled again and lowered her head.

"It's perfect, honey," I said, and Don draped his arm around my waist and pulled me closer to him.

"Mom obviously likes you." She paused and looked at me. "I just wanted to say, it's cool, I mean okay. I'll get Kevin and Rick."

"Thanks, Myesha. Let's eat. I'm starving," Don said.

He stuffed himself with food, and I was too nervous to eat. He tickled my thighs and smiled a knowing smile. My stomach did flip-flops. I wanted to kick myself for acting like a starry-eyed teen in front of my children. Don complimented me on the food, which he had cooked, until Myesha and Kevin made enough-already-faces.

"You guys are worse than Hakeem and me."

Hakeem is Myesha's boyfriend. I like him, but when I think about the things I did with Bobby, which Ida Mae told me not to do, I get goosebumps. Kids aren't into heavy petting these days. In the old days, pregnant girls were treated as though they were contagious. Most were shipped away to aunts or to special schools for unwed mothers until after they gave birth, but nowadays some flaunt their pregnancies and babies like trophies.

After dinner, Myesha had a ton of homework and a term paper to finish. She asked Kevin to help her with something on the computer. I doubted if she needed help. Kevin was killing Rick on the video games. He couldn't resist the opportunity to tell him to go practice.

"Dang, I got stuck with the dishes," I said even though I was thrilled to be alone with Don again.

"I'll help you," Don said.

"I can handle it. Niki is probably waiting for you to come home," I said.

Don eyes darkened, his jaw tightened and he flinched not in a good way when I mentioned Niki. He walked around the counter where I was already loading the dishwasher. He took my hands in his and stared into my eyes. "I don't want to go home to an empty house before I thank you properly for taking your day off to help me out." He smiled and kissed me on the forehead. "Thanks. I feel one-hundred percent better."

"You're welcome," was all I could murmur.

"Is there something I can do to repay you? I'm handy around the house. My uncle was a plumber."

I wanted to get laid; why the hell else would a nice Southern girl tickle a man's balls? "Clean the table." I gave him a damp dishcloth.

Okay, so I chickened out. It's been two and a half years since I made love to a breathing man. Omar doesn't count--that was a "get off" to keep from going all the way.

"Is that all?" he said as though he was daring me.

"For now, unless you want to do some plumbing."

Big Mama and her friends used to tell a joke about the best kind of man to have around--a milk man who brings food, a mail man who brings you stuff every day, or a plumber who dibbles and dabbles with your pipes all the time. I didn't get it when I was young.

Don smiled the whole time he was cleaning the table, the island top and the counters. When he finished, he wrapped his arms around me, brushed my wild hair to the side and nibbled on my neck and ear while I squirmed. He worked my shirt tail loose and his hands were quick to find my already taut pebbles. He stroked them through my French-lace bra. I was putty in his skilled hands.

"You wanna show me how to slow dance before or after I take care of your plumbing?" he whispered. His joy stick was poking me in my back. I didn't answer. He turned me around. We kissed until he ended the kiss by pulling my bottom lip between his teeth. I said, ahhhh, and he said, "God, you're sweet."

I leaned on him for support and whispered. "You, too."

"You're different from most women I meet. There's something about you that I can't shake."

"What?" My voice was squeaky and sweat or something was already trickling down my thighs.

"I like the way you make me think. I can't believe I didn't get your number the first time we met."

"You didn't ask."

"So, do you wanna slow dance or should I check out your pipes?"

I couldn't resist the hungry puppy dog look in his eyes. I needed and wanted to slow grind. I decided not to leave any room for error. I said, "Both."

I was shocked because my voice didn't squeak and I was looking dead into his eyes. I didn't want to sound eager. I wasn't sure what he was offering, but Ida Mae didn't raise any fools. Even though I never paid much attention to her prim teachings, I usually did what was proper. I looked away and said, "But not here, and the kids must never know." I pictured Sharon in my mind clapping her hands and chanting "get the dick, get the dick" like an old-time gospel song."

Don's smile showed all thirty-two teeth. "I saw a Marriott."

When I realized without a doubt what I was agreeing to do, I said. "I, aghhrr, can't leave the kids tonight."

"Rick can stay with them. Don't worry, I have it covered." Don rubbed my hand and stared into my eyes. "It's okay, you can trust me."

I wanted to trust him. I need to get over Charles and get on with the rest of my life. Tonight, I can have Don. I'm not looking for a commitment. I just want to get over my blues. "I, uh, need to change—when the sun goes down in Connecticut this time of year the temperature can drop twenty, thirty degrees in an hour or two. I'll be ready in ten minutes."

Don kissed me and smiled. "I'll tell Rick."

We stared at each other for a few moments. I couldn't distinguish between the trust and lust in Don's eyes. It didn't matter, this wasn't about starting a fire, this was about putting one out.

I ran upstairs. Myesha was busy doing her homework when I peeped in on her. "I'm going out with Don. Don't stay up too late."

"Don't do anything you wouldn't want me to do," she joked.

I took a few deep cleansing breaths when I went to my room. Then I changed into my favorite ripped jeans, my lucky heart with angel wings belt, a white silk blouse, a red silk jacket and my blue Ugg clogs. Thank goodness I had caught Victoria's Secret's semi-annual panties and bras sale. I was matching, sexy, but not sleazy. I threw the condoms and the K-Y lubricant into my bag, then I brushed my hair and teeth and added perfume to the spots Don had been nibbling on. When I went downstairs, Don was standing in the doorway of the family room talking to Kevin and Rick while they played video games.

I eavesdropped before I turned the corner. Rick agreed to stay with the kids while Don and I took a sight-seeing tour around town. Don told Rick we should return before midnight. I had four hours to get Don stroke'em and leave'em Stokes out of my system. I touched his shoulder and whispered, "I'm ready."

"Wow! You look great. Red looks great on you. So, you want to test drive my Ferrari and give us a thrill ride?" He wiggled his eyebrows. I hadn't missed his hidden innuendoes.

"I was thinking that we could stop for cappuccinos." I glanced at Kevin and searched for a reaction. He continued to play. If I could get him to maintain that intense concentration level with his homework we wouldn't fight half as often.

Don winked. "Stopping for cappuccinos sounds great."

I was as nervous as a virgin. I shouldn't be doing this, but what the hell--it's only for one night!

CHAPTER 12

Name Calling Sex

One kiss from Gina and I wanted more--a whole lot more. She exudes sex appeal in an emotional way that could make even a man like me settle down. My heartbeat has been erratic and my bone has been on standby since she stroked my cheek to see if it was numb. I've been celibate since the night I flipped Candy, but I haven't gotten premature erections since I was twelve. A song by DJ Drama, Chris Brown and two other rappers called "Wishing" was playing. The radio was set to the uncut rap station. I reached to change it but Gina slapped my hand again.

"Leave it."

I made a mental note of that and the eerie way she hugged the door and stared ahead as if I was driving her to death row. "You're supposed to be driving, you know. You're awfully quiet," I said. "I hope you're not changing your mind."

"I was thinking about the forces pulling us together."

"Forces?"

"Yep. The moon is in Venus and that song pretty much sums up my naughty dreams so this could be our destiny," she said as she stared out the window.

"Damn! So, we are getting down like that in your dreams. You putting a little pressure on a brother?" I teased.

She turned toward me and blushed again. I covered her cold hand with mine and squeezed it. She smiled and looked away again.

"I'm sure you have it all under control. I've always been able to say no, but this reminds me of my first roller coaster ride--I'm terrified and thrilled but I don't want it to stop."

I love the way Gina explains things in roundabout ways. I prefer to think about things and draw my own conclusions. I like her open yet mysterious nature.

"You're supposed to be a bad boy, but that's not what I feel in your kiss. I'm drawn to your fire, but I can't afford to get burnt."

"I like your honesty, it's rare. We can act on these feelings or forces if we agree that's the ride you want to take." I glanced at her. "It hasn't been easy but I've changed. I like you a lot, Gina."

"Spare me the like talk--this is a grownup ride between consenting adults."

I liked that, and I might have been stepping out on faith myself when I said, "My gut wants this to be a whole lot more than what happens tonight."

Gina's head snapped around again and her eyes had a shocked look in them so I said, "We can get cappuccinos if you want me to slow down." I wanted her, but I didn't want to rush if sex was all she wanted. I squeezed her hand; the ball was in her court.

She shivered and said, "I want to feel your spirit and all that fire in your eyes."

"Damn! That's deep."

"You can handle it, Mr. Stokes?"

Our eyes met as I pulled into a parking space. Fear was in her eyes, and probably mine as well when Gina said she needed a favor. I ran my "anything for you, my sweet" line. I was ready to explore her mind, body, and soul. She was nervous. I was afraid she was going to change her mind.

"Connecticut towns are very much like small towns in Mississippi," she said, "and you're, well, you know who you are. Anyway, my office is close by, and I have patients who work here so can you check in and text me the room number?"

"Gina, you're too much. Trust me, I understand."

I was filled with anticipation when I bounced out the car and headed to the lobby. I checked in under an alias even though this didn't have anything to do with basketball. My heart was beating faster than a hummingbird's wings until I got back to the car and saw the solemn expression on Gina's face and tears rolling down her cheeks. I kneeled by her side and coupled her face in my hands. "Tell me what's wrong; I'll try to make it better."

She wiped at her tears. "I was thinking about the tough times when Charles first died. I'll be okay." I leaned her head on my shoulder.

"We don't have to do this," I said. "I'd like to take your pain away, but I can wait until you're ready."

That was bull, but with the way I was feeling I couldn't afford to take a one-way trip.

Gina put her arms around me and whispered, "The stars are aligned for love, and the fire in your eyes is scorching the fringes of my heart, Mr. Strokes."

"Damn! So, who the hell are we to argue with the stars?"

Gina kissed my forehead, and I screamed "yes" in my mind. I stole another kiss and put the key to room 1187 in her trembling hand. She managed a smile and I took my gym bag from the trunk and bounced back to the room.

I stripped down to my boxers and ordered champagne. The bubbly came, but no Gina. Twenty minutes later I heard someone fiddling with the door. I opened it. She walked inside. I smiled. She closed the door and leaned on it while she gasped for air and fanned herself. I asked her if she was okay. My heart was racing again. She couldn't believe she was in a hotel room with me. I locked the door and leaned her against my chest. We embraced for five or six minutes, maybe longer while I rubbed her back. My heartbeat slowed when she relaxed in my arms. I thought she had run off. One of her patients had stopped her at the reception desk. I ran my fingers through the corkscrew curls in her thick hair. She looked at me with her sad seductive eyes, and clung to me like a frightened child.

"If I kiss you right now, I doubt if either one of us will have any control over what happens next," I said. She shivered. "Some things are meant to be, Gina. We can ignore the forces, the stars and the fire and slow down, or we can go for broke. You tell me." I wasn't sure if I was trying to seduce her into trusting me, or if I was beginning to believe the "forces, stars, fate" bullshit that was coming from my mouth. She was right about my fire. I've never wanted a woman as much as I wanted her.

Gina's eyes begged me to kiss her. I didn't. I wanted her to decide. She tip-toed and pressed her lips to mine. I didn't part my lips or deepen the kiss. She stepped away, but our eyes held steady. She smiled and kicked her shoes off. I smiled when she took off her blazer and peeled off her jeans. She unbuttoned her silk blouse and slid it off slowly as she held my gaze. Full breasts spilled from a lacy peach-colored bra that matched her pale skin. I turned to drool when her clothes fell to the floor. Her small raisin-colored nipples puckered under the thin lace, and we stood before each other in our underwear and shivered.

She giggled and walked into my opened arms. We kissed and I squeezed her to verify that she was real. I've never lost my cool like this--maybe there were higher forces pulling us together because if this was a game—I was losing. I took her sweaty hand in mine and led her into the suite. We sat on the sofa. She straddled me and kissed and rubbed the damp crotch of her silky panties up and down my thigh. Then she smiled innocently and pulled me up and led me to the bedroom.

I poured two glasses of Cristal and gave one to her. We clicked our glasses together. "May the forces be with us," I said. She took a sip and sat the glass down. "You don't like it?"

"I don't need anything else to impair my judgment."

I'm not a man who has to have his ego stroked, but Gina had me playing a different game. If she was talking about me, I wanted to hear it from the kitten's mouth.

"The forces," she said then she sat on the bed and patted the spot next to her.

I didn't know what forces she was talking about, but I was willing to bet that she was going to need a force to keep her from wanting more. I sat on the bed and massaged her feet. She hummed, moaned, giggled, and said it felt great. She was ready to get to the nitty-gritty, but she seemed tense so I ran my hands up and down her long sexy legs and teased her some more.

"Were you a dancer?"

"Good genes and track. Charles used to say I had the prettiest legs on campus."

I wanted to say fuck Charles, but I figured by the time I was done she would be over him. I gripped the twin peaks in my hands like miniature basketballs and had my way with them. If Charles was a breasts man, like me, I can see why she is still in love with him. It has been a long time since I had my hands on a set of hypersensitive real ones as big as hers. Some men don't know the difference, but real breast men, who have been around the block a few times, can spot silicone a valley away. I don't care if they are big or small, but I feel better when I know I'm dealing with a real lady with real parts. I want them to be there twenty years from now, and I don't particularly want a fifty-year-old lady with twenty-year-old breasts, unless they invent a twenty-year-old boner for me. Gina has nice genes to pass on.

I brushed her hair back so I could investigate her interesting tannish-pink face while we kissed. I usually don't kiss on first dates, mostly because I don't have to, but I liked kissing Gina. I've been known to kiss breasts, fingers, behind the knees, and even downtown, but this mouth-to-mouth, staring into big brown sad eyes shit isn't my usual game. But Gina has great boobs and legs, and she's strange in interesting ways, and I love kissing her. I can't wait to feel her pouty lips all over me.

"If I were a painter I would paint you in the nude, but I wouldn't be able to capture your inner as well as your outer beauty." I thought about how corny I must have sounded until I thought about Gina's forces.

She blushed and stared into my eyes until I was hypnotized. She wrapped her arms around me and I rolled on top of her. We kissed and kissed, and I couldn't believe I was doing so much kissing.

"I want to kiss you all over," I said instead of letting her know that I was too aroused to get right down to it.

She kissed me again and I got lost in her sweetness. I tried to slow things down by kissing her eyes, ears, nose, and throat, but her moans, sighs, hums and giggles fueled me more. I worked my way from her shoulders to the twin peaks again. I even kissed every finger and sucked every toe. We were swap kissing each other's hot spots when I kissed her pelvic bones. She is the better kisser so I skipped her epicenter. I couldn't handle that just yet, but she arched her back and tugged on me for more. Her body felt feverish, and as her love heat perfumed the air with wild raspberries, I thought about Candy and decided to just go for the gold. I stopped myself just in time--even nice girls need protection.

I left the room to retrieve my gym bag. I checked the bag--no condoms. I checked my wallet--no condoms. "Oh shit!" I said to myself. The last time I had unprotected sex I ended up with Jason. I always protect myself and my partners. HIV isn't a joke--that shit will kill you. I wanted to make love to Gina, but I don't fuck around when it comes to that. Gina walked into the room.

"Did I do something wrong?" she asked. Her raspy voice and the concerned look on her face tugged on my heart. I wrapped my arms around her and enjoyed the simple comfort of having her there.

"I don't have any condoms," I whispered. "I need to run to the gift shop."

She gave me a CVS bag from her purse that had a box of ribbed extra-large Trojans in it and His and Hers K-Y lubricant. She had never purchased condoms before, but she'd had a feeling she would need them tonight. I asked her if she really is clairvoyant. She said she is intuitive so I asked her what she saw in our future.

She put her index finger to her forehead and pretended to be in deep thought. "I see us making mad, passionate, love, and you shouting my name when I make you shoot off like my daddy's shotgun!" She laughed and ran into the bedroom. I followed. Gina did a Simone Biles hop, skip, and jump into the bed. Then she did a fancy tumble and covered herself with the duvet in one smooth movement. She pulled the covers completely over her head and a few seconds later she threw her bra and panties at me.

My cock was so hard I nearly hurt myself when I took my boxers off. Gina was tense when I slipped under the covers and tried to pick up where I left off. Instead of meeting my kiss with a fever she tickled me. I didn't know I was so damn ticklish. Fighting back was hopeless. Gina laughed and cried until she got the hiccups. She was ticklish as well, but I didn't have any mercy on her. She started it, and I was determined to have the last laugh, and anyway it slowed my roll and gave me time to regroup. I tried to kiss her hiccups away. It didn't work. She said she needed water. I gave her a glass of champagne. She drank it fast as she pinched her nose. I was surprised when it worked. Everything about her amazes me.

"That was fun. Thanks for the drink. Most men are afraid to laugh in bed." She kissed me, but I pulled away.

"I'm not most men, and you're nothing like most women I hang out with." I smiled. I almost said fuck. Gina is different in a nice way. "I didn't finish kissing you. So, should I start over or pick up where I left off?" I couldn't wait to hear her screaming my name. She sounded sexy saying, "Stop, Don, I can't take it anymore!"

She flashed another innocent smile and said, "Pick up where you left off."

I smiled and started over. I love a challenge. I doubt if I will call her name, that shit just isn't going to happen, but after all this kissing I will be damned if I don't hear my name being called. I started from the top. I have skills and I used them. Recess was over!

I had shown Gina how hot my flames were by the time I kissed her everywhere but where she hungered for my touch the most. I kissed her toes and worked my way back up her body again skipping her epicenter. I sucked the twin peaks until she arched her back and moaned for me to take all of her. I wanted her to beg. I wanted her to be sure she wanted me. I was already lost in her big brown eyes. I was making damn sure she was lost in mine. I left the lights on so I could see the moment those eyes fell in love with me. I rolled my hot tongue along her stomach around her navel and then I touched her there. She let out a low moan and out came, "Ooooh, God, yes! Yes, Don! Jesus!!!"

She was moaning, kicking, and bucking like she was having a seizure, but I didn't stop. I had to hear that sweet sound a few more times. I ripped open a condom. She begged me to connect our souls. Her moans ignited my fire, and we danced like dogs in heat. Then Gina wrapped her long sexy legs around me, and pulled me deeper into her rhythm and slowed my ass down. I was at the breaking point when she said, "Roll over," between moans.

In the superior position, she rocked her hips and did smooth figure eights on my cock like the dance moves she showed me last fall. She made circles on her nipples with one hand, and circles on her clit with the other, while she rode me near oblivion. I slow burned out of control. She took me to the edge and stopped. Gina smiled wickedly as she looked down at me. She had total control of her muscles. "Don't move," she demanded as she rocked and rolled to a beat of her own. She kissed me, and her eyes asked, do you like me? Mine said I do, and we rocked a little more. "Not yet!" she said. I was on the edge, but I told my pubococcygeal muscles to call off the horses. I had some control, but this was Gina's show. I kissed her belly and gripped her thighs and let the rhythm of her moans and groans distract me. Our music was perfect. I was hungry for her but she showed me how to slow dance.

She kissed me and rocked me, and I did as she said. Her pupils were fully dilated revealing the gates to her essence. She rarely blinked. She kissed me occasionally. She smiled and rocked me into her soul. It happened so quickly I couldn't stop my emotions from showing. I gripped her ass and shuddered when my horses jumped the fence and galloped wildly toward her pearly gate before they realized they were on lockdown.

I grunted her name at first. She was turning me, Don fuck'em and leave'em Stokes out! Her name got louder and clearer with each groan and damn, girl! I had goosebumps of love all over my body. Gina read those suckers like Braille as I trembled out of control. I sang her name in falsetto like Michael Jackson. She had forced me to let go of my well protected emotions. Luckily for me she was riding the waves of her own frenzy. I doubted if she heard me--her muscles pulsated around me like a vacuum when she shuddered and collapsed in my arms.

She shrieked, "Hallelujah, Lord have mercy!" and pounded the mattress with her fists and feet. "Halle-lu-jah! That was fan-fucking-tastic!"

I figured if she could let go of that much emotion, and still sound happy, and not feel any shame, then so what if I did a little high pitched name calling. I held her until she relaxed, and while we lay, sweaty bodies still tangled, she whispered "Thank you. Thank you, Jesus. Amen."

I didn't know how to respond. I didn't even know if she was talking to me. "Thank you" followed by "goodbye" are my classic lines after I've received what I want, and I have one foot in the bed, and the other foot out the door. Gina knew what she wanted, and she damn sure knew how to get it. I liked that.

"You give good love, Gina. You put some moves on a brother." The next time I'll be more prepared, and she'll be singing my name.

She giggled as though she was reading my mind again. Then she flashed an innocent smile and said, "Big Man, you made me get the Holy Ghost!" Her eyes told me I was the man. Well, me and Jesus. I slapped her on her naughty butt before I went to the bathroom to double flush the condom. Sorry about the beaches, but ain't nobody freezing my shit although making a baby girl with Dr. Hill could be interesting. She put a hurting on me. I looked in the mirror to see if I looked differently. I was still humming, "Wishing" when I splashed water on my face. Brothers are always bragging about how we're going to hit it, but the way Gina took control was as hot as it gets. I couldn't believe this was happening to me.

Gina had her bra and panties on and she was pulling up her jeans when I came out the bathroom. That took me for a loop. I've never had a woman walk out on me. Never! I wanted to say, what the fuck is up, but I said, "What's up, Dr. G?"

She smiled coyly. "Aghhrr, I'm, aah, getting..."

I kissed her hard and long before she could finish.

"Are you trying to run out on me?"

"I have a confession to make," she said. She looked away, but I lifted her chin. I had to see what her eyes had to say about this after they had begged me to love her.

"I, we, shouldn't have..."

I kissed her again. I couldn't let her go--not after what she had done to me. I pulled her in my arms and kissed and nibbled at the spots that had made her purr. She tried to wiggle her way free, but I wasn't having it.

"I've been infatuated with you since I kissed you last fall," she said. "I wanted to get you out of my system. I don't want to get hurt." She squirmed, but I held on. "This is not how I do things, Don. Let me go... We can't possibly have a future together, and I can't risk falling in love with someone like you."

I wanted to say, "What's wrong with me?" But I said, "Ssshhh." I kissed her with all I had to give. I couldn't let her go.

"The way you loved me, Gina, you can have whatever you want." She stopped squirming, but she had a bewildered look in her eyes. "The forces are with us." I was starting to believe that forces shit. Something was going on, and I sure as fuck didn't have a clue. "Give us a chance, Gina."

I took her back to bed and I tried to get her out my system, but I fell faster than I ever thought I would fall. I gave what I knew how to give. I even prayed.

Gina said she wanted to commit me to her memory. Then she kissed, sucked, rubbed, nibbled, licked and savored me from head to toe. She told me things about me that I didn't know. "Your birthmark looks like a toad attached to the base of your spine; if I kiss it will you turn into my prince?" She did and I started singing Prince's "I Wanna be Your Lover."

My body was Gina's private wild kingdom and she knew she could have me when and how she wanted me. It was frightening knowing that I was vulnerable to a woman who was turning me into a fucking memory. I was sensitive everywhere she touched. She wouldn't let me talk, didn't want me to move, and it turned me on more than I wanted to be turned on. I was trying to get her out my system, but I let her make me a memory I will never forget. After she finished, I committed some things to memory myself.

Gina had touched that part of me that I thought Jason's mother and Niki had destroyed forever. I prayed that I had done the same. We talked between our loving, which was a first for me. I asked her a few questions about what she wanted in a lover and in a relationship. Yep, I said relationship. All her answers began and ended with Charles. I shocked myself again--I lay in bed and listened to the woman I was falling in love with talk about a dead man. That scared the hell out of me, but I would be damned if I let some shit like that show.

Gina fell asleep in my arms. I had put a smile on her face and a glimmer in her sad eyes. She snuggled up to me and wrapped her arms and legs around me. I played in her messy hair while she snored lightly and drooled on my shoulder. It was a comfort I had never experienced with another person.

She woke up at four a.m. and yelled at me for letting her fall asleep. Like Cinderella, she was supposed to be home at midnight. She was worried about how to explain our indiscretion to her kids? I was groggy, but the dread in her voice snapped me awake.

Myesha was waiting up for us with tear soaked eyes when we walked in at 5 a.m. My heart opened again. I was completely hooked on Gina, and I didn't have a clue about how she felt about me? She was trying to get me out of her system.

CHAPTER 13

Love and Pain

*M*yesha's red puffy eyes brought me back to reality. "What's wrong, sweetie?" I asked as if I didn't know. Don and I rushed to her side. Between sobs she blurted out that she had gotten suspended. I was shocked. I tried to hug my guilt away. She hadn't told me before I left with Don because she didn't want to ruin my evening. She had waited up all night for me to come home.

Don rubbed her back and said, "Myesha, your mom told me how much she loves you. I'm sorry I kept her out. We found a nice quite spot, and we were sitting in my car talking about you, your brother, and your dad, and before we realized how much time had passed, the sun was coming up."

Honesty is important, but it is also important to be discreet with children. I made eye contact with Don and wished that I could lie with a straight face like him.

Myesha had skipped gym class and met with Hakeem. They got caught kissing behind the football lockers. I need to talk to her principal before she can go back to school. I sent her to her room to get dressed. I wanted to hear the full story before I punished her. She hugged me and whispered, "Did you run out of the wild raspberry shower gel I gave you for Valentine's Day? You smell like that ginger soap they had at the hotel we stayed in when we went with you to your dental convention." She ran upstairs before I could answer. Well at least I'm not raising a fool. Thanks to Sharon I would have never randomly revealed anything to Ida Mae that I thought I might know.

"So, can a hard-working man get breakfast?" Don asked. His question brought me out of my musing about how to handle Myesha. My knees got weak when my eyes met his come-hither stare.

Jill Scott's song "Whatever" was stuck on replay in my head. I'm so not cut out for one night stands, too emotional, too trusting, too vulnerable. Instead of running the other way I wanted to fuck him again, right now, right on the kitchen counter. God knows I loved every second of last night. I smiled. Don smiled and our eyes locked again. The intensity in his made me swoon again. Like the song says, he represented in the fashion of the truly gifted.

I grabbed a box of Cheerios from the pantry and gave it to him. "Knock yourself out." He laughed as though I had said a dirty joke. I rushed upstairs to keep from making a bigger fool of myself.

I put on a demure pantsuit, and twisted my hair into a professional looking French twist. Don came up carrying a tray with breakfast for two. Jill Scott was still on replay in my mind. Don still had that intense look in his eyes. He sat the tray down, wrapped his arms around me, and nibbled on my neck as he whispered. "I think I love you, Gina."

I fucking froze! I didn't know what to make of his declaration. I'd kept myself from thinking. We had a chemistry thing going and I couldn't deny myself any longer. I broke all my rules. I lived out a fantasy. I made love to Don fuck-em and leave-em Stokes, basketball player, playboy extraordinaire. I smiled. Now what the fuck do I do? I don't want to fall in love with someone with his player reputation, not to mention his high-profile lifestyle. I doubt if I can survive another heartbreak, and I sure as hell don't need any more drama in my life.

I smiled when I thought about the Quasimodo faces Don made when we came hard together. I wanted to laugh when he called my name. His eyes crossed and he looked stupid, but cute, and I knew I still had some pussy powers. Girls rule! I gave him goosebumps--brothers can't fake those. He turned me in his arms and brought me back to his fantasy world.

I couldn't make eye contact when I said, "Don't. I'm not stupid, don't say you love me." He is everything that scares me about a lover. I've seen pictures of him in the tabloids with Niki Jones, and more than a few groupies. I'm not going to fool myself into thinking I'm in his league. He didn't deny that he has been with his share of women but he said he has learned enough from them to know that I'm special. Oh, and he was smooth. His voice was low but tight so

I wrapped my arms around his waist and said, "Last night was great, but I've been loved and I've been pained, and I'm not sure if I can handle either with you, Mr. Stokes."

The muscles in his jaw flexed and he mumbled something about our breakfast getting cold. After he ate, he wanted to get a nap before he left for practice. I showed him how to set the alarm and let himself out. He kissed me and told me he would see me next Wednesday. I smiled and thanked him again for taking my blues away. He stared at me as though he was searching for the right words or deeds to prove that he is worthy. I didn't know what to feel because this is not how a night of hot sex with a person like Don Stokes is supposed to end. I almost confessed that Charles was not the saint I had painted him to be. The problem is, it will take a saint to get me to trust again after Charles's betrayal, his lies and his secrets. Don is as far from a saint as a man can get. I wanted to bang my head into the wall for thinking that I could fuck Don Stokes and then just get on with my life like it never happened. Stupid! Stupid! Stupid!

I'm active with the P.T.O. and Myesha is an excellent student. Mr. Warren reviewed the school handbook's sexual harassment policy and sent me on my way. Hakeem had tried to keep Myesha from getting in trouble by saying he forced her, but when he got suspended for sexual harassment, Myesha came clean. Things sure have changed since I was in high school.

When I went back home, I wanted to tell Don to be patient. Rick was still knocked-out on the sofa in my family room. He could have slept in one of the guest rooms. I tiptoed upstairs to check on Don. He was stretched out across my bed. He was hugging my pillow and holding his junk. He looked content, happy even. I kissed him on the cheek before I left for the office.

I called Sharon for some sisterly advice. Thank goodness for the hour time difference. I used to think my sister hated me because everything just seemed to fall into place for me and nothing seemed to work for her. She had gotten her life back on track before Charles died and my glasshouse fell apart. Sharon could tell from my happy mood that I had done something naughty before I even mentioned Don. It was nice to listen to her scold me about finally dropping my tight ass drawers and advising me to be careful all in the same breath. She had gone out with a rapper who wanted a golden shower and a hell storm so she wanted to know if Don was a freak-freak. I told her about his declarations of love, but she told me not to fall for the okeydokey. The last time she fell for that mess she ended up with Erica. She changed her tune and tried to get deep in my business when I told her Don lied for me and made breakfast. She wanted to know what kind of freak shit I had put on him. I told her the two years past due slick panties trick, then I changed the subject to my parents.

Daddy has been begging her to bake him a chocolate cake knowing that he is not supposed to have it. He makes her feel guilty by saying she is depriving an old man of one of the few pleasures he can still enjoy. Ida Mae would have killed them if she had known Daddy used to let Sharon get away with smoking pot, cutting class, and shoplifting. I wondered if staying with them was cramping her love life, but she said Ida Mae encourages her to go out so she and Daddy can knock boots. I remember hearing Ida Mae lose her cool when Daddy bounced her around on their squeaky box springs--she used to say she was helping him with his bath. It wasn't a bad thing knowing they still had some loving between them as much as they used to fight about Daddy's drinking and gambling and his other woman. I had to go but Sharon wanted the lowdown on what had happened after Don popped my elastic.

Don had the hardware and his power drill certainly got the job done. The man has Ph.D. skills, and he was gentle, considerate, and intelligent. He listened and responded with his whole body, and the first time we did it the big O was an out of body experience. He tasted everything I have and I'm not talking food groups. He made me hotter than Mississippi on a hundred-degree day so I wasn't surprised when I did things I thought I would never do again. We did it three times and a quickie this morning and every time we made it mo better.

I only go into details with Sharon. She made some mistakes along the way, but she used to tell me what to do and what not to do. I learned from her mistakes. I still made my own, but I always listened to Sharon. My problem with Don is, I'm already hooked. Hell, I was dickmatized before the first big O. Sharon knew it too--she said she was going to pray for me. She thought it was funny so I asked her about Memphis.

"Don't even go there, Gina," she snapped.

"What happened?"

"We got busy all weekend. I'm talking mo better sex like you were talking about earlier. But on the way home, the muthafucka said he was gonna try to work it out with his wife. He said he was staying for his kids and because of his religious beliefs. I asked his ass what the fuck was this weekend about? Do you know what his ass said?"

"No. What?"

"He said he wanted to let me down easily. So, I said, the next time, pick up the damn telephone and say, 'Sharon, it's over.' Don't wine and dine me and try to screw my brains out and then tell me the shit's over. That ain't how you fucking tell a girl she's history. Hell, that's generally how I start a good relationship."

I would have laughed, but this seems to be Sharon's life history, and after last night I was in no position to judge. I asked her if she was okay.

"Hell, yeah. This ain't my first rodeo. At least he told me. Ain't like I didn't know the brother was married. Besides, I've never been lucky in love like you."

I cringed. Sharon is always rubbing that lucky mess in my face. I'm no luckier than the next sister. I'm a helluva flirt, and a tease, but I usually think about what is going to happen next before taking the plunge. Luck doesn't have anything to do with it. It's about taking risks, rolling the dice, and being prepared for whatever happens. Bobby said it best, "The only difference between good sex and great sex is what happens next."

"Call me if you need someone to talk to."

After I said good-bye and hung up, Doris walked in and asked me why I was so happy. She couldn't believe she had missed Don's emergency visit, but she could tell from the way I was blushing that I didn't need any help.

"Tall, doofus, nervous Adam is waiting for us," Doris said. "Remember the first time he came in? He was sweating bullets, but by the time we were done, he thought we were the best kept secret since false teeth."

Laura walked in and said, "A Mr. Stokes is on line one. I tried to take a message because Adam is getting antsy out here. Mr. Stokes says he has to ask you a personal question, and he needs your answer right now."

CHAPTER 14

Pussy Whipped

I pretended to be asleep when Gina kissed me. I knew the loving couldn't have been that good if she wasn't feeling me. Her receptionist gave me the third degree before she would even consider giving Gina my call. I would have texted or called her cell but that's too easy to ignore.

She greeted me in a professional tone. I asked her about Myesha's school. She was having as many problems explaining last night as school policy. She appreciated my concern. I went ahead and invited her to come to the city for the weekend. She used Kevin game, Myesha's dance class, and her book club meeting as excuses not to come. She is worried about her kids' reactions to her spending the night with me, and I get that. I offered solutions to all her other excuses. I wasn't taking no for an answer. I invited her and her kids to Friday night's game.

"I take an African dance class on Friday nights, but lately I've been avoiding Omar--I mean class," she said. "I'm afraid to drive in the city. I usually drive to Stamford and take the train in, but I don't like to be on trains late at night."

"Okay so spend the night and take the train early Saturday morning."

"Myesha and I can share a room, but I can't trust Kevin in a hotel room alone overnight."

"You all can stay at my place."

"That would work, but you'll have to pretend that we're just friends. I can't sleep with you and you'll have to get up early and take us to the train station. I have a patient waiting; if you can live with my terms call me after nine tonight."

She clicked off before I could give her one hundred and one reasons why I'm not going to behave. I didn't miss her Omar slip. I'm not going to stop this roller coaster ride so she can avoid me. Hell to the no! I'm going to make my moves while the getting is good.

I went to Gina's family room to get Rick. He had fallen asleep on the sofa while playing video games. He didn't think Gina was the type, but he knows I can walk into a room and panties will start flying all over the place. I've changed, but he doesn't believe it.

He sat up and looked me square in the eyes. "Don't tell me my rusty ass slept on this couch and you didn't tap skins. Don't tell me you've changed that much."

"We had a good time, but it wasn't like a freak thang. I could make Gina a major part of my life."

"What's with this future nonsense?"

It sounded crazy to me as well so I tried to explain. "Everything feels right when I'm with Gina. The sex was great, but kissing her and discussing our deepest desires was just as stimulating. I think I love her, man." Rick looked at me cross-eyed. "Gina said there were higher forces pulling us together so we both went for broke."

"Hold up!" Rick yelled. "The lady did a root canal. What if she put some roots on you? That's it--she slipped a potion in your food. You have to watch out for those country girls."

I couldn't picture Gina cooking up anything this powerful--she could use some help in the kitchen. Rick knows all about the freaks; if this was one of those women, I would have my head examined. Gina is nothing like that. She's a professional. She has her own shit; she isn't trying to be a trophy on my arms. Hell, she wants the same thing I used to want, but I want it all with her, and the only way I know how to get it is to come to her correctly.

"What about Niki?" Rick asked.

Niki is gorgeous when she steps out on the streets. Rick couldn't understand how I could choose someone like Gina over her. I never told him about Niki's dark side. I didn't know how to explain it, but like Mom said: something just clicked between Gina and me.

"We better go before we get fined," Rick said.

"Give me a minute. I want to leave Gina a note."

"Damn, man, you must be in love--leaving notes and shit, talking corny. Gina must have laid some game changing loving on you. Man, your rep is so tight--I've gotten dates just because I'm your boy."

Rick was in the same spot when I returned from leaving a note on Gina's pillow. "Why are you looking at me strange?"

"Is this your first time?" Rick asked.

"I guess so, if you mean falling in love."

"You ain't in love--you's pussy whipped," Rick said and he was laughing so hard he bent over and stumbled.

I laughed it off and headed to the car. After I backed out, Rick closed the garage door from the kitchen and came out the front door.

"You're slipping, homey," Rick said when he got in the car. "You didn't even get the keys?"

I let that slide as well.

"As many hoes as you've dogged out, you should know that you have to keep your guard up with a sweet honey like Gina. She looks plain and innocent at a glance, but she's sexy as hell around the edges. Are the titties real? I bet she's been dick whipping niggas since those babies popped out. The pussy was tight, huh?"

I certainly wasn't going to disrespect Gina by participating in a conversation about her body parts.

"All I have to do is tell women I'm your friend, and all of a sudden, they're all over my jock. You're the king, man. I'm just a knight in your court. Don't worry--I'll give you a week and a road trip to fuck-up. See the problem with women like Gina is--once they know they have the only pussy you want, they use that shit to make you play'em straight. You called her name when she busted your nuts, didn't you?"

I didn't answer, but we both busted out laughing.

"Name calling pussy will make chumps even out of playas like you, homey. Just wait until she won't let you touch it."

I laughed again. "That shit'll never happen to me, man."

"We'll see... the worst part is when your children start calling some other nigga uncle so-and-so, and y'know he's busting out your pussy, and spending your cash, and there ain't jack you can do about it 'cause y'know your ass wore sorry out like a nickname."

"Yo, man, I know I made it look like fun, but if I can make this Gina thing work, I ain't trying to be sorry."

"That's what I'm trying to tell you homey--don't get caught out."

CHAPTER 15

Slap Your Mama

I was giddy all day. I hated to admit it but a night of great sex makes life a lot less stressful. Nothing was getting on my nerves, not the big stuff and definitely not the small stuff. I had a smile on my face and everyone smiled back at me, and if they didn't—screw'em.

I went home to take a nap during my lunch hour. Don's male scent greeted me at my bedroom door. A small piece of paper was on my pillow. He had left me a note saying I had completely changed the way he feels about dentists.

I dialed his number and left a message. "Hey, stud, it's Gina. I can't wait to see you on Friday. Thank you for...," I paused to giggle, "taking away my blues."

After I hung up, I called Rolonda and told her about the large deposit of the heart I had made. She screamed and said it was about time, then she reminded me that Don is not the type of guy I should fall in love with. I was supposed to get what I needed and move on. Ro is right--a baller like Don probably has a woman in every major city, but that didn't explain why she was so grouchy until she let it slip that she had caught Edward in bed with someone else.

It was the most disgusting thing she had ever seen. When she let herself in his apartment, she heard noises. She thought he was watching a porn flick. She opened the door and the chick he was doing jumped up and ran out of his apartment screaming. Rolonda said she was swearing like her daddy on a Saturday night and throwing his stuff all over the place until the cops came. Rolonda laughed so I joined in. She loves drama. Instead of lying about doing a pelvic exam Edward asked Ro to marry him. He has known about her other men for a while. He cheated on her to see how she would react. She decided to keep his keys while she thinks about his offer. We laughed while she gave me the details about how she had wrecked his apartment. She is leaning toward settling down and here I am getting reckless.

I was greeted by four Birds of Paradise in a beautiful crystal vase from Don and another note when I went back to my office. He said I touched him with my sweetness, and our lives will never be the same if only I would stop being afraid and let him love me. I pressed the card to my heart.

"You're a smooth criminal who is stealing my heart, Mr. Stokes, but can you give up all your other women and love me only?"

The Wild Apricot specializes in baskets filled with edible and pleasurable goodies. I ordered a basket filled with my favorite fresh raspberry flavored shower gels, lotions, massage oils, candles, teas, and chocolate flavored condoms. I sent it to Don with a note with a smiley face no words.

The afternoon flew by. I did two implants, five crown preparations, and six veneers. I rushed home with just enough time to eat a cold slice of pizza and drive the kids to their music lessons at the Artist Connection.

Kevin went downstairs to check out the dancers in the ballet class after his lesson. Myesha was in her piano lesson working on a duet with one of the other students. Omar used the opportunity to give me feedback on Kevin's progress. Since I couldn't avoid him forever, I figured I would be a woman and get it over with while I was still under Don's spell.

Omar locked us in his audition room and pulled me into his arms. He planted one of his convincing kisses on me, and the memory of that night, the horror of my reaction and Don rushed to my mind. I pulled away.

"Rough day? You're tight," Omar said as he massaged my shoulders. God knows he has golden hands. "I could take care of that if you let me."

I couldn't--not yet anyway. I gazed into space and thought about Don. I don't like sneaking around, and I hate lying to my children. Omar is like a big brother to Kevin. I can't take advantage of him. He cares about me, and I definitely respond to him, but the price seems way too high.

"Kevin knows about us," Omar said.

I couldn't believe he had confirmed a damn rumor and Kevin had said nothing. Kevin has been more disrespectful than usual lately and after what I did with Don I can forget it. Omar tried to kiss me again. I turned away this time. Kevin is not the silent type. I unlocked the door and went back to the hallway. Omar banged the wall a few times then he played a bluesy tune, which I didn't recognize on his saxophone.

My eyes were misty when Myesha asked me if I was okay with so much concern and passion in her tone of voice it made me want to burst into tears for not being the parent I wanted to be in Charles's absence.

"I'm just tired," I mumbled.

Myesha raised a brow. She has been asking me hard questions since she was old enough to speak. "Are you in love with Don?" she asked timidly.

I'm certainly in awe of falling in love with him.

"Don had the look of love written all over his face when you all walked in this morning. I want you to be happy, Mom. I talked it over with Kevin, and we decided that we like Don. He's cool people, but don't let him play you. Rick says that Don is trying to change, but until he does he is still player number one."

Myesha gave me her perfect report card when we got home and Kevin looked at her as though she had broken a sacred trust. I hugged and praised her. Kevin tried to sneak out the kitchen. I asked him how he had done before he could escape.

"I passed everything," he said as if life is something one can pass like gas.

I opened his report: A's in PE, Band, and Art. D's in everything that counts, and comments about no effort, missing homework, and a disruptive attitude.

"What is this crap about your homework and your attitude?"

"The work is hard, Mom. Damn!"

"Life is hard, but you get out, what you put in, and from the looks of this the problem is you."

"Leave me alone!" He yelled. "Why should I care? You don't!"

"This is your life, Charles Kevin Hill. How can you be so lackadaisical about it?"

"Things changed when daddy died. It should have been you!"

"I wish it had been!"

Myesha ran out the kitchen. "See what you did? What kind of mother are you?"

"What is this really about, Kevin?"

"You don't love Myesha and me."

"That is not true! Everything I do is for you and Myesha."

"Fucking that goofy white guy, Omar, and Don ho was for us?"

I slapped Kevin so hard my hand stung before I hit him. I regretted it the minute he slapped me back. He stormed out the kitchen and ran up the stairs before I could react. The sting pinched my brain and gripped it. My hand shook, my face stung and my feet felt as though they had shackles on them. I'm tired of losing everyone I love, which is why I can't risk falling in love with Don.

I listened at Kevin's door before I knocked. "Go away!" he yelled. I opened the door and peeped in. Kevin and Myesha were sitting on his bed hugging. Myesha was crying.

"I didn't mean to hit you," I said. Kevin's eyes pierced mine. He needs his father and I'm a poor substitute. I looked around his room. The only experience I had with adolescent boys were the ones I encountered in high school. I realized that I don't know my son at all. I try, but teenage boys rarely talk to their mothers about the things that matter to them.

A month ago I caught my housekeeper cleaning his room. I should have listened to her warning when she said, "You can't treat adolescent boys like girls. Perhaps if you cleaned his room or spent some time with him you would understand him better." She gave me a well used copy of Playboy, a stack of Victoria's Secret's catalogues, a joint, and an empty box of condoms and walked out. I stood in his doorway looking and feeling as stupid as I had that day.

"I don't know why you're upset--I did better than my friends."

I chuckled, but I maintained my cool. "Kevin, I'm more upset about your lack of effort and your attitude than I am about your poor grades. You're a smart kid. You tested into all AP classes. It's not that you can't do the work, it's that you don't."

"That's just it, Mom. I'm not a kid!"

"Sweetie, when I push you to do your school work and keep your room clean I'm trying to make you a responsible adult. You can still make your father proud even if he is not here."

"I'm supposed to be responsible when you're not?"

"Please don't say that, Kevin," Myesha said. "Remember what I told you."

I sat at Kevin's desk. A drawing pad I had given him two years ago was laying there. "Do you mind?"

"Ain't like I can stop you."

The first few pages were drawings of cartoon characters and cars. There was a portrait of Myesha and a portrait of me, which had caught the agony etched in our faces right after Charles's death. I could barely look at them, but I needed to take a critical look at how my son sees me.

"Your drawings are good."

"I know. You should see my new stuff." He pulled another pad from under his bed. It contained a haunting picture of Charles and several pictures of nude Victoria's Secret's models, and several of Niki Jones. I frowned at the pictures even though Kevin's talent was obvious. "These are excellent, but you have to develop your academic skills as well as your artistic and athletic skills."

"I'll do better when you stop sweating me."

"I don't--" I wouldn't call it hassling, but if that's how he feels then I'll acknowledge his feelings. "I'll try, but I expect you to do your school work. You can do better." I hugged and squeezed Kevin until he returned my hug. "My baby is almost a man."

"I am a man, Mom. I'm almost sixteen." Kevin poked his chest out and smiled. "I'm sorry I said those mean things and hit you."

I hated looking like a floozy to him so I told them I would tell Don we couldn't make it to the game. Kevin and Myesha's eyes met. "We wanna go," they said in unison. Watching basketball and football games is one of the few things Kevin and I enjoy doing together.

The wall next to my Jacuzzi has a full-length mirror. I studied my reflection. My breasts aren't as perky and my hips are wider, but Don made me feel like a twenty-year-old brick house. The pulsating water caressed my body, Coltrane's "In a Gentle Way" caressed my ears, and my mind drifted from Charles to Don. The telephone rang. I waited for Myesha to answer, but her punishment is no phone calls in or out for one week. The machine picked up. Troy was coming home a week early. He never leaves a return number. The phone rang again. It was Don.

CHAPTER 16

More Than a Big Dick and a Smile

$\mathcal{G}$ ina was on my mind, my bone was on standby and I didn't give a damn
if it was voodoo, a mojo, or good pussy--I was in love. My doorman had
given me a basket filled with raspberry goodies she had sent. I can hardly wait
to make her sultry body mine again. She was breathless when she answered
the phone, and I was under her spell again. I've never felt like this before, but
when I told her she said, "Don't say that until you mean it. It's way too early to
call this love and anyway, we have to slow down." My conversation with Rick
flashed through my mind.

"I don't say things I don't mean, and it's too late to slow down."

"If you want some more of my loving, mister, you'll do as I say."

"In that case, I'm all ears."

"I want to know everything about Don Stokes the man, not the famous basketball star. I want to get inside your head and get to know the man behind the
dark eyes that sucked me into his soul and took my love."

I was touched. Most women are more interested in the other Don. Gina
wanted to know everything from the information on my birth certificate, if I'm
father material, and what makes me laugh.

"My full name is Donald Godfrey Strokes, III, and my birthday is November
fifteenth, and if you ever call me Godfrey, we're done," I said.

"Oooh, Godfrey!" Gina whimpered as if she was in the heat of the moment.
Then she laughed at her antics. "A Scorpio and a Cancer. That explains the hot
sex. So, uh, tell me about your first love, Godfrey."

"First love would be you, my sweet, and don't make me get in my car and
drive to CT right now to kiss my awful middle name out of your mouth."

"I guess I had better behave then, because my whole body would explode if we repeated last night so soon. Tell me the truth, Don. How can you say you love me if you can't tell me the truth?"

"I've had lots of lovers. Most said they loved me, but this, my sweet, is the first time I've experienced an insatiable need to care."

"You're confusing lust for love, sweetie."

"It's like lust but it's not about sex--I cared about you before we surrendered to our desires. If I didn't love you, trust me, you would have been home long before midnight. And nobody gets away with calling me Godfrey but Mom." She got quiet after I said that. "May I ask you something or do you get to ask all of the questions?"

"I would be offended if you didn't ask me anything."

"Why did you try to leave?"

"I was scared."

"You don't have to be afraid of me."

"It's not you that I'm afraid of--it's us."

"Don't let my reputation fool you, Gina."

"I sexed you Don... My loving is not about sex, it's about making love."

"I don't understand."

"Then it is true--you've never been in love, because when you're in love after the orgasm ends the love making begins."

"That's what I meant by needing you before, during, and after." She got quiet again. "Tell me about the forces you talked about last night. Rick thinks you put a mojo on me." She chuckled but I was serious. "Are those voodoo dolls under your pillows?" She laughed again and asked me if I believe in God. I said, "Sure, but what did God have to do with last night?"

"Everything. Didn't you get God-like feelings last night? Other worldly feelings like higher powers were guiding our way?"

"God made you sex me? Isn't that blasphemous?"

"There is a thin line between the flesh and the spirit. Even nice Christian girls have a propensity to sin in the flesh and in their thoughts. I've been struggling with my sexuality and cussing since I can remember, but spirituality and life has always been based on the same principles. We're spiritual beings trapped in human bodies for a short time, but our spirits and the things that we do while we're here can live forever."

"So we sin and our spirits have to deal with the consequences."

"That's one way of putting it. Guilt, going to hell and fearing going blind were a mutha. I believe love, trust, purpose, and commitment are the most important ingredients to living a content and joyous life. When you have those principles in your heart you have faith, and when you have faith you can handle whatever comes your way. That's why I can't separate my spiritual self from last night. My preacher says 'Love is just faith dressed up in work clothes, love gives and lust takes.' Everything that I am is based on those principles."

"Umm. Well, last night you opened the doors to my soul and they had turned to stone years ago."

"Your soul is your spirit--your essence. And if you keep talking like that you'll be living with the consequences for a long time, mister."

"Is that a prediction or a promise?"

"Some things are more predictable than others. I'm very unpredictable when I'm in love."

"Thanks for the warning. So, what do you see in our future?"

"I predict that you will play well tomorrow night, and after the game you will play even better."

I chuckled. "Now I know why I love you."

"Love is the greatest gift God gives us. It's blasphemous to use it in vain--so don't."

"Maybe those God-like feelings you felt were love." She didn't argue after that.

I gave Gina the information about where to pick up their tickets, and where to meet me after the game. I tried to sweet talk her again. She liked me but she wanted me to behave. She will need to tie me up if she wants me to behave because I wouldn't be able to control myself around her even if I tried.

"Myesha and Kevin are not crazy, Don. Kevin reprimanded me about my behavior."

I couldn't conceal my alarm. "Are you okay? Is Kevin okay? What did he say?"

"He said I couldn't tell him anything after the way I've been f-ing around, but I'll live."

I was silent. Gina made it sound like there had been other nights like ours, and I didn't want to think about that. She had slapped Kevin and he had wished she had died instead of his father. Gina started crying and I wished I was there because I remember having scenes like that with my mother when I was around his age. I asked her not to cry. She sniffled and said she would be okay. I understood where Kevin was coming from so I offered to talk to him.

"I don't want you playing with my children's hearts. I'm a grown woman. I'm capable of raising my children." I made another offer to help but she said, "You can help by behaving yourself. Big Mama used to say, 'After you let the hen out of the coop, she's bound to find somebody's hands around her neck, and her ass in the frying pan.'"

I pictured Gina in a pair of cut off shorts and her grandmother telling her to keep her loving to herself so she wouldn't get hurt. I laughed and she joined in. "I'll talk to Kevin."

"Maybe we should chill-out for a while," she said.

"No! We're already in the frying pan. Together. If we chill out now, I'll be a fried chicken, and you'll be a burnt one. We can't go back."

"You don't understand, Don, my children come first."

"I lost my pop when I was ten. I know how it feels to depend on my mother, and wish it were my father, and wish I was man enough not to depend on neither."

"If you're down for the long haul I suppose I can show you what true love is all about even though we started at the finish line."

"I want to get to know you and your children better so we can continue to cross the line together. If Kevin and Myesha have a problem with me, chilling out is not going to solve it."

"I can see that I'm gonna have to tie you up and whip you to make you behave, Mr. Stokes."

"I would enjoy that with you, but on the serious side, there is one other question I'd like to answer for you."

"Please don't tell me you're married and have a house full of kids in some remote town in Illinois."

After I told Gina about Jason, there was no more doubt in my mind that I was in love with her. I'd had a crush on my Math teacher. It was Valerie's first teaching job. She had a great body and she flirted more than me. She was married, but her husband was stationed in Iraq. She asked me what I was going to do for my eighteenth birthday. I wanted to spend it with her. She took me to her apartment. The next morning when she dropped me off Mom was livid. Mom threatened to ruin Valerie's teaching career by turning her in to the police and the school board. Needless to say, it never happened again. Anyway, I didn't think anything about it when Valerie started showing before the school term was over. Mom is a social worker. She was at the hospital checking on a teenage mother and her baby when she saw Valerie with a baby who looked like me. Mom did the math and confronted Valerie. Valerie dropped Jason off and disappeared when he was three months old. I was away in college by then and Mom has pretty much raised him. Jason has no memory and no contact with his mother. Valerie lives in New Orleans now. Gina is the first woman I've ever told about Jason, that's why I know she is the one.

"Thanks for sharing," she said. "Does Jason ask about his mother?"

"Sometimes. That's why I found her location on the internet. We have a decent father-son relationship, and you know how grandmothers are so I've probably had more of an issue with the fact that she never said a word to me before or after she left."

"Don't try to sound modest. I bet you're a great father."

"I don't spend nearly enough time with him. It seems as if he was a baby one day and almost a man the next. I want to do better."

Gina yawned. I offered to drive up and help her get her second wind, but she wanted me to save it for the game.

"I'm not coming to watch my team lose, mister. I'm a fan. If you win, I'll show you the difference between fucking and making love."

"You're not hearing anything I'm telling you, Gina. Look, if you think I'm saying I love you just to screw you again, don't bother to come. Groupies throw pussy in my face twenty-four-seven. When you say, we weren't making love, you downgrade it to fucking, not me. I'm falling in love with you, not with what we did. Pussy barely matters anymore. What we shared was different. I'm offering you my love. It's up to you to decide if you want it. Don't answer now. But if your seats are empty tomorrow night, I'll know you play a good game, but you don't want to hang with me. I won't bother you anymore if you don't come." I clicked off before she could say another word.

CHAPTER 17

The Only Difference Between Good Sex, and Great Sex, Is What Happens Next

The fans booed when I ran on the court. Gina blew out an earth-shaking whistle and yelled, "Don't worry about it, sweetie, I got your back!" Seeing her there charged my batteries. I not only finished the night with a triple double, we walked away with an unexpected win. I headed in Gina's direction when it was over. The reporters who had accused me of choking in the last game headed in my direction. I gave statements to reporters from ESPN, MSG, The Sports Channel, and NBC. Gina was waiting when I finished. I extended my arms. She walked in, pressed her lips to mine and said, "You were awesome."

I owed it all to her.

Myesha gave me a hug. Kevin gave me a high-five. I figured I had made it over a major milestone when Gina smiled. Kevin loved my three pointers and my turn-around jumpers. I promised to teach him some smooth moves. His smile and Gina's wink was all the thanks I needed. I was getting good at reading Gina's nonverbal clues. She stole a kiss before I headed to the shower.

I put on a gray Armani suit and a pink monogrammed shirt. Gina was wearing the hell out of a royal blue bodysuit, classic Levi's and some sexy alligator boots. I whispered sweet things in her ears about making love to her with those boots on all the way to my Navigator. She warned me to stop before Kevin and Myesha overheard me begging. She claimed that I had promised to behave. I hadn't. Hell, I wasn't even sure if she was going to come.

Mom and Jason were thrilled when I told them I had found someone I want more than a quickie with. They couldn't wait to meet Gina. They surprised me and flew in for the weekend.

We were at my place in no time. I hated putting Gina on the spot. I didn't want to scare her off.

"What's with the poker face?" Gina asked.

"Mom and Jason couldn't wait to meet you. They're upstairs. I would rather have you to myself, but it's cool."

Gina searched in her bag and took out her phone. She dialed somebody's number.

"What's wrong? You don't want to meet my family?"

She looked at Kevin and Myesha. "Do you have enough room for everyone, I'm calling Rolonda."

I wrapped my arms around her and whispered, "Don't worry, I won't tell Mom about Wednesday night." She cleared her throat and reminded me that we weren't alone.

The elevator door opened, and the smell of Mom's cooking announced that I was home. Mom was sitting on the sofa watching my highlights on ESPN. I kissed her on the cheek.

"Where is Jay?"

"Jason!" Mom yelled, "They're here!"

A few minutes later he entered the living room. His shorts were sagging and his feet and chest were bare.

"Like father, like son," Gina whispered.

"I can't remember the last time Donald brought someone home to meet Jason and me," Mom said.

Gina smiled and squeezed my hand.

"Try never," Jason said.

"I've been praying that he will settle down, and give me a few more grand-children," Mom added.

Gina squeezed my hand tighter.

"You're going to be my stepmother?" Jason asked.

I waited for Gina to say something clever, but she seemed surprised. I kissed her on the cheek and whispered, "I'd like that."

She went from blushing to looking like she had seen a ghost.

Jason took Kevin to his room. Gina and I went to the kitchen. We left Myesha and Mom in the living room chatting. Gina leaned on the stove. I nibbled on my food and her. After a while, I sat her on the counter. She wrapped her legs around my waist and we were in the middle of a provocative kiss when Jason busted us.

Gina hopped down and flashed an innocent smile. She was blushing and her nipples were pressing against her tight bodysuit like two big eraser heads.

"What's up, Jay?"

His eyes were glued on Gina. She folded her arms. "Kevin invited us to come to his baseball game tomorrow. He says we can spend the night if it's okay with Gina."

Her plump lips eased into a sexy grin when she looked at me. "It works for me. I'll have to take you all to Stamford, come back for practice, and drive up later, but I can definitely make that work."

"Thanks, Dad. You should probably take Gina to your room before Mom catch you all making-out."

Gina was embarrassed, but I picked up where I left off. "Maybe we should go upstairs," I suggested after I got her hot and bothered again.

"I don't think so," she moaned.

"Why not, girl? Stop squirming. You know we can't slow this down."

"I don't want to be too embarrassed to show my face tomorrow, Don. Stop that." She swatted my hands away.

"You worry too much." I continued to nibble on her neck. "I want you to check out my new sound system and my vintage CD collection. I love to make you blush, but embarrass you, never. Come with me. I'll massage your feet." I smiled like a helpless puppy. Women always fall for my needy boyish look.

"Okay, but no funny business. There are minors in the house. If you mess with me, I'll scream."

I led the way. My bedroom suite is up the spiral stairs located in my art deco style living room. Myesha and Mom were still chatting so we joined them.

Mom passed on the trip to Connecticut. Myesha hinted that she needed her beauty rest because her dance class is drudging. My penthouse has three bedrooms downstairs, and my suite upstairs. Gina kept Mom company while I showed Myesha to the guest room I used to entertain Candy in. After I rejoined them on the living room sofa, we watched TV while Mom bragged about me. Gina slid her hand in mine and rested her head on my shoulder.

Mom wanted Gina to call her, Edna, but Gina said she didn't feel comfortable with that even though she sometimes slips and calls her mother Ida Mae. Gina's family owns a funeral home and everyone in their part of town called her mother Miz Ida Mae. She used to hang-out with her great grandmother at the business. Her Big Mama had to constantly explain to everyone that Gina was Ida Mae's daughter because of her pale skin. And to make matters worse, she was always carrying messages back and forth to her mother from her Big Mama and the customers. No one noticed when she took to calling her mother Ida Mae the same as everyone else. Gina said her folks taught her to respect her elders, and her Big Mama would pay her a visit from the other side if she got too big for her breeches. Mom and Gina laughed and exchanged down South stories and by the time Mom yawned and stood up on cue, Gina had progressed naturally to calling her Mom.

"Be patient with, Donald. He needs a good woman. I can tell that you have a good heart," Mom said. She winked and left the room.

I grabbed Gina's hand and pulled her up from the sofa. "Are you ready for a repeat of Wednesday night?"

"That would be highly inappropriate, Mr. Stokes, what will the kids and your mother think?"

"It's not like it used to be, Gina. I doubt if Kevin and Myesha think we talked and held hands all night. We were too happy when, we walked into your kitchen, and found Myesha crying."

Gina blushed and said, "I'll sleep with Myesha."

It didn't seem right for her to sleep in the same bed I had screwed Candy in. I eased her mind about the kids, but she was still worried about Mom. My suite is completely private. Even if she screamed, and I did intend to make her scream, no one would hear her, except for me of course.

"We don't have to make love," I said. "I just want to be near you."

"Okay, but you have to leave when I get sleepy, and don't think for one minute that I forgot about my foot massage. Where are you going to sleep?"

I pointed to the sofa and flashed my boyish look again. Then I practically pulled her upstairs. I opened my door and waved my hand for her to enter.

"After you my sweet."

She gasped when she entered my room. "Oh my God! You have the 18th century mahogany poster bed!"

I noted that she said "the" instead of "a" poster bed. My bed sits in the middle of my huge space. It is covered with a zebra print comforter and cheetah print cotton sheets. It commands attention. Gina was in awe because she had seen "my" bed in her dreams. Just the thought of it made her blush. I didn't push her for details; I didn't need to with her.

I opened the two large glass doors that extend from the floor to the ceiling. Gina stepped out on my terrace. The air was chilly. We went back inside. She straightened and studied an original painting called "Endangered Species" by Dexter Griffin. It has two rare tigers surrounding a queen mother baring her breasts. She nodded when she checked out my degree from GW and pictures of Jason on the other wall. One corner of the room contains workout equipment--free weights, a treadmill and a Soloflex machine. The wall facing the bed has a large entertainment center with a 65-inch TV, a CD player, an iPad, my travel Kindle, and tons of books, and movies. She perused my books, and CD's, and my office. She was impressed.

I was like an adolescent boy on the verge of getting his first piece while Gina checked out my world. I don't allow anyone in my space. Her antique bed, those horseshoes and crosses over the door, the dolls under her pillows, and the foundation in his name confirmed volumes about her love for Charles. I wondered what was going through her head while she examined my things and thus me. She pulled a novel from the shelf, sat in my brown leather chair, put her feet on the ottoman, and started reading.

I programed my iPad with jazz and old rhythm and blues slow jams. My home theater gives the music a live feeling. I stripped down to my lucky boxers and sat on the bed. She ignored me until I asked her to join me. When she sat down, I put my feet on her lap and smiled.

"You earned the foot massage and anything else you want tonight," she said.
"Anything?"

"But that. Your place is nice. Did you decorate it yourself?"

"I hired an interior decorator to do the living room, the kitchen, and the bedrooms downstairs. This room is all me."

"You have an artistic eye. I like the way you pulled everything together. I even like the picture."

"Thanks. Do you like Coltrane? I heard him playing in the background last night." My One and Only Love was playing.

"I love him, 'Soul Eyes' is my favorite."

I didn't have to wonder why. Gina's eyes are always filled with questions, answers, love, pain, passion and lust.

"Would you like to get comfortable?"

"I would, but I didn't bring anything to sleep in."

"I don't have a problem with that."

She slapped my foot. "Why don't you ask me some questions? And don't ask me what my favorite flavor popsicle is. There is more to me than great sex, you know."

Damn, how did she know I was thinking that? "What do I have to do to make you love me as much as I love you, Gina?"

"You don't know anything about me or love, Don, and I don't know enough about you to explain Wednesday night. We need to figure that out before we start falling in love?"

She was right about that so I decided against telling her that when I woke up on Thursday with her in my arms, I knew I wanted her in my life. I feel a completeness when I'm with her that I've never felt before, but I can't explain that either. I guess this is the what happens next part that I've been missing.

"You're the first man I've gone all the way with since Charles died. I needed to be loved again. I guess I gave much more than I had intended, but let's stop confusing great sex for love, okay?"

"It apparently was just sex to you, but in the middle of it, you showed me how love feels, Gina."

She massaged my foot and mumbled, "I'm trying to be serious, Don. Don't start flipping shit on me--Charles used to do the same thing."

"Look at me, Gina. Do I look like Charles?"

"Well, since you like the way I make you feel, let a sista know what she did to make you think you love her."

I played with her hair while I talked. "I like the warmth in your eyes and your cheerful disposition even though you seem sad deep down inside. I like the way you take charge without being pushy. I like it when you're playful, but I also like it when you're serious. I like your spiritual side even though I don't understand some of the things you say. I like the mystery though. How am I doing?"

"Not bad. Keep going."

"You're honest, kind, giving and you don't seem to have a hidden agenda." I pulled her on top of me and rubbed her behind while she squirmed. "I love your slamming body and the way you work it."

"I'm trying to be serious, Don."

"It's true. I love everything about you. I don't care about your past so are you gonna take a chance and fall in love with me, or are you afraid to let Charles go?"

She shivered, but she scooted closer. "I think it is clear that I rolled the dice Wednesday night. Giving you my body, and risking my heart, is as big a gamble as I've ever taken," she said. She kissed me passionately, and I didn't feel bad about throwing Charles back in her face. "I get my risk-taking genes from my daddy, the Craps King of our hood." She smiled wickedly but quickly lost it. "Yeah, baby, I can get down in the hood, but I get my cautious-genes from my mother, Mrs. Strict Southern Girls Rules. And that makes me a rebellious risk taker."

"A rebel."

"A little or a lot of both, more like a preacher's kid." She flashed a sly grin again. "I should tell you some things about me before we go any further," Gina said as she stroked my hand. "When I love, I love deep, and when I hurt, I hurt just as deep. I follow my instincts. I need love, trust, honesty and good communication to keep me happy. Are you with me so far?"

"I can satisfy your soul," I said, but when she smiled I was thinking damn, she already has me talking eclectic and shit.

"So you're saying you can satisfy my physical as well as my mental and emotional needs?"

"Did I stutter?"

"Are you sure you're ready for me and love? After I rolled the dice, I was all in. I played to win, and I seem to have the upper hand after game one. If I were you, Mr. Stokes, I would listen up and try to understand what you're getting yourself into."

When Gina was young she struggled to find inner peace. She had horrible nightmares about the turmoil in Mississippi. She says she was trying to understand it and herself. Raise two kids. Keep Charles happy. Start her practice and maintain a house. She wasn't happy so she started reading self-help books. She made some changes, and put her life into perspective. She found some outlets, which were just for her. They sounded selfish to me but she said she had to find self-love before she could give good love. She had finally found inner and outer peace when Charles died. She wants it again. She wants to be sure we are looking for the same thing in a relationship. She says she needs my unequivocal love. She needs the love and support of her family. She needs the love and support of her friends, and she needs the love that she puts into her work.

"I'm not trying to play twenty questions, Don. I'm trying to give you good love, and good love grows from good communication. Our bodies communicate great between the sheets, but if our minds can't make that same connection, it won't last long."

I kissed her on the forehead, "I want to know every cell that makes up your luscious body and your great mind, Gina."

"I have to go to a meeting with my Sisters and Friends book club Saturday night. It usually last three to four hours, but I promise to take you to one of Hartford's jazz clubs after the meeting. Will you be okay with me leaving you with the kids for a few hours?"

I wasn't thrilled, but I was sure she was testing me. I vowed to do whatever pleases her, at least for now. She loves to read and she was impressed with my selection of books. I had read all of them, including a few of those relationships novels on my Kindle. A real player keeps up with what women are thinking and their secret kinks.

"Good. Intelligence is extremely sexy, totally irresistible and a terrible thing to waste," she said as she straddled me and kissed my nipples. And when she kissed a trail from my navel to my lips, she had me, of all people, shuddering from a kiss.

"Would you like to slip on my robe?" I asked.

"Where is it?"

"Hanging on the door hook in the bathroom."

She took a cosmetic bag from her purse and headed to the bathroom. Her phone went off as soon as she closed the door. She stuck her head out and asked me to get it from her purse. Her journal fell out while I was searching for the phone.

Gina was working my silk robe, and I was still reading her personal thoughts when she walked into the room. I put her journal behind my back. She frowned and rested her hands on her hips.

"Did you find what you were looking for?" she asked.

"She's standing right in front of me. Wow! You look great in black." I laid one of my best kisses on her.

She pulled away. "Your Jacuzzi is awfully big, Mr. Stokes. I can just picture you in there with a few of those groupie's you mentioned or," Her hands were on her hips again. "I could believe that you love me, and only me, and picture you in there with me, champagne, Coltrane, and many repeats of Wednesday night." She sat on my bed and continued, "I'm not here to play games, but I'll go psycho bitch on you in a minute if you try to fuck over me and my kids. If we're gonna do this, we need to be honest about our feelings and everything else. If I can't trust you, I sure as hell can't fall in love with you, so did you find what you were looking for in my journal?"

She folded her arms and pouted. I couldn't think of anything clever to say, so I said what was on my heart. "I love you, Gina. This is new for me, I looked because I care."

"I'm here tonight by choice, so don't tell me you love me again unless you mean it, and you're willing to do the work necessary to make me want to trust you. Did you find my phone?"

I handed it to her. "I didn't mean to pry. I thought you said you weren't serious about Omar?" I sat next to her.

"Omar is Kevin's saxophone teacher," she said in a nervous tone that indicated that it wasn't that cut-and-dry. And I had read her entry about how she had missed his crush on her all these years.

"Is that all?"

"I went out with him once."

"What about Troy?"

"He's a friend. He wants more. I was considering it, but I don't feel as if he's right for me. I thought you didn't care about my past? I let my guard down with you, but I don't sleep with everyone I go out with--I hope you don't either."

A chill went up my spine, but I didn't let it show. "Did you tell Troy about us?"

"He's in Paris."

"Gina, I'm serious about you. Let the forces work their magic. Tell Troy to get lost."

"I don't have his number."

"Maybe that's him. Do patients call you this late?"

"I had a life before Wednesday, Don." She looked at the caller ID. "It's Rolonda."

"Rolonda, is everything okay?" Gina asked. "Wow, Ro, that's great news! I told you it was love. Edward is finally going to make an honest woman out of you." Gina covered the phone and said, "Ro just got engaged." She nodded. "I don't know, Ro. It's after midnight. I'll run it by Don. Hold on."

My robe slid off Gina's shoulders and gave me a clear view of the treasures inside. I pulled her in my arms, slipped my hands inside the robe and placed a firm kiss on her lips. I made her purr so fast she forgot Rolonda was on hold and Mom and the kids were downstairs. I tried to prove that I am the only man for her. And after I had written my signature on the smile in her eyes I didn't feel corny talking about my feelings. Gina hinted at hers just enough to give a player something to dream on.

She told me to go downstairs around three a.m., but I stayed. Her head was on my shoulder and she was still wrapped around me when the morning sun woke me up. I got up, and dropped to the floor to do my daily sit-ups and pushups.

Gina tried to sneak up on me. When she reached for me, I grabbed her and pulled her into my arms. She greeted me with a sloppy kiss. We made love right there on the floor. The passion was so hot and raw we didn't think about protection. I had a carpet burn on my behind, but we were two mingled, sweaty out of breath, satisfied souls. And when I didn't think my life could get any better it did.

She tightened her arms around me, smiled and stared in my eyes and said, "I think I love you too."

She was all choked up, and I knew she meant it. Then she cleared her throat and put back on her game face and said, "Don't you dare get a big head. I'm not one of those waiting to exhale chicks, and I'm not a damsel in distress. I've been loved. And I've been alone. I know what real love feels like and if I think for one minute your shit ain't right, I'll be gone faster than the wind."

Those three words coming from her were like winning the National Championship trophy, so if she thinks I'm going to let her get away, then she is right--she doesn't know me at all.

"I wish we had more time. I'd like to make you a regular part of my workout."

"Don, sex is just another way women get cheated."

"You don't look cheated."

She blushed and got up. "When a man has an orgasm, he burns enough calories to run four laps around the track, whereas a female orgasm equates to only one lap, unless she masturbates. Therefore, sex is not an excuse for a girl to stop exercising. Did you know married men and men who have active sex lives live longer?"

I didn't, but for a fleeting moment I was glad Charles had died in that car crash.

Gina helped me up. We shared a warmer shower than I desire. She put aloe on the passion marks on her knees and my butt. I wore jeans and a T-shirt, and packed a suit to wear to the jazz club. Gina wore a different bodysuit and the same jeans, and she put her hair in a bushy ponytail. I stared at her and wondered how she could be so wholesome one minute and so lascivious the next.

CHAPTER 18

The Hardest Work I've Ever Done

*D*on stared at me and smiled. I wondered what in the hell I had gotten myself into. He was so sweet when he was apologizing. I wasn't all that upset anyway--I would have answered my own phone if I hadn't been snooping around in his medicine cabinet. A single man's bathroom can tell a woman a lot about his habits and lifestyle. He didn't have any prescription or illegal medications. No extra toothbrushes. No strange hairs or feminine products. His box of condoms was unopened. He had dental floss. He owned a Bible. He had a karma sutra kit. I decorated his bathroom with my red toothbrush and pink razor, and an emergency tampon and pad. We were both wrong for prying, but I would be a fool not to check him out and leave my mark. He stared at me and smiled again. "What?" I asked.

"I'll start breakfast. You can wake-up the kids." My phone rang when he turned to go downstairs.

"What in the hell happened to you?" Ro yelled when I answered.

"I uh, Don uh."

"I thought I was your girl. You got a hard one and dropped me like a two-dollar ho. If it wasn't for me, you would still be in your big ass house in Connecticut drowning in your own tears. I asked you for one favor, and you just left me hanging!"

"What can I say? I'm sorry."

"I love you, Gina. Don is a dog! I wanted you to come share in my happiness. Was I asking too much? Was he that good? You couldn't wait until later to get your groove on? Who do you think is going to pick your sorry ass up when he breaks your heart?"

I didn't bother trying to get a word in until she finished her tirade. "Why don't you and Edward join us for breakfast? I'll make mimosas. So, what do you say, girlfriend?"

"Don't girlfriend me!" she yelled, and then she added a very sarcastic, "Did you clear this with your man?"

"It was his idea."

Don gave Rolonda directions and apologized. We walked downstairs together afterwards. I made sure the kids were awake before I went to the kitchen to help Don. He had everything under control so I sat at his breakfast nook and kept him company. Watching him move around the kitchen effortlessly made me wish I were a better cook.

"I can't wait to meet Rolonda again," Don said as he cracked several eggs using only one hand. He put them into a bowl.

"You'll love her. She's nice if you don't upset her."

"She gave you an ear full, huh?"

"Yep. This is going to be her second marriage. She was totally in love with her first husband. She hung in there a long time, but when he got strung out on crack he cleaned out their bank accounts and sold half their stuff; she had to let the brother go."

"How did you all meet?"

"At the gym. She had taken a less stressful job with the FDIC while she was getting divorced, but Connecticut wasn't her cup of tea even though we became quick friends."

Don smiled and I was open to letting myself love him. I stood up. "What do you want me to do?"

He stole a kiss and laughed. "I have it under control. Tell me some more about Rolonda."

"I'm sure you have someone to help you manage your money, but Rolonda is a great financial planner. She helped me double my savings. We tried to start an investment club, but Ro moved back to the city when her mother was diagnosed with breast cancer. She died three years before Charles." I got teary eyed until Don stole another kiss.

"Are you sure you don't want me to help?"

The intercom buzzed before he could answer. Don gave the okay and a few minutes later Ro and Edward were stepping off the elevator.

I met Ro and Edward at the door with tight hugs, kisses on each cheek, and cheerful congratulations. Ro showed me her two-carat diamond solitaire ring. I screamed, and then I took Ro and Edward by their hands and led them into Don's home.

Rolonda and Edward were immaculately dressed. Ro's flawless dark skin and long hair didn't have a strain out of place. She was wearing a pink Prada pantsuit, and her perfectly applied makeup made her look as if she was going out to dinner at one of New York's finest restaurants rather than having breakfast with Don and me. Edward was as sharp as a tack as well. He has come a long way since our struggling medical and dental school days at UCONN. I introduced Ro and Edward six years ago. Rolonda had told me she was afraid to go to the gynecologist because of her fears about breast cancer. Edward was a super nerd and Rolonda wouldn't give him the time of day at first. He had a thing for her from the moment he met her. He transformed himself, with Ro's help, into the man she wanted.

Don stayed in the background, but I noticed him checking Ro out. She is probably closer to the type of glamorous women he is used to dating. I felt like a country bumpkin in my Levi's, no makeup, and curly wild hair until Don wrapped his arms around me. Myesha went through the same routine with Ro as I when she came into the room. Don invited everyone to his dining room. I served the drinks and juice while Don finished the eggs and pancakes. Myesha set the table, but Don still wouldn't let me help him prepare the food.

Don fixed a plate and a mimosa. He put them and a rose on a serving tray. He took it to his mother's bedroom. Everyone else sat at the table. We all held hands while Don did the grace. He added special congratulations to Rolonda and Edward, and he surprised me when he indicated that he hopes to marry me one day. I played it off by proposing a toast to Ro and Edward for many years of happiness.

Rolonda and I were making girl-I-have-to-tell-you-something eyes and giggling like school girls when nothing was funny. Don looked at Edward and shrugged his shoulders.

"I wonder if it is contagious," Edward said.

"You guys did this to us." I said.

Don and Myesha cleared the table. "You can chat with Rolonda while I do the dishes," Don said. "Maybe you all can figure out what's funny." Ro and I looked at each other again and laughed.

"I'll help with the dishes. I think it's a girl thing--you guys wouldn't understand," Myesha said.

"I can take a hint," Edward said.

"So can I," Jason added.

"Don, you and Myesha don't need my help with those dishes, do you?"

"Kevin, I don't know why you're frontin'. You never help with the dishes or anything else for that matter," Myesha said.

"That's because it's women's work."

"I do the dishes all the time. It's no big deal," Don added. Then he winked at me. "Helping the ladies out can be very beneficial, but Myesha and I can handle it."

Don and Myesha took the dishes and left for the kitchen. Everyone else scattered.

"Girl, I see why you left me hanging. Did you put Spanish fly in his anesthesia?"

I couldn't believe I had let myself fall for Don Stokes.

"Don's nose is wide open, and I can see that Kevin and Myesha like him so don't try to use them as an excuse. Are you prepared for this?" Rolonda asked. "Don't think I missed his comment about getting married, or the look on your face."

"We're moving so fast I haven't had time to think about the future. I don't seem to think at all when I'm with Don. Girl, I'm enjoying the here and now. Isn't that what we're supposed to do at our age?"

"When Don mentioned marriage, you looked like you had seen a ghost."

"Maybe I did. I just wanna be Don's lover. This feeling probably won't last, and anyway the thought of marriage to someone like him scares the hell out of me."

"Why? Talk to me, girl."

"Marriage to Charles was good, but there are still some things that scare me about marriage. I'm not trying to scare you, sugar. Everyone is different and if

Charles were alive, I would still be happily married even though he fucked up. When you get married you give up some of your identity. You become somebody's wife, somebody's mother, somebody's everything. And most of all it is on you to make them all happy. I used to joke about needing a wife to fill all my needs. You often give up some of your dreams and make their dreams your dreams. When I was twenty I was willing to do that, but now I don't know if I can give up all I've worked for to live someone else's dreams. Don't get me wrong, I'm infatuated with Don and for now that's all I want from him. The relationship is young, who knows, if he can keep this smile on my face, I'll just swear I never said I wasn't interested. At this rate, I'll probably beat you to the altar."

"Yeah, girl when men love us right they make us weak. I swore I would never get married again either. I tried not to be in love with Edward. That's why I always had a tenderoni on the side. My first marriage was never great. I know all about being a giving wife. I gave all I had and some. All I didn't give the drugs made him take anyway. I feel good about Edward and me, but I'm keeping my eyes wide open this time."

Don walked in while I was hugging Rolonda and pointed to his Rolex. It was time for us to hit the road.

"Okay, sweetie. Ro, the next time I come, we'll hook-up for a real party." I walked over to Don and pressed my body to his. "You still wanna be my lover?"

"I wanna be your lover and a whole lot more," he said, and I will be damned if I didn't have to admit that he looked dead serious.

It was another warm sunny day. We piled into Don's black Cadillac Escalade, and since it was early, it didn't take long to get to Stamford. I gave the kids the keys to my Land Rover so Don and I could have a few moments alone. The kids sat in my car and made silly faces while Don and I made out like teenagers.

Two beautiful females approached him when he walked me to my car. One gave him her stylist card. She asked him if he remembered her? She was a friend of Niki's. She had helped with a photo shoot Don and Niki did last summer. The other asked for an autograph. He signed her arm. She planted a kiss on his cheek. I wanted to scream, "Don't kiss my man," but it wasn't my place. Don threw the numbers away and said he was sorry. He used to think occurrences like that were about him, but now he knows it's all about the game. I told him I wasn't worried--I lied. The girls got into a black SUV, and I suddenly got a bad case of horripilation.

Don had to go. We kissed, and then I drove away. I was oblivious to the kids' chatter on the way home. I kept checking the rearview mirror for the girl's SUV. I dropped Kevin and Jason off at the house and drove Myesha to her class. I rushed back home and cleaned out my medicine cabinet.

I took my butt to the gym. My sex workout with Don wasn't going to be enough to compete with all the beautiful women offering him their services. After my workout, I stopped by Patrice's office. She was sitting at her desk with her head between her hands and her lips poked out like a whiny child. My better instincts told me to leave her alone. Misery loves company, and since I had just ended a long affair with it, I didn't want to go back.

"Hey, girl!" I said using a cheerful tone. She barely spoke so I entered her office and closed the door.

"Quincy has been avoiding me. I went to the club last night, and he was all over some bitch and then the dog took her to our secret place."

Quincy is a married man. What in the hell did she expect?

"Have you all talked? Maybe he can explain," I offered.

"He called me a fling."

"Forget him and find someone who appreciates you."

"I'm not like you, Gina. It's not that easy for me."

"It's not easy for me either. Take some time and get your life in order. Take it from me, things will feel easier for you when you're feeling better about yourself. If you helped me, you can help yourself."

"I helped you?" She seemed surprised. I ordered her to get rid of that pitiful face and get it together.

"Is that the trick?"

"There are no tricks, but considering the consequences before taking the plunge helps."

I rushed back to Hartford to pick up Myesha. Don's Ferrari was sitting in my driveway when we got home.

CHAPTER 19

Silk Stockings and Stilettos

$\mathcal{I}$ loved the hustle and bustle of normal family life around Gina's house. She drove us to the game. I was comfortable in the stands until Kevin hit a home run. Gina jumped up and down and shouted, "That's my baby!" Then she put two fingers in her mouth and blew out the loudest whistle I've ever heard. Kevin waved at her as he trotted home. She screamed and whistled again.

"I thought you said you didn't like baseball."

She sat down. "I said it's not my favorite sport. You don't listen, Don."

I put my arms around her and kissed her when she pouted. A woman and her son were headed in our direction. I wanted them to know I was busy, but they were waiting when the kiss ended. A few more fans came over during the game. Gina appeared to take it all in stride.

Kevin's team won three to one. His girlfriend kissed him. They held hands and giggled as they walked toward us.

"Did you see that kiss? I think he has been sneaking her in his room while I'm out on Saturdays?"

It still hasn't sunk in that Jason is sexually active, and that I didn't have any real advice for him on the subject.

"I talked to Kevin about girls, but he wouldn't open up. I miss the little boy who used to think I was the greatest mom on earth. Now all we do is argue." Gina frowned. "Will you talk to him? You don't have to get technical. Kevin is easily influenced. I'm afraid some of these aggressive girls will take advantage of his situation."

Kevin introduced Tracy to me. I wanted to help, but other than telling him about protection, there isn't a lot I can say on the subject without being a hypocrite. Tracy has a pretty face, nice curves and she is flirty. The usually mouthy Kevin was now shy guy.

Myesha, Jason, Hakeem, and Myesha's best friend Timara rejoined us.

"Kevin, were you embarrassed when Mom whistled at you or what?" Myesha asked.

"I thought it was cool, when she whistled at me last night, she got me going." The kids stared at me as though they didn't believe me. "My mom couldn't come to my games because she had to work or go to school. I used to wish she was there to cheer me on."

"It was cool. Did you see me wave at you, Mom?"

Gina smiled and squeezed my hand. "I saw you, baby." The kids laughed when Gina called Kevin "baby." He asked her not to call him that then Tracy kissed him on the cheek and said, "Come on, baby. Let's go find my mom."

The children laughed and teased each other as they walked away. I picked up with my kissing while Gina and I waited in the car. She was determined to go to her book meeting. I was trying to change her mind.

When we got home, I stayed downstairs with the kids while Gina showered and changed upstairs. The kids played video games, and listened to Drake, J. Cole, and Jeremih while they discussed the senseless murders of black youth by the police. Tracy was all over Kevin while he was playing video games with Jason or me. I enjoyed hanging out with them. I had gotten used to family life as quickly as I had gotten used to kissing Gina. I didn't know what was going through Kevin's mind, but mine was on kissing his mother in all the places that made her call on the Lord.

I went upstairs to see if she needed help with her zipper. She was singing an off-key version of "In Common" by Alicia Keys when I entered her bedroom without knocking.

I stopped dead in my tracks when I saw her in a black silk chiffon dress which was low cut in the front, lower cut in the back and about six inches above her knees. She had on sheer black nylons and three-inch stilettos, which made her long legs even longer. My sex swelled when she propped her leg up on the chaise lounge by the marble fireplace and ran her hands over her stockings to make sure they were smooth.

"You need help with that?"

She swung around and gave me a better view. "Sweetie, don't sneak up on me like that; I thought you were a ghost."

"Oooh baby, you look good in that dress. Are you sure you're going to a sister meeting?"

She sashayed over to me and kissed me on the cheek. "The dress is for you, silly."

"In that case--" I swept her off her feet and kissed her hard enough for her to feel it on her g-spot.

"If I leave now I'll get back sooner," she purred.

I let her slide down me so she could feel what she was missing. She blew me a kiss and walked out before I could change her mind. I followed her downstairs like a dog in heat--tongue wagging, sex ready.

Gina gave Kevin money to order Chinese food for dinner. "Myesha is banned from using the phone. She might try to get over on you, don't let her." She blew me another kiss and flashed a mischievous smile my way, and then she was gone.

I hung out with the kids, got dressed and called Sloan while Gina was out. The kids ordered pizzas. They stuffed themselves while they played video games and listened to rap music. Kevin told me about his art. Then he asked me if I wanted to see it.

His room was as messy as Gina had described it. His bed wasn't made and books and clothes were scattered everywhere.

"Mom used to tell me that if I couldn't be responsible for the bed I sleep in, I shouldn't sleep there. I used to wonder if she was talking about more than beds. What do you think, Kevin?"

"Mom says the same thing. Well, not exactly, but she's always nagging me about being responsible. I guess I should clean up since I have company."

Kevin had done a fantastic job capturing the pain in Gina's eyes in his drawings.

"Do you love my mother?" he asked.

"Yep. Do you?"

"Mom was a basket case after Dad died. That's when I drew that picture. I hated seeing her unhappy, but I didn't know how to love her so I withdrew.

Daddy used to tell me to be tough. He was always telling me to be a man. I could always count on Mom to hug and kiss me without judging me. She used to say it was okay for me to cry on her shoulders. But after it happened she needed me to be tough."

"I lost my father also, but our mothers don't need us to replace our dads. The best way to make life easier for them is to be sons they can be proud of. When Gina cheers for you, she's not doing it to shame you. She's doing it because she is proud to be your mother."

Kevin sniffled. "What do you think about my art?"

"It's impressive. I love this picture of Gina. Is it for sale?"

"It's not, but I'll draw you one because at least for now you seem to make Mom happy."

"So are you in love with Tracy?"

"Tracy wants to run things, but Dad told me to take my time. She's always talking about love, but I don't know if I want to be in love. How did you know you were in love with Mom?"

I expected Kevin to tell me to mind my own business. I couldn't tell him my attraction to his mother was equal parts lust, astonishment, and mystery so I said, "There was something in your mother's eyes that calmed my spirit. I'm not sure if it was the sad empty stare that you captured in her picture that pulled on my heartstrings or the way her smile made me feel that got to me. But there is something about your mother that made me stop and take notice."

Kevin chuckled and said, "You have it bad, don't you?"

"Yep, it's kind of spooky too."

"Mom has that effect on people. That's what Daddy loved about her."

"So why are you afraid of love?"

"I'm not afraid of love. Dad said sex and love for men are different things. Sex with Tracy is fine, but I ain't trying to feel no love."

"I used to feel the same way until I met your mother. Falling in love was scary, but I'm not complaining."

"Tracy used to date a senior. He turned her out. Then he dumped her. I'm scared to fall in love with someone like her. Were you in love with Mom before you did it?"

"I'm in love with her now--that's what matters."

"So do you think it is okay to fall in love with someone who has been around?"

I was definitely on the wrong end of that question. "Sometimes we judge ourselves and others too harshly. People can change."

"Thanks, Don, you verified what Dad told me years ago."

"You should talk to your mother about this. Mothers are much better at this relationship stuff than you may think. My mother used to tell me to listen to my heart, but I never did until I met Gina."

"You used to talk to your mother about sex?"

"Nope, but she used to talk to me about relationships. I didn't listen until I woke up one day and couldn't figure out what I was doing wrong."

We heard a vague rumbling sound in the background. Kevin looked at his clock. "Wow, Mom really likes you--she never comes back this quick from her girls and books meetings."

Kevin and I went downstairs. I stood in the doorway while Gina scolded Myesha and extended her punishment for talking on the phone, then she looked at me and scolded me for letting Myesha wrap me around her little finger.

"I was upstairs talking to Kevin," I said in my defense. Myesha pouted like Gina and left the kitchen. I told Gina with my eyes that it had gone well.

"How was your meeting?" I asked.

"It was okay. My friend Patrice tried to turn it into a pity party, but I put my foot down so we could get on with it."

"You missed me, huh?"

"Maybe or maybe I'm just in the mood for a little jazz tonight. Are you ready?"

"Yep."

Sloan recently signed a new saxophonist from Hartford named Omar Fisher to our label. He is probably the same Omar Gina is sweet on.

CHAPTER 20

Who's the Boss

$\mathscr{G}$ ina had an ill look on her face when I parked in front of the club. I gave myself bonus points for being able to read her well. When I asked, what was wrong, she mumbled something about not checking to see who the entertainment was before we left home. Ensorcelled, starring Omar Fisher on saxophone was in bright red lights.

"Is Omar Kevin's teacher?"

"Yep."

"Is there a problem?"

"We, never mind. He understands why I can't go out with him again, but I didn't mention you. I wouldn't want him to think I'm parading you in his face."

"Why would it matter if nothing happened between you all?" She blushed and looked away. I lifted her chin so I could see her eyes.

"He's Kevin's friend, and he's a nice person," Gina said. She blushed and our eyes disconnected. She is a terrible liar. Omar's contract has been signed, but it is not too late to introduce myself to the competition. I got out the car and walked around to help Gina out.

"I want to check this cat out, but if you really don't want him to see you with me, we can go back to the Marriott." Her eyes widened. "Come on, girl." She pouted and slid into my arms.

Quincy seated us at a VIP table. Sloan and I own a small label, which isn't making any money yet, but we're committed to keeping young people interested in jazz and blues. Omar's group opened for Wynton at the Blue Note. Sloan started wooing Omar that night. Omar sent his demo, and Sloan signed him. I couldn't confirm the connection until I saw the worried look on Gina's face. I should be honest with her about what I'm doing, but the way I see it, she didn't tell me the truth, and if she did, it wasn't the whole truth. Besides, she really turns me on when she is nervous. Gina is smart--she'll figure it out sooner or later.

We ordered dinner after our drinks were served. Gina got a Caesar salad with jerk chicken and I ordered the prime rib. I teased her about doing a couple of laps with me later. She sipped wine and ignored my comment until I offered to take her to the Marriott again.

She crossed her legs and nervously shook her foot after she finished her first glass of wine. I loved it. I polished off my bourbon and ordered refills.

"Your legs and those stockings are making it hard for a brother to keep his hands to himself." She giggled so I sat back and enjoyed the view.

The emcee looked and sounded like an Eddie Murphy wannabe. He asked the audience to give me a warm Q's Place welcome when he introduced me as the head honcho at D&S Music. The crowd applauded. He asked me to say a few words. I wasn't here to be lionized tonight. I waved my hand to indicate that I would pass. Gina's eyes were dead on me until the emcee said, "I see you're here with my lovely dentist. All you, snaggletooth muthafuckers out there who need to fix your damn teeth go on over to her office. Doctor Gina will hook you up! Look at her. Hot body and the prettiest legs I've ever seen." The crowd laughed and Gina turned beet red.

She gulped her wine down and shook her foot. I scooted closer and put my hand on her thigh. She switched legs and said through clenched teeth, "Why didn't you tell me Omar was signed to your label?"

"I figured you already knew."

She smiled but her teeth were still clenched when she said, "And how was I supposed to know?"

"The same way I'm supposed to know you have feelings for him when you told me otherwise?"

"It's not what you think."

"So why don't you school me."

"I've known him since he was a kid. We had a hot moment, but I came to my senses before it was too late."

"Is that it?"

"That's it. I'm ashamed. I shouldn't have let it go as far as it went."

"And how far was that?"

"Nothing happened."

"You didn't have sex?"

"That depends on your definition. I know better. So can we drop it?"

"Were your clothes on or off?"

"You already have too much information."

Our dinners were served. The band came out. Omar came out smoking.

"Damn, Gina, he's young, but the kid has skills and stage presence. So, you like tall, young and handsome?"

I wiggled my eyebrows and tried to make her giggle. I have to hand it to the kid, he can play. Jealously was kicking my ass when I scooted my chair closer to Gina. Her legs were giving me flashbacks of our first time. I rubbed higher up her thigh. She shivered. I relaxed. She grabbed my hand when I got into the heavy petting zone.

"Pay attention to the business at hand," she said without looking in my direction.

Omar played a series of classic jazz tunes by John Coltrane, Thelonious Monk, Dexter Gordon, Donald Byrd, Jackie McLean, and Miles Davis. I had finished my dinner by the time he played "Soul Eyes." They obviously had gotten close enough for him to know it was her favorite. My eyes and Omar's eyes were on Gina. She picked over her food, which I wrote off as one of her nervous reactions to me. I put my hand around her shoulder. She leaned her head on my chest.

"Are you angry with me?" Gina asked.

"Nope, I'm a business man--I understand that business is business. I was upset because I thought you were lying to me after you made a big deal about us being honest with each other."

❧

Omar announced a break. He asked the crowd to stick around for some original songs from his up-and-coming CD. He was way too cool for my ego as he made his way to our table. There was no mistaking the unfinished business look in their eyes when he said hello and kissed Gina's hand. She shivered and I moved my hand from her knee back to her shoulders and pulled her closer to me.

"You look stunning tonight," Omar said and he blatantly swept his eyes over Gina again. I would have punched him, but I was sure that wouldn't have gone over well with Gina. She cleared her throat and got his attention.

"So, Omar, you're signed to Don and Sloan's label. When you said you were signed to D&S I didn't make the connection."

"You're a lucky man to have such a lovely date, Mr. Stokes," Omar said, but his eyes were still focused on Gina.

"Thank you. Why don't you join us?"

He pulled up a chair, flipped it around, and straddled it. I checked to see what he was working with.

"You're a very talented young man. Sloan and I are lucky we signed you. You played some of Gina's favorite songs." I paused to kiss Gina, she turned and I had to play it off by kissing her cheek. That shit pissed me off, but I damn sure didn't let it show. "We can't wait to hear your next set. Isn't that right, sweetheart?"

Gina looked at me as if she had seen me checking out Omar's package and said, "I'm going to the lady's room so you boys can discuss business like men." She winked and strutted away. We watched her back as she disappeared behind a swinging door. Soon our table was surrounded by women seeking autographs. Omar excused himself under the pretext that he had to prepare for his next set.

I excused myself from the ladies to go to the men's room. Gina came out the lady's room as I made my way to the door. She glanced in my direction before she disappeared with Omar behind a door with a private sign on it. When I reached the door, it flung open.

"I never picked you for a gold-digger. You're just another link in his long golden chain," Omar said.

Fire was in Gina's eyes! I grabbed her before she could do or say something she would regret. She shivered. I locked eyes with Omar. Mine said, back the fuck off.

A DJ played dance music between sets. I led Gina to the dance floor. "Nobody But U" by Jeremih was playing. I tried to bring her out of her compunction by singing along with the rap and clowning around while I danced. Her hips gyrated and she moved around me like a belly dancer. I brushed my body against hers until my blood pressure rose. She stopped teasing me when I showed her she wasn't the only one who could get down and dirty on the dance floor. We went to our table when the second set started.

Omar poured his emotions into his music. His second set was better than the first. He dedicated the last song to Gina and me. It was a jazzy tune with a sad blues twist. He called it "Ensorcelled" the same as the band. He said it was about a mystical woman who had bewitched and encouraged him since he was a kid.

Gina fell asleep on the way home. I tucked her in. She was out again before the lights. I didn't go downstairs, and the next morning her loving kisses proved that the best part of waking up is having someone you love in your arms.

CHAPTER 21

I Know What I Want, and I Want You

$\mathscr{I}$ planted kisses on Don's closed eyes, nose and his soft lips. I usually take my time, plan things out, think about the consequences, set goals and kept my guard up. I rose on one elbow and watched him sleep while I drew kisses on my favorite places.

He pulled me closer. "A penny for your thoughts," he said without opening his eyes.

"I hope this roller coaster ride you have me on is worth a lot more than a penny."

"Are you enjoying the ride?"

"Too much." I straddled him.

His eyes opened. "What's wrong, Gina?"

"It's not like me to be this harum-scarum."

"You're not. The forces are still with us." He tightened his arms around me. "What are you afraid of?"

"Who said I was afraid?"

"Your eyes and the way you're chewing your bottom lip. I love you, Gina. I need you to love me back. Is it Omar?"

I chuckled. "Don't be silly. I love you so much I don't know what to do about it. I lose all control with you, and the sex is incredible."

"It's not the sex that's incredible, it's you."

"Me?"

"You! When I touch you, and you get those sparks in your eyes, I get a rush. The sound of your voice and your laughter caresses my heart. I love it when you tease me. I love the way your hips sway when you walk, and when you dance, and good God when you love me. I love hanging out with you and your children. I love the way you think. I love all the things that make you unique."

I rolled away and lay on my back. "You shouldn't say those things, if you don't mean them."

He turned and stared into my eyes. "You are as rare as a blue lobster. You do know I don't have to have a rap to get with women. Hell, it sounds corny to me too, but it's true. You have some kind of a mystical, sexual, spiritual magnetism about you that's baffling yet totally irresistible."

"I've seen some of the beautiful women you've gone out with, Don. You're supposed to be Niki Jones's man."

He kissed me like a dog in heat.

"I don't kiss everyone like that and I don't have to use the "L" word in vain. And as far as Niki goes don't believe any of that shit you see in the tabloids. I like your honesty--it makes it easy to love you."

"It's easy for a girl to lose her wits around you. When I'm crazy in love, honesty and being myself is the only way to go." I kissed him this time to stake my claim and soon we were making raw passionate love again.

It was slow burner lovemaking. I shrieked. Don slowed down. The slower we moved the hotter and louder I got. Don sucked my neck--like Charles. He moved--like Charles. The air even smelled--like Obsession cologne. I was wrapped in their love and as much as I tried, I couldn't stop my love cries. Don matched my moans and moves. Charles's presence was strong. It was an orgy of satisfaction and as soon as we climaxed, I sprang up and scrambled to my side of the bed. Charles was smiling at me!

Our anniversary picture was on my dresser--I didn't put it there. The air smelled like Obsession and a light lingered over me.

"Oh, my God!" I shouted.

"What's wrong?"

The light whisked around the bed and me. The picture fell to the floor. Don rolled over and hugged me.

"What are you looking at?"

I pulled the covers around me. The light disappeared, but the smell of Obsession lingered.

"Is everything okay? Whatever it is, it's gonna be okay."

"It's not okay, Don. The kids probably heard us and Charles is not resting in peace! You were supposed to sleep in the guest room. Get out! Why are you doing this to me?"

"I don't get it, Gina. A minute ago you were turning me out. You, baby. You gave. I took!"

"This isn't right. Charles hated for the kids to hear us." Tears rolled down my cheeks. "This is his bed." I tried to hop up and ran from the bed, but Don wrapped me in his arms.

"I'm sorry--I can't do this!"

Don rocked me and whispered, "When I was twelve I heard noises coming from Mom's room in the middle of the night. I grabbed a butcher knife and busted into the room. I thought someone was hurting her. I was tall for my age, but skinny. I pulled dude off her, and I would have stabbed and killed him if he hadn't been strong enough to fight me off. Mom screamed, and she cried for hours afterwards. We were all traumatized. Mom never had male callers after that. I won't let that happen to us."

"What am I gonna do?"

"Situations like ours are much more common these days and kids are much smarter about them. I'm sensitive to your concerns."

"What if we don't work out?"

"I love you, Gina. If you want me to sleep in the guest room, that's what I'll do. It's your call. I'll do whatever it takes to make this work for us."

"How do you do that?"

"What?"

"You're so damn smooth. You say the right things at the right time, and you make me do things I shouldn't do."

I hopped up and headed for the shower. "I'm going to the early church service--I need to pray on this."

"I'll go with you."

Kevin and Myesha didn't seem to notice how anxious I was or care that Don had spent the night in my room. I still vowed not to let it happen again. Charles had been in bed with us! There were moments when I couldn't tell who was making love to me.

Reverend Knight and the Crossroads A.M.E. Church gave me strength during my time of need. All eyes were on us while we made our way to our seats. The congregation sang "We've Come This Far by Faith." I held Don's hand and led the way to an empty pew near the front of the sanctuary. Reverend Knight was preaching from John 15:7-12 about love. He can pick apart bible verses and relate them to normal life situations. I always leave his services feeling inspired.

"God gave us the ultimate gift of love, and if we want to receive love, we have to give love," Reverend Knight said.

Don squeezed my hand while the congregation sang "Blessed Assurance, Jesus is Mine." I never paid much attention to the words until today. While we sang lyrics like "perfect surrender perfect delight," and "caught in His rapture and being happy and blest," from verse two and three I thought about Don. Words like those make it difficult to separate the spiritual from the emotional me. I sang from my heart and I couldn't tell if Don was smiling at my off key singing or if he was reading my thoughts.

Reverend Knight asked the teenagers to stay for a few minutes after the service. A teenage boy from the congregation had been shot and killed. Reverend wanted to pray for his family and create some Christian dialogue with the kids.

Don and I waited in my SUV. I gazed out the window. Why had I let myself fall in love with Don Stokes knowing full well that if he breaks my heart, it could easily drive me insane for real?

His hands were visibly trembling when he reached for my hand. "I think we should—" He cleared his throat. "Maybe we should, ah—" Small beads of sweat popped up on his noise and his hands were as sweaty as they had been when he was sitting in my dental chair.

"We should what?"

"Get married."

I replayed his words in my mind. "Are you proposing, Mr. Stokes?" My voice quivered and I got a sudden case of heartburn and grabbed my chest. "Stop playing!"

"I'm serious. We should do it."

He removed the small hoop earrings from my ears and replaced them with the three carat diamond studs from his ears. "Consider yourself engaged, Dr. G.—let's, let's legalize it. No more games for you or me."

"Are you sure?" I felt his diamonds in my ears. "Are these things clean?" I looked in the rearview mirror. "Wow! These are nice. But if you want me to do 'it' again you'll have to buy me a rock so big I'll need two midgets to hold my hand up." I joked because that is what I do when I don't know what else to do. "Wow! I don't know what to say. You caught me off guard again."

He stroked my cheek and stared into my eyes. "I know I'm moving fast, Gina, but I don't want you to worry about holding back your feelings because you're afraid the kids will hear us. I don't want you to worry about me leaving you. I want us to be a family. I want the world to know I've fallen in love with you—say yes, Gina. Don't let fear keep us apart."

I placed my hand over my heart and pretended to take it in my hand while I looked deep into his eyes. "Here is my heart. It's fragile. Please don't break it." My voice quivered and now my hands were trembling. The sweet illusion of new love had me believing I could go wherever Don's magic took me.

With shaky hands, I placed my earrings in Don's ears and said, "Consider yourself engaged, Mr. Stokes."

Myesha tapped on the window and interrupted Don's kiss. "No phone calls for two weeks for making out in the church parking lot."

I ignored her comments. "Where are the boys?"

"Talking to girls--where else?"

"Tell them to hurry up? Don and Jason have to leave soon." After Myesha left I asked Don if we really were engaged. He touched his ears and smiled. "I'll give you that rock you requested on Wednesday, but I'm not sure about the small people."

"I was joking earlier. I don't wear rings because of work. I'm not into flashy jewelry."

"When we get married... Wow! Married! Anyway, I hope it will be soon, and when we do your only job will be taking care of me and our children," he said. "I've invested my money well. I own several lucrative businesses. You can sell your house and your practice and we can all live together and add a few more to our clan... The way you loved me this morning, little Gina probably hooked up with little Don and Dongina is probably already on the way."

I turned away when he tried to kiss me. He wants babies! Sell my house. Not work. Well, that brought me out of my love fog.

"What's wrong?"

The kids were back before I could respond to Don's question. Myesha broke the silence while I was driving home.

"You traded earrings with Don? Cool!"

"Better than cool--I only paid fifty bucks for Mom's. They were on sale and I had a coupon," Kevin added.

Don rubbed my hand. "Well, they are priceless now."

My head was pounding by the time we got home. I ran upstairs without giving Don an explanation.

"You better get it together, girl," I said to myself. I kicked my shoes off, stripped down to my underwear and laid across the bed.

How can I be in love with Don? I'm still in love with Charles. What if I lose Don too? I must tell him I can't have his babies. Maybe I could have one of those less invasive surgical procedures they treat fibroids with nowadays. Forget that—I'm not a spring chicken anymore? Shit, I'm damn near forty. It's too soon for this. Will he change his mind when he finds out? Oh my God, what should I do?

Don knocked. I didn't answer. He banged on the door and yelled for me to let him in. I put a T-shirt on before I opened the door. He pulled me in his arms and held me until I stopped trembling.

"Whatever it is, we can work it out together. Let's talk about it. Okay?"

I sat on the bed and patted the spot next to me. He nodded when I asked him if he was ready to listen.

"I think I love you, but I'm not ready to be a wife again, and I will never be anyone's possession."

"Possession?" He frowned and tensed the muscles in his jaw.

"I want to have a life with you, but I want my own life, Don. I love what I do. I don't want to sell my practice and my house. Why can't we build a life together here?"

"Maybe we can, but not in Charles's house."

I flinched.

"I don't want to possess you. What's mine will be yours."

"Until your attorneys convince you that you're a fool if you don't have me sign a prenup. It doesn't matter, I don't need your money, when I tell you what is really bothering me, you'll probably change your mind anyway."

"Gina, there is nothing you can say that will make me love you less. Now that I found you I don't want to waste any more time."

"I can't have any more children. Charles and I tried for years. I haven't used birth control since Myesha was born," I blurted out. I didn't miss the disappointed look in his eyes.

"You are everything I want in a woman and a wife. Yes, I'd like to see you pregnant, but I don't want to lose you over it. I have Jason and you have Myesha and Kevin. We all blend well together. I'm more concerned about being separated from you. Let me be your husband and take care of you."

"Don, we met five days ago." I held up one hand.

"Jesus died on the cross, rose from the dead and forgave us for our sins in less than that because he loved us."

I had to grin. "You'll wonderful, mister, but you ain't Jesus. I want to believe that I love you, Don, but I can't marry you and walk away from everything I've worked for."

"Gina, you've been on my mind since I meet you last October. My feelings for you have been brewing since you kissed me and hopped out my car. The more I tried to shake your kiss, the stronger my wonderment for you became. Now that I've gotten to know you, I have to have all of you. I know I'm moving fast, but I already know I want you forever so why waste any more time?"

He stood up and paced the room. His head was bowed too low for me to read his eyes. His hands were stuffed in his pockets, and he kept kicking at something imaginary. I bit down on my lip and wished I could say something to make him grin--I couldn't. A big fat tear rolled down my cheek, but I didn't make a sound--not even a whimper. My mouth was cotton dry. Don looked up. Our eyes met. His eyes were sad. I wiped my face with the back of my hand and took in a quick breath of air. He paced the room again before he plopped down on the bed beside me.

"I love you, Gina. I want to marry you."

"It's too soon. You have my heart, but I can't--"

He stood up and pulled me into his arms. Then he looked deep into my eyes, and backed away. "I have to go."

I sat on the bed and watched him prepare to leave. I wanted to run into his arms and say, "yes," but I didn't move. I walked him to the door. He kissed me on the forehead and backed away again.

"Call me?" I pleaded because the look in Don's eyes said he was done wondering.

CHAPTER 22

Giving Up Is Hard to Do

I hopped in my car with Jason and burned rubber. What's the point of calling you, Gina? It's over. I love you, but it's obvious to me that you're not over Charles. You can't have my babies. You're mutable. And I'm not comfortable with the power you have over me. I made a headlong offer at a weak moment. You're not ready so to hell with you!

"What's wrong, Dad?" Jason asked.

"Nothing I can't handle."

"Kevin thinks Gina is in love with you. He said she has been floating on a cloud since you took her out on Wednesday."

"Really? What else did he say?"

"That she never walked on air when she went out with some square named Troy."

"Did he mention his saxophone teacher?"

"Don't worry, he's Kevin's friend. Besides he's too young. He's had a crush on Gina for years."

"Gina is concerned about what Kevin and Myesha think about me."

"Don't worry--you're cool. It was disgusting when you all were making out yesterday and this morning, but they like you. You put a hurting on her this morning, huh?"

"Do you like Gina?"

"She makes you happy and that makes me happy."

"She's erratic and she drives me crazy, so what makes you think she makes me happy?"

"The way you look at her, the smile on your face when you say her name, and the fact that she matters."

"I give up on her. She's too much work."

"No, Dad! I promised Kevin that I would look out for Gina. She's perfect for us."

"Us?"

"Yep. Kevin said she is strict about school, and she is always talking about responsibility and what not, but she encourages them to develop their creative sides and to be independent thinkers. She respects their privacy for the most part, and she's cool about rap with positive messages."

"I proposed… She turned me down."

"How long have you known her. I thought this was new."

"We meet last fall."

"Oh. Kevin said Gina's father tried to scare his dad away with a shotgun. All you have to worry about are her changing moods."

"It would be easier if her father chased me away. She tells me what is bothering her, but her eyes tell me it's a lot more complicated than what she says. She says stop but her lecherous gaze says take me now. Sometimes I think she is possessed. Rick thinks she must have put a spell on me, and I'm starting to believe it. She has cable, but did you notice that the TV gets static every time she gets near it?"

Jason chuckled. "I can't believe you're trying to blame your feelings for Gina on a mojo. I saw you kiss her, that's a love bug biting you in the butt, Dad."

"Love bugs are for children—this is more like a deadly virus. That's why I'm quitting while I'm ahead."

"I don't know, Dad, something made you propose. Don't you think it will be a mistake to give up without a fight, and if it's that lethal you probably can't anyway."

"You're probably right. I can't explain anything about Gina. She has a strange magnetism about her for sure. Her eyes draw me in, man, and you're right I was sprung after our first kiss. She's the strangest woman I've ever encountered and the more bizarre she gets the more I'm drawn to her fire, her description, not mine. Last night she turned her stereo off with her remote control, and when she walked by it, the damn thing came back on. She says stuff like that happens to her all the time when she is charged up about something. Last night she said I had her all fired up so I let it slide. She can't even wear watches because they tend to keep erratic time depending on how she's feeling. And she's always talking about forces and stars drawing us together. And music making her blood rush and giving her this intense pleasure like sex or chocolate. Stop laughing—I'm dead serious—I don't know what she's done to me. For all I know she could have put one of her spills on you too." Jason was laughing so hard he was in tears.

"Stop making excuses, Dad. You're always talking about visualizing stuff and thinking positive and nobody is calling you strange."

"True that, but I can't lie and say the stuff Gina says and does don't spook me sometimes."

I played a fierce game of basketball while I worked out my anger, then I hung out with the twins after the game just to prove that I could. Gina hadn't called when I got home and that pissed me off again. My mood was so sour; Mom and Jason decided to go home early. Mom told me to give Gina some time because marriage is a huge step, and we need to think about it long and hard before we jump into it.

I bought the ring on Wednesday after I admitted to myself that my life has been a living hell since I cut off all contact with Gina. And to make matters worse, I played like crap tonight. The chances of my contract being renewed are probably as slim as my chances of convincing Gina to marry me and move. Instead of going home after the game I ended up in bed with Bee and Tee again. I had hoped that the twins could help me forget about Gina, but their efforts only made me fantasize about her more--the way her kisses make my belly hungry for her, the way her eyelids flutter like butterfly wings when she comes, the way she blushes when we make eye contact--little shit that's just me and Gina.

She turned me down so it's her call to make. Our relationship is already too complex for our current lives. She must know that we and our children are already emotionally invested. I couldn't concentrate on the twins so I didn't bother to make excuses.

The answering machine was blinking when I got home. The first message was from Niki—the last person I wanted to see or hear from. The second message was from Mom and Jason. My caller ID indicated that Gina had hung up six times before she finally said, "Hey, big guy, it's me, Gina... I was watching the game, and, uh, seeing you touched my inner core. You played as bad as I feel. I miss you. Maybe we can cheer each other up. Call me—we need to talk."

I grabbed my overnight bag and headed to Connecticut. It was four a.m. when I rang Gina's cell and told her I was outside. She cracked the door and when her sad eyes met mine, I knew she had been crying. My diamonds were in her ears, and she looked sweet and sexy in her pink nightgown.

I brought her red and yellow tulips and Godiva chocolates from the 24-hour deli. I have an eight-carat Harry Winston diamond in my pocket, and a bottle of Cristal to celebrate if I can get her to change her mind. I'm prepared to get down on my knees and propose right this time. She opened the door and smiled.

"I'm surprised to see you—I've been calling you for hours... I thought... you don't want to know what I thought. Why didn't you call me? I could have slept until you got here."

She wrapped her arms around me and laid a kiss on me that was filled with passion and hope. I gave her the chocolates and the tulips.

"I wanted to give you time to figure out what you want from me."

"You tortured me, Don. I was beginning to think you were kicking it with someone else. I called your ass twenty times." She grinned coyly. "You'll have to forgive me for leaving F-you messages on your voicemail."

"You turned me down, Gina; I was waiting on you to change your mind. Do you want me to come in?"

She pulled me inside, and we tiptoed upstairs. She slid under the covers. I sat on the bed next to her. She asked me if I was going to join her. I was wiped out after the game, the twins and the drive, but I needed her answer before I got caught up in her rapture again. I kneeled on one knee, and knitted her fingers with mine.

"Marry me, Gina."

She didn't answer--it wasn't coming out right again. I searched my soul and forced my words to come from it.

"Let me be a part of your world. Let me pick up where Charles left off. Let me love and cherish you for the rest of our lives."

Her lips inched into a smile. I kissed my way up her arm. She sat up and embraced me. I wanted her to say yes. I kissed her and held it just in case it was my last.

"Yes. Yes, Don. I would love to be your mate."

I slid the ring on her finger.

"It's beautiful." She held her hand out and admired it.

"Like you, my sweet," I said and I couldn't believe how corny, and in love, and happy Gina makes me. We kissed until we both shivered. I was beat and she hadn't slept either. We decided to wait until the kids left for school to celebrate, but she pulled me in her bed and undressed me. Tomorrow was her day off.

"Are you sure?" I asked.

"Yeah, but no hanky-panky." She kissed my cheek and wrapped her arms around me. "You smell like cheap perfume."

I pretended to be asleep. She kissed me again and whispered, "I'm glad you're here." She was snoring a few minutes later.

I took a shower after the kids left even though I smelled like Gina now. She was admiring the ring when I came back into the bedroom. "So how long are you going to make me wait to be your husband?"

"I always wanted to be a June bride. What about my birthday a year from now?"

"Your birthday this year sounds better? There is no way in hell I'm going to sleep in your guest room for a whole year. We should have a small wedding with a few friends and family this June and get on with our lives."

"Since you know what you want and you obviously know how to get it, why don't you plan the wedding? I'm going to be busy searching for a business partner. Will you have time? Do you have any basketball obligations or anything during the summer months?"

"I'll start making calls today." Sleeping in Gina's guest room wasn't the only thing I feared.

"My family went overboard when Sharon got married. It barely lasted through the honeymoon so Charles and I eloped. I don't want you to put more emphasis on the wedding than our marriage." She held her hand up and admired the ring again. "You do have good taste; just tell me when and where, I'll be there."

We went downstairs and made breakfast, and then we made wedding plans and made love in the guest bedroom. I fell asleep but Gina startled me when the phone rang. I could tell from the twisted look on her face that it was a male caller.

"You caught me at a bad time," she said. "Give me your number. I'll call you later." She glanced at me.

I wanted to stay, but I should have left for practice an hour ago.

"Not now, Troy, I have--" She stared at the phone. "He hung up. He's on his way over. He is flying out again tomorrow. He wants to see me today."

"That's good. I'll tell him to get lost."

"It will be better if I tell him. I had better get up and get dressed." Gina put my shirt on and ran upstairs.

The doorbell rang a few minutes later. Homeboy probably saw my car and wouldn't take no for an answer. I pulled on my jeans and answered the door. Troy and I sized each other up a few moments before speaking. He wanted to know who the hell I was. I flexed my muscles and boldly told him I was Gina's fiancé.

He laughed and said, "What would a classy woman like Gina want with someone like you?"

I played it off, but I'm getting sick and tired of people spot judging me.

"Did I hear the doorbell?" Gina asked when she came down the stairs and startled Troy and me. "Troy must have called from his cell phone." She stepped around the corner still wearing my shirt, diamond earrings, the big rock on her finger and nothing else. Troy's eyes were fixed on her legs as she approached us. She stroked my cheek and placed a kiss on my lips. Then she asked me to wait in her family room. I flashed Troy my best fuck-off look before I left. The door was cracked. I couldn't understand what they were saying so I stepped into the hallway. Troy was kissing Gina and groping her behind. Gina was struggling to get away. She rammed her knee into his groin with a force to be reckoned with.

A subconscious male reflex made me grab my nuts, and probably made Troy punch Gina. Damn, that had to hurt.

Troy howled like a wolf and doubled over. Gina ran into my arms and smudged the blood dripping from her busted lip on my bare chest.

Troy's voice was four octaves higher when he asked, "Why did you do that?"

"Get out!" Gina yelled. She grabbed me around the waist when I rushed for Troy. "No, Don! Please, baby, let it go."

Troy straightened up slowly and adjusted himself. He gave me a threatening look and swept his lustful eyes over Gina again.

"I'm sorry I hit you." He said. "You felt so good in my arms; I guess I got carried away."

Gina walked to the door and opened it. "Goodbye, Troy."

He walked to the door and leaned over to kiss her. She flinched. I stepped between them.

"I'll call you later about the Paris trip, and update you on my investigation in Mississippi." He adjusted himself again and walked out with his head high.

"Where do you find these guys, Gina?"

"They find me. I wasn't looking for any of this." She threw up her hands and waved them. I knew she was including me.

"If I ever piss you off, remind me to stay clear of your knee. You should stay away from that dude."

"Enough about Troy. You're gonna be late for practice." She turned and ran back upstairs.

I drove like a mad man and I was still fifteen minutes late. Coach fined me five grand. He asked me what was my problem, and said something about not being able to count on me in the stretch. I didn't appreciate that shit. I worked on my shooting for three extra hours. Nothing feels better than making naysayers eat their words.

I called Gina when I got home. Her machine picked up. I packed for my road trip, called again, put my bags in the car and drove back to her house. Kevin answered the door with his baseball bat in his hand.

"I thought you were Troy. Congratulations, but I hope you'll protect Mom better in the future. I wouldn't let a fool like that get away with hitting my woman."

"Don't listen to Kevin. Mom didn't want you to get in trouble. I think it is way cool that you guys are engaged. Mom is so happy!" Myesha added.

"Where is she?"

"She went to a Dental Society Meeting. She called earlier and said Troy was at the meeting, but she told him to leave or she would tell everyone he hit her and busted her lip. He left in a huff," Kevin said.

The kids thought they had seen Troy's car near the house when their pizza was delivered. Gina came home while I was removing my bag from the trunk. Her lip was swollen and she had a purplish bruise around it. She was wearing a low-cut peach dress. I smiled at how innocent and sexy she looked even with a busted lip.

"Did you see a car parked on the street when you got here, sweetie? A car pulled away from the curb, it's dark but I'm sure it was Troy's Lexus," Gina said.

"I didn't notice anything, but your smile."

Her smile got broader. "Even I'm a believer in good luck today." She whirled around. "The Foundation won another cold case, and your fiancé is the new VP for the County Dental Society. Let's go inside and celebrate!"

Myesha and Kevin went upstairs to do their homework. Kevin wants a car for his sixteenth birthday. Gina told him she would think about it if he got all A's and B's on his next report card. He hasn't given her a hard time about his school work since. It's only been a week but it seems to be going well. Gina and I went to her family room to smooch. I didn't say anything about Troy's car but it was heavy on my mind along with the comments he made about Paris and Mississippi. Gina removed her shoes and stockings and curled up next to me on the sofa. She was in a frisky mood. I tried to behave. Her peach colored dress reminded me of the first time I made love to her. She stood up and shimmied until her dress fell to the floor then she said it was my turn. She was wearing the peach colored underwear and I forgot all about Kevin and Myesha upstairs. Gina took off my shirt and pants. Then she chased me around the sofa wiggling her fingers while I laughed and begged her not to tickle me. I surrendered and we laughed until we cried.

She was positive that she had seen Troy's car pull away from the curb. I'm going to be out of town more than in the next three weeks. I should have kicked Troy's ass when I had a chance. I'm not sure when I will be able to see Gina again, which is why I drove up tonight. I don't have time to worry about Troy coming around.

We went to the kitchen to get Gina a glass of wine. I had to leave before daybreak so I passed even though I wanted to help her celebrate. I went upstairs to run her a bath. She was out of breath when she came up a few minutes later.

"Somebody was watching me from the deck!"

"You saw someone?"

"No. I felt them."

"Oh. It's probably the wind, but I'll check it out."

Loose dirt was on the deck and footprints were on the landing so we called the police. One of the officers asked Gina about her lip. She made up an excuse about bruising easily, and chewing it after having some dental work done.

I'm sure the officers mistook my surprise for guilt. Gina flashed me one of her sexy smiles after they left and said, "Would you like some of the wine Troy sent me from Paris? It's good. He told me to save it for the first time he made love to me. You want some?"

I wanted some all right--I should have punched that muthafucka out when I had a chance. "Nawl, I'll pass."

"Are you sure? The glass I had last Wednesday night put me in the mood. Troy says it's an aphrodisiac."

Gina poured the wine. I nibbled on her ear and whispered, "So, you were under the influence."

"Your influence," she said as I put my mark on her neck. Why the fuck did she cover for Troy?

"Did you say you were going away for a few weeks?"

"Yeah. I wish I could take you with me."

"We'll just have to make the best of tonight."

Gina took a sip of wine and gave me a shot from her mouth. Then she slipped her panties off and stuck them in my pocket. She hopped up on the counter and wrapped her legs around me, and pulled me into her circle. I stole a kiss. She took another sip and gave me a taste. She finished her glass and smiled wickedly. Then she hopped down and pulled me toward the laundry room. I grabbed the wine bottle and her glass. She locked the door, started a wash cycle, and hopped on the washer.

I refilled the glass. "There's no point in wasting good wine." She put her finger in the wine and ran it between her breasts. I smiled wickedly and licked her finger and the spot.

"Oooh, you know what I need?"

I smiled again and gave it to her hard. Why did she let those policemen think I had hit her? What is going on with her, Troy and Omar? What kind of investigation in Mississippi would drain the color from her face? I was too in love to ask my questions so I buried my anger between her hungry thighs.

CHAPTER 23

Phone Sex

*T*he garage smelled like Versace Eros when I put the wine bottle in the recycle bin. The prickly radar hairs on my neck alerted me that someone had been there. Don had whipped some loving on me that will have me craving him for the rest of my life. I shook my intuitive radar off. My wires were probably still short circuiting from Don's sweet loving.

I didn't squeal on Troy to those officers because I want to know what he has uncovered about what happened at the swamp near my house in Mississippi. Smearing his or my name in the papers just didn't feel like the best thing to do with all things considered.

Don tucked me in, and then he went to the guest room without being told. He said he just needed a nap before he left and he didn't want to disturb me. I tossed and turned in my sleep. You're tainted. The boys were crying for my help. Gunshots. Dinner. Conversation. Sex! Blue eyes. Sex! Cheap perfume. Sex! And finally--peace after I went downstairs and climbed into bed with Don.

The phone rang at 4:00 a.m. and scared the hell out of me. Don answered it. He slammed it down and said, "Tell your men not to disturb me if they didn't call to talk."

I pulled one of his numbers and pretended to be asleep.

The phone rang again at five a.m. I grabbed it this time. There was a minute of silence before Troy told me not to hang up. I sat up. Don pressed the speaker button.

"Forgive me for hitting you," Troy said. I was silent. "You let that boy spend the night at your house. Where are your precious children, Gina?" I glanced at Don again. "You teased me. You never intended to give us a chance, did you?"

"I should have known you wouldn't understand my reasons."

"I checked out your reasons. I even have some leads. Call me when you get tired of your boy toy. I'll show you what a real man can do."

I got a dreaded feeling in my gut when he slammed the phone down. I didn't want Don to go. I would never forgive myself if something happened to him. I told him about my feelings the morning of Charles's accident. Then I begged him not to go, but he said nothing was going to happen to him even though I told him when I get feelings this strong, I'm rarely wrong. Don left but he called me less than ten minutes later to tell me he had an accident!

He had braked at a red light and his car wouldn't stop. He swerved into a ditch to avoid hitting an oncoming car. He was okay, but that didn't stop me from getting excited. His bumper was fucked, but he said he didn't have any scratches. He was more concerned about getting back to the city. I offered him the use of my extra car. He asked me if I thought Troy was capable of tampering with his car.

His scent was in my garage, but why? Troy had mentioned that he used to rebuild foreign cars as a hobby. I couldn't understand what I could have done to him to make him do something to Don's car. Could trying to burst his balls, and maybe crushing his ego drive him to do something so uncharacteristic for a professional? Is the male ego that fragile? I doubted if that would make him put his reputation on the line, but he is arrogant enough to believe he could get away with it. The cops arrived so Don clicked off. I put on my jeans and left.

We had his car towed to Import & Luxury Auto Repair. Then I drove him to my house to get my SUV. Don thanked me with a kiss when I put the keys in his hand.

"If you need a place to crash in the city my place is now your place," he said when he gave me the keys to his house.

He was surer about our engagement than I was. I hugged him until my 36DDs were flat against his chest. "Remember you promised to grow old with me," I said.

"The police will take care of it. I'm not worried about Troy, but the next time you get those feelings I'll pay attention."

I squeezed him tighter. "Troy is a world renowned forensic dentist and detective, he's too smart to leave evidence. But I'm not gonna let him get away with coming into my house and doing this. I need to feel safe in my home. I'm not gonna let Troy or anyone else take that away from me." I kissed Don and turned to walk away.

Don spun me back around. "I see fire in your eyes, Gina. Promise me that you won't do anything rash."

"I promise, but trust me, it ain't over!"

I called my niece at the University of Alabama School of Dentistry. She will be graduating in a few months. I called to see if she would be interested in becoming my partner as soon as I got into my office. I've been like a second mother to Erica all her life. It's funny how life repeats itself. Sharon is thirteen years older than me, and I'm thirteen years older than Erica. I dialed the number and waited for Erica to answer.

"Hey, Aunt Gina, I was just thinking about you. Are you coming to my graduation?"

"Wouldn't miss it for the world. So, Miss Lady, what are your future plans?"

"I applied for an oral surgery residency. I didn't get it. I got accepted for a general practice residency here in Birmingham though. What about you, how are you and the kids doing? I've been so busy trying to get outta here without any problems, I haven't talked you or Mom."

"I'm actually thinking about getting married again. I'm looking for a partner who can start in a few months. My practice is doing great. I should have gotten an associate a long time ago are you interested?"

"Wow, Tee Tee, that's what I love about you! Has it been that long since we talked?"

"It's been a while. I cried over Charles for so long I don't blame you for not letting me bring you down with me. Anyway, I finally met someone strong enough to pull me back to the other side."

"I like the way you dive right into things, heck I wish I could do that. I'll call you tomorrow. Congratulations. I want all the details, but I have to get back to the trenches."

I called Rolonda next to spread my good news. She fussed at me about letting Don rush me into marriage. I told her I was keeping my house and my practice and she chilled out. We planned a shopping trip to the city so she can help me pick a dress. She doesn't want us to look wacky on Facebook and Instagram.

After work I went to my room to put my ring on. The answering machine was blinking. I pressed play. It was Don thanking me for letting him use my Range Rover and for the present I left in his pocket. He sent me some love and he promised to call back. I hit save before I rushed downstairs to take the kids to their music lessons.

Omar kept Kevin in his lesson extra time. When they came out, Omar congratulated me on my engagement. Don had asked him to play at our wedding.

I called a family conference when we got home. My palms were sweaty and I was more nervous than I was comfortable when I told Kevin and Myesha, Don and I were planning to tie the knot in June. I wanted my children to voice their concerns. They were okay about me dating Don, but they wanted to know how long I had known him.

"We met last fall," I said. "It's still sudden, but I have a sixth sense sometimes, and this is one of those good times."

"I can see why you would be flattered by sleeping with him, but why would you want to marry someone like that?" Kevin asked. "Why would Don Stokes want to marry you when he has hundreds of fine thots to choose from? Get real, Mom." Kevin threw a tabloid on the coffee table. "The man is screwing Niki Jones!"

Kevin doesn't shock me anymore., but I can't lie and say I wasn't rattled. "There is a strong sexual attraction, but we are getting married because we love each other. He's ready to make a commitment—he asked me, and he set the date."

"I just don't want you to get hurt so before you flip completely out over Don, take your own advice and think about the consequences first," Kevin said, "And if you decide to do it, don't even think about changing our last name."

"Don is cool, but he can never replace Dad," Myesha added.

I doubted if Don would love Kevin and Myesha any more, or less if they did or didn't change their names.

Myesha was willing to give Don and Jason a chance to be a part of our family, Kevin was harder to sell. He said, as long as Don makes me happy, and respects me, he will be cool with him. Kevin promised to protect me and Myesha if Don screws this up. That was the last promise he made to Charles.

I hugged Kevin and Myesha and sent them to their rooms. Then I made a cup of chamomile tea and went to my room after I made sure the doors and windows were locked.

Don called every morning and every night, and Kevin and I watched all his games. By the middle of the second week, I was missing him badly enough to initiate phone sex. I asked him to do something special for me. He said sure, so I told him to caress Big Man for me while I caressed Hot Mamma for him. The line was silent for a dead man's minute. Don coughed and asked me if I was propositioning him? I sure as hell was. He didn't think he would be too good at it, but when I told him I was wearing a lacy red bra and a matching thong and a pair of three inch red stilettos he got with the program. He had to pretend that he was blindfolded and his hands were tied behind his back. I wanted him to use his imagination. I said I was hiding in his dining room, and he had to describe how he was going to make love to me after he found me. I swear I could feel him plotting his actions through the phone line. I was in the mood for freaky. I sent my spirit to him so he wouldn't have to feel guilty. He wanted to know why he was blindfolded and why the dining room.

"They say blind people have acute senses. Close your eyes and pretend that I'm really there. I'm sipping champagne and eating cherries. I want to feel you all over me."

"I'm supposed to use my senses to find you?"

"And your imagination. Close your eyes and touch all the places you want me to touch."

"All of them?"

"Keep your eyes closed and pretend your hands are mine. Now tell me everything you're doing so I can do it for you."

My body heat perfumed the air with my raspberry love scent and directed him to me. He ripped my panties and bra off with his teeth, but he left the shoes on. He found my inner lips and parted the soft folds. I imagined him enjoying me. He kissed my face and neck. He climbed the twin peaks with his tongue and feasted on their chocolate peaks. He teased them, and pinched them, but he stopped short of biting them. I moaned into the phone and stroked the sensitive areas with his spirit. I could barely say his name when he asked me if he was doing okay.

I moaned and told him I was sliding off his lucky boxers and kissing my way to Big Man's head. Don moaned and said, "Now you're talking."

I slid my Mr. Wonderful into my moist heat.

"Ooophs, you knocked over the chilled champagne," I said. "It's soaking through my wool blanket and cooling your bath."

"Damn, Gina, you're making me hot!"

"I need help cleaning up this cold champagne?"

"Can't you feel me lapping it up?"

"Yes, baby. Yes! My legs are over your shoulders and around your neck. Give it to me now!"

I moaned into the phone.

"Spread them legs and let Big Man strip search you doggie style."

"Hot mamma is already prepared and ready, Captain. Don't forget to run your hot tongue up my spine and squeeze my tips when you knock on the backdoor. Explore my depths slowly, and don't forget to massage my hills and valleys with one hand and steady my hips with the other. I'll lean against you for support and make circles on my clit. Nibble on my neck while you power drill me to ecstasy for best results, Sir."

He moaned, "Is my spirit working its magic on your end?"

I was at my breaking point when I heard a knock on my door. I grabbed the covers and turned Mr. Wonderful off.

"Mom, are you crying?" Myesha asked.

I covered the phone and said, "I'm okay. I was playing a trick on Don."

Myesha shook her head and closed the door. Don was still moaning into the phone.

"Don, Myesha just busted us." He continued to moan. "Sweetie, you're traumatizing my child."

He let out a hardy laugh and said, "Baby that was fun."

"Did you?" I asked.

He took the fifth, but he said he learned some things. I had a good time and I thanked him for making a marvelous day better.

"Anytime. Anytime at all, my sweet."

"Donald Stokes, you need a spanking."

"Big Man has a whipping waiting for Hot Mamma as well."

"How did a nice girl like me fall in love with a bad boy like you?"

"I don't know, but I wish my nice girl was here to clean up the mess she made."

"The next time we will do FaceTime or Skype, okay?"

Don made a few midnight-runs to see me after that. He has planned a small wedding, which is going to take place on Sloan's private yacht during a four-hour cruise. I'm hooked on Don's loving, but the thought of marriage to someone like him still scares the hell out of me.

CHAPTER 24

Flashbacks and Going Too Far

Rolonda and I found wedding dresses at Bergdorf Goodman. Mine is a Vera Wang white V-neck silk chiffon number with a court train. Ro says the dress looks like it was made especially for me. I don't always agree with her opinions, but girlfriend knows fashions, and if I could get married in my jeans and boots, I would be good to go. Ro picked the bridesmaids gowns, and I chose the perfect shade of pale peach.

We shopped for our trip to Aruba after we finished shopping for our weddings. The trip was supposed to be a "get Gina out of her rut vacation." Don has already taken care of that problem, and more. I made a mental note to tell him about my girls only trip.

Kevin, Myesha, and Rolonda ganged up on me and insisted that I update my wardrobe. They wanted me to look good for Don's games. I bought two pair Balmain jeans and a few dresses and shoes. I renamed everything my freak-um outfits. My credit card was on fire. I had my own personal shopper by the time I left the store. We all had crunchy fried chicken form Red Rooster Harlem before we went to Don's place. He left me a note and a piece of chocolate on his pillow. His answering machine had messages from Jason, Sloan, and from someone named Bee or did she say Tee. She couldn't wait to hook-up with him again.

Don wasn't thrilled about me going to Aruba without him. He had gone to a similar festival in St. Maarten and he had been mobbed by half-naked women at the beach parties. He had to concentrate on basketball right now, but he promised to tighten me up before I leave. I'm going to Aruba to relax and to see the concerts.

I wanted to look good for my wedding and for my trip. I went to the gym every day. I hadn't seen Patrice since the Sisters and Friends book club meeting. The rumors floating around the gym had her damn near on her death bed. She looked poorly when she slammed the phone down. I was already standing in her doorway. I walked into her office and closed the door. Her eyes were bloodshot and her pallor didn't look healthy. I asked her if she was okay?

"Shut the fuck up, Gina. Everyone doesn't live life on easy street like you. Some of us have real problems."

She began to cry. "I really messed up this time," she said.

I walked around her desk and rubbed her back. "I'll help you if you let me. But you have to remember that I'm still your friend even when I don't say what you want to hear."

She dropped her head and cried louder. Then she whispered, "I'm pregnant." I rubbed her back faster. "Quincy?"

"Of course, I'm not a whore; he told me he and his wife were in the process of getting divorced. I didn't have any idea that he already has five kids and four baby Mamas. He told me to take care of it. He's sending someone over with the money."

I wanted to help her in more ways than I knew how. I wanted her to be the confident sassy sister I met last fall. She reminds me of Sharon. They are beautiful and talented, but they are always selling themselves short. They can understand why I can live and love like I do, but they don't believe they can do the same things. I continued to rub her back.

"How can I help?" I said softly.

Patrice sounded like a helpless child when she said, "I can't tell my grandmother. Will you go with me?"

"Sure. Do you have an appointment?"

"Friday. I've been as sick as a dog. My grandmother is starting to get suspicious." She stood up. "I have to teach an aerobics class."

"It will be okay, you're stronger than you think."

I took Patrice to The Women's Clinic the following Friday. I don't know why they call it that--it's not like we create these problems all by ourselves. Patrice had a lost childish look in her eyes after it was over so I took her to my house. I made tea, gave her Campbell's chunky chicken soup, and played jazz until she fell asleep.

Don isn't going to be able to see me again until his season is over, but he promised to make it worth the wait. Kevin and Myesha went to a party. Patrice was still sleeping. I haven't seen Don in two weeks. Living on his promises has only made me horny. I've been craving ice cream.

I drove Don's Ferrari to Baskin 31 Robbins. I bought a double scoop cone to lick, and two pints to get me through the weekend. I stopped by the office to get my business checks and the bills that I don't pay online. I didn't bother to lock the door it was only going to take a minute. I grabbed the bills and the checks and the door chimed indicating that someone had come in!

I rushed to the front and bumped into Troy. He squeezed me close to him and smiled the same lustful way he had the first time he met me in my office.

"What are you doing here?"

"I saw you come in. I brought your airline tickets."

"I can't accept these."

I gave the tickets back, but he pulled me into his arms and kissed me. I willed myself not to respond. Lord knows I miss Don. My body deceived me as Troy kissed and fondled me through my snug fitting bodysuit. I tried to wiggle away, but he tightened his grip and kissed me again.

"Let me love you at least once," he whispered between kisses. "You owe me that much."

He fondled me again and a sigh slipped out. I chastised myself for being weak to his touch.

"I used to imagine us making love in your dental chair."

I broke free when he said that, but he was stronger and faster. "Don't ever kiss me like that again," I yelled.

"Your eyes say you like it."

"They do not!"

"Don't deny yourself. I heard how sensuous you were with that playboy. You need to let a real man in your bed. I can take you to your greatest heights every time."

He pulled me toward the dental suites.

"No, Troy! Please? You don't want to rape me."

"He grinned again, then he frowned. "How could you make love to that boy and drink my five-hundred dollars a bottle wine?"

"Damn! No wonder it was so good. Is that why you tampered with Don's brakes?"

Troy chuckled. "You've been leading me on for months, Gina." He kissed me again. I turned away, but he held me with one hand and stroked my crotch with the other.

I couldn't believe the adrenaline rush the danger was giving me. It was like teasing jocks back in high school. Troy freed his manhood, and pent me against the wall. He kissed me and put my hand on his wooden cock. My legs turned to cooked noodles. I didn't know if he was capable of rape, but I sure as hell didn't want to find out.

My first instinct was to yank and squeeze it as hard as I could and ram my knee into it again, but my legs didn't feel strong enough to run.

"You're known all over the world," I said as I stroked and kissed him. I figured I had a better chance, if I used my sex appeal to save my ass. I heard somewhere that most rapists like to be in control so my intent was to flip the script. "Show me how much you want me," I said as I rubbed his member up and down.

Troy captured my lips again. I deepen the kiss. He kissed me on the neck and groped my chest again. When Don does that my flesh turns into his putty.

He grew in my hand and Troy smiled and said, "As you can see, brothers don't have anything on me."

He unzipped my jeans, but he couldn't do anything with my bodysuit. Ida Mae knew what she was doing when she brought them for me back in high school. He worked with what he could reach.

"I've always been curious about how we would be together. I was waiting for you to offer me love and commitment. I need more than sex from the men in my life," I whispered. I continued to stoke him. He seemed to like it.

"I offered you love the first day I met you," he said as he kissed my neck and stroked at me.

"You offered me casual sex, and I couldn't get pass what those men did to me in my nightmares."

Troy stopped stroking me and stared into my eyes. "You wouldn't give me a chance because I'm white?"

"That had nothing to do with it," I said flatly. "My skin is paler than yours. I just didn't want to get screwed, "I said as I choked his thing and rotated it in a circle like Big Mama used to wring the chickens' necks she killed for Sunday dinner. "I needed to know that I was being loved," I said between kisses intended to distract him from what I was doing. He seemed to like the roughness but when I turned it up a notch he put his hand between mine and stopped me from squeezing him.

"There is an unsolved case of two missing police officers and some farm workers in May of 1964, but they weren't from Sweetwater," he said.

"I didn't tell you my damn story so you could go out and try to solve it. Some shit don't need to be solved!"

My anger must have surprised him because he let go of me.

"Gina, this case doesn't have anything to do with you. For Christ sake you weren't even born!"

"I wanted you to understand why I have a hard time committing to relationships with men. Those men say and do terrible things to me in the nightmares."

"I don't understand."

"I didn't think that you would. You practically accused my father of murder when I told you. It's just a dream that won't go away. And anyway, those men were wrong!"

"I would never accuse anyone without proof. From what you told me it sounds like self-defense, but I still don't understand what it has to do with us."

"Troy, the men said no one would ever love me because of how I look. Most men are more interested in sexing my body than they are in me, you included!"

Troy dropped his head. "It's been a long time but I can find the answers for you."

"It doesn't take a rocket scientist to figure out what happened if it happened at all. Daddy and I are fine. In the dreams those wicked men are at the bottom of Dead Man's swamp with a bunch of dead black boys they put there, and one pretty little girl who looks like me, and anyway like you said, it happened long before I was born!" I didn't bother to tell him I had given Charles information from my dreams that had helped him solve some of the cases with the dead boys.

"You think those officers were dumping bodies in the swamp?"

"Duh. What else would make them travel that far? There are no fish in the swamp and the water is too murky for swimming. The only thing that was ever found there were the bodies of dead black boys no one in Sweetwater knew."

"How did you find that out?"

"They told me."

"Who?"

The spirits of the dead boys. "Some boys told me when I was little. They made me promise not to tell."

"Do you know where they are now?"

Heaven. "I'm not sure. I haven't lived in Mississippi in twenty years."

"Your dreams and what you're telling me fit the unsolved case. If I give you some proof will it make a difference?"

"Maybe. Maybe not."

"Damn you, Gina, you're a tease!"

Troy pulled me in his arms again, and I looked deep into his lustful eyes and saw visions of those men right before their blood spilled all over my little girl face.

"I love Don." *Bang!*

"How long have you known that sissy?"

"Long enough," I snapped. *One of the men shot at Daddy.*

"I was straight with you about my affairs in Europe. But I made it clear that it was you that I wanted. If you would let me love you I wouldn't need other women." Troy said as he wrestled me back into his arms.

Bang! The man who shot at Daddy chest exploded first.

Troy kissed me before I could get away. He's a good kisser, no make that a great kisser. There was something about his kiss that felt right or was I that horny and delirious? I struggled to regain control of my body and my mind while Troy kissed and fondled me.

You're tainted. No one will ever love you. Bang! The other man's chest exploded. Blood rinsed my dusty face. His eyes were filled with hate. Their eyes were soliciting me to help them. Hatred is stubborn--it dies slowly. Troy's eyes and that man's eyes laughed while they kissed and rubbed my full lips, breasts, and butt.

"*You're an ugly little thang,*" the man said.

Troy stroked my cheeks. "You're so sexy," he said as he moaned. Who should I believe?

You're tainted. We don't want you. Stay on your side of the tracks.

"Let me love you, Gina. That's it. Touch me. I've never wanted anyone as much as I want you. Ahhh—"

Here and there was spinning around in my head. *A gun was in my hands!* Troy squeezed my breasts and moaned. His eyes. *Their eyes.* Begging eyes. Wanting what I couldn't give. I was scared. *A gun was in my hands!*

"Let me love you... If I'm not all that I promised, I'll leave you alone. Don't deny yourself... Ahhh, that's it—"

"It's too late for us," I said, but lust had built up. "I have to go home."

"No! Don't stop. You wouldn't be kissing and touching me like this if you were in love with Don."

I was confused, delirious, crying and I didn't even realize that I had slid down and taken him in until I gagged.

Troy moaned, "Oh, God! Oh God! Come home with me. Let me love you like you deserve!"

My jaw clamped down. He screamed, "Oh God!" in a higher pitch.

I shoved him away and shouted, "I'm happy with Don and our love life!"

He grabbed my arm and penned me against the wall and started nibbling on my breasts through my bodysuit.

"Stop," I said, but it felt good, and I wasn't convincing. *There were three gunshots. A gun was in my little hands!*

"You like it rough, don't you?"

Bang! He bit my taut nipple. "Ouch! You're hurting my arms."

I thought about the rape cases he told me about months ago. I kissed Troy. Nibbled. Stroked. Spread DNA. Wished he was Don. Moaned. I licked and rubbed until he moaned again, then I bit into his neck like a vampire until I tasted his salty sweet blood!

Bang! He pushed me away. I ran for the door this time. I didn't give a damn about leaving him in the office. I was trying to protect my ass. *Bang!*

Troy chased after me. I hopped in the Ferrari and sped away. I was out of sight before he could get to his car. The rush was thrilling. My body had said yes even though my mind knew I was only supposed to tease him until I could weaken him. How did that gun get in my little hands? How did his thing get in my mouth? Did *I* pull the trigger? Did I fuck Troy with my mouth? Shit! What have I done?

CHAPTER 25

Guilt Trips

I went back to the office to get the checkbook and the bills. I locked the office, and then I stopped at my favorite Chinese takeout and got dinner. By the time I got home, ice cream had melted all over Don's leather seat.

Patrice had a killer look on her face and she was in the middle of my bed rocking and hugging a pillow when I walked into my bedroom. "Are you okay?" I asked. "You didn't call, Quincy, did you?"

"You make me sick!" Patrice shouted.

I asked her what I had done this time. Then I sat on the edge of the bed and sulked.

She rubbed my back. "I'm sorry, Gina. I appreciate everything you've done. You're my mentor." I was surprised. "Why didn't you tell me you were fucking Don Stokes?"

I flinched. "I'm not. We're in love," I spat out!

"Well, you could have told me. I thought I was your friend. Damn, girl you have all of the luck."

I stood up. "Did you talk to him or did the machine pick up?"

She said machine. I pushed play. "Hey, baby. Where you at, girl? Pick up the phone, it's Don. You know I needs my fix before the game. Where you at?" Don laughed. "I hope you ain't letting nobody touch my stuff." I always joke like that when I get his voicemail. "Just kidding," he said. "We're leaving early tomorrow. I'll call you when I get to Miami."

"So, where have you been for the last two hours?" Patrice asked.

"I picked up dinner."

"You could have made dinner in two hours. Don Stokes is your secret lover, and you're screwing Troy behind his back, aren't you?" Patrice chuckled and waved her fist. "You don't have to answer--it's written all over your face. Power to you, sister! All these lying, cheating ass dogs need to be taught a lesson. Power to you!" Patrice burst out laughing, and then she fell back on the bed and kicked her heels up and down. I would have laughed at her antics if I didn't feel so guilty.

Later that night, I was bumping and grinding with Troy and sucking him off when he turned into the men. "You're tainted. Stay on your side of the tracks." Bumping and grinding. Bang! Bang! Blood all over their chests. My face. Bang! Blood everywhere. Darkness. Om..., om..., om..., a thousand fucking oms screaming in my head. The boys were singing and chanting.

I woke up in a cold sweat. The boys continued to sing but I was afraid to go back to sleep. The next morning, I dropped Patrice off at the gym and rushed back home so I wouldn't miss Don's phone call. I wanted to tell him what I had done, but he was already in a funk because the team had lost the game and he got suspended when he joined in a fight that cleared both benches.

Don and I talked twice a day. Guilt was kicking my behind. I needed him now more than ever. I've been having the nightmares every night. I can't shake the guilty feelings about what I did to Troy. Now I feel like the little girl was the reason for whatever *went down* at the swamp. I didn't burden Don with my problems though. I don't want him to think I'm a slut in addition to being peculiar.

I'm not good at faking the funk so I inadvertently drew Don into a funk with me. I couldn't play phone sex games with him and soon he stopped asking. The team lost three painful games in a row. Don had promised me some good loving after his season was over so I waited up all night for him to show up. He didn't show or call. That was three days ago.

Sharon came a few days before my trip to Aruba. We had plans to hangout before I left. I took her to Q's Place to get away from my walls rapidly caving in. It was a slow night, but Quincy used his seductive Italian stallion, gangster brotha moves and his best champagne to lure Sharon. Since I couldn't strangle him for what he had done to Patrice, I coochie blocked all evening. I wasn't about to let Sharon fall for his lies. She wanted to sample his mixed flavors, but I wasn't about to finance his cause. I drank his elixir, protected my sister and stuck him with his mack daddy tab.

Sharon brought me breakfast in bed the next morning. I had drunk more than my share of Quincy's champagne, but between worrying about Don and those stupid nightmares about Troy and shooting people I hadn't slept a wink.

"You look terrible," Sharon said. "If I were you, I would get my ass to New York in the first thing smoking. I would help Don get over whatever is bothering him, and I'm sure he is the only one who can help you get pass that Troy thing."

I took a sip of juice and a bite of toast. "You're probably right, but I don't wanna leave you alone."

"Don't worry about me. Give me the keys to the Benz, and a hundred bucks for the mall. I'll find something to do and somebody to do it with. And I promise to be home when Myesha and Kevin come home after school."

"You ought to quit."

"Ida Mae and Johnny Lee didn't raise quitters so get your rusty behind out of bed and go and give Don some loving, or go take some loving, or whatever the hell y'all need to do, because I didn't come all the way here from Mississippi to feel sorry for your ass this trip."

"Yes ma'am."

"You know I wouldn't give you any bad advice."

I got up and got it together, and then I drove Don's Ferrari to his penthouse. I called Sharon to let her know everything seemed to be in order when I arrived. Don's phone rang while I was checking out his place for signs of foul play. I cringed at the female caller's phony accent when she asked if he was home.

"No he's not. Would you like to leave a message?"

"Tell him Niki called. Are you his housekeeper?"

"No, I'm Donald's fiancée," I said with confidence. I have the keys to his house and his car. His ice is on my finger and in my ears and I wasn't about to give her the satisfaction of knowing she had ruffled my feathers.

"Well, tell him my doctor is Edward Wilson. Tell him I changed my mind about aborting his baby. Never mind. I'll tell him when he gets here." She chuckled and clicked off.

Okay, she got to me. I filled Don's Jacuzzi, lit seven candles and programed Don's iPad to play Beyoncé's "Lemonade" CD. I pulled the shades, bumped up the volume and set the jets for twenty minutes. My hot romance with Don flashed through my mind while I sang along with Beyoncé and tried not to cry over what I should have seen coming. The worst thing about my so- called gift is being able to see everybody's shit but my own.

CHAPTER 26

A Love Supreme

I ran up the stairs two at a time when I smelled raspberries. My clothes fell to the floor on the way. I stopped dead in my tracks when I found Gina in my Jacuzzi singing *Hold Up* along with Beyoncé and crying. She was off key, but she looked like an angel in the candle light. Her words were as sad as they were sweet. I wanted to sweep her up in my arms and keep her there forever.

Her eyes popped open. She wiped away a tear and pushed her hair back. We stared at each other like pieces of forbidden fruit. Ted and I had discussed all the fine points about my trade to Phoenix over lunch. Gina is adamant about staying in Connecticut. I'm afraid she will change her mind about marrying me when she finds out about the trade.

"Hey, sweetie, I needed a place to crash. I hope it's not a bad time," she said. She flashed a phony smile and I knew something was wrong. I walked toward her like a tiger in pursuit of his prey. I can't explain why I love her like I do, but I can't imagine life without her. Instead of smiling when I sat on the side of the tub, she captured my full mouth with hers. I sucked her lips and tongue and savored her sweetness. She pulled away. I caught my breath and surveyed her again. Her eyes were full of tears and fears. I started a path of kisses from her shoulder to the crook of her neck. Between kisses I told her I don't ever want to be away from her this long again.

"Why didn't you come to me? I waited up for you," she said. I could feel the disappointment in her dead doll's stare. I was ashamed of my actions. I had needed some time alone to regroup. I stroked Gina's face and stared into her sad eyes. It wasn't my intent to shut her out. I simply don't know how to tell her about the trade.

"Do you love me enough to understand the things in your life that you fear the most?" she asked of all things.

I kissed her again. I needed her to understand.

"Are you getting cold feet, Don?" The jets stopped. She stood up. I wrapped her in a towel.

"We can get married today. How long will it take you to get dressed? Put your jeans and boots on, let's go." She relaxed when I said that. "Where are the kids?"

"They're with Sharon. I can't wait for you to meet her. She put me out of my own house so I could make sure you were okay."

"I owe you some supreme loving; Come with me," I said.

Gina's smile touched her eyes when she said, "I can't imagine our loving being any better."

"I want to obliterate any doubts you have about my love, faith or trust."

She smiled again. "In that case, let's get it on!"

She laced her hand with mine and led the way to my bedroom. I programed my iPad to play "A Love Supreme," and "The Gentle Side of Coltrane." Gina lit my patchouli candle and placed it on my night stand. She stretched out on the bed while "The Gentle Side of Coltrane" played. I removed the sweet almond stimulating massage oil from my karma sutra kit and warmed it with my hands.

"Close your eyes and listen to the music while I give you a full body massage."

I started with a slow, broad gliding movement over her back and shoulders, and slow circular movements using both hands over her back and buttocks. She relaxed but her muscles were tight. I asked her if I was using too much pressure. She said it was wonderful. I used a kneading motion to loosen the tension in her shoulders and leg muscles, and then I finished with a pressure technique using my thumbs and fingers over her entire back. I turned her over and used the towel to cover her precious parts. "Close your eyes and concentrate on the music and the movements of my hands."

I kissed her and continued by massaging her temples, shoulders, arms, the palms of her hands and her fingers. I skipped the twin peaks and moved on to her legs. Her face was relaxed and she moaned, but her muscles were tight. Gina loves my foot massages. I saved the best for last. I tied her feet together with a silk scarf, and finished by massaging, kissing and tickling them with a feather.

"I loved every minute of it," she said. "But it felt like sexual torture." She smiled and my heartbeat became erratic.

"I enjoy pampering you."

"You make me feel beautiful. Lay down, it's your turn."

"Having you with me after the way I treated you is enough for me."

I stole a kiss, but she pouted and begged me to let her pamper me. "You are not allowed to hog the ball in this relationship if we want us to keep winning," she said. Then she tied my hands together with the scarf, and tied me to the bed-post. Her soft oily hands floated along the paths of my muscles. She applied just enough pressure to stimulate the blood flow. Her hands were lethal weapons, but I already knew that. She tickled me with the feather, and teased me with kisses, and her naked aroused body.

It was sexual torture. She called it tantric loving. She said it is an artistic form of sexual expression. She promised that it would help us learn to trust each other physically, emotionally, and mentally, but most of all, it would deepen our connection to our self, and to each other. I was ready to explode when she untied me. I took her in my arms and showered her with kisses. She begged me to love her. I did. She wanted me fast and hard, but she had taught me how to slow dance. We held each other tight and barely moved. I nibbled on her neck, ears, shoulders, and bottom lip, and held back long as I could. She locked her strong legs around my back and pulled me deeper into her soul. We made one heart, one love, as the passion flowed from one to the other. "A love Supreme" caressed our ears and our bodies embraced the rhythm. We climbed to the edge slowly, and when we climaxed Gina whispered, "Now you are my love supreme."

I squeezed her closer, if that were possible. I wanted to say something dynamic as well. I knew what she meant. I was all choked up when I whispered, "I love you, Gina. No matter how complicated our lives get, know that I will always love you."

We cuddled with our legs intertwined for about an hour. We didn't talk--we didn't need to. My mind drifted while the music continued to play. I got up to go to the bathroom. The phone rang while I was refilling the Jacuzzi. I stuck my head out the door and yelled for Gina to answer it.

"Are you sure? What if it's—" She picked up. "Stokes residence." A big smile lit up her face when she said, "I'm fine, Jason." I smiled and went back to the bathroom. When I came back into the room, Gina was blushing and smiling like a kitten. "Are you sure he said he can't wait to marry me?"

I took the phone. "What's up, champ. I told you to get your own woman."

"I was trying to help you out. You have to let your woman know how you feel or some other dude might try to get in your business."

"You were helping your old man out?"

"Yep. Was it working?"

"That depends on what you were saying?"

"I told Gina that you love the way she dances, and you always feel better when she is with you." Gina flashed mischievous smiles every time I looked in her direction. I clicked off the phone and took Jason's advice. I wanted to take her out dancing, but she didn't have anything to wear. I gave her my silk robe. We selected a playlist on my iPad. I asked her to dance with me. The Isley Brothers' "Mission to Please" was playing. We danced for nearly two hours in my bedroom. We danced fast. We danced slowly. We danced to rap, rhythm and blues, and jazz. We even danced to no music at all. But Gina wasn't her usual playful self. I wanted to ask her why she was crying.

It is not going to be easy to convince her to come with me to Phoenix. I practiced telling her about the trade while I was downstairs getting two bottles of water. She had a strange look on her face when I returned. I asked her if I had done something wrong.

"Niki Jones called. When were you going to tell me about the baby?"

The shit I had gone through with Niki rushed to my mind.

"She said Edward is her doctor and something about changing her mind about aborting your baby."

Gina was using Niki's phony British accent and the timing was so fucked up all I could do was laugh. "I'm sorry, but it's such an outrageous lie. I don't know how Niki got my new numbers. Crazy bitches like Niki track your location using your phone number, it's a good thing I never brought any of them here."

Gina flinched. I wanted to take back my words. Just the thought of Niki pisses me off. I pulled Gina into my arms. "Is that why you were crying?"

"Some women like to play games, Don. I don't." She tried to wiggle her way free. I wanted to tell her about the trade, but the timing wasn't right. Gina and I are good at reading each other's emotions. I'm hiding something more important than Niki Jones. What is she hiding?

"Niki is beautiful. She can give you the babies you want." Gina's eyes were misty and so were mine. "I love you, Don, but—" She struggled to take off her engagement ring. "I must be retaining water."

I talked fast as I forced the ring back on her finger. "My heart belongs to you, Gina. I haven't been with Niki since the night I met you. She's been out with Rick and I've heard rumors about others."

"You should check Niki's story out. Women like that can hide their pregnancies well into the third trimester."

"I know better than to trust Niki. All those pictures you see of us on the tabloids lately were taken by her people last year supposedly for a magazine article. They took hundreds of pictures. She has more tricks up her sleeve than Houdini. Niki was born and raised in Texas. She lived in London for a year so now she calls it home. She is beautiful but everything else about her is phony. She may even be behind that shooting last fall. She definitely has some violent tendencies."

I talked Gina into staying. It was late and she was too tired and upset to drive. She didn't want to leave anyway. We decided to watch a movie. She wiggled her eyebrows and licked her lips in a playful manner. I popped her on the butt and said, "Get in the bed, girl. I'll take care of the rest." I smiled. "You're on my court now. You haven't seen irresistible yet. I'll be back in a minute."

The movie watched us while I proved to her that she is the only woman I love. After the movie, we drifted into a well-deserved sleep, but the sound of thunder, and Gina screaming and talking in her sleep, woke me up. Each time the thunder roared, Gina retreated deeper under the covers.

"Leave my daddy alone! He didn't do anything. Let me go! No, Troy, don't kiss me." I put my arms around her and tried to comfort her. She jerked away and retreated deeper to the foot of the bed. "The gun was in my hands. Tell me what happened, Daddy. Please?" She curled up in a ball and started sobbing.

Every time I tried to comfort her she pulled away and said, "How did that gun get in my hands?"

"Ssshhh, baby. What gun? Let me help."

"Don't touch me. She's having your baby, and I can't—"

"Ssshhh. I love you, Gina. I won't let anybody hurt you, and there is no way in hell Niki is having my baby." She stopped fighting. "What did Troy do now? What gun?"

Lightning lit up the room. Gina sat straight up in the bed, and said, "Beano, I want you to take care of your mother until I get back." Beano was the nickname my father gave me. Jack and The Beanstalk was my favorite fairytale, and I used to call the book Beano when I was a toddler. Gina spoke using the playful voice she uses when she mimics me. "Get over here and help me scrape this mustard off these sandwiches your mother made, and put some mayo on them. Now just because I let you help me with my little covert operations, and ask you to keep it a secret between us boys it don't give you authority to sass your mother when I'm away. We are lucky to have a woman like your mother. She's a five star, you know? Nawl, you don't know nothing about that yet, but one day you will." Gina laughed a haughty laugh, not hers, my father's. "Go on and hook those sandwiches up for your daddy, your mama got me running a little late this morning." She winked and laughed again, this time it was the kind of laugh a man has when he knows he has a good woman who treats him right. Those were some of the last words my father said to me before he left that morning to haul a load from Chicago to Dallas. He never returned. Lightening flashed again. Gina had a strange look on her face as she stared into space. My mind was reeling from what she had said. I wrapped my arms around her and pulled her close.

"I guess my secret is out," she said in her normal voice.

I squeezed her closer to me. "What secret?"

"I'm afraid of thunderstorms. Storms are violent in Mississippi. I used to hide under the bed. The nightmares and spirits always come during storms."

She sounded and looked serious, and the fear in her eyes told me that was just the tip of the iceberg. The spirit of my father had spoken through her. I was so stunned and taken aback I didn't know how to react. "What did Troy do, and why did you have a gun?"

Gina slipped her arms around me and rested her head on my shoulder. "Troy showed up at my office. It was my fault—I should have locked the door. He kissed me. I didn't slap him so he pushed for more. I told him I love you, but he kept coming on to me. He said I teased him."

Gina's tone of voice expressed her fears. Her lips trembled and my gut got fighting tight.

"He forced himself on you?"

"He was more arrogant than forceful; I got away. I've been leading him on for months. The poor guy probably didn't know the difference between my 'no' and my 'yes.'"

"Poor guy? I should have jacked him up when I had my chance! If I did that shit to somebody my ass would be in jail and my name smeared all over the damn news. Why didn't you press charges?"

"I'm okay except for the nightmares."

"Well, I'm not fucking okay with this. What nightmares?"

Gina kissed me and changed the subject. "Calm down, sweetie, you didn't tell me what your greatest fears are?"

"Losing you. Now that I have you in my life I can't imagine it without you. You are my number five. What are yours?"

"I'm not sure but I think a man molested a little girl who either looks like me or is me. I think she killed them, Daddy was on the ground. I was only six." She looked at me, but I somehow knew she didn't see me. Terror filled her eyes, and I finally understood the sad scared look in them. All this time I thought it had something to do with her losing Charles. Now I know it is a lot deeper than that. Gina doesn't remember exactly what happened, but in her latest nightmares, the gun is in her hands and she pulls the trigger. I squeezed her close to me. Silent tears rolled down her cheeks while she told me about the nightmares she has been having since she was a child. We talked while the rain poured outside. I tried to convince her that there is no way she could have killed two men when she was six, and even if she did, the men deserved to die. It was either her and her father or them. I asked her some of the fact finding trivial questions she wanted me to ask when we first met. I knew where my heart was at--I thought her past didn't matter.

Gina grew up fearing that men in hoods would come in the night and take her father away because of what she thought they had done at Dead Man's swamp. The only proof she had were the nightmares, which are just starting to make sense. Her father wouldn't discuss it one way or the other. At first she thought they were just dreams that scared her in the night, but as she got older she knew in her heart that something bad had happened. She still isn't clear exactly what, but she fears the worst. She couldn't figure out how they had gotten away, and why her father wouldn't talk about it. She used to believe that he had saved her even though he is on the ground getting beat up in most of the dream.

After she pieced the dreams together she bounced back and said, "I love to laugh. I often laugh until I cry, but I've never cried until I've laughed."

"That's deep. Is there some hidden meaning that I'm missing?"

"No, but I'm seriously in love with you, Donald Godfrey Stokes, and if we don't laugh sometimes, then we might as well be at the bottom of Dead Man's swamp with those boys and that little girl who looks like me." She kissed me and said, "What did you mean when you said I was your five?"

"Did I ever tell you about my last conversation with my Dad?"

"I don't think so."

"I didn't think so either. My dad told me that my mother was his five and that I would find mine one day. Are you sure I never told you that?"

"That is so sweet, I'm sure I would have remembered."

"Did I tell you my father was the only person who called me Beano?"

"Beano? No, you never mentioned it. Give me some sugar, I think the thunderstorm has put you in a melancholy mood too."

I wanted to ask her more, but she started a tickle fight and we chortled and made love. She drifted back to sleep after we did some name calling. I kissed her on the cheek and hoped that none of the things she said about the little girl and her father were true. She didn't seem to remember that my father had spoken through her. I wondered if she could ask him to tell me and Mom about his accident. I can only pray that the extraordinary love Gina and I share will last.

CHAPTER 27

Sex, Secrets, And Burnt Waffles

*D*on was obviously hiding something so I stopped short of telling him about the visits from Charles and the boys, and I don't ever plan to tell him what I did to Troy. I know I'm not crazy. God just has a strange way of protecting me. I grabbed Don's robe and slid out of bed. Last night was fantastic, but I still have a nagging feeling that something is wrong. Don could be wrong about Niki, just as I pray I'm wrong about what happened all those years ago at the swamp.

I burnt the Belgium waffles and omelets I made to go with the fresh raspberries and freshly squeezed orange juice I had whipped up. I trashed the waffles and eggs and made pancakes. Everything was on the serving tray when Don came in the kitchen. I wanted to surprise him with breakfast in bed but the smoke detector woke him up. He smiled when he saw his less than perfect breakfast.

"Don't get excited," I said. "I was hungry."

He pulled me into his arms. "So you weren't trying to spoil me and make me fat to scare off the chicken heads?"

"Nope. I was just making sure you'll have plenty of energy so you can hang with me in bed all day."

He kissed me and untied my robe. I served him. He did the same for me. Before long we were making out on his kitchen counter. The phone rang and broke the spell. When Don answered, I wiggled away.

"Hello!" he snapped. "Sloan? Sorry about that, man. Hold on... Sloan wants us to meet him for lunch."

"I would love to, but I don't have anything to wear. You can go. I need to run a few errands while I'm here anyway."

Don released the hold button. "Why don't you come over? I'm sure I have something edible here..." He winked. "I have some unfinished business to take care of... One o'clock should be good."

I wiggled my way free but Don threw me over his shoulder like a caveman and carried me back upstairs. Hours later we woke up to the sound of his alarm clock. We showered and dressed. I was glowing from his good loving--great sex always has that effect on me.

Don ordered lunch from the corner deli. The intercom for his door rang. He buzzed Sloan up. We didn't bother to put on our shoes when we went downstairs to greet him.

Sloan stepped inside, pulled me in his arms, and kissed me like I was his woman. I figured it was a test. He gave me some tongue. I gave him some right back. "Wow!" he said. "So now you'll have to wonder if you picked the right man." I blushed. "Do you know how many women have tried to get this guy to the altar and failed?" He patted Don on his back. "Did Don tell you he tracked you down after my party? My boy doesn't track honeys."

"Don't listen to him."

"Man, you could have told me Gina was here." Sloan slapped Don on his back again. "I hope that burnt smell isn't lunch."

"Gina made breakfast. I didn't get lunch yet."

"You know, man, we can do this another time."

"No, No, we all have to be comfortable with each other. I ordered lunch from the deli. You can walk with me to pick up the food."

"Don't they deliver?" Sloan asked.

Don winked and said, "They were short staffed today."

"I'll set the table." I walked away, but I could feel their eyes on my behind. I cleaned up the breakfast mess Don and I had made. Sloan went upstairs with Don to get his shoes. He seems to know Don well. I'm sure this won't be the first time he has walked into one of Don's love nests, and judging from that kiss, I wouldn't be surprised to learn that they have shared a few lovers.

Don's agent called while he was out with Sloan getting the food. He congratulated me on our engagement then he said he had some more marvelous news for

Don. I gave Don the message. I even told him it was good news, but he looked at Sloan, and Sloan looked at him, and neither looked at me. I asked them what was wrong. Don said everything was cool, but his eyes dodged mine.

"Let me help you with the food. You can call Ted while I set everything up."

"Let's eat. I'll call Ted later," Don said and he still didn't make eye contact.

"Gina, Don tells me you're a good dentist."

"Good? That's not what he said this morning. Donald Stokes, have you been lying to me?" We made eye contact. Don should know by now that it is hard to keep a secret from me. I searched his eyes for answers. What I saw scared me.

We feasted on a deli platter with a variety of meats and cheeses, fresh baked rolls, and homemade vegetable soup. Don and Sloan had a beer and I had a glass of wine to tame my confusion. Sloan asked me a shit-load of personal questions about my family, Charles, and growing up in Mississippi. Don seemed to be oblivious to the conversation. Whatever is bothering him must be major.

"I wish I hadn't told you about the nightmares," I blurted out. "I didn't mean for them to come between us?"

Don squeezed my hand. "I'm not gonna let anything or anyone come between us, Gina."

"Then, why are you so miserable?"

Don looked at Sloan. "Everything is cool... don't worry... we will be married soon and everything will be perfect." He looked at me, but his eyes were filled with a plea I couldn't read. I didn't know what, but no words came out. My eyes got misty, then I rushed out the room. I wanted to call Edward, but I would never ask him to do anything unethical.

I took a cab to the bridal shop. The color of the bridesmaids' dresses was perfect and so was my fitting. I bought a Yves Saint Laurent little black dress, and the sexiest pair a of Christian Louboutin pumps I could find to keep in Don's closet for emergencies. Exactly what did he mean when he said, "I never bring them here?" What the hell is that supposed to mean? Why didn't he call Ted back? I love Don and I want to marry him, but what is going on? What if Niki is having his baby? What if Kevin was right?

Don and Sloan were working on business proposals when I came back. I said hello and ran upstairs. The dress and shoes looked out of place in the front of his closet, but it was there for him and whomever to see. I worked out in one of his T-shirts and a pair of his boxers. I was in a funky mood thanks to the man downstairs and those nightmares. I walked for twenty minutes and ran for another twenty on his treadmill. Sweat was dripping everywhere but I did my sit-ups and crunches and some light weightlifting. I can't let myself go with Niki banging on the door. Damn him! I didn't ask for this. After I gave in to my tears I felt better, but I was thirsty and ready for a fight so I peeled my behind off the floor and went downstairs to confront Don.

"Did you have a good work-out? Come here. I miss you," Don said.

"I'll be right back." I wished Sloan would take his ass home. I grabbed a bottle of water and went back to the living room.

"Are you finished with your work?"

"Not yet," Don said.

"I don't want to disturb you."

"You're not. Come sit with me."

"I'm sweaty."

"I like your sweat." Don spread his legs and patted the spot between them for me to sit. I sat down. He wrapped his arms and legs around me and caressed my breasts and nibbled on my neck. That's the shit that landed me in his bed from the get-go. I stood up.

"Sweetie, I need to go home earlier than I thought."

I didn't give Don a chance to protest. I showered and changed. He came upstairs while I was dressing.

"Can you stay until I finish with Sloan? We're almost done." He looked sad, but instead of telling me what was wrong he pulled me in his arms and whipped a kiss on me. I got weak in the knees. I wanted to stay, but my intuition was telling me that he had secrets and I wasn't going to like his anymore than my own.

"I want to beat the rush hour traffic," I said, but the truth was I was running scared.

"I'll come up before I leave for Chicago—I need to take care of some business before the wedding."

"Chicago? Business?" I wasn't thrilled about that news, but what could I say? I'm going to be in Aruba for two weeks with Rolonda.

"I'm confused, Don. I love you. But how can I say this? When we're together, it's great, but because we jumped into it tails first, I need to be sure I'm not confusing great sex for love. I do think I love you, but something has happened to our bond."

"What are you saying, Gina? Nothing has changed."

"I need some think time, Don. When I make love to you, I don't think—I feel. I don't want to sound childish, but I need to know if these feelings are the real McCoy or just some superficial almost mid-life guilt free great sex. Maybe we should abstain until our wedding night." My words surprised me and when I looked up, Don had that defeated look in his eyes again.

He hugged me and whispered, "I don't want you to be confused. The reason we are great together is because the force that pulled us together was love. I'll give you all the time you need."

I kissed him with all the passion I could muster up and walked out. Maybe I was getting cold feet. I love Don. The sex is a nice bonus, but it doesn't mean that we should rush into marriage. What secret could he have that would make losing me his greatest fear? What could be worse than possibly killing someone or watching your father do it? Even if it wasn't me or Daddy it has to be connected to my family. Troy said there was a case in 1964 that could be a match. And when I was home Ida Mae's cousin said I looked like her daughter. But when I asked about her daughter, no one would talk about her.

I called Ro on my cell phone and gave her the lowdown on Niki and Don. She reassured me that she could get the truth from Edward without him suspecting a thing. She was going to tell him Niki was one of her clients and Rick was the baby's daddy. We figured Edward would either confirm it, or deny it, and no harm would be done.

It took me three hours to get home. Don had called twice before I got there so Sharon was worried. I filled her in on my visit.

"Sis, your tight ass ain't getting any younger. And you ain't got it in you to hang tough like me, so I suggest you go with the flow. Even your chances of hooking up with another good-looking, dick popping, fine ass brother like Don are slim to none." Sharon clapped her hands in front of my face and said, "Get with the program, girl!"

I jumped back to keep her from bitch-slapping some sense into me. The phone rang and saved me from having to give her a comment. I grabbed the phone, it was Don.

"What's wrong?" He said.

"Nothing. Sharon was talking some sense into me."

"About this celibacy thing?"

"Not exactly, why?"

"Baby, I can't let you go to Aruba in need. I wouldn't want you to be tempted to do something you might regret. Why don't you let me give you some more supreme loving before you go?"

I considered his offer—warm climates make my libido rises faster than the temperature in Mississippi on an August afternoon. "You trust me, don't you?"

"I trust you--it's the G-string wearing brothers on the beaches that I don't trust."

"You should pop over to Aruba so I can jump your bones."

"I'm saving my bones for my wife--I want her to be sure."

I will never be sure after the dreams I had last night.

CHAPTER 28

Sometimes When You Win, You Lose

y gut made tight knots when I signed my new contract. I got the bucks
I wanted and some to play three years in Phoenix. Mom had helped
me focus on what is important, and I worked hard and prayed. Look at me now,
I found a great woman, and signed a fantastic contract. Now all I want to do is
convince Gina to come with me. I can't make midnight runs from Phoenix to
Connecticut just to be close to my lady.

I passed on lunch with Ted. If Gina gets wind of this before I have a chance
to explain, I'll be up shit's creek for sure. She suspects something and now she
won't let me whip my loving on her so I can make it better.

My heart ticked like a time bomb while I drove to her house. Sharon
answered the door. She's a chocolate version of Gina. They even have the same
naughty laugh.

"I can see why Gina flipped over you. You're even more drop drawers
gorgeous in person," Sharon said. "After the stunts I pulled as a teenager, Ida
Mae made sure Gina was as prim and proper as they come. But you romped
her stomp from the jump. It's about time somebody knocked her back to the
real world." She looked me over. "From the looks of you, she probably bit
off more than she can handle, but don't go thinking you can get over on her.
Gina will have you in an emotional headlock before you know you cared."
She chuckled again. "The boy she used to date in high school has been married two or three times and he has eight or ten kids, but every time I see
poor Bobby, he goes on and on about how sorry he is about screwing things
up with Gina." She smiled and extended her hand. "It's nice to meet you.
Don't mind me—I don't know what Gina does to y'all men, but judging

from that big ass smile on your face, you're sprung." She chuckled again. "Gina told me all about you."

"I hope everything she told you was good." I wanted to know more about Bobby; from the sounds of it dude still has it bad. "Is Gina home?"

"She's getting dressed. She went to the gym earlier. Come on in. I'll see what's taking her so long."

Sharon came back a few minutes later and said, "She'll be down shortly. She wants you to wait in the family room."

Gina came downstairs an hour later, but it was worth the wait. She was wearing a red mini dress, a pair of matching stilettos and her toenails were painted red. I pictured her in red underwear, but it was that sad scared look in her eyes and the pout of her lips, which reminded me why I loved her and why I must find a way to take her to Phoenix with me.

She walked into my arms and kissed me. We were lip locked like it were our last kiss. I nibbled on her neck and whispered, "Baby, you're making Big Man's head ache. My offer is still good."

She unbuttoned my shirt and rubbed her hands over my chest as she pressed her body to mine. I groped her butt. She kissed me again. I thought I was going to get lucky, but she whispered, "Thanks, but no thanks." Then she pulled away and put her hands on her hips. Fire was in her eyes--fighting fire! "You wanna tell me something?"

I froze. She is full of fire when we make love, but after she is satisfied she is as cool and as sweet as ice cream.

"Uh, did you have dinner? Can we go somewhere private?" She slammed the door and locked it.

"You said you loved me, Donald Godfrey Stokes! You promised to always tell me the truth."

I wrapped my arms around her. "I love you more than I thought was possible." She pushed me away as if I were contagious.

"Don't patronize me! I know about the damn contract and the trade, and I sure as hell didn't hear it from you." She pounded my chest with her fist. Tears rolled down her cheek. I wanted to catch them with my kisses.

"How did you find out?"

"I was jogging on the treadmill at the gym when I saw you on ESPN. I read what the announcer was saying at the bottom of the screen. I was floored when I read that you had signed a contract with Phoenix for sixty million dollars for three years! How could you sign a new contract without telling me?"

"I was afraid I would lose you."

"How can you stand here and say you love me when you don't trust me enough to tell me what is going on in your life? I don't know about you, but I can't marry someone who doesn't trust me with simple shit!"

I pulled her to my chest. My heart was beating a mile a minute. "I didn't do this to hurt you," I whispered. "I couldn't find the words to tell you. I love you, Gina. I know you love me too." My voice cracked; I didn't give a damn. I had gotten over feeling corny.

"You're right. I love you. I let myself trust you, Don."

I rubbed her back while she cried into my chest. "I should have trusted you. I blew it. Sloan said this would happen."

Gina pulled away from me again, and sucked up her tears, but she still had a hurt look in her eyes. My eyes were stinging, but I'm too much of a man to let my lady see me cry.

"You told Sloan yesterday, didn't you?" Her tone of voice had an unfamiliar edge. "You trust Sloan more than you trust me?"

"I tell him everything. We're like brothers."

"Let me get this straight... You trusted him, but not me? Maybe you should—"

"Should what?"

"I've read all those E. Lynn--never mind. Just leave. I need to think. I don't want to say something while I'm angry that I will regret later. I'll call you when I get back from Aruba."

"I can't let you go to Aruba angry."

She wiped her face and her hands found her hips again. "Well, my brother, you have two days to win my heart and my trust back. Otherwise, you'll have to trust me on the beaches of Aruba in this scandalous dress and a few others Rolonda picked out. Maybe I'll call you when I return. Maybe I won't have to."

"If you love me you won't let this keep us apart, Gina."

"Don't try to flip this shit on me. I can't stop loving you because you chose to move away. Hell, I wish it was that damn simple, but don't blame me for the choices you've made."

"I'm not blaming you. I want you to come with me."

"You messed up, mister." Her finger felt like an ice pick stabbing my chest as she punched in each word. "How could you let me fall in love with you knowing we could never be together?" She unlocked the door and said, "Get out!"

I pulled her in my arms and gave her a pleading kiss. It seemed to weaken her but she didn't give in. "I was wrong, but two wrongs don't make a right. Please don't make me leave. I'm no good without you."

Her eyes said stay, but it felt like she was typing in each letter when she said, "You should have thought about us when you signed our future away. I need some time to decide if I can live with this."

Sixty-million seemed like a lot of future when I scribbled my name even though my stomach churned and I feared I was going to lose something immensely more important. I walked out proudly. Trust was banging me upside the head, but faith kept telling me to hang in there. I thought about what Sharon had said about Bobby; I wasn't about to go out like that.

I drove around for a while and planned my next move. Then I checked into the Marriott and requested suite 1187. I fell across the bed and replayed the first night I spent with Gina in my mind. We had a good time, good conversations and great sex. Two days. What did I do right that night?"

I sent Gina a bouquet of Calla lilies and a card that said:

Gina,
My life changed the day we met. We're on this roller coaster ride together. It's scary right now. You're probably wishing you hadn't trusted me, and I'm wishing I had trusted you. I'm in room 1187. If you love me and trust me with your heart come over for a tickle fight. Give me a chance to make the ride "mo' better." I love you, Gina. I need you in my life.
Love Always,
Don

I read the note and sent it with the flowers. Tickle fights. No condoms. Gina tried to run out on me. I tried to get her out my system and she rocked me into her soul. That was one helluva first date. She committed me to memory. She needs me as much as I need her.

I saw a billboard for Lux, Bond & Green with a diamond tennis bracelet and a woman with a big ass smile on her face. I googled the address to find the nearest store. Gina likes rubies and bracelets. I told the sales clerk I wanted something that would put a smile on my lady's face. I bought a Favero platinum, diamonds, and rubies bracelet that would set most brothers back a few years, but since I had signed our future away I said, what the hell, I might as well use my money to get my woman back. The clerk gift wrapped it while I wrote a note.

> Gina,
> When I saw this bracelet, I immediately thought of you. The diamonds represent my love for you; it will last forever. The heart-shaped rubies reminded me of the day you gave me your heart. I promised to take care of it. I said I would never hurt you. I did. Now I understand why trust is one of the main ingredients of true love. Everything I know about love, you showed me. Please don't stop loving me now.
> Love Always,
> Don
> P.S.--I'm still in room 1187. Please come. Let me make it better.

Gina didn't call or come so I called her house to make sure she had gotten the flowers and bracelet. She wouldn't talk, but Sharon said, "She gave me the keys to her car and told me not to let her out the house. The surface stuff doesn't count with Gina. So, unless you want to join Gina Anonymous, you had better dig deep, brother. Well, good luck."

Dig deep. I called Gina's office at seven-thirty and told her answering service I was in extreme pain. Then I paced around the room and prayed while I waited anxiously.

Gina called at eight o'clock and asked me if my pain was real. I moaned. She offered to call in a refill, but I lied and said I had cracked the tooth and the medicine wasn't working. She said something about teeth becoming brittle after the nerves are removed. I moaned again. She called me her poor baby. I played it for all I could get.

"I was angry with myself for the way I messed things up. Will you look at it tonight? Please? I don't trust anyone else."

"Are you saying you trust me in that respect, Mr. Stokes?" She sounded professional but I could hear her smile.

"Yes. Only you."

She agreed to meet me at her office, but she promised to hurt me if I was pulling a fast one. If I could get her back in my bed, I would show her who the boss is, on second thoughts, I had better play this straight. I left immediately.

Lustful thoughts entered my mind when I saw her wearing the bracelet and that red dress. She looked at me leery so I grabbed my jaw, moaned and pretended to be in pain. She opened the office, turned on the lights, and locked us in. Then, she put on a lab coat and snapped it all the way up. She didn't say anything.

She pointed to the chair. "Sit!"

I obeyed. She put the nitrous cone on my nose. I took it off. "I don't need it when I'm with you."

"Suit yourself," she said, and then she rammed the needle into my jaw without putting that jelly stuff first. I tried to be a man, but that shit hurt. My eyes got misty and my hand found her bare leg and gripped it. My jaw got numb and a familiar tingle run through my body straight to where I wished Gina was sitting. I smiled lopsided when my jaw became heavy. She gazed into my eyes while I rubbed her knee and she finished my root canal. I prayed that she wasn't finishing it so she wouldn't have to see me again.

She climbed into the dental chair with me afterwards and kissed my numb lips. I couldn't tell how hard I was kissing her, but the kiss was packed with emotions. I was so lost in her sweetness my hands were under her dress before I realized I was making a mistake.

She hopped up, pulled her dress down, blushed and said, "We better go."

I rubbed my finger over her engagement ring. "We need to talk about our future. Come with me to the Marriott." She shivered, but this time I didn't know if that was good or bad.

"Not tonight… Maybe tomorrow."

"Why not tonight?" I smiled coyly. I wanted to see her thong panties.

"I can't. I'm too in love and too angry with you right now." She looked deep into my eyes. I tried to look pitiful but I was too happy to hear the love part.

"I'm sorry, Don. I'm not doing this to hurt you. I'm doing this for us. I need to figure this out with a clear head. You know I can't think when you, when we, oh you know what I mean."

I held her face between my hands; anywhere else would have interfered with my thinking as well as with hers. I pressed my lips to hers. She didn't resist.

"Did you have dinner? Please come with me. We have to talk."

"You can talk, but don't be surprised if I don't have anything to say."

I kissed her again. "Thank you."

"I'll call Sharon and the kids. I didn't tell them I was meeting you, although Sharon saw me wearing this dress and figured it out."

"You mean you don't tease all your patients by dressing like that? It could be good for business."

"The dress and the shoes are for you. I wanted to make it hard for you to say, 'Gina, it's been real. But, baby girl, I signed a phat ass contract--sorry I forgot to mention that shit. Phoenix is gonna pay me a shit-load of money. I love ya, but it bees that way sometimes. See ya!'" She was mimicking my mannerisms when we tease each other, but this time she laughed, and then she cried.

I wrapped her in my arms. "Baby, I would never look that good in that dress." I got a rise and pulled her closer. "We better go before I have to see what color thong you're wearing."

She stepped back, reached under her dress, and tugged off a tiny red thing and stuffed it into my pocket. Then she grabbed her keys and said, "It was making me horny. Enjoy it. That drop of pussy on it may be your last."

We went to Buddy's. I ordered food and drinks. She ordered a triple ice cream sundae.

"I lied about having a toothache," I said when we were alone.

"I know. That's why I tried to hurt you."

"I had to see you tonight. What I did was wrong. Baby, you are so cool when you're doing your dentist thing. You're large and in charge. And when we do our love thing, you're awesome and some." She blushed but she didn't comment.

"I wanted to stay in New York. I told Ted I had to know about my future before we got married." I stroked the ring and wished it could grant my wish. She flashed me a searching gaze.

"I want to marry you. I want us to be a family. I want to be with you as much as I can, Gina." I kissed her hand and looked away into space, into the perfect future we could have together.

"You made your choice when you signed that contract."

"I know, but I never intended to make you decide between the other things you love and me. Marry me, Gina. You can stay here if you don't want to come to Phoenix. My businesses are in New York. It makes sense for me to keep my place there. It's a three-year contract. When it's up I'll retire and pursue other interests. Please, talk to me."

"Why should I? You obviously don't value my opinion."

"I was afraid I would lose you. I haven't felt like that since I lost my father, I'm sure you can relate to that. You brought these emotions out in me. Come with me, please?"

"How can I? We would be drinking champagne and making love right now, if you had trusted me and had faith in my love for you. It hurts me to know that I'm nothing more to you than a brainless sex kitten."

"That's bull and you know it!" A man and his young son stopped and asked for an autograph. I scribbled something quickly and lowered my voice. "I was in love with you before we made love. I understood your pain and your fears. I hung in there when you talked about Charles and when you were unsure. I filled the empty spaces he left in your heart. If I didn't have faith in our love and trust you, I wouldn't have done any of that. You fill my voids as well. We need each other, Gina."

"You have selective trust, Don. When you can share all the things you share with Sloan with me, then you will be ready to get married. A good marriage is a partnership, too. Let me know when you're there. I'm there."

I was out of words. I had a quiet dinner, and she blamed me for making her eat every drop of her sundae. I followed her home, and then I went to the Marriott to think of plan B. I couldn't believe she had accused me of wanting a bed partner knowing she is hooked on my sex. I'm going to make Miss Gina an honest woman before *I* say I do. I've been playing your game, baby. It's time you learn to play mine.

CHAPTER 29

Playing Your Game, Baby

*D*on had thrown the ball in my court. Get married. Don't get married. Move. Don't move. We should make these decisions together, but he messed up and kicked it to me in the name of trust. If I was twenty I would have been angry for two, three weeks, maybe longer. But at forty, hell, I don't have that freaking long. I didn't know what to do, but I wanted to believe he loved and trusted me enough to let me decide.

The next day I received another special delivery while I was packing for my trip. Don had sent two CDs, "The Best of Love" by Luther Vandross, and "In the Mood" by The Whispers. He also sent a pint of black cherry ice cream and a note.

> Gina,
> Play Luther Vandross "A House Is Not a Home" first. Close your eyes and listen to the words. The choice is yours. Don't let my mistake keep us apart. If you love me, let me turn your house into a home. I need you as much as you need me. (Stop, play the CD.)
> Okay, now that you have listened and thought about what you want to do, you can play The Whispers, "Say Yes." Don't forget to close your eyes and think about me. Pretty lady, do you think about me in your fantasies? Say "yes" and I will do the rest. (Stop, play the CD.)
> Did you say "yes" at least one time? If you did, open the second compartment of the Luther CD. Did you find the key for room 1187? You did? Okay, now here comes the hard part. You can

say yes to my love and I will do the rest, or you can enjoy your
ice cream, and Charles's empty side of your bed.
Please tickle me, Gina. Let me make your laugh reach your
eyes again. Give it to me—I'm gonna make you my wife.
(Whispers songs 1 and 12.) It's your choice. Supreme love
or ice cream.
Love,
Don

Shit! I thought I was running things but Don is playing hard ball. "A House
Is Not a Home" not only made me wonder what life would be like without
him, but it reminded me of how painful it was to lose Charles. It took me a
while to compose myself before I played the Whispers. The song asked the
girl to say yes and the guy promised to make all her fantasies come true. I
said yes seven times.

Since I had on sneakers and a baseball cap, I tried to pretend that I was on
my way to the gym. Sharon came into the kitchen before I could get away. I gave
her the ice cream and said, "Don challenged me to a tickle fight."

"Well, go and get him, and remember there are no losers in a good
tickle fight."

We hugged and Sharon pointed to the door. "Get your butt outta here and
go give Don's fine ass some loving before some ho takes your place."

I played both songs again in the car. My heart was pounding by the
time I knocked on the door. Don was wearing a big smile and red boxers. I
leaned against the door, but before I could compose myself, he covered my
lips with his.

I didn't have any answers, but I wanted him in a sinful way. He kissed me.
I tickled him. He held on. I took control. I wanted to get busy, but we needed
to see if we could have a future together. We tickled each other until we cried
and I got the hiccups.

"Please, baby, baby, please, marry me," Don begged.

I giggled and held up my ring. "I'm not giving up this Rock of Gibraltar or
you. I'm angry, but I'm not crazy."

He pulled me into his arms. "Marry me on your birthday." We kissed. I tickled him again, but I was too torn inside to handle the laughter.

"I don't know, Don. I love you, but maybe we're rushing it. How am I supposed to give up everything and uproot my family when you left me out of your decision?"

He held my face between his large hands and looked me dead in the eyes. "I don't wanna wait. I didn't tell you because I knew it would be hard for you to make a choice. You don't have to come with me if you think you'll be okay here. But you'll never find another man who loves you more than I do. I want you now."

I sat on the bed. Don's intense stare was more powerful than his words. Even Sharon said I couldn't be that lucky. Damn, he is cute when he is vulnerable. He stood next to me and stared while my mind raced. He sat down and stroked my cheek. I kissed him, leaned back, and pulled him down on top of me. He rolled away from me onto his back.

"I have a confession to make," he said.

I raised a brow. "What?"

"I have business in Chicago, but it's personal."

I sat up. "Personal as in, I will tell you all about it; or personal as in, you'll just have to trust me?"

"Jason's mother and his half-sister need his help."

"What's a half-sister? When we get married I will treat Jason the same as Kevin and Myesha. Jason is a great kid--he's not a half anything. When I was a kid people used to call me and Sharon the Ebony and Ivory twins. They used to ask us if we were half-sisters. They should ban that term. I'm sorry, what were you saying?"

"Jason's mother contacted him because her daughter has acute lymphocytic leukemia. Valerie asked Jason to donate marrow. She hasn't called him in fourteen years, but now she needs his help. Mom is against it, but Jason wants to meet his mother and help his sister."

I moved behind Don and wrapped my arms and legs around him. "That explains the strange call I received from him a few weeks ago. He asked me if I knew anything about donating bone marrow. He wanted to know if I would donate marrow if I knew someone who needed it."

"What did you say?"

"Yes." I stood on my knees while I massaged the knots out of Don's muscles. "There's a need for more African American donors. Marrow types are unique to people of specific ancestry. You can match a donor to any racial or ethnic group, but you're more likely to match a donor within your own group. The first step is to take a simple blood test that determines your tissue type. Your tissue type is then added to the National Marrow Donor Program Registry. When a donor is needed, the registry is searched for a match."

"That sounds simple enough."

"If a match is made you'll have to get a physical and donate some of your own blood to receive back after the marrow is collected. The marrow is removed from the lower part of the back in a surgical procedure using anesthesia. You'll probably stay in the hospital overnight and experience some soreness in the lower back for about a week, but I would do it to save someone's life. Wouldn't you?"

"You know how I am about needles."

I continued to massage his shoulders. "Is it the surgery you're worried about or confronting Valerie?"

"Both. I never had a chance to talk to her about Jason or what happened between us. It shouldn't matter now, but I felt as though I had been used and betrayed."

"I think you should support Jason. I'm here if you need me. I'm a good listener, and you know I have your back."

"I should have known you would understand. I'm sorry I didn't tell you about the trade. Please forgive me?"

"You hurt me. I want to forgive you, but it's hard for me to make a choice when you make major decisions without considering us." I kissed Don on the cheek. I patted him on the back. "I have to catch a limo tomorrow and I didn't finish packing. Sharon is making dinner. Why don't you join us?"

Don smiled and stole a kiss. "Come home with me instead of taking the limo."

"I want to spend the evening with the kids and Sharon."

"Okay, but I'll drive you tomorrow."

We had a nice down home soul food dinner. Sharon cooked fried chicken, collard greens, cornbread, macaroni and cheese, and peach cobbler. After dinner, she put food in Tupperware containers for me to take to Aruba.

"The flight to Aruba is long and that crap they serve on planes is barely edible. You might as well take a little snack just in case," Sharon said.

I didn't want to hurt her feelings, but there was no way in hell I was going on the airplane smelling like fried chicken. Old habits in my family die hard.

Don chuckled when I frowned at Sharon. He knows me better than I would like to admit. He flashed Sharon a wicked smile. I thought they were reserved for me only. Then he said, "I'd like a doggie bag. Your fried chicken and peach cobbler is slamming." He looked at me and flashed the same smile. "Baby, why can't you cook like this?"

I rolled my eyes. "You're marrying the doctor in the family. You can't have everything." He chuckled again.

Don hung out with the kids while I tried to fit my stuff in two suitcases. Sharon kept me company while I packed. When Don got tired of losing video games to Kevin, he joined me in my room. We all watched "Power" on Starz from my bed until Angela and Ghost got busy on a table, and Don started massaging my feet. I moaned and Sharon left. Don excused himself when things got hot.

He picked me up the next morning and drove us to his place. He packed quickly and we were into some heavy petting when the limo arrived early and saved us from getting our swerve on. We were back in the heavy petting zone when Rolonda got into the limo.

"Unless you plan to make this a threesome I suggest you cool it," she said.

I let out a raucous laugh and patted Don's roaming hands. We made a scene in the boarding area until someone flashed our picture. Don kissed me again and I boarded the plane.

"Damn, girl, I didn't think you were going to make it," Ro said. "Look at you blushing and shit, nipples all hard. You should have taken care of your business last night."

"Shut up, Ro, we're in first class; let's act as if we have some." I rolled my eyes, gave my carry-on bag to the flight attendant, and sat in the aisle seat next to Ro.

"Your country ass was in the lobby making love to your man, and I don't have any class? Please!" She rotated her neck and put her hand in front of my face like a stop sign.

I rolled my eyes. "We weren't making love. We were making up. I guess you didn't hear the latest."

"What's the latest, Gina?" Ro said sarcastically. And I thought: aren't we off to a good start--two black women with bad attitudes.

"Don was traded. He's moving to Phoenix. He didn't know how to tell me, so he didn't. I heard it from ESPN."

Her mouth and eyes opened wide. Now she looked like she had seen a ghost. "You're kidding. What are you going to do?"

"I don't know. I love him too much to let him go alone. But I have responsibilities to my patients, my business and the foundation. I can't just walk away. I've worked too hard the last ten years. I want it all, but this time I don't know how to make it work."

"Damn, girl. Are you going to postpone the wedding?"

"No. I love him. I'm afraid I'll lose him. He said I can stay in Connecticut, but he doesn't want to wait. I'm supposed to use this trip to come up with some solutions. We took a hiatus from sex to make sure we're making the right decisions."

"Damn, girl."

"Is that all you can say?"

"You're lucky to have someone who loves you as much as Don. I can tell from the way you guys were kissing that the sex is hot. You have the full package--tall, dark, handsome, pocket full of cash, great lover, so what's the damn problem? What else could you possibly want?"

"Trust, commitment, good character, intelligence, honesty, integrity--someone who cares emotionally as well as physically."

"Isn't Don all of that?"

"And some."

"You're the luckiest person I know, Gina."

"Ro, I believe in a lot of things, some of which are a bit outlandish, but I never believed in the luck of the draw. I believe in making good choices and living with the consequences."

"Anyway, girl, watching you all go at it made me want a hungry man. Edward is such a dud in bed. That's the real reason I always had a tenderoni on the side. I've been straight since we got engaged, but if I slip in Aruba it's between you and me."

"I don't know, Ro. I don't judge you, but have you told Edward what your needs are? When you kick it to him, does he respond? When you give good loving, you get good loving in return. I know I act prim and proper, but when it comes to sex, I get buck wild, 'cause that's how I like it."

"I usually follow my man's lead, but with Edward I can't seem to get in my zone."

"Maybe you should take the lead sometimes. He's probably not getting in his zone either. If you fake it, girl, he'll continue to do the same shit and you'll find yourself faking it every time. The man is a gynecologist. He's up to his elbows in coochies and breasts all day long. You need to give him something to come home to. Make it special. Talk dirty. Spank him. Do something different. Let him know he's the man. Stroke his ego. If none of that works--pack your shit. Find somebody new, masturbate before, during and after, but don't go out once a month to get your world rocked."

"Masturbate? Girl, you're a trip."

"Whatever. The first time I did it with Don I was tripping my ass off. The next time he knew just what I liked. He loved it and the rest is history."

"How do you know so much with your no experience self?"

"I have lots of experience. Bobby showed me what to expect and what men want. Charles was an incredible lover. And I shonuff get my world rocked with Don. We're taking a break so we can manage the other issues in our relationship. You're the one hopping from bed to bed, maybe you should get to know yourself first."

"Don't go there, Gina."

"You started it. If you love Edward, you have to work it out together. You're both my friends."

"Speaking of Ed, girl, you know I love your stank behind. You should have seen me seducing the information you wanted about Niki from him. My poor baby didn't know what hit him. Girl, if you let a man talk about his work, you can't shut him up. I told him Niki told me she was having Rick's baby. But he said I must have heard her wrong because the only thing Niki has is severe endometriosis and a cocaine problem. Her boyfriend used to give her coke to help her relax during sex because it was too painful for her. Now she is in love with a different brother who won't give her the time of day because of the drugs. Edward suggested that she leave the drugs alone and have a baby. He said the condition sometimes corrects itself after pregnancy, but if that doesn't work she may need laser surgery or a hysterectomy. She's been trying to get off the drugs. He saw her a few weeks ago. She wasn't pregnant. It's amazing how many things can go wrong with us women. I felt sorry for her by the time Ed explained her problems."

"I forgot all about Niki and Troy when I heard about the trade, but thanks, girl. Maybe we should continue this conversation later. You never know who may be listening. Someone took a picture of Don and me in the lobby. I sure wouldn't want my last comments printed in one of those tabloids."

"Gina, do you think we will ever see the day when men will drop their careers to let us advance ours?"

"Some men will but the alpha men we deal with probably will not."

"Why not? A lot of women make more money than their men these days."

"True that, but their man thang would still get in the way."

"What's a man thang?"

"A man thang is everything we prayed for in a man when we were little girls, but we grew up and discovered our needs had changed and theirs hadn't."

"Oh, well. I need a nap. I don't know why I've been so tired lately."

"Ro, you work way too hard. Let's make this a forget about men trip. I was finally in a peaceful state of mind after I decided to marry Don. I need to do some soul searching in Aruba." Rolonda fell asleep on my shoulder before I finished talking.

We arrived at the Costa Linda Resort five hours later. We were shown to a beautiful suite which was decorated in rich corals, violets, and aqua. It was a calm place. It had two large bedrooms, two bathrooms, a full kitchen, a living room and dining area, and a private balcony. I walked out on the balcony overlooking the pool and beach and let the trade winds and the clean smell of the ocean breeze caress me. This was my first vacation without Charles, going to Mississippi doesn't count. I went back inside and called Sharon and the kids before I got teary eyed.

The next morning, I was hungry and horny. I dreamt of Charles and Don, and happy days and thrilling nights. A long walk on the beach helped me to sort out my feelings. The crystal-clear water and the clear blue sky were the same turquoise blue. The sand was white and grainy like uncooked grits with a pinch of gravy, and the trade winds were wonderful. There were no seagulls, but there were plenty Divi-Divi trees, and the natives all smiled and said "hello" or "good morning," and no one looked at me suspicious or made me feel tainted.

Rolonda was still asleep when I got back to the suite. I ate outside on the balcony and finished reading a love story about a hoodoo woman and a blues man. Rolonda woke up around noon. We went downtown and shopped at the Royal Plaza Mall opposite the harbor. This was our routine the first three days.

On the fourth day, I did my usual walk on the beach while Rolonda got her beauty rest. Walking worked wonders on helping me find inner peace. I still missed Don, and even the pesky seagulls.

We went to our first beach party which turned out to be a freaknik for all ages. The DJ was jamming when a couple of recent graduates from Howard University invited themselves over. Kenny and Marcus were twenty-one bursting with hormones and willing to share them with a couple of older sisters whom they hoped were trying to get their groove back. Rolonda stroked their oozing young masculine egos. I kept my eyes glued to the latest Eric Dickey installment.

I woke up the next day excited about seeing one of my favorite groups. My love for the Isley Brothers and Barry White is one of few things that I have in common with my mother. I had worked my way to the front of the crowd by the time The Isley's came on stage. They were rocking and I was in a zone so deep,

I was lightheaded. I've done just about everything worth doing while listening to their music, but making love, dancing, and driving tops my list. I love to play "Summer Breeze" when I'm driving. On a nice day, I will open the windows, crank up the volume, let the breeze blow through my hair and trick my mind into believing that I'm twenty again. I was in that zone that only Charles, Don, and the Isley's could take me. My knees buckled but I caught myself before I went down. I'd had more than my share of Patron by the time The Isley's were getting down playing "Summer Breeze." The wonderful breeze and the music caressed me as my life flashed before me. I was in a different place a different time with a different love. I blinked to keep from passing out. I saw Charles and our wonderful years together--a great love affair, that only lives these days in my dreams. Suddenly, everything was black. I was a goner. My legs were weak, but I refused to let myself faint--not in this crowd. Rolonda was somewhere in the back. I fought to stay coherent. I took a few deep breaths. The music swam in my head and so did Charles and Don.

Everything was a big blur. Then I imagined their warm delicious lips touching mine. I saw a bright light. Summer Breezes. Charles? Don? The Boys? They gave me strength in a deja vu way. Suddenly everything was clear, my right palm was itching and the smell of love was in the air.

Ernie Isley was doing a solo to the tune "Voyage to Atlantis." My body was his guitar string and each cord was a piece of my life. "I'll always come back to you," swirled in my mind. I threw my hands up in the air and swayed from side to side. I had been saved by the summer breezes, the boys from the swamp, Charles, and Don. There was magic in the air and love in my heart.

When the concert ended, I pushed my way through the crowd to find Rolonda. She was with Marcus and Kenny.

"Are you okay?" Rolonda asked.

"I'm fine. I'm high from the music--the experience."

"You look as though you just had a round with a great lover."

"I wish. No, I had a round of great music."

We went with Marcus and Kenny to the City 1 Club. We danced and drank until the wee hours of the morning. I'd had one too many sweet sex on the beach drinks when Marcus stuck his tongue in my ear and his hand made a power play for my cookies. I mentioned Don and hoped that Marcus would slow down. He continued to nibble on my neck and ear. He swore up and down that he had seen Don, Rick King, and a light-skinned dude at the concerts with their arms around some fine ass twins--his words not mine. Ro was our designated driver. She sensed my mood change and snatched my inebriated behind away from Marcus so fast he almost bit off a piece of my ear.

CHAPTER 30

Trying to Figure It Out

I wanted to surprise Gina, but instead I got more than I bargained for. Sloan and I made it to the concerts in time to catch the Isley Brothers. Gina loves the Isley Brothers. I was sure she was in the crowd somewhere but I'd be damned if I could find her. While we were wandering around in vain, I spotted Rolonda sitting on a blanket laughing and talking to two young brothers. Gina wasn't with them, but I figured she wasn't far away. I didn't tell Sloan what was going on, but it didn't take him long to figure out something was foul. We waited in the cut until the concert was almost over. Gina never showed up. Sloan suggested that we wait at her hotel since the crowd was thick. I dosed off on the sofa in the lobby and dreamt about Gina and Rolonda doing the old-school freak to those young innocent boys. Sloan and I went back to his yacht around four a.m.

The next day the beach party was at the Radisson Resort Hotel. I hadn't slept well and my mood was fucked-up. Sloan and I combed the beach looking for Gina. Fans interrupted me to take pictures and to sign shit; they didn't even care about my bad attitude. I stood stiffly in the pictures and continued to search the crowd since I was wearing dark sunglasses and my Chicago Cubs cap. My lips curled into a smile when I saw Gina's legs.

"You see her?" Sloan asked.

"I think so."

Sloan smiled and followed me. Gina was lounging on her belly in a chair, reading a book, and talking to Rolonda. She had on a cheetah print bikini, which reminded me of my bed sheets and that was exactly where I wanted her to be. Her top was untied and her tan looked yummy. I ran my finger up her leg until I felt a familiar tingle. She leaped from her chair into my arms. I grabbed her and kissed her hard.

"Baby, this isn't the topless beach," I whispered. I held her close while I tied her top.

"And this ain't Phoenix."

"Is that what Mom told you?" We gazed at each other. Her eyes said, I missed you. And mine said, I can't live without you and where the hell were you last night?

She smiled and I stole another kiss. "I can't believe you're here," she said.

"I told you I don't trust the men at these parties."

The two brothers who had been sitting with Ro were walking in our direction wearing purple and gold G-strings showing off their brawny bodies and the Omega brands on their huge biceps. They smiled slyly when they greeted us by our names. I was leery of the quiver in Gina's tone when she spoke to them and smiled.

"Did you get my messages?" she asked.

"Yep," I said but my eyes were on the young men. I didn't like the way the curly haired one looked at Gina or the way she smiled at him.

"Why didn't you call?"

"You weren't in. That's why I'm here. You know those creeps?"

"They're nice boys. You know I can't stand it when I don't talk to you. So, when did you get here?"

One of the things I love and hate about Gina is the way she can ask me a simple question, lift her brow and look at me cock-eyed in a way that makes me believe she already know the answer and everything in-between so I had better come clean.

"I waited for you after the concerts." I stammered as though I was the guilty party. "So where did you sleep last night?" The boys looped around and passed us again. I followed them with my eyes.

"We went to the after party." She grinned coyly. "Why are you looking at me like that?"

"Like what?"

"I could feel you looking at me like that if I were blind. You're looking rather good yourself with these swim shorts riding low on your sexy hip bones." Gina ran her finger around the inside of my waistband and pressed her thighs to mine. "Those gold hoop earrings in your ears make me want to throw caution to the wind." She kissed me and wiggled her pelvis on my thigh.

"Baby, your tan looks good--yummy good," I said.

"You look like my favorite flavor Popsicle as well."

Sloan and Rolonda cleared their throats when Gina and I started to kiss and slow grind. We apologized for being rude. Gina put on a sarong and grabbed my hand. We strolled away like young lovers. When we were out of the crowd, she stopped and kissed me, then she sat in the cool damp sand and stuck her feet in the water.

"I miss you," I said. I wanted to say something to tell her how lost I am without her but that was all I could come up with.

"I miss you, too. I can't live like this--missing you all the time. I'm too old to play this game." She covered her feet with wet sand and looked away. Far, far away. And I knew she was still torn between two states and two men.

"How is the regrouping coming along?"

"Okay, I guess." She looked away again, but not fast enough to keep me from seeing the pain in her eyes. Our hearts are split between my world and her world and I don't know how to bring our worlds together without one of us taking a huge loss.

"How are things in Chicago?"

"Jason did the initial blood test. He didn't match. But he wants to meet his sister and his mother. We're flying out on Tuesday."

"Did you take a test?"

"No, why should I?"

"To support Jason and you might be a match."

"You think I should be tested?"

"I think it will show Jason how much you love him and support his decision."

"Okay. I'll do anything for you and Jason."

Gina smiled, but it didn't last long. "Can I ask you something?"

"Sure, anything, but make it easy. My cup is full."

"How does Sloan feel about us?"

"He thinks we're perfect for each other."

"Why does he look at me strange and drill me with questions now? Did you tell him about my dreams?"

"He's just looking out for me. You are his type, and that kiss you gave him, went a long way. He wished he had gotten his chance with you. He is fond of you, and happy for us."

"I thought that kiss was just a test to see how strong you all's bonds are." Gina turned and looked at me. "Am I your type?"

"I don't have a type. You're my everything." I kissed her on her sun burnt nose. Gina is sensitive about her skin color or lack thereof, but I'm in a money position now where those kinds of hang-ups about people are overshadowed by far more important things. I see beauty as something deeper, and she has an abundance of that deeper something-something that I've been looking for.

"Maybe I'm envious of the special bond you guys have."

"Sloan and I have been through a lot together, but you have to know that you are pretty damn good at reading my mind and my heart. Come with me to his yacht, after you spend some time with him you'll see how much he likes you."

"You guys cruised over?"

"Sort of, all the hotels were booked, so we took Sloan's yacht from Puerto Rico--come with me. Please?" I hugged her and rubbed her special spot while my eyes begged.

"I can't leave Rolonda. We're roommates. She's vulnerable right now. Besides, I'm still regrouping."

"Let me help you regroup. Isn't that what you told me?"

"Okay, but only if I can invite Ro. We better get back. My yummy tan is starting to burn."

On the way to her seating area, I saw Bee and Tee, the super-freaky twin sisters from my past. They were wearing matching hot-pink bikinis. Their long curly hair blew in the direction of the trade winds and their long barely legal rust-brown legs and full breasts were headed straight for me and Gina. The twins flashed me a Rembrandt smile and panic rushed through me. I squeezed Gina's hand. Bee and Tee were a good time from my past when I was freaking harder than Rick James. The first time I had hooked up with the half black half Puerto Rican twins we had a sexual smorgasbord weekend. The twins screamed when they were in front of me. They grabbed me and started kissing my face and chest.

I was probably blushing when I said, "Time out! Hold up! This is my fiancée, Gina. Baby, these are a couple of old acquaintances." I raised Gina's hand to show off her ring, but the twins were not fazed.

There were a few moments of awkward silence. Bee, who is taller than Tee by an inch, older by five minutes, and a hundred times bolder said, "Congratulations, Don." She smiled directly at me and did a suggestive trick with her pierced tongue, and there was no way in hell that Gina had missed her signals. I slid my arm around Gina's bare waist and pulled her closer to me.

I couldn't stop what Bee said next, and since we weren't standing on quick sand, I prayed.

"Before you get married, we should get together for another orgy. You can bring Ginger. The more, the better." She winked, and my hand tightened around Gina's waist.

She tensed and the spot where my hand was touching seemed to burn. I stood there like a fool and said nothing. Part of me wanted to take Bee up on their offer--if Gina was down--that shit would have been a wet dream come true. Then I thought about me freaking it with Gina and those two big ass brothers--that's some shit you just don't do with someone you love.

Gina slid her hand into the waist of my shorts and rested it on my ass. I got excited. My baby definitely has some freak in her.

"Thanks for the invitation, but we don't need any assistance. We do extremely well all by ourselves. Isn't that right, sweetie?"

She was talking through clenched teeth and pinching my ass at the same time. There was a cute smile on her face, and if I hadn't felt the pain in my behind, I would have thought everything was straight. I stood there like a fool and said nothing. She pinched me harder and I knew I had to say something clever quick.

"That's absolutely right, baby. We got so much love between us we don't need to do that freaky stuff. You girls need to stop that nonsense and find someone who will make you as happy as Gina makes me."

I thought I had done well. Gina was pinching me so hard my butt had gotten numb. She smiled at Bee and Tee while her eyes pierced theirs. They stared each other down for a few moments. The twins scrambled away without saying another word. Sand flew everywhere.

I had a sinking feeling when Gina tightened her eyes and stared at me. She spanked the spot where she had been pinching and the pain returned. A drop of sweat rolled down the side of my face in slow motion. The breeze dried it. I hadn't been that scared since I knocked over Mom's curio cabinet. My stomach even seemed to hurt as hopelessness took me over. Gina didn't say anything, and her emotionless stare cut into my soul. She didn't blink. She didn't even look hurt. Another drop of sweat trickled down my temple.

She finally said, "I hope you will get better at getting rid of your whores before we get married or we won't stay married long."

"Baby, don't let my past scare you. I've done things most men only dream about, and none of it compares to what we share. I would never risk losing you over some freak. Never!" I tried to kiss her. She turned away.

"I want to trust you. But the thought of you being alone in Phoenix is something I'll have to rethink. I've been walking the beautiful beaches of Aruba for nearly a week. I think about us and I think about how it was with Charles."

I frowned. Fuck Charles, I thought. Mom taught me not to speak ill of the dead, but I was damn sick of Charles.

"I know you're tired of hearing about Charles, but I think I had an epiphany last night at the concerts. I have to tell you this before I can move on."

"Okay, I said not planning to listen.

"Charles loved me. We were in love for nearly twenty years and I was content knowing that someone had truly loved me the way that he had. He wasn't perfect, but neither am I. When I met you, I believed you were sent to me by an angel. I believed you could love me the way you promised. The way I need you to love me. I'm picky, Donald Godfrey Stokes, if you want me, make good on your promises. I can't let go of my past until you start trusting the power of our love."

"You mean you won't let go of Charles."

"Last night I was ready to let Charles rest. I'm trying right now. I want to trust you. I want to share all my thoughts and fears with you. It's okay for us to bring the knowledge of our pasts to our futures, but let's try to bring only that which will make our futures better."

We piled into my rented jeep and went to Sloan's yacht. The Lady Geneva is named after his mother. It is seductively luxurious and perfectly private. Sloan took Gina and Rolonda on a tour of the yacht. The technical stuff, such as engine power, and knots cruising seemed to go right over their heads. Lady Geneva has seven staterooms and can sleep fourteen people plus a small crew. The wedding will take place in the salon. It looks like the lobby of a five-star hotel with an adjoining semi-private formal dining area and an imaginative sky-lounge. The interior of the salon features raised African cherry panels that give it a traditional feel even though the cream-colored leather sofas and chairs that dominate the salon have a contemporary design. The wedding planner will add a few more formal dining room tables and chairs for the wedding and place fresh flowers all around to make it more romantic and cozy.

Gina and I relaxed in the Jacuzzi on the sun deck for a while before going to our room. Sloan gave us the master stateroom which had an off-white queen-sized platform bed with matching his and hers dressers, a queen-sized sofa and a full sized private bathroom.

Later that evening we went to another concert. I wrapped my arms around Gina and sang along with Jeffery Osborne while he sang "We Both Deserve Each Other's Love." She turned around and I stole a kiss even though she seemed distant.

After the concerts, we went to The Royal Cabana Casino for a dance party. I used my celebrity status to get us in without standing in the long line. I was surprised when Gina didn't protest.

She said she hates standing in lines, and if you ask her, it is the only part of my stardom worth writing home about.

"What about the money?" I asked as we walked by two ladies who let us know they had been waiting in line over an hour.

"It's good when you control it and it doesn't control you," Gina said. "Everyone knows the best things in life are free."

I decided to drop the conversation but Sloan said, "Name three."

"Trust. It doesn't cost anything unless you lose it. Freedom. We can vote for whoever we want, and we can voice our opinions about them good or bad, and we don't have to worry about repercussions. Big Mama and them fought hard for our freedom. I don't take it for granted. Air. You can't do shit without that. A few years ago, I would have said water, but have you checked the price of bottled water on this island?"

We all laughed. Sloan doesn't know Gina as well as he thinks. Hell, I don't know her all that well myself. I thought she was going to say love, sex, and laughter, although I'm sure they are in her top ten. She probably could have named twenty things without thinking about it. She had switched to one of her cloud nine moods and I was grateful to be a part of her purple haze.

We found a corner VIP table and ordered champagne. The music was thumping and I was ready to get Gina on the dance floor. She said she had been practicing and Myesha had taught her how to do the butterfly.

The DJ played "Flashlight." Gina pulled me to the floor. I was impressed with her new moves and I picked them up easily. Her booty and long legs were all over the place. Her little brown dress was fitting her like a coat of paint. I could see why I lose my cool every time I make love to her. When she cuts loose, all I can do is enjoy the ride. Her legs moved in and out and her ass and hips gyrated with the beat. I got down and dirty with her. The other couples cleared the area and cheered us on. The DJ played "I Want to Thank you" by Alisha Myers. Gina danced and serenaded me. I was honored even though she was off-key. After the song ended I pulled her into my arms.

"Whew, you're killing me out here. Keep it up and I'll take you on this dance floor." She let out a raucous laugh and led the way to the table. I love to hear her laugh.

Rick was sitting at our table with his arms around Bee and Tee. They were drinking champagne and chatting with Rolonda and Sloan.

I squeezed Gina's hand and said, "Let's go to the yacht?"

"And miss the fun? Hell no!"

Gina flashed Bee and Tee a chilly smile. I poured her the last glass of champagne and whispered, "Behave yourself."

The twins held out their hands and said, "I'm, Bee. And I'm, Tee," as if they had never meet Gina before.

"I remember the message you left on Don's machine," Gina said. Sloan flashed me an oh-shit-look. Gina flashed a chilly stare in my direction, and said, "It's nice to meet you again. Are you all having a good time?"

"The best. Rick is nice." Tee said.

"But Don is better," Bee added as she did a suggestive trick with the little balls in her tongue. I doubt if anyone saw Gina flinch, she was subtle, but that's one of the other things I love about her. On the other hand, Ro's smile looked and felt more like a pit bull's snarl than a friendly gesture.

Gina took a sip of champagne. "Don is great. There is no point in disputing the truth." She ran her fingers through her hair and held her hand up until the light caught the fire in her engagement ring and her eyes. Sloan smiled.

"You're one lucky ho," Bee said. I said a prayer. Sloan said oh shit out loud and Ro growled like a rabid dog.

Gina cocked her head. "Excuse me?" She was calm, cool and collected, but her right eyebrow shot up and the fire in her eyes erupted into flames. She took a quick breath and lowered her eyebrow. I realized I was holding my breath and exhaled.

"What did you have to do to hook that golden rod? All the hoes are gonna cry if y'all get married," Bee said.

I held my breath again, along with Rick and Sloan--I know them well. Gina leaned toward Bee and looked her square in the eyes. She took a sip of champagne. I thought she was going to toss it in Bee's face. I should have said something because my boys were looking at me, but they don't know Gina. She looked at me the way she did right before our first kiss, and then she smiled and turned to Bee.

"I suggest you invest your money with Kimberly-Clark, because there are no ifs, ands, or buts about Don and me getting married. Isn't that right, sweetie?"

I spoke up quickly. "That's right, baby. One kiss from Gina and she had put her mojo on me and stole my heart forever." I winked at Gina. She had done well. She smiled at me and I figured I had done okay. Rick and Sloan let out a sigh of relief and Rolonda relaxed in her chair.

Rick and I went to the bar to fetch champagne. When we returned to the table everyone was talking and laughing like longtime friends. The twins made goo-goo eyes at me all night, but I only had eyes for Gina. Rolonda wanted to take it to the streets, but Gina kept reminding her to be a lady. I kept Gina on the dance floor long as I could stand it.

"It's amazing how pleasant people can get when you don't let them take you to those dark places where they live," Gina whispered while she nibbled on my ear and rubbed my bone. Everyone was watching us yet they were oblivious. We hung out until four in the morning.

Sloan invited everyone to the yacht for breakfast. I was the head chef and Rick and Sloan were my assistants. By the end of the night even Rick understood why I was head over heels in love with Gina, and Bee and Tee seemed to like her as well. They kept telling her how lucky she is. Gina fell asleep on the sofa before the eggs were ready. Ro wasn't buying Bee and Tee's bullshit. After I put Gina to bed, all hell broke loose.

CHAPTER 31

Direct and to the Point

T he next morning, I lay in bed next to Don and studied him while he slept. He looked serene wearing nothing but my earrings. There is nothing gawky about Mr. Stokes. Everything about him is proportionally big in a nice way. I still can't believe he chose me out of all the beautiful women who have obviously crossed his path. Heck, some of them did more than cross it. Some of them did some things I've only dreamed about. That's my Don, he knows how to make the impossible possible. He rocked my world and nothing has been the same since. I propped up on my elbow to get a better view. He didn't open his eyes when he pulled me closer and asked what I was smiling about.

"Us." I pressed my naked body next to his. "Hold me tighter--I'm in the mood for love."

His eyes popped open and he smiled from shore to shore. "When I make love to you again, Gina, I want you to be absolutely sure you're ready for all the love I have to give and all the changes that go with it."

"I'm sure about us. It's the changes that I'm working on." He kissed me on my forehead and said, "In that case go back to sleep."

"What! So it's like that? If I agreed to do a threesome, and pierce my tongue, and nipples, would that make your blood flow?"

"No, Gina. It's too early in the morning to get into that now. Go back to sleep." He pulled the covers over his head and turned over.

I choked back tears. "What if I pierced my clit? I'll have to make the ultimate sacrifice for our love anyway. My heart is ready and willing to give up everything to be your wife, but my mind--now that's a different story."

"We'll have to discuss this later--I'm too tired to get into it now."

"Sweetie, I want to find a way to make it work between two states, but you're not making it easy, and scenes like yesterday make it impossible. Right now, I want to be so deep in your love that nothing else matters."

He didn't say anything so I kicked him. "Are their clits pierced too?" He still didn't answer. "I saw a patient who broke her front tooth with the metal balls in her pierced tongue, you wanna explain that shit to me, Don!"

"Go back to sleep, Gina, I just got in the bed. We can talk about this later."

"Did Rick and the twins spend the night here? Did y'all have an orgy without me?"

"Rolonda threw them overboard. Now will you go back to sleep?"

I sat up in the bed and pulled the sheet with me. "What!"

"After you fell asleep Tee decided to massage my shoulders. Rolonda called Bee and Tee disrespectful whores and a bunch of other lewd names that I can't repeat this early in the morning. She called me a few as well."

"I slept through all of that?"

"Not quite."

"Did I say something to them? Sometimes I talk in my sleep."

"No. the commotion woke you up. You staggered to the room, took off your clothes and fell into bed."

"Too much champagne. What else happened?"

"I loved you all night long that's why I'm so tired. You don't remember?" He turned around and slipped his arms around me and tickled my butt with the tips of his fingers, but a five-star alarm had already gone off in my head.

"Liar! I would have woke-up for that. Why did Ro call you names?"

"She said she was looking out for you."

Anger rose in my throat like vomit.

"I love you, Gina. Your girl was bugging. You should have heard her. I thought she was Wall Street, not alley trash. We were just hanging out. Tee was with Rick. I want to marry you. I would never disrespect you. I love you." He sat up and looked me in the eyes. The plea in his eyes was real.

"What did Ro say?" I asked through clinched teeth.

"She said I had better start acting like I love you and stop flaunting my hoes, or I would lose you."

"And what did you say?"

"I told everyone to leave including your girl. I told Rick to take Tee and Bee home because Rolonda was going off."

I wrapped the covers around me tighter. My head fell back and my eyes rolled to the ceiling. Men are so damn stupid sometimes--even when they love you--shit, mostly when they love you.

"Because my girl was going off? You should have fucking gone off on the bitches at the damn beach!" I yelled.

I snatch the sheet off Don, hopped out the bed, wrapped the sheet around my shoulders, and ran to the bathroom. The door slammed. I locked it. I need privacy when I get pissed off, which is why I try not to let too many things upset me. I'll fuck a bitch up before she or I realize she is getting her ass kicked. I leaned on the door and did my deep breathing exercises. The shit wasn't working. I was ready to kick ass yesterday on the beach and last night--that's why I drank too much champagne. Hell, all women have a little bitch in them. I try to keep mine under cover--I'm a professional. I'm not one of those, I'll-fuck-your-man-just-because-I-can bitches, but I'll fuck a bitch up if she messes with my stuff; just ask that skinny white girl I caught Bobby with--that bitch showed me how to suck dick using cucumbers. She told me to give him fellatio, then she gave him the whole shoo-bang--she was supposed to be my friend.

Don knocked on the door. "Gina, are you okay?"

Hell nawl, I said, but not out loud. I was starting to cool off. I don't like being angry with Don. He's just a playboy who doesn't know a whole lot about love, but he's trying.

"Gina, I'm sorry. Please come out."

I took a few more deep breaths. It was starting to work. I unlocked the door and walked into his arms.

"She wasn't trying to seduce me. She was massaging my shoulders. What was I supposed to do?"

"Sending them home with Rick doesn't mean a damn thing to girls like that. You have to take away their last hope. Otherwise every time they see a crack in the door they're going to try to creep in. You have to be direct and to the point--you can't be nice!" Don squeezed me closer and tried to kiss me. I turned away. I wanted to kiss him but he wasn't kissing his way out of this after he had turned me down.

"Women like that don't mind creeping. They don't give a damn if we're married, or engaged, or whatever. You let them think there was a slight possibility and that was all they needed. You need to nip that crap in the bud before it gets started. I'm not going to be with you all the time. You have to prove to me that I don't have to worry."

"Are you angry?"

What the fuck do you think, I thought, but I didn't say. Instead I said, "Nope."

He made another motion to kiss me. I turned away.

"You have to let those bitches know you're no longer available."

"You want to make love?" he asked while he nibbled at my neck.

Hell yeah. I was as horny as a nymphomaniac. But I said, "Nope."

"Are you sure you're not upset?" I didn't answer.

"Baby, if I can be this close to you and keep my hands to myself you don't have to worry about me creeping, because you got it like that."

I flashed Don a salacious smile. "I got it like that?"

"Gina, I love you like that." He smiled. "This is torture, but I want you to be sure you can live with the consequences. Baby, I will never love anyone else knowing that you love me."

"Are you sure you're ready for only one woman in your bed?"

He kissed my forehead. "There's a lot more to my loving than what is between the sheets. I'm not gonna blow what we have over some crap."

"You learn fast, Mr. Stokes." I tiptoed and kissed him. "Now go back to sleep. It pisses me off to blow a whole day angry."

Don laughed and hopped back in the bed. I followed with my sheet. He started a tickle fight. We laughed until I begged him to stop. Afterwards we kissed until I was at the breaking point, but he stopped and said, "I'm sure that I love you. I want you to be as sure as I am."

"I'm sure about us. Trust me, if I wasn't, last night would have been a different story. I was so glad to see you there was no way in hell I was going to let a couple of your hussies ruin our day."

"Gina, women have used me for their pleasures as much as I have used them. You may have even been guilty. I think we got past the sex and found love. Baby, I just want you to be sure. Being a basketball wife can be hard. I've seen several friends go through divorces. You don't have to worry about me risking this good thing we have going over sexing some groupie. I can't promise you prefect, but I can promise you my best because you bring out the best in me. If you come to Phoenix it will be easier for us to be together, if you stay in Connecticut we won't see each other often, but at least Myesha and Kevin's lives won't be disrupted again."

He stroked my cheek and played in my wild hair. His eyes said he was being honest but most of all they wanted me to understand that he understands. I drifted back to sleep while he rubbed my back and I listened to his heart pounding in my ear.

Later in the day we went to the last beach party to relax and to work on our tans. Don's fans kept stopping to say hello, ask for autographs, or to take pictures with him. After a while, he asked me to take a walk.

We stopped at the Pelican Pier an open bar on the beach with a rustic straw roof. The Reggae was too loud, but we took a seat at the bar and ordered two pinã coladas. Don sipped on his drink and tapped his fingers to the beat even though his mind seemed to be elsewhere. A few of his fans strolled by and stopped. After a while the place was crowded. The bartender gave us more drinks on the house. I suppose I could add freebies to my super-star benefits list, but I doubt if it matters to someone who makes sixty million bucks. The bartender sat a third round of drinks before us. Don drank four drinks then he took me by the hand and led me to the beach. He had been quiet since our morning fight.

"Are you okay?" I asked.

"I have to leave tomorrow. I didn't know what to expect when I came, but I had prayed for a miracle."

"What exactly did you pray for?"

"I prayed that you would come to Phoenix. I want us to be one big happy family under one roof. I don't want to pressure you. It's still your decision. You can trust me, but it feels like you're slipping away."

He had stated exactly what he wanted and I couldn't deliver. Later that evening we went to the last concerts featuring George Clinton. We tried to recapture the magic of the previous two nights. We weren't in a party mood so we went back to the yacht.

The first time we were together there had been higher forces leading the way. Those forces were stirring us when Don pulled me up from the sofa in the salon. We slow danced but there wasn't any music. We didn't need any. We swayed back and forth to the beat of our hearts while our bodies screamed, "surrender." When we met again in April, I had surrendered. I wanted to get over my blues. I wanted sex. I wanted Don. Now, I need to surrender to our love fully or set it free. Those are my choices. We held each other tight and rocked from side to side, afraid to speak, afraid to let go, afraid to surrender. We swayed and eased fears. Then Don's warm sweet lips covered mine. His hands were all over me. Mine had already memorized every inch of him. He pulled me to him, then he let me go, yet his eyes begged me to stay. A clock ticked loudly in the background and reminded us that time was running out. I removed Don's shirt. He unbuttoned my blouse one button at a time. His eyes asked if I was ready. The pain of losing Charles was still fresh, and this new pain Don had put in my heart was like a fresh paper cut. He unhooked my bra and slid it off so gently it felt like our first time.

Sloan entered the room. Don and I searched franticly for our discarded clothes.

"We thought you guys went out," Don said.

"Rolonda wasn't feeling well. I dropped her off. I didn't mean to interrupt. I, uh, need to talk to you for a minute."

"Go ahead. Gina and I don't have any secrets."

"Gina was letting you have it this morning when Jason called so I didn't think it was a good time to tell you his sister has gotten worse. He went ahead and changed you all's flights to go to New Orleans a day early. All the flights out of Aruba are booked. We'll have to go to Puerto Rico tonight."

Don covered me while I slipped my arms back into my blouse. Sloan didn't appear to be bothered, but I pushed my bra between the sofa cushions. I packed my things and told Don to fetch my bra when Sloan wasn't around. I wanted to go with him. There should be an easier way for us to be together. We kissed, and kissed. Our time had run out.

When I went back to the resort, Troy had left me five urgent messages. The dead police officer's truck had been found in the swamp, exhumed, and his investigation was proceeding full speed ahead.

CHAPTER 32

Satisfy Your Woman

$\mathcal{L}$ ila's head was bald, but it was her wide set eyes and rich brown skin like Jason's and Valerie's that made my chest heave. Jason had tears in his eyes when he hugged them, and I wished with all my heart that Gina could have us a baby. We brought Lila roses, a Beanie bear, and gourmet jelly beans. "I hope you don't get cavities from the candy," I said.

"Don't worry. My mom can fix them," Jason added.

I was pleasantly surprised when Jason called Gina Mom, but I hoped he wasn't suppressing any anger toward Valerie. God knows that I was.

After our first visit, I had blood drawn. I wasn't a match, but I couldn't sit around New Orleans for a week and do nothing. Jason liked Lila and so did I. We went to Channel 6 where I made a public appeal on Lila's behalf. Valerie thanked me for my efforts when we returned to the hospital. I made sure she knew I was doing it for the children and for Gina, but I didn't mean to make her cry.

"I'm sorry I abandoned Jason," she said. "The only peace I've had since that day has been my love for Lila."

I put Jason in Lila's place. Where was her heart when he needed a mother? I wanted to hate her; she's lucky Gina has cracked my heart of stone.

"God hates me for what I did to you and Jason. Lila's father died in Iraq before she was born, and now she is dying."

I held Valerie while she cried in the hallway of Tulane University Medical Center. People passing probably thought someone had died.

"Jason is a great kid. I don't have any regrets," I said even though I didn't feel sorry for her.

"I didn't want to leave Jason, but your mother threatened to tell the school and my husband. I couldn't take that chance."

"What?"

"Edna let me see Jason when he was a baby, but when he started school she said it was better for him not to see me."

I knew Mom had threatened Valerie, but I didn't know she had tricked her into giving Jason up. Mom loves kids.

"Your mother sent me pictures, and I always send him gifts for his birthday and Christmas. I wanted him back, but she said you would fight and I would lose in more ways than one."

I thought I had created another burden for Mom while I was away in college. She loves Jason and me. She was wrong, but she did what she thought was best for us. She did what any loving mother would have done. Didn't she?

I hated Valerie, but Jason was always a joy. I used to shut down whenever he asked about his mother. I couldn't think of anything positive to say about a mother who would abandon her child.

"Don't cry. I'll help you find a donor for Lila. I promise." I gave her my handkerchief. "Lila needs you to stay strong." She wiped her face. "Let's check on the kids," I said.

Lila was asleep, and Jason was standing by the window staring into space. "Would you like to spend some time with Valerie before we leave?" I asked.

"Sure, why not?" Jason said.

"Is that okay with you, Valerie?"

She looked up from her paper. "I would love that. Thanks."

"What are you gonna do, Dad?"

"I'm gonna find myself some Gumbo and a cold brew. Then I might go shopping for a little something-something for Gina."

"Could you get her a thank you gift for me?"

"I can handle that. I'll pick you up around eleven."

I went to Dooky Chase, and since I was feeling sorry for myself, I ordered gumbo, a seafood platter with the works, and praline pudding for dessert. I downed three glasses of sweet tea before it sent me to the men's room. I was deep in my misery, when a guy bumped me from behind just as I was getting ready to take a leak.

"Watch out, man."

"Maybe Gina isn't the classy woman I thought she was. Why she took up with someone like you is beyond me?"

The night of the thunderstorm rushed to my mind. Gina said she had vexed him, but that's beside the point.

"Look, man, you don't want to fuck with me!"

"Why are you wearing Gina's earrings? Are you one of those funny bunnies who can't decide which side of the fence to hop on?" He grabbed his nuts and made a hunching motion toward me. "You want some of this?"

I had to piss too bad to laugh, and this muthafucka was blocking the urinal. I was already mad at the world, and this prick was in my face begging for an ass whipping. "Look, man, I don't want to hurt you."

He chuckled. "Now I understand why you can't keep a woman like Gina satisfied."

I laughed in spite of my other urgent needs. "She's gonna marry me. I must be doing something right."

Troy grunted. "That's not how it looked the last time I saw her. I kissed her and her nipples were as hard as rocks. She kissed me like she was starving for love."

I wanted to feed that muthafucka my right hook, but adding assault and battery to my growing list of problems wasn't going to help me convince Gina to move to Phoenix. I flashed Troy a threatening look, then I stepped around him and used the john.

"Stay away from my woman," I said. "The wedding is June thirtieth, at six p.m. I don't recall getting your confirmation back."

Troy grunted again and left in a huff.

When a woman says no, she means no. I don't give a damn how taut her nipples are. She may have been cold, or scared. Hell, nipples don't have a brain any more than pricks like him. Sometimes the brain gets its adrenaline rushes crossed. One time I hit one of those incredible shots and my shit got hard as a muthafucka.

I was hanging out in the French Quarter when a woman dressed like a gypsy approached me and said, "I have information about your future that you need to know." I'm not a believer but I was curious so I let her read my palms. She said

I'm going to marry someone with strange but special qualities, and we're going to have five children. She was off on the children, but on the money about Gina. She said we would be separated for a while, but in the end things would turn out better than we dreamed. For a small fee the priestess hooked me up a gris-gris bag, and she gave me instructions that amounted to praying and having faith to help her predictions along.

I found bubble bath, scented candles, and a red silk night gown for Gina. She looks cute in peach and pink, but red, black, and animal prints--have mercy!

I didn't go into Valerie's apartment. I stayed away from the same lonely eyes she had years ago when we made Jason. All I wanted was to go back to the hotel, crawl into bed, and listen to Gina's sweet voice and giggles.

Jason was quiet when he got into the car. "Is everything okay?" I asked.

"Yep."

"You wanna tell me about it?"

"Did you love Valerie when--you know?"

"I love you. That's what matters. Did you ask her?"

"Wanted to ask you." Jason stared out the window and sat on the edge of his seat the same nerve-racking way as Gina.

"You didn't ask Valerie any questions?"

"Nope. She has enough to worry about."

"Are you worried about Lila?"

"Yep."

"Are you okay about Valerie and me?" He gazed out the window and didn't answer. "It was a long time ago, Jason. I love you. Mom loves you too, probably more than you will ever know. I don't have any regrets. I hope you won't have any regrets about coming here."

After ten minutes of silence he said, "Valerie is a good cook." I jumped from the sound of his new manly voice. Jason has grown into a man with very little help from me or his mother. "Is Gina a good cook?"

I chuckled. "Tell Mom to give you some cooking lessons."

"That bad, huh?"

"I'm not complaining." Jason had dried tear streaks on his face when he got out the car.

CHAPTER 33

When I'm Not Around

The nightmares have been keeping me awake since Troy left that disturbing message about exhuming the policeman's car a few days ago. He caught me off guard again when the ringing phone woke me from yet another night of restless sleep. He wanted to know if the names of the boys and the little girl come to me in my dreams. I hadn't washed the crusty stuff out the corners of my eyes, and the drool off my face, and I certainly wasn't in the mood to talk to him. "No names, I just see how they all died," I said flatly.

"Didn't you say your father was on the ground when the shots that killed the police officers were fired?"

"I don't remember telling you they were policemen. They were white men, with blue eyes like yours! They're fucking nightmares. They change. I'm on vacation, for God's sake! Do we have to talk about this now?"

"I didn't mean to ruin your vacation. I was trying to help. Did I tell you there were no skeletal remains in the missing car that was exhumed from the swamp?"

"No, and I don't want to hear anymore? You're the damn expert, just do what you do, and leave me out of it! Look, Troy, I don't want your help anymore. You're making the nightmares worse not better."

"I'm sorry, Gina, when I started this investigation I didn't expect to find anything, but I have to admit that cold cases really get me excited. I'll fill you in when you're in a better mood. Enjoy your vacation, if I were your man I would be there with you." he said, and then he hung up.

My last night in Aruba was filled with the worst nightmares of them all. The boys and Big Papa were talking at the same time. It seemed as if hundreds of voices were telling me what to do. They were praying, arguing and shouting at the same time. Then all the voices blended into oms. The oms got louder and louder as they took over my body. Then the praying, shouting, and the oms stopped. The little girl takes the gun from that officer's holster. The boys shouted, "Do it--it's you or them!" Big Papa shouted, "No! She's too young," but the boys said, "Kill them so they can't do it again." And Big Papa asked, "Who will take care of her?" And the boys shouted, "We will! Do it! Do it before it is too late!" A fetter deep within me squeezed with all its might. I was the little girl who looks like me again, my little guts did things my mind didn't command it to do. The officers' chests exploded. Blood covered my skin, and blue eyes stayed suspended in my mind while the boys sang "Amazing Grace."

My screams scared the hell out of Ro when I sprang up from my sweat soaked mattress. I couldn't wait to go home. I wanted to be in Don's arms, but I didn't want to marry him with this hanging over my head. If anyone can prove that my family, dead or alive, killed those men Troy can!

I watched Don's appeal for Lila on CNN and caught up on the news while I unpacked. I'm treating Sharon to a day at Lady Ester's Spa tomorrow. We're getting full body massages, facials, our hair styled, and I'm getting an herbal mud pack to counter the effects of too much sun. The phone rang when I slid under my covers.

"I know it's late, but I wanted to make sure you got home okay." Don sounded like soul music to my ears even though he was wining the blues.

"Is everything okay?" I asked.

"I need you beside me, Gina. It's rough when we're apart for too long."

"It's rough for me, as well. Is Lila okay?"

"She's stable. Do you still have my back?"

"Of course, I do. What's wrong?"

He told me the long version of what happened with Edna and Valerie, and the short version about running into Troy.

"Jason is a wonderful kid, and Edna has done a great job raising him. You can't change the past, sweetie, but you can control the way it affects his heart. The important person is Jason, and he is doing fine."

"That's why I love you, Gina."

I decided not to confirm that I had done more than kiss Troy that evening. Hell, I'm still kicking myself for telling Troy about my nightmares.

"Are you okay? You don't sound like yourself," Don said.

"I'm okay. I miss you. I didn't sleep well after you left."

"I wish I could see you tonight. Do your nipples get hard when I'm not around?"

I giggled. "Do I have to swear on a stack of Bibles? Why do you want to know that?"

"No Bibles, but I just need to know."

"Yes, usually when I think about you, but sometimes when I'm excited, cold, or scared. What about you?"

"Same answer. Gina, you keep me centered. You're my strength. Your words kissed my pain and made it better."

"Is that your way of saying you love me?" I grinned from ear-to-ear. His words were better than "I love you." Don had finally stopped fighting this thing we have about us. He had finally given me his trust. His words were from the heart. He was letting me break his fall. He was letting me know that he has my back, and now I'm the one who doesn't trust him with my secrets.

"It's my way of saying I more than love you. I need you. We should be together, Gina."

He lifted a huge burden when he said those words. Now we have the kind of love that will keep us together over the long haul. We can make it through the better and the worse. We have what it's going to take to keep us together long after sex becomes good more times than great. Now I can rest easy at night knowing I can count on him when I need to get through a crisis so why can't I tell him what I did?

I didn't have any nightmares that night, just knowing that Don would be there if I need him helped me rest better. The next day at the spa Sharon cut off her long gorgeous hair and saved it to make a wig for her best friend who has ovarian cancer. I used to wish I had Sharon's long silky hair and beautiful black skin when we were little girls. Other than those two things we could pass for twins. I grew up hearing, "black is beautiful" and "the blacker the berry the sweeter the juice" mostly from Sharon, but with our huge age difference she has always been my big sister/mother. She always gave it to me straight and I've always loved her more than I let her know. I was a raspberry in a blackberry world. I felt out of place. The funny thing is: Sharon used to wish she looked like me. My eyes got misty, not because my sister was almost bald, but because we had wasted so much time worrying about the wrong things.

After we left the spa we stopped at the Westfield Mall to take pictures for our parents. The Ebony and Ivory twins were back. We skipped lunch for ice cream sundaes at Friendly's before going home. A red Flying Spur Bentley was parked next to my Land Rover when we got home. The license plate said MRS DGS. I ran inside to find Don.

Jason was in the kitchen. We hugged. "Thanks for convincing Dad to take me to see Lila and Valerie." His eyes were emotional. I was still hugging him when I noticed Don in the doorway.

Our eyes met. He smiled. I smiled. The smell of his cologne made my mind drift back to the last time we made love. I needed some big time.

He removed my hands from Jason's shoulders. "Sorry, kid. Get your own girl." I pulled him into my arms and hugged him tight. His hard body felt like my Astrabeds mattress pressing against me. He found my lips, and when we came up for air, Sharon and Jason had disappeared.

We smooched in the kitchen until Kevin and Myesha came home from school. I hadn't seen my babies in two weeks. I jumped from Don's lap to give them a few hugs and kisses. I told Kevin and Myesha about my trip even though there wasn't much to tell after the concerts, Don's brief visit, my walks on the beach, snorkeling, the damn nightmares, my suntan which was already peeling, and my shopping sprees with Rolonda.

We went to my bedroom. I divided up my borrowed treasures. The kids left with their Aruba T-shirt and caps, and diamond and gold goodies. Don pouted until I placed an 18k gold chain with a gold lock and a charm that said "MARRIED" around his neck. He said it was a scarecrow to keep his other honeys away. I doubted if it would work without some help on his part. Sharon broke up our reunion when she gave me the phone and said it was Ida Mae.

"I hear you're still trying to be Little Miss Independent," Mother said.

"I'm at the crossroads and I don't know which way to go." Don left the room. "I love Don, but I've worked hard to make my business a success."

"If you love him you'll have to be his wife first."

"Mom, that's so old school. Why can't I have both?" I pouted even though I hated that she could still make me feel like a child.

"Sugar, there are women who won't care if Don is married, and some who will be happy that he is. Don't make it harder on yourself than it needs to be. If your father was tempted don't think Don won't be."

"Humph." I remembered the rumors about Daddy cheating. That was the other cause of my teenage rebellions and fears.

"You can't tell me you get that much satisfaction from pulling teeth and doing root canals. There are plenty people in Arizona who have teeth that need fixing."

"You're right, but I can't walk away from a lucrative business. Besides, it's only three years."

"Life doesn't wait on you, sugar, you have to grab it when it's given to you. Look at poor Charles."

"I'm not a kid, Mother, I'll find a way to make it work. I've talked to Erica. She is going to join my practice. We can create a family legacy with the practice like Big Mama did with the funeral home. Who knows maybe Myesha will join us down the road."

"That would be wonderful, but don't ever forget that a woman's primary duties are her family. I don't care what profession and how many degrees you all have if things aren't right at home you're not going to be happy."

"Humph. I'll find a way to keep my business and Don."

"I hope so because if you don't, some other woman will."

"Is that what you did, Mother?" I didn't want to know about that part of my parents' lives. It was my way of reminding her that our lives weren't as perfect as she taught me to pretend.

"It's not the same. Your daddy had a lot of pressure on his back. He was a different man after we moved out of Big Mama's home. Besides, I had my--comfort."

I knew Ida Mae had it in her. I thought about the old blues song she used to play that asks: Who's making love to your old lady while you were out making love?

"I love you, Mother. Take care of my Daddy. And don't worry about me--I'll do what I can live with."

"I know you will, sugar. Don't worry about your daddy. With all the running around he did he always found his way home to me and you girls." I grunted again and clicked off. His body was there, but he sure as hell wasn't, at least not for me. He would shut me out every time I tried to talk to him.

In the meantime, Sharon had cornered Don in the kitchen. "Cute charm. So, Gina is gonna marry you after all. Well, let me tell you what you're getting into," Sharon said. Don frowned.

"Don't worry, she loves you, Bro. She can be a pain in the ass sometimes, but if she gives up everything to be with you--you better keep her happy."

"That's not a problem," Don said.

"I used to be jealous of Gina because she appeared to have it together in the relationship department. I never realized all the sacrifices she made to keep it together. That's how she ended up in Connecticut. Now, here she goes again following her heart. You guys are moving too fast for me. I don't think I could stand seeing her heartbroken again so you better be a man and stand by your words."

I peeped around the corner and continued to eavesdrop when Sharon continued. "She doesn't look tough, but she'll kick your ass and cry doing it."

"I know what you mean."

"She can be soft and sweet one minute and a hell raiser the next. I used to think she had multiple personalities. Did she tell you about the ghosts?"

"Ghosts? No but I've seen her feisty side."

"So, are you one hundred percent sure she is the one and only one for you?"

Eavesdropping was proving to be a good way to get information. Sharon continued before Don could answer.

"Gina and I have had our moments of jealousy; all sisters have them. She used to cling to every word I said. I made mistakes along the way and I didn't think I should give her advice, but she told me my advice saved her from a lot of heartache. Didn't help my black ass none, but Gina did okay. I protected Gina, we all did. That's what big sisters do best. I don't know everything about you, Don, but I know Gina loves you. So, here's the deal--if you break her heart, I'll break your gotdamn neck!"

I stepped around the corner. They looked as guilty as sin; I probably did too. I walked over to Don and nibbled on his ear. "I want to feel you touching me there," I whispered.

"Now?" He licked his lips. "I can't spend the night. I'm gonna make a national appeal for Lila on Good Morning America." He pursed his lips again and I wished I could make him a baby girl with his dimples and soft lips and my legs. He would have more trouble keeping the boys away from her than Daddy had with Sharon and me. He can kiss me anyway, anywhere, anytime and we should have something to show for it.

He glanced at his watch. "We don't have enough time?"

"Not now, silly. By the time I get to Phoenix," I sang.

"You're coming?"

"Can't let my man go alone. There are too many skeezers who would love to make things hotter than they already are out there."

"I knew you would come." He smiled broadly and said, "You know you're hooked on me, girl." He slipped his arm around my waist and pulled me to him. "I bought you a wedding gift."

"You did?"

"The Bentley is for you. It's loaded so you can get around town in style."

I kissed him. "You knew I would come?" We kissed again. "You think you know me after this short time? Well, let me tell you something, mister, Sharon gave you a few hints and warnings, but stick around, I promise to make your life seriously interesting." He cupped my butt and squeezed as he pressed me to him. "I see I'm not the only one who is hooked."

"Baby, I was hooked on you the first time I got lost in your big sad eyes." He licked his lips again. "I took the sadness out of your eyes even though sometimes I'm not sure if you are making love to me or to Charles."

Sharon held up a finger and tiptoed out the kitchen with her head bowed like the little old ladies do at church.

"I appreciate the way you take time to understand me and my problems and lend your support. I meant what I said last night. I love you and a whole lot more. I knew you would come; I can't be the only one feeling like this."

"I have to phase out of my office gradually. My niece is finishing dental school next month. She was planning to do a general practice residency. She will get just as much experience working with me. She is coming soon to take the Northeast Regional Boards, if she pass, she can get a license to practice in Connecticut. It will take some time. I would like to stick around for a while to make the transition smooth. Even though I can't move right away, at least I have a good plan."

"I hope it won't take too long."

"I'll need something to keep me busy while you're traveling. I'm not gonna be your typical housewife. I tried it when Myesha was born--being a full-time housewife and mother was the hardest work I've ever done. I envy women who can do it and be happy, but it's not me."

"We can work the details out later. I want you to be happy."

"Okay, I'm ready to test drive my Bentley." I held my hand out. "Keys please."

"I ain't like them other niggas, and I ain't 'bout to play no games." blasted from the speakers when I turned the ignition. Don turned the sound down and blamed Jason. I turned it back up and sped away. *"Who you love? Tell me who you fucking love. Tell meeee who you wanna fucking love?"* We bobbed our heads to the lustful sounds of Big Sean, Chris Brown, Ty Dolla $ign and me. I was in the mood for a fast ride and some good loving. *"Hit you with the 99 like it's fucking primetime."* A quickie in my wedding present would be nice after two weeks of sun and beach and no sex. *"I got some thangs I wanna do to youuuuu…"* I rubbed Don's thigh as I sang along. I hopped on Route 9 and headed to Hammonasset Beach where we could watch the sunset and smooch in the back.

I soared at 80mph up the hills and cruised down them. Don was quiet and probably scared shitless from the look on his face. Charles hated my driving. Men think they are the only ones who can be reckless. Ida Mae had her secrets, and I have mine. I jammed the brakes. Don looked at me as though I was crazy. I laughed like the wicked old witch from the West. I was in a rare mood.

"I got a two-hundred-dollar ticket over this next hill." I reached for Don's hand and placed it in the heavy petting zone. "You down for a quickie in the back?"

"Hell no! What if we get caught?"

The cops were waiting at the bottom of the hill. I creeped by them doing a cool 55mph, then I took the next exit and turned around to go back home. I pushed the pedal to the metal all the way home. My mood had changed. It didn't have anything to do with multiple personalities. A woman in love, and a true Cancer, is a euphemism for moodiness. It's the stuff that makes us tick, and the stuff men like Don crave. He thinks I'm adventurous. Hell, I'm just horny for him.

I came to a squeaking stop in the garage. "I love it." I gave Don a make-me-wanna-holler-throw-up-both-my-hands kiss like our first kiss, and hopped out. I was in the mood again, but I would be damned if I was going to make another offer.

"Chicken," I said. I flapped my wings. "Baaark, bark, bark, bark bark!"

"I ain't scared of nothing."

"Except dentists, needles, and police. Baaark!"

Don reached for me. I ran into the kitchen and locked him in the mud room. That will teach him to be cautious when I'm in the mood.

He hung out with the kids while I helped Sharon make seafood gumbo. I made the rice and chopped the onions and okra.

I gave him another make-me-wanna-holler kiss and he forgot about being angry. We smooched and made plans for our futures after dinner. We decided to spend the summer between Connecticut and New York except for the two weeks of Don's basketball camp in Chicago. We picked a long weekend for me to fly to Arizona to look at houses and schools. Don gave me the gifts he purchased in New Orleans, and since I was still in the mood I slipped on the silk gown and lit the candles. I threw in a few I-wanna-holler kisses, but Don Stokes got me hot and bothered and said, "Baby, there are too many people around."

I threw a sweater over my shoulder and slipped on my red hot-mama sandals. I didn't care if I looked like a lady of the night, I grabbed my purse and said, "Let's go to the Marriott I'm in a screaming mood."

"I have to get back to the city. If we go, I'll never make it back in time."

"Let's go to the Grantmoor and get a quick stay."

"I'm not gonna take you to some sleazy motel. What do you know about those places?"

"Forget you, Don." I flung my sweater off and kicked my shoes across the room like Patti LaBelle. He ducked, and I missed his big head. I slumped on the chaise lounge next to the fireplace and pouted.

He reached for me and pulled me up. "I want you to be sure hot sex isn't the only thing we have before we get married."

We decided not to make love until I was sure. I'm sure now, so what's your problem?"

"I have to get up early." He put on his shirt.

"I'm hooked on you because you're a wonderful caring man who happens to be a fantastic lover."

I gave Don a few more please-make-me-holler kisses, but he pulled his pants on, kissed me on my damn forehead and left me horny and confused.

CHAPTER 34

When Something Is Wrong
with My Baby

*S*omething was different about Gina, and it is going to bug the hell out of me until I figure it out. She didn't bother to walk me downstairs. I kissed her goodnight and she slid under the covers. Her eyes were begging me to love her, but I wasn't about to make love to her again in Charles's bed with that scared hungry look in her eyes.

It was late. I sent a text to let her know I was home. She texted me right away.

> Gina: Why wouldn't you make love to me
> Don: Why don't you tell me what happened after I left Aruba
> Gina: I didn't sleep well
> Don: Why
> Gina: Nightmares
> Don: The same one
> Gina: Worse
> Don: I trust you, but I'm not sure if you still trust me
> Gina: I don't want you to think I'm crazy
> Don: Do you see ghost

She didn't answer right away. I was trying to make sense of what Sharon said about ghosts and the men in Gina's past.

Gina: Sometimes

Don: Are you afraid of them

Gina: Afraid of the truths about how they died

Don: The nightmares show you how they died

Gina: Yes

Don: Real murders

Gina: Yes

Don: Family

Gina: Only my great grandfather so far

Don: OMG

Gina: I think that there is a family connection with the little girl dreams. The nightmares about her have always been the hardest on me because she looks like me

Don: Why are the nightmares worse now

Gina: All the police killings in the news lately and Troy found some information about a case that happened in 1964 that seems to match

Just the mention of Troy's name made my blood boil. I wanted to call Gina but she was finally sharing her deepest secrets with me. I was careful not to sound angry with my response text.

Don: Troy is helping you find answers

Gina: I feel foolish for getting him involved, but the boys pointed me in the right direction to help Charles solve their murders

Don: So, Troy found something. You think it involves someone in your family. Now you don't know what to do

Gina: Correct, it happened before I was born but it may involve my father

Don: I'm here to help, okay, if you can't sleep, call me if you have a bad dream, call me, I presume you already tried talking to your dad

Gina: Years ago, but maybe I should try again. Thanks for loving me like this

Don: It's not like I was given a choice

Gina: You always have a choice, mister

Don: Baby, you were so overwhelmingly irresistible I couldn't stop myself from devouring your sweet pleasures

Gina: So, what happened tonight

Don: I didn't finish what you started

Gina: I don't start things I can't finish

Don: You know you seduced me from the start. I ain't complaining though

Gina: I did not seduce you

Don: Yes, you did. You seduced me and you thought you could live with the consequences, but you turned a brother out. You took off your shoes and tempted me with your bare legs and feet. You threw this dog a bone. You drew me in with your big brown sad eyes. Then you put your feet on my lap and teased me. While I was massaging your feet, a calm look came over you. You said, that feels great, but it's not enough. Give me some damn loving. Kiss me, fool, bring me back to life. Just one kiss and I'll make you mine. Come on, sucker, I dare you. And I took what you gave and now I need all of you.

My phone rang two seconds after I pressed send.

"Donald Stokes, you are so full of it."

"It's true. You seduced me. You knew what you were doing."

"I did not!"

"Who had to take a break to think straight?"

Gina let out a shrill laugh. "Don, you are so not right."

"I'm joking, our thang is one hundred percent. We may have started at the finish line but our stuff is tight. Tell Sharon she don't have to worry about breaking my neck. I love ya, girl."

Gina chuckled. "I love you, too, liar."

"Baby, I have to go. I don't want to look as though I made love to you all night. Everyone isn't as beautiful as you after intercourse."

"But you would have had a helluva smile on your face on national TV if you had let me have my way."

"I'll take you up on your offer the next time. Although I don't know when that will be. I have to take care of a bunch of loose ends before we move."

"Go ahead and get in your big old bed all alone. Sleep tight. Don't let the bed bugs bite. If you can't sleep call me. I'll be here in my red gown thinking about my sadomasochistic lover and what could have been." She giggled again and hung up.

Jason woke me up when the limo came to take us to the studio. My mind was on Gina's texts and I had overslept.

Candy jumped into my arms when we walked into the lobby. She smacked me dead on my lips. A camera flashed as she slid down my thigh.

"Long time no see." She still had her nasty girl smirk. "What is up with the rumors about you getting married?"

"All true. The last Saturday in June, you're invited, bring Link." I rested my arm around Jason's shoulder. "This is my son. Jason, Candy is an old friend."

"I love your movies," Jason said, and for a fleeting moment Candy's smirk was for him.

"Don, you're an enigma?" She stared at me and at Jason, and then she burst into laughter. She stopped laughing on a dime and walked away.

The interview went well. I got my plug in for Lila, and when Robin asked about my charm, I told the world I was getting married without giving any details.

Jason and I flew to Chicago after the interview. Jason had school and home-work to make up. Everyone was trying to get in my personal business after I let the cat out the bag. I went to Phoenix to look for a house. Gina had mentioned going to a dental conference in Scottsdale. I checked it out. She had instructed me not to buy anything too extravagant. I had to outdo Charles. I didn't care how much it cost.

I was like a bee buzzing back and forth between Chicago and Phoenix. Gina called every day, twice a day. She still hadn't given me a definite date when she could move to Phoenix. She was busy going to Kevin's games. Taking him and Myesha to music and dance recitals. Helping her niece prepare for the boards and her move to Connecticut. And preparing for our wedding.

Lila was moved to St Jude Children's Research Hospital to try a new clinical trial the day before Gina was supposed to fly to Phoenix for our last premarital fling. I had found a three story 15,000 square feet Mediterranean style eight-bedroom mansion with ten bathrooms, three fireplaces, a media room, gymnasium, game room, and a swimming pool and spa. I had planned to do the closing the morning she arrived and to make love to her in a different room the rest of the weekend until every room had been christened.

I tried to convince Gina to come to Memphis with me and Jason. She had a summer cold that she has been trying to shake for a couple of weeks. She hasn't been sleeping well since she went to Aruba. And lately she has gone from being irritable to damn near evil. I think she needs to see a doctor. She said all she needs is some good loving. She thinks she is just stressed out about the changes she is going through to prepare for marriage to me, and sexual withdrawal. She said she can go without sex for years, but after she gets it good, she needs it like a drug. I figured my plan was working.

CHAPTER 35

Conspiracy Theories

*S*omething was wrong, and I couldn't deny it any longer. Even when I go to bed early, I still can't get up in the mornings. These cold-like symptoms have been lingering for weeks. It was eight a.m. when the phone rang. I should have been up at seven. I moaned, "Hello." My body felt like aliens had invaded it and Don's cheerful disposition didn't help this time.

"Baby, are you okay?"

"I hope you didn't call to pluck my nerves about selling my house because if you did, goodbye."

"You're gonna love the house. So, ah, do you know when you're coming?"

"Christmas, but it makes more sense to wait until the kids are out of school next June. Did I tell you Myesha got accepted into Miss Porter's School? Now Kevin wants to stay here until he finishes high school. Erica can help me out, but I think it will be best to keep the house until everyone is settled."

"Christmas! Next summer! But, I thought..."

"Sweetie, I told you it was gonna take a while. Maybe we should wait until next year."

"Gina! Why did you let me buy this big ass house if you were going to change your mind? What in the hell is wrong with you?"

Bile was in my throat and venom was on my tongue when Don flipped. "I didn't let you buy the frigging house. I told you not to buy anything extravagant. We're not married yet and you already stopped listening!" I slammed the phone down and ran to the bathroom. I regurgitated all over the place. The phone rang again, but by the time I got the virus or panic attack out my system, it had stopped. Don didn't answer when I called him back.

Lila was stable, but Don stayed out West to make sure the house was ready. I had given him the go-ahead to buy the house and hire an interior decorator, but I avoided telling him when I planned to move until now. I showered and got dressed before I called again. He still didn't answer.

I wanted to go back to bed, but bed rest was not an option. Erica was flying in today to prepare to take the boards next week. After she gets the results, she can apply for her license. She will be able to practice by August if all goes well. In the meantime, I will have her shadow me in the practice. By the time she gets her license, we will already have patients scheduled to see her.

Don didn't return my calls. I had nausea almost every morning. The Echinacea tea and burnt toast I had for lunch made me feel better until Patrice rushed into my office. I was helping her write a business plan to get a loan. She wants to start her own personal training and fitness group.

She panted and fanned herself. "There's a fine man with roses in your lobby asking for you, Gina."

"Don is here? That explains why he isn't answering my calls." I grabbed my mirror to make sure I didn't look as bad as I felt.

"It's not Don. It's that fine ass white guy. He looks so much better in person."

My intercom buzzed. "Dr. Hill, Dr. Devaux is here to see you."

"Send him to my office." I released the button. "Stay here, Patrice. Whatever you do don't leave!"

Troy had a bouquet of red roses and a sly grin on his face. He had a great tan. I could see why I hadn't written him off completely. Patrice smiled at Troy and my matchmaker genes were hard at work. "Troy, this is my friend, Patrice."

They gazed at each other and smiled. He undressed her with his eyes, which wasn't hard since her green dress was hugging her perfect body in all the right places.

"It's nice to meet you, Patrice." He kissed her hand. Her eyes seemed to undress him as well. "Will you excuse Gina and me? I need to speak to her alone for a minute."

Patrice seemed to float out of my office. Traitor! Didn't she sense my fear?

Troy gave me the roses and sat on my desk. The smell of the flowers made me feel sick again. "Why did you bite me?" He asked, and I didn't miss the lustful grin on his face.

"Reflex reaction."

"It ruined the moment, but it didn't hurt nearly as bad as your knee."

"Did you come here to tell me that? Yesterday you said it was important."

Troy hopped off my desk and paced the room. "I'm fairly sure that the events you described in your nightmares really happened." We made eye contact and I could feel the burn of his stare on my cheeks. I maintained my poker's stare even though my heart was beating rapidly. Troy cleared his throat. "I've replayed what you told me hundreds of times in my head and I think there is a possibility that the girl may have been the shooter."

I focused on taking normal breaths and holding eye contact while he checked my reaction.

"Your story checks out until that point. You said the men were beating the girl's father, and he was on the ground, which leaves the girl to pull the trigger. It's the only thing that makes sense."

"You're wrong. The boys did it," I said and no one was more shocked than I.

My heart pounded against my chest at three times its regular rate, but my voice didn't quiver when I looked dead into three sets of blue eyes as I spoke. I saw the officers' chests exploding, and I knew the boys had helped the girl do it. I didn't blink while Troy's sharp detective eyes evaluated me. The boys were with me. I could feel them. They have always been there when I needed them most.

"The boys did it?"

"Yep, and they are all dead now, so let it go." They were dead when it happened but everybody knowns that Dead Man's Swamp is haunted. There are more black boys and men bodies dumped there than the morgue, that's how it got its name.

"Why didn't you tell me this before?"

"I wanted you to understand why I was having a problem falling in love with you. Those boys saved the girl's life. You didn't need to know that to understand my story."

"I don't understand what any of this has to do with you loving me. I thought you needed answers."

"I'm sorry I bothered you with it."

"Two policemen are missing, we have their car; did the boys tell you what they did with the bodies?"

"No, but I remember my grandmother saying there were over a dozen skeletons found at the bottom of the swamp after a dry spell in 1968. Maybe they weren't all black. My guess is, there were multiple killings spanning many years. One monkey never stopped the show in Mississippi."

"Troy crossed the room again and stared out the window. "I couldn't find any information about any murdered boys. Are you sure they were murdered?"

"Sheriff Parker classified them as accidental drownings. That's what was put on their death certificates. Do you have any idea how many black men were lynched in Mississippi for looking, saying, or just being black around the wrong people? Nobody on our side of the tracks, were in a position to question Sheriff Parker's findings--anybody who was bold enough would probably end up dead themselves." Charles had found that bit of information.

Troy turned away from me and stared out my window. "You've been living with these nightmares all these years?"

"Yes. We all lived in fear on our side of the tracks. My parents and grandparents didn't trust white people, lots of people still don't. I'm sorry if it's hard for you to comprehend, but trust me, if this information had gotten in the wrong hands my whole family and some probably would have been killed. People are starting to change, but it takes a long time. Lots of people where I'm from are still afraid of change."

"I think I get it now. I don't like it. It's not right. I'm European, none of it makes sense to me."

"Well, if it helps I didn't understand your attraction to me anymore than you understood my fears."

Troy was out of my life, and maybe Don as well. He hasn't returned my phone calls in days.

CHAPTER 36

Time to Fall Out of Love

I called Edna since Don wasn't answering or returning my calls. I needed to know what was going through his mind. Missing him has made me as pitiful as I had been when Charles first died. Kevin and Myesha are worried. When I called Edna, she said Don and Jason had gone to the movies and judging from the way I sounded, Don and I were suffering from the same sad blues.

"I don't know why I'm so scared."

"Honey, you don't have to be afraid. Don is so in love with you, he's beside himself."

"I want to make him as happy as he makes me, but I have baggage, and I can't give him any more children."

"The Lord doesn't always give us everything we want, Gina, but He gives us what we need."

"My Big Mama used to tell me that when I was a child."

"You have a good heart. That's what Don needs most. He has driven a few cars himself, but he says you're a keeper. He loves Kevin and Myesha, and Jason is absolutely crazy about you all."

"I wasn't given a chance to fall out of love with my husband. I made Don compete for my love. He deserves better."

"He understands all of that. My Don was an honor student, very smart, street smart too. I told him to be patient with you. It's only natural to struggle with your feelings in these situations."

"I'm a basket case when we are apart, but I'm scared to death about walking away from life as I know it to start over."

"I didn't think I deserved the luxury of falling in love again. Now that I am old and soon to be alone I wish I hadn't passed on my opportunity."

"I'm not so sure I can make him happy."

"Stop talking nonsense. I've never seen him this happy, or I should say sad lately. The only negative thing I've ever heard him say about you is that you can't cook, and you sing off-key. He wasn't complaining, he said it was endearing."

"I'm not all that bad. Cooking isn't my forte, but I won't let him starve."

"I'll write out his favorite recipes for you. He said you guys eat a lot of pizza. Most of my recipes are easy--fish, chicken, sweet potatoes, greens, easy stuff. I'll email them to you. Practice them and surprise him, okay? We girls have to stick together."

"I'm afraid that won't do me much good--I have tons of cook books. When we get settled in Phoenix you're invited to come and give me a few lessons."

"You have yourself a deal, Gina. Don and Jason just walked in. He smiled for the first time in days when I said your name. Hold on. He's gonna take the call in his room."

My heart ached when I heard Don's sad greeting a few minutes later.

"I'm sorry, sweetie. I was throwing up and I couldn't answer the phone in time."

"Gina, if you really think marrying me is what is making you feel this bad, maybe we should just forget it."

"No! No, sweetie. I want to marry you. I love you. I don't know why I'm so scared. Well, okay, I do--You're Don fuckem' and leavem' Stokes our night of great sex wasn't supposed to end in marriage. Everything happened so quickly. It's taking my logical brain time to catch up, but God knows I love you." I paused to wipe my silent tears. "Okay I'm scared as fuck but let's do it, Don Stokes, will you marry me?"

"I didn't mean to pressure you into marrying me--I just wanted you to be sure."

"I've gone through every possible scenario for us to be together without me leaving Connecticut. My friends think I'm a fool to give up all I've worked for to please you, but in all honesty, I'm doing this so you can please me."

"I'm sorry you have to choose," Don said.

"I wish it didn't have to be this way either, but if you leave me now I'll go crazy for sure."

"I want you to be happy and lately you haven't been."

"It's not that I'm not happy. Something is wrong, I made an appointment to get a physical, even when I do sleep through the night I can't seem to get going in the mornings."

After I talked to Don, it seemed as if our wedding day would never come. I couldn't blame being tired and queasy every morning on the nightmares so I blamed it on fear. Don couldn't explain why he wouldn't answer his phone, or why he hadn't returned my calls. Maybe he really was trying to forget me. That's what men do when they lose interest in the relationship, and they are too much of a coward to tell you it's over.

We're back to talking everyday on the phone. Our conversations shifted from phone sex to raising children, blending our families, business practices, political views and money management. At first I thought Don still wanted me to prove that I want to marry him for more than his looks, money and good loving, but our conversations proved that we will be great partners in and out of the bedroom. There is nothing wrong with good loving between two people in love. Even after learning that the net worth of his business and real estate holdings is approaching the billion-dollar mark, I sure as hell wouldn't marry him if the loving wasn't good. He stopped teasing me with promises of nights and days filled with loving after we are married, and he certainly didn't make any effort to hookup. All the serious talk also made us acutely aware of the fact, that rushing into marriage will be a major life changing event for all of us. I'm finally ready to marry him, but like Sharon always says, this is not my first rodeo. With our wedding day approaching in a few days, now my greatest fear is, Don is also keenly aware of the magnitude of our coupling, and might not be as sure anymore.

CHAPTER 37

Kiss and Say Goodbye

$\mathscr{I}$ received another wedding gift from Don. It was his pencil-post bed and a note saying, "I can overlook you living in "his" house for now, but I'm not going to sleep with "my" wife in "his" bed ever again." The wrought iron bed went back to the curb where Charles and I had found it one day while we were out jogging. Charles used to say I was tough, malleable and relatively soft like that old discarded bed. I can only pray that I still am, because marriage to a man like Don, with a woman like me, will require those qualities and many more.

I was relieved when Don, Jason, Edna, and Sloan arrived twenty minutes late for the rehearsal. I had chewed the inside of my lips until I drew blood while I waited on the Pier in Westport with my family and friends. I hadn't seen Don in nearly a month. Time stands still when he is away. We will be husband and wife in twenty-four hours. I can only pray that everything will be great in our worlds after we say our I do's.

Don's smile removed all my doubts. We hugged and I trembled in his arms. We went to his stateroom after our rehearsal and dinner. I wanted to love him, but he just tortured me with tantalizing kisses. I didn't think our hiatus would last until our wedding night, but it forced us to grow emotionally and that's always a good thing.

"Now that we know our love thang is tight, I can hardly wait until tomorrow," Don said. "I read somewhere that women glow when they are in love. You're lighting up the room."

Charles used to say that when I was pregnant. Sloan kicked me out so Don and the men could do their bachelor thing.

I looked in the mirror when I got home. It was countdown time and I was still dithering. I didn't see a glow at all. I was pale, paler. My stomach was grumbling, my knees were shaking, and I still couldn't separate my feelings for Charles from my feelings for Don. How is it possible to love two men this hard at the same time? I climbed into my bed. Sleep came to me in waves. The smell of Obsession and dead fish was in the air, and I had a strange dream about Don's love deep inside of me, and Charles caressing my stomach the way he used to do when I was pregnant. It was weird, even for me, but it was a happy dream and I was happy in it. I got up to go to the bathroom and bumped into a light that smelled like Obsession.

"Charles?"

His warmth wrapped around me and gave me an angel kiss.

"Am I doing the right thing?" I whispered.

He kissed me goodbye.

"I'll always love you." I whispered.

The light disappeared, but its warmth lingered. I got back in the bed, and closed my eyes and there I was in my pink Easter dress. Clear memories flooded my mind. Ida Mae had dolled me up so Daddy and I could go into town to get ice cream. Our neighbors owned a general store on our side of town that was doing well until somebody set it and the house the family was sleeping in on fire. The whole family burnt like roasted hogs while they slept. Big Mama said the fires had Klan written all over them. Both fires were the same night, but the newspaper said it was faulty wiring. Everybody on our side of Sweetwater was antsy. I'd had the heebie-jeebies the whole week before the fires. I wanted Daddy to go the long way around the swamp, but it was late and he took the shortcut. I could always feel the boys' uneasy spirits there even though I didn't know how to explain that when I was six. Daddy and I sang the blues and enjoyed the breeze blowing through his truck. Then I saw two boys hanging from the bridge. Daddy was still singing a Howlin' Wolf song about superstitions and black cats. I told him to turn around twice before it registered. The men cut the ropes and the boys' limp bodies fell in the water like cement blocks. The water splashed and hit the bridge like a gigantic seismic wave. Daddy was speeding on the narrow gravel road when a man ran toward us. Daddy said, "What the hell," when another man stopped a car about a mile ahead of us. Both men had guns. One man ran to the driver side of the car and pressed his gun into the driver's window and fired. The taillights went off on the car. Daddy tried to whip his truck around. The other man jumped in front of the truck. I wondered how he got there so fast. The man was fighting mad. He smelled like stale whiskey. I had learned enough from the ghost boys to know that Daddy and I were in trouble, and whoever was in the car ahead of us was probably dead. I curled up against the passenger door and covered my eyes and prayed. The swamp is in a remote section of our side of town. The only things around were water that smelled like fart, tall cypress and old oak trees covered with low hanging Spanish moss, humid stagnant air, crickets, lightning bugs, mosquitoes and the creatures of the night singing their songs. The orange and purple sky turned night blue as soon as the man told Daddy to get out the truck.

The boys' straw hats, and the vapors floating around the water like genies, were the only things moving, and even they were moving in slow motion. A buzzard flew by and a night owl's eerie cries broke the silence.

"Looker here," the blue-eyed man near me said. I stopped praying and removed my hands from my eyes. "We got us a little mulatto!" He chuckled and stroked my cheek. I fought half my first-grade class for calling me that name and worse.

"My wife is colored but she is as pale as you, boss," Daddy said. I wondered why he would say such a thing.

"Ain't no way in hell a boy as black as tar could make this gal with another Colored even if she looks white, and I know you ain't implying that a white man done been with yo wife," the man with his gun held to Daddy's head said.

"I ain't saying that at all. All I'm saying is, that's my baby."

"Her mamma must have some of them big ole mammy titties?" the man said as he cupped his hand in front of himself like he was gripping imaginary breasts. It didn't matter that I was only six; I wanted to knock him out! I started praying again. I had overheard Big Mama and her friends talking about how they had hoped the killings would stop after the pictures of Emmitt Till were printed in Jet Magazine. The boys and Big Papa had told me how the Klan had killed them. It was Daddy and my time to die!

"Answer me, boy, and say, sir, when you talk to me!" the man said to Daddy.

Daddy swung at the man wildly and the man whacked him in the head with his gun. My screams echoed against the surrounding woods, they didn't travel far. Daddy kissed the ground. The man aimed his gun for Daddy's head again and said, "I'll kill you when I'm good and damn ready!" He made a nasty sounding chuckle and said, "Her mammy must be sumthing if you're still fighting for her after what she done to ya. She must have sum of them big ole pointy titties and a big jiggling booty, and I bet she rides ya slow and steady like a mule. Is it true that Colored pussy sucks back?"

Daddy hopped to his feet. He was angry. I understood the man's filthy talk. I guess that's why his filthy words have always been clear in my nightmares. Daddy kicked the man like Bruce Lee and knocked the gun from his hands. They dove to the ground for the gun. While they were rolling around in the dirt like dogs in heat, the gun went off!

"Run, Angie, run!" Daddy yelled.

My heart was beating so fast it felt like it was going to bust out my chest. "Angie?"

Daddy and I had in fact turned around. We were home! I was delirious about what I had seen or what was coming to me in my visions. Ida Mae and Big Mama gave me a strong tea concoction that made me sleepy. They put me to bed but the visions didn't end.

Poor Angie couldn't run. The man next to her had moved from stroking her cheek with his rough trigger finger, to playing with the curls her mother had put in her long dark hair, to pulling up her pink Easter dress, and rubbing between her thighs.

"You're an ugly little thang," he said as he reached inside her panties.

She sucked in a breath of air and let it out slowly while she smiled at him just like Daddy taught me to do the kids at school when he showed me how to catch more bees with honey.

"We can have your kind anytime," the man said and he put his finger inside her sweet spot. She couldn't move. All she could do was stare into his pretty blue-eyes and smile. She was mesmerized by their centers. They opened wide like doors and swallowed her soul.

"Don't worry, we don't want nothing to do with the likes of you. No one will--you're already tainted."

He pushed and wiggled his finger deeper until she cried. Her lips trembled when she peed all over his hand. He got a thrill from the feel and smell of her hot pee. She kept staring into his eyes and the nasty smirk on his face. She eased his gun out of its holster thinking that she could give it to her father. She was still fixed on the man's eyes and the sickening smirk on his face. He continued to molest her with his hand.

Bobby touched me there in first grade. Daddy whipped my behind and told me never to let anyone touch me there again. He promised to inflict bodily harm to any boy who wanted to touch inside my panties before he married me.

Angie managed to blurt out, "Stop! Please stop," but the man said, "You best stay on your side of the tracks. You could get some poor unsuspecting white boy in a heapa trouble. You gonna be a hot one when you grow up." The nasty man laughed and pressed something down there until Angie screamed! Her father hopped to his feet like a mad man and reached for her and the gun in her hand.

"Leave her alone!" he shouted. "She's an innocent child."

Before Angie could give her father the gun the man behind her father pointed his gun and pulled the trigger. Angie didn't have time to think, and anyway she probably couldn't think for the noises, the screams, the oms, and the boy's telling her to pull the trigger before it was too late! Her father somehow managed to get the gun and fired it twice!

Something deep inside of me reminded me that God sends guardian angels to protect us. All these years I thought I was Angie. Daddy and Uncle Seddie Lee were twins. All I had ever heard was, he left Mississippi in a hurry before I was born. His first shot hit the shooter that was aiming for him. His second shot hit his beautiful daughter's molester, but it was too late. The man's shot had already lodged in Angie's gut!

Angie's father rushed her home. She died in his arms. Aunt Pearlie Mae called Big Mama. She told Aunt Pearlie Mae and Uncle Seddie Lee to get out of town and never come back. The boys chanted and Daddy and Uncle Wydell put the bodies of the white men in the hearse. Then Daddy drove their truck into the guardrail of the raggedy bridge and knocked it out of gear. They gave it a shove, and then they hauled ass to safety. They blocked the entry to the bridge with several big logs, and put a homemade "DANGER DO NOT ENTER! BRIDGE OUT OF ORDER" sign there. They took the bodies and the guns to the funeral home and placed them in the coffins with the bones of the burned victims. The funerals were the next day at Sweetwater Baptist. Reverend Shorter preached about the tragedies of the day and for brotherly love, peace, and equal rights in the future. The choir sang "Precious Lord" and "Amazing Grace." The bodies were buried in the Colored cemetery and covered with rich black soil and a rainbow of flowers. Angie was buried next to Big Papa. Pearlie Mae and Seddie Lee left Mississippi an hour after the tragedy with all the money they had and the clothes on their backs. First to Chicago, then to Montana.

I chanted the twenty-third Psalms and the boys sang until I drifted into a deep, deep sleep. I had suppressed and misinterpreted Angie's nightmare for mine for thirty-four years. Probably all she wanted to do was to protect me from repeating our family's tragedy.

CHAPTER 38

You Played Me, Baby

*M*y palms were sweaty. My heart raced. I had nausea. It was my wedding day! Sharon brought me breakfast in bed. I got a whiff of the bacon and eggs, and barely made it to the bathroom. My boobs bumped into the cold porcelain toilet bowl while I made a return deposit of my rehearsal dinner. The pain was bad, but the shock was worse.

My breasts were engorged and tender. I couldn't remember the last time I'd had my period. I checked my calendar and the last red star was before Don gave me a love supreme. Sharon and Ida Mae brushed my unsettled stomach off as a bad case of wedding day jitters. I didn't tell them I had upchucked my dinner, missed a period, and was past due for another. I've missed periods during stressful times, but the soreness in my boobs wasn't normal.

My glam team wasn't coming until mid-afternoon. I pulled on my jeans, and grabbed my phone, and keys. My first stop was CVS to pick up an E.P.T. pregnancy kit. My second stop was my office. I locked the door, and took the test.

Positive!

I reread the directions to make sure I had done it correctly. I didn't want to get my hopes up until I knew for sure. I called my gynecologist and begged her to check me out before my wedding. She was on call. I met her at Yale-New Haven Hospital. She did another urine test. It was positive. She did the pelvic exam, and drew two tubes of blood.

"How did this happen?" I said as I overflowed with joy and fear.

"Well, you choose a good man, and then you open your heart and let him water your forbidden garden with his holy water, and if you're lucky, beautiful flowers will grow." Pam teased.

"Pam, you're nuts. I've been trying to get pregnant since Myesha was born. We thought my fibroids were blocking my tubes remember?"

Pam regained her professional demeanor. "I always say probably blocking, nothing is a hundred percent. Have you had any abnormal bleeding, abdominal or pelvic pain, or nausea?"

"Nausea, but no pain and no bleeding. I've had cold-like symptoms, and I've been tired, and irritable, but now that I know--I'm sure it is just morning sickness."

"You've lost a lot of weight. Sometimes that may make a difference or maybe the problem wasn't you. Did you and Charles ever do any fertility testing?"

"Nope, we had a boy and a girl. We left it up to God if he wanted us to have more."

She did a sonogram and checked for the baby's heartbeat. "You have a miracle baby growing inside you," Pam said as she pointed him or her out on the monitor. "You're going to be fine."

I was surprised by my new development, but I was even more surprised about how happy I was. This baby was conceived with a love supreme. Don had changed my life more than he knew.

I'm getting better at lying under pressure. I was smooth with Troy. I haven't mentioned what I did, or my visits from Charles. I told Sharon and Ida Mae I had taken a long drive to clear my head. They are aware of my Summer Breeze/ Zoom escapes. I didn't want the world to think Don Stokes was marrying his forty-year-old bride on her birthday because she was having his love child. I ran upstairs before Sharon and Mother could question me about my disappearing act.

Ro had on her slip. She was staring into the mirror, and crying. "What's wrong, girl? It can't be that bad—it's my wedding day." I wanted to say more, but I didn't. She wiped her face with the back of her hand. I gave her a tissue to wipe her snotty nose. "Girl, you're looking rough."

Ro cracked a smile. "I'm sorry, Gina, but I can't fit my big ass in that skinny ass dress you picked."

"Excuse me—you picked the dress. So, what's up with your sudden memory loss?"

"I'm pregnant. That's why I slept so much in Aruba. You were so love sick you didn't even notice. And I thought you were my friend."

I thought about all the tequila I consumed in Aruba and touched my tummy. I sat on the bed next to her. "Wow, Ro this is great. Isn't it?"

"I never thought it would happen to me, but here I am. Edward and I went to a justice of the peace a few weeks ago. I was gaining weight so fast we decided not to wait. Girl, I've been craving everything. I think it is the vitamins he prescribed."

I tightened my hand on my purse containing my prenatal vitamins and thought about the fifty pounds I'd gained with Myesha. It took me forever to lose that weight, truth be told, I didn't lose it until recently. My children are a joy. It hit me that I was willing to gain fifty pounds, clean hundreds of stinky diapers, breast feed, live off a few hours of sleep a night, and love every minute of it. Why—because I love my babies and their daddies more than anything in this world.

"Why didn't you tell me sex was great while you're expecting? Edward is so excited. He loves my big butt." We giggled like school girls. "I'm sorry about the dress. I can't zip it. Check out my boobs—Edward thinks he died and went to heaven. They're almost as big as yours. I take that back, yours have gotten bigger. Maybe they just look bigger. Since you loss all that weight, you're all tits, legs, and ass. Keep it tight, girl, and you won't have to worry about Don looking elsewhere. He'll be too busy trying to keep tabs on you." We chuckled again.

"I tried to call you about the wedding. You can see the pictures before you leave for Phoenix." Rolonda started to cry again. "Gina, I'm going to miss you. Will you be my baby's godmother?"

"Of course I will. Don's keeping his place in the city, and I still have this house. Don't worry; you'll probably see more of me than you do now. Myesha can wear your dress. She was upset when I didn't make her a bridesmaid anyway."

Sharon knocked on the door and peeked in, "Gina, your glam squad is here."

"Show them to my room, I'll be there in a minute." I gave Ro a hug. "Find Myesha and give her the dress. If she needs adjustments, Ida Mae can take care of them. When she is ready, send her to my room to get glammed up. She will like that."

Omar's band was entertaining our guests with his rendition of Bob Marley's "Could You Be Loved" when the white Excalibur limousine Don had sent for me dropped me off at the yacht. Daddy held my hand and led me up the aisle while the band played "A Love Supreme." My eyes were misty, but I had a grand smile on my face. I was one scared but lucky woman. An emotional tear slid down my cheek.

Don caught it with a kiss and said, "Don't cry, my sweet."

I was all choked up with a grand smile on my face and eyes so misty I couldn't focus. I should have worn a veil or skipped the mascara and eye-lashes. Don smelled like Armani Code and fresh baked cookies. I wanted this to be quick. I'm ready to tell him the good news and love him tender. The salon smelled like roses and expensive perfumes. The smells were not helping my situation one bit. Reverend Knight sounded distant when he cleared his throat and said, "Okay, lovebirds we didn't get to the kissing part yet."

Don stole another kiss and when I opened my eyes he was beautiful brown and white wiggly lines in front of me. I leaned on Daddy for support and prayed that I wouldn't faint.

"Are you okay?" Don asked.

My eyes were misty and unfocused and I didn't trust my voice. I nodded and tried to slow down my pounding heart.

"Hurry up, Reverend. I've been waiting all day to kiss my sweet lady."

"Dearly beloved: we are gathered together here in the sight of God and in the presence of these witnesses, to join this man and woman in holy matrimony."

Everything seemed distant, but Daddy supported me.

"Will you have this woman to be your wife to live together after God's ordinance in the holy estate of matrimony? Will you honor, and keep her, in sickness and health; and forsaking all others, keep you *only unto her*, so long as you both shall live?"

"I will," Don said and he squeezed my hand.

Reverend Knight repeated the same words to me while I tried and failed to bring everything into focus.

"I--do." I couldn't control the quiver in my tone of voice. Don squeezed my hand. I still couldn't focus.

"Who gives this woman to be married to this man?"

"I do," Daddy said and he stepped away and sat with Ida Mae. I still needed his support; I never stopped needing it. My legs were weak. Don squeezed my hands. Tight! I tried to focus.

Reverend said, "The couple has written their own promises to each other to be read before God."

"I, Don, promise to love and cherish you and only you, Gina, for the rest of my God given days. You are the force that touched my heart and showed me what true love is. You are the star that aligns with every cell in my body and makes us a couple like no other. You are the Venus that fills my days and my nights with love. Gina, you are the fire that inspires me and makes me a better man for you, our children and our families. With you by my side, I no longer have to worry about having a bad day. Your smile is all it takes to make me better. I will love you today, tomorrow and always. Will you be my wife and trust me to deliver on all I promise you this day and forevermore?" Don said as he squeezed my cold clammy hands.

My turn. I still couldn't focus. Now I was crying.

My lips didn't move--not even a quiver. Don squeezed my hands. Tight! I bit down on my lip. Everything was quiet. Everything!

"I--" Don squeezed tighter. "Yes."

I trembled and a drop of sweat trickled down between my breasts. Don held my hands while I slowly stated my vows to him.

"Don, I promise to love you with all that I am, and all I have to give. You understand me when I don't understand myself. You soothe me when I don't know I need soothing. You awaken my soul to endless possibilities. You know my heart and my soul..." I couldn't bring Don's face into focus. I squeezed his hand while my voice shook and my already misty eyes filled to the brims with built up emotions. "Yes, I will marry you, and love you, and be there for you today and forevermore."

He slipped a diamond wedding band on my finger that looked like a thousand stars through my misty eyes.

"With this ring I thee wed--" he said.

I placed a matching diamond wedding band on his finger. My voice and my hands wavered. "With this ring--"

Reverend Knight prayed, "O Eternal God, send blessings upon this man and this woman, and may they remain in perfect love and peace together." Don squeezed my hand. Reverend Knight continued.

"Those who God has joined together, *let no one come between them*." I tried to focus when Reverend Knight continued. "I pronounce that they are husband and wife together. Now you may kiss your bride."

Don's warm sweet lips touched mine and gave me new life. I squeezed him. He was my support now. I had to let him be that for me. I'm his and he is mine. When the kiss ended a bigger crowd than I had expected cheered and Don smiled a grand smile and stared into my misty eyes. I kissed him again while Reverend did the closing prayer.

Omar's band played "Ensorcelled" while Don and I danced our first dance as Mr. and Mrs. Stokes. We moved to the sensuous beat totally in sync with each other.

"I wasn't sure if you were going to make it through it. Are you okay?" Don asked.

I wrapped my arms around him and pressed my tender breasts to his chest. He kissed the sensitive spot on my neck and we started to slow grind.

"We're married, but let's not get busy in front of my parents and your mother."

"It's hard to hold your soft body and not want you. It's been a long time. Let's get out of here."

"We can't leave." Our feet continued to dance but our hearts moved on to a loving beat. "Bend over. I need to tell you something. You have to promise not to tell anyone."

"I'll do anything for my wife."

"Bend over. I have to whisper." Don bent over and nibbled on my neck. "Stop, you're making me hot. I'm trying to be serious."

"So am I."

I pinched him in his side. "Ouch! Okay. No more joking around." Our guests banged on their glasses. I kissed Don.

"What's the big secret?"

I nibbled on his ear and whispered slowly so I wouldn't have to repeat myself. "Sweetie, you're, going, to, be, a, daddy."

He stopped dancing, smiled and lifted my chin with his index finger. My eyes were misty and unfocused again. Don was so choked up, I didn't recognize his voice when he said, "Pregnant?" He stroked my face and looked deep into my eyes. "You?" He pointed his finger to his chest. "Me?" He looked at me with a knowing smile. "I knew there was something different about you. Do you feel okay? Is that why you looked like you were about to pass out? Why are your hands cold?" I covered his lips with mine to keep him from spilling the beans.

"Ssshhh. We should keep it to ourselves for a while. You promised." Everybody banged their glasses again and I covered Don's luscious lips again.

We willed our feet to dance. "I thought you said you couldn't."

"Ssshhh. I didn't think I could do a lot of things until I met you."

The song ended and Don led me out the room.

"We can't leave. The reception just started."

"If you don't want me to get freaky with you on this dance floor and embarrass you in front of Ida Mae and our guests you better come on, girl?"

We went to the master stateroom. I told Don about my visit with Pam without mentioning Charles or the dreams.

"We can't tell anyone until after the results of the blood work, and we still have to pray and keep the faith."

Okay, but you're not staying here. I'm gonna be with you while your belly is growing. I'm gonna be there to listen to her heartbeat, talk to her, and feel her kicking. I missed everything with Jason. You're coming with me to Phoenix tonight, and don't even think about coming back before my child is born."

I giggled. "I'm all yours for two-weeks, and if you would rather spend our two-week honeymoon in Phoenix instead of Bora Bora on our own private island skinny dipping with exotic fish before I get pregnancy fat, I'll leave it up to you." I held up two fingers and flashed Don my sexiest smile. "Sweetie, you promised me Bora Bora but since we absolutely have to be back in two weeks for our first prenatal appointment together it's okay." I pouted and slipped my hand in his. "I have to run my office at least until Erica can take over." I flashed my sexy innocent smile again. "And we also need to have our attorneys make sure our combined business and personal assets are setup so we are protected from lawsuits." Don frowned so I continued quickly. "We are going to have two teen-age boys driving soon, anything can happen. I think we can squeeze in a family trip to Phoenix before the kids go back to school. And I'll let you, Edna, and Jason decide if he wants to join us in Connecticut." Don looked defeated, and I hadn't even gotten to the hardest part yet. "Sweetie, I know this is not what you want or what we discussed." I wrapped my arms around him, gave him a sweet kiss and flashed my sexiest smile. "We've been given the best un-expected wedding gift of all, and it is not a good thing for me to be pregnant and stressed, so don't fight me on this, and don't count on any major moves until after our little bundle of joy is born sometime around Valentine's Day, okay?" I put his hand on my stomach and flashed a pouty-sexy smile again.

His dark eyes pierced mine. I bit down on my lip, I couldn't or didn't want to read what was going through his mind. He ran his finger over my lip. I shivered. He didn't smile, not even a twitch. Poker face and piercing eyes. Warm heat rushed through my entire body. Don's poker face didn't give away anything. He stared, and said nothing. I could feel the burn of my cheeks blushing. He put both his hands on my arms and held me at a distance. He continued to stare with piercing unreadable eyes. After what felt like an hour, but was closer to a minute, his thumbs began to make slow sensuous circles on my forearms. I felt a jolt in my girly parts and goosebumps appeared where he was stirring.

First there was a little twitch at the corners of his luscious lips. Next his lips blossomed slowly into a sexy smile. I thought he was going to kiss me. He bent down, but before our lips touched, he let out a bellowing laugh from deep in his gut. It reminded me of our first tickle fight.

"My wife just played me!" He shook his head and continued to laugh. "Damn, Gina, you had me at our first prenatal appointment. Baby, I can't even fake being angry at you today. You still don't have any idea about how happy you make me." He stopped laughing and flashed me a sexy smile that stole my heart.

"Well, since the only thing I get to decide is the honeymoon, I say it starts right now, Mrs. Stokes." He kissed me wantonly, and I fucked him right back with my tongue.

"I've never made love to a pregnant woman.," he said as he moved his kisses to my neck and ear. He unzipped my wedding dress and started nibbling and feeling my breasts and stomach. "I feel like a virgin."

"We is married now, Mr. Stokes, give me all that loving you been saving for your wife," I teased. "Ummm...! You don't kiss like a virgin!"

He slipped my dress off and kissed all the places his virgin lips and my pregnant super sensitive body had been missing. I wiggled away and said, "We should go back to our reception, sweetie. I haven't seen Gretchen, and Gabby at the same time since we were in college. Everybody used to call us the three G's. I must introduce you to them, and I want to introduce Sloan to my cousin Gianna. And did you see Omar and Erica eyeing each other, and Sloan's Uncle Bo flirting with Sharon, and Patrice and Troy holding hands. Don't you want to eat, and take pictures of our wonderful day, and all the love in the air?"

"I'm not going anywhere until I lose my virginity. The only picture I want, is of my beautiful wife coming with her husband for the first time. I think I will take a private picture, it will remind me of the slice of heaven I'm missing when we are apart." He pulled me to him and kissed me again.

"Ummmm! Okay, but make it a quickie. I'm hungry."

"Do you have any predictions for our future, Mrs. Stokes?"

"I predict that we don't have anything to fear, and that if we keep this love thing up you're going to keep me barefoot and pregnant for the next three years." He continued to kiss me while he removed my bra.

"Ahhhhh! Those are tender."

"Hey, I'm a virgin." He stroked and kissed me with less urgency. "So are we gonna live happily ever after?"

"Ummmm, I don't know, but if you keep kissing me there you won't be a virgin much longer."

He put his phone under the pillows. Then he took off his tuxedo jacket and shirt and kissed me in one smooth movement.

"You slow dance pretty good for a virgin, Mr. Stokes."

"Barefoot and pregnant--see what batting your sad doll-baby eyes and tickling my balls with your toes got you?"

"Us, Mr. Stokes… Us…" I placed his hand on my flat belly. The one I had worked nine months to get back. He slid his hand lower and connected our souls.

"Yes, that's it. Right there…take it slow, baby…ummmm…yesssss, like that…"

"Baby, you are incredible. Heaven has to be missing an angel."

I thought about Angie, the boys, Don's father, and Charles. My heart opened completely for my new husband.

"I'm the luckiest man on earth."

Don and I came apart and came together simultaneously. The good Lord was having triple-double mercy on us today. My guardian angels could go home to glory, and from now on, they could watch over Mr. and Mrs. Stokes from heaven.

Author's Notes

$\mathscr{B}$irth to delivery of this novel has taken me twenty years. The first draft was handwritten. This draft comes to you on computer number four. I had to do two complete rewrites after losing one draft to a computer virus and another to a stolen laptop. I also took a ten-year break after divorce, mostly because my spirit wasn't in the right place. Thanks to friends and family, and another computer approaching retirement, and the ability to publish on my own terms, I can now take publishing my novels off my bucket list. I hope you enjoyed the journey as much as I did. I have already written two follow-up novels to complete my Living with the Consequences series. I have many more stories in my head waiting to be written if you all give me a little encouragement. Please leave a review and tell a friend.

I updated most of the story after my ten-year break, however I didn't have the heart to cut Gina and Rolonda's girlfriend's trip to Aruba. It was based on my trip to Sinbad's Funk Festival in 1997. I even had a few cameos in the HBO special. I don't want to confuse the timelines for other readers who attended the festival. I also had to keep Gina younger so therefore she would have attended Tougaloo College long after I graduated. I updated Don's interview and changed it to The Daily Show with Trevor Noah. In the novel, Don does the interview while he is away on a road trip to the West Coast whereas the show is located on the East Coast. I'm not sure how often professional basketball players practice, I just know that when I played I had to practice if I wanted to get better and last through a game.

Thanks again for reading Playing Your Game.

Acknowledgements

$\mathcal{T}$his has been a long wonderful journey. There were many people who helped me along the way. First I would like to thank my writer friends who read and critiqued bits and pieces, gave me pointers or encouraged me to continue writing. Eric Jerome Dickey, Colin Channer, Valerie Wilson Wesley, Donna Hill, and Dwight Fryer thank you, your workshops and critiques were helpful and greatly appreciated. I would like to thank my Hurston Wright Workshop Group lead by Jeffery Renard Allen. Thanks to the Hartford Writer's Group and the Hartford Public library. Thanks to the Russell Library and the Russell Writers. To all the agents who told me I was on to something but I wasn't there yet, thanks for pointing me in the right directions. To the editor in California who told me no one is interested in reading about women who look and love like Gina, thank you. I wrote two more novels about women like her. We have stories to tell, and who better to tell them than someone whose life it is to live.

Shout-outs to my many early drafts readers, Alicia, Lala, Tonja, Marisol, Jacqui, Patricia, Roz, Michelle, Ashley, Rene, and Gigi. I hope I didn't leave anyone out, but if I did my apologies. Special thanks to my sister Deloris and my friend Yvonne for giving me permission, well, telling me that I needed to step Sharon and Rolonda up a notch or two. To my sisters, Peggie and Barbara thanks always for your encouragement and special prayers. To my brothers Nathaniel, Charles, Bright, Willie (RIP) and Henry thanks for keeping the bogeymen away and for helping me identify the many variations of men. To Alfred Sr., thanks for your encouragement early on, I can't be mad about the twenty years we shared and the two wonderful children we produced. To Alfred and Alicia thanks for helping me with my many computer issues. Why do I need to enroll in a computer class when I have you? Mommy loves you too. To Bobby thanks for introducing and sharing my vision with your VIP clients. Bryan, I finally got it together and got it done, thanks for your encouragement, prayers, and help.

Special thanks to Sister 2 Sister and Soul Passages: A Book Club, our book discussions give me invaluable insight into what is important in a book and what works and doesn't work. At the end of the day, it is the readers that count. To all my family and my readers, thank you, I love you, God bless you.

Gloria
gperryauthor@gmail.com

About the Author

Playing Your Game (a Consequences Novel) is Gloria F. Perry's first published novel. **Playing Your Game** is book one of a three book series. Gloria has published short fiction and non-fiction stories in various local magazines, newspapers, and anthologies. She has earned local recognition for her commentary and non-fiction stories. Gloria was a co-organizer of the Soul Passages: A Book Club Community Book Read and Book Festival in New Haven Connecticut (2012). She was the chairperson and brainchild for an Author's Luncheon and Southern Style Tea to raise scholarship funds for the book club scholarship fund (2014). Gloria attended Tougaloo College in Mississippi where she grew up. She graduated from UCONN Dental School. Dr. Perry owns and practices dentistry in Connecticut where she lives with her family.